A finalist for the 2004 PEN / Hemingway Award for Fiction

A *San Francisco Chronicle* Best Book of 2003

"Reading Murad Kalam's *Night Journey* is a windows-down, whipping, 3:00 AM ride that pushes the odometer too easily over a hundred miles per hour. . . . Its obvious inheritance might be from Richard Wright, but the novel should also be compared to Leonard Gardner's classic, *Fat City*."

—LINDA WAGNER MARTIN, president of
the Ernest Hemingway Foundation, and
PERRI KLASS, chair of PEN New England

"A remarkably assured and tightly plotted first novel."

—*Booklist*

"An impressive debut. . . . On page after page, Kalam offers up sharply observed and vividly rendered set pieces, making this a solid first by a writer who bears watching."

—*Kirkus Reviews*

"Murad Kalam will be compared to Richard Wright and with good reason. Like Wright, Kalam explores with an extraordinarily moving directness neglected facets of African-American life. He shows a sharp eye for the telling visual detail, a keen ear for arresting dialogue, and an uncanny ability to portray dramatic action in ways that make a reader keep reading. *Night Journey* announces the presence of a major new figure in American letters."

—RANDALL KENNEDY, author of *Nigger* and *Interracial Intimacies*

"Just as Richard Wright's *Native Son* and James Baldwin's *Go Tell It on the Mountain* did in their times, *Night Journey* gives narrative expression to the everyday experience of a new generation of African Americans."

—*Jacksonville Free Press*

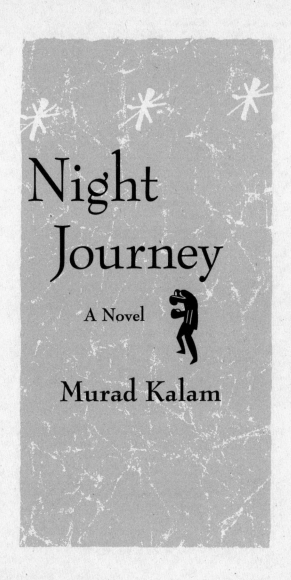

Night
Journey

A Novel

Murad Kalam

Simon & Schuster Paperbacks
New York London Toronto Sydney

SIMON & SCHUSTER PAPERBACKS
Rockefeller Center
1230 Avenue of the Americas
New York, NY 10020

First Simon & Schuster paperback edition 2004

SIMON & SCHUSTER PAPERBACKS and colophon are registered trademarks
of Simon & Schuster, Inc.

A part of this novel has been previously published
in slightly different form in *Harper's* magazine
and the O. Henry Awards 2001 Prize stories.

For information about special discounts for bulk purchases,
please contact Simon & Schuster Special Sales:
1-800-456-6798 or business@simonandschuster.com.

Designed by Jeanette Olender
Manufactured in the United States of America

1 3 5 7 9 10 8 6 4 2

The Library of Congress has cataloged the hardcover edition as follows:
Kalam, Murad.
Night journey : a novel / Murad Kalam.
p. cm.
1. African-American boys—Fiction. 2. Phoenix (Ariz.)—Fiction.
3. Boxers (Sports)—Fiction. I. Title.
PS3611.A69N545 2003
813'.6—dc21   2003042466

ISBN 0-7432-4418-4
0-7432-4419-2 (Pbk)

For my wife, Rashann

To have lived and died as one had been born, unnecessary and unaccommodated.

V. S. Naipaul, *A House for Mr. Biswas*

From the beginning, I went with that boy. Sure he has deficiencies, some of them big ones, but in that ring he took what he had and laid it on the line. He moved you.

Cus D'Amato

Acknowledgments

Big thanks to two big mentors: to Robert Cohen for being an amazing teacher, friend, and writer; to Jamaica Kincaid for all of the same and for her early belief in my talent, and almost maternal guidance; to Denise Shannon, for incredible patience and for guiding this novel to publication. Rarely does the first-time novelist find both a great editor and a no-nonsense advocate in one agent. To Denise Roy, for her energy, enthusiasm, and brilliant editing. I also want to thank David Rosenthal, Victoria Meyer, and Aileen Boyle. I would like to express my appreciation to Dr. K. Anthony Appiah, Henry Louis Gates Jr., Harbour Fraser Hodder, and Zaheer Ali. My law school classmates, Minoti Patel, Josh Bloodworth, David K. Min, and Justin Herdman were kind enough to look at drafts of the novel for me.

Night Journey

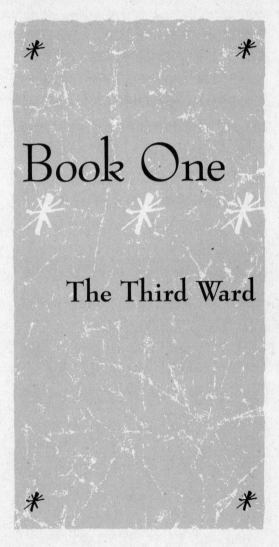

Book One

The Third Ward

Part One

An Awkward Boy

*T*he neighbor woman died, and it was all that Eddie could take.

He found her, returning from the New State Variety, with his big brother, Turtle. Turtle came upon her first, discovered Mrs. Walker in full rigor, facedown dead, her arms and legs splayed out like open scissors on the ruddy red carpet of her parlor. They'd let themselves in through the front door of 51 Woodland, to find her obese body laid out at the bottom of the stairs in the hot room, her aluminum walking cane angled on her back, glowing in the parlor light. Eddie had knocked twice, as he always did, Turtle running in ahead of him, Mrs. Walker's grocery bags in his hands, stopping short, dropping the grocery bags on the floor, standing two minutes silent above the old woman, who'd loaned Mama sugar, who paid the boys $5 a week to fetch her groceries. Eddie ran in after Turtle and then he saw her, the neighbor woman dead, staring at her unmoving face, her eyes wide open, left eye staring at the carpet! He gazed at the waxen brown flesh, dead calves slanting against the bottom stairs.

The old woman had that morning tripped, tumbled down the stairs, and broken her neck. She lay upon a bloated, hyperextended arm. The ceiling fan shook on its joint. Turtle ran screaming out of the front door, down Woodland Ave., Eddie after him.

They sprinted two blocks home, across the hot, broken sidewalk to Nana's house. God, Eddie thought, Daddy ain't run off a week ago, and now Mrs. Walker fall down the stairs and die—and they had found her, Turtle and him, and Eddie had looked into her dead face.

Eddie followed Turtle up the front stoop, into Nana's house, storm door slapping at his back. Nana stood in the kitchen, a wet rag in her hand. "What is it, boy?" Turtle went to Nana and hugged her fat hips until Nana pushed him away, and Turtle told her, each word forming slowly on his pale lips. "Mrs. Walker dead," he muttered, and what came next was a flood of useless sounds. Nana took a sigh, set the wet rag on the counter, and patted Turtle's back. "Okay, boy." Nana went to the telephone to call the police.

The police were just arriving at the dead woman's house when Mama came home from work and found Nana, Turtle, and Eddie at the kitchen table. Nana told Mama the story as the coroner pulled up in a twenty-five-year-old Chevy station wagon, and Mama, like the whole snooping street, watched, from behind a kitchen curtain, the white uniformed men, necks pink from the sun, drape Mrs. Walker's body and take it out on a gurney. "Turtle come screaming down the street," Nana said as Mama stared. "I heard him screaming from two blocks away. He been crying like this all day." Turtle drank beers and cussed, picked playground fights, tore the tails off lizards; he lured and tortured stray cats in the E. Monroe St. Church parking lot. And today he had been crying at the death of an old woman. Eddie watched Mama smile at Turtle in the same way Nana had smiled, as if she thought Turtle's grief was sweet. Then Mama turned to look at Eddie. Nana saw her looking. "This one here ain't let out a peep," Nana said, pointing. "I almost forgot he was here. It beginning to spook me. Christ, you'd think something like this would make him talk."

Eddie was ten, and Turtle was twelve, and Eddie had not said a word since his daddy ran off the week before. It was Turtle who could not set two words together without stuttering, but now Eddie had stopped speaking. No one thought they were brothers. Turtle was lank and frail and light, and dirt stupid Mama called him, and Eddie was hefty and black and handsome, strong like Daddy. Quiet. Eddie was a giant. Nana thought it was odd to see such a hulking boy, a boy who could pass for twelve, fourteen, sit silent at his bedroom window all day, hurt on his face. Just the day before Daddy ran off, Mama had sat behind Eddie on the sunny stoop, rubbing his head. "Look at you, boy," she told him. "You watch, you'll be big like your daddy. Won't nobody ever bother you."

Eddie woke the next morning to find Turtle smiling at him, pointing at the bedroom window. "He run," Turtle said. "That son, son, son of a bitch, I told you he would!" Eddie went to the window and stared out at the empty, oil-stained concrete of the driveway, and laughing, Turtle ran into the kitchen. Eddie found him there with Mama. She was cutting up all the clothes Daddy had left behind, old Kodaks, tossing them into the wastebasket.

That night Eddie was too worried to eat and went to bed without eating the dinner Nana had scrounged up. Turtle waited until nightfall and snuck out through the bedroom window as Eddie lay on his back, staring at the ceiling. "You best, best, best say something when I come back," Turtle said. Turtle spoke in slow bursts because anger made him stutter, made him breathe and think out and pronounce each word, until Turtle was staring at Eddie from the grass outside. Eddie watched him wander across the street and disappear into darkness, imagining Turtle gliding across Woodland Park and beyond to Van Buren Ave., his head bobbing beneath the swaggering hustlers, the prostitutes strutting in spandex, like Eddie had seen him do a hundred times, zipping up and down the street, running his fingers across the chain-link fences of the hooker motels, smoking half-smoked menthol cigarettes he found ashed in the Circle K parking lot. When Turtle came home Eddie was still lying on the bed, suffering, staring at the water stains on the ceiling. Turtle slapped Eddie's face. "Say, something, you crazy overgrown nigger. Say, say, say . . . !" Turtle slapped him again. Eddie tried to speak, but the trauma of the morning had not left him; it was a panic, a child's midnight anguish, a nightmare, and he decided that he would not speak again that summer no matter how many times Turtle beat him.

Three days after Mrs. Walker fell down her staircase and died, her sons drove down from Texas in a pair of four-door sedans to collect her belongings. Turtle and Eddie peered at them from the shade of Nana's porch. "They will sell it now," Turtle stammered at Eddie. No! Eddie thought. From the shade of their stoop, Eddie and Turtle watched Mrs. Walker's sons stare at the front of 51 Woodland Ave. The sons did not recognize the street, the condition of their boyhood home, the street a slum, the house nearly worthless. Upright Christian types in polo shirts and deck shoes they were, the two sons come down from Texas, climbing the front steps, removing from the house Mrs. Walker's most precious belongings, those things which seemed in an instant to represent her spirit, and leaving the house to rot. Eddie watched them, praying they would not come back, smiling when they drove off two hours later, sedans packed with boxes, as if never to return. Eddie was smiling. Turtle was, too. The house was theirs if they could claim it.

Boys from Maryvale watched Mrs. Walker's sons packing too, trailer park white boys watching from the curling grass of Woodland Park, others orbiting the street on dirt bikes, boys younger than the pimps in do rags and bright shirts who rode their bikes along Van Buren Ave., older, meaner than Turtle. Eddie saw the boys and he nudged Turtle, and then Turtle saw them and cussed. They'd come before, a phalanx of ugly, pimple-faced boys on dirt bikes, casing the houses of Woodland Ave., fatherless boys like Eddie himself. They'd made forays into Woodland Ave., held the street, the park, for a few weeks each summer, only to realize that they lived too far to hold the street for good. They would glide down the street and grit their faces at Turtle and Eddie sitting on their stoop, Turtle gritting back, gritting when Eddie, sitting behind him, knew he could only be afraid.

The Maryvale boys came that very night. Eddie heard them breaking into the back door of the dead woman's house—Eddie from his pillow heard distant smashing windows, the shrill shouts of wilding boys. Eddie sat up, and he thought, God, God, Turtle, don't you go over there and try nothing. Turtle heard them, too. His eyes popped open. Boys whispering in the backyard of 51 Woodland, scurrying across weeds, the dead woman's back door the next moment shoved in.

Eddie watched Turtle climb into his shirt and jeans, take a baseball bat from under his bed. God, he running over to the house, Eddie thought. Turtle opened the window and climbed out. Eddie got dressed and followed him. Turtle grabbed Eddie's foot. "No. You, you, you can't," Turtle muttered. "What if Mama find out?" Eddie said nothing. "All right," Turtle said, passing Eddie a flat-head screwdriver from his pocket, "but they ain't gonna fight you soft cause you ten." Eddie nodded, climbed out of the bedroom window. From their stoop they watched the Maryvale boys, the dark silhouettes of their sneaking bodies in Mrs. Walker's living room windows, bouncing flashlights. The boys had claimed the house already. If they fought them now, the boys would beat them down, and if by chance they beat the boys, the boys would only come back with more boys. Turtle was cussing. There was nothing they could do.

Turtle had an idea. Turtle and Eddie took their bikes from the backyard. Eddie felt his pulse beating in his temple as he pedaled his bike after Turtle to the farmhouse of Turtle's best friend, Adolpho, a mulatto boy who lived on the dirt fields under South Mountain.

They parked their bikes inside Adolpho's gate. Adolpho heard them crunching chicken feed and came out onto his front porch. Turtle, gasping, caught sight of Adolpho. "Adolpho, Adolpho," he said. It was all Turtle could do not to stutter. "The house, they claimed it, the Maryvale boys."

Adolpho waved Turtle and Eddie inside. "Well," he said, "come on, then. We best make us a plan."

Early in the morning, at five, they appeared at the dead woman's house, Eddie, Adolpho, and Turtle, and found it empty and smelling of urine. The boys had broken the back window and painted gang signs on the white kitchen walls. The red parlor smelled of weed. Eddie looked at himself in the crack of the parlor window. "Those motherfuckers," Turtle shouted, looking at the broken windows. "They, they, they will be back soon. Tonight."

Adolpho gave Turtle a look. "Eddie, you go home and get a hammer and nails. We got to board it up by noon. Turtle, come on, we needs to get some boys to help us."

A week passed. Others came to claim the dead woman's house, young boys in would-be gangs, boys from the adjoining wards, boys from Apache Junction, from Broadway Rd., brandishing sticks and knives, none older than fifteen, and for days the house was lost to Turtle, Eddie, and Adolpho, until they could gather enough South Phoenix delinquents to reclaim it; there were small street scuffles, rocks hurled from slingshots, young boys sniped at from the almond trees with BB guns, drunken melees, raids of screaming boys, the smashing of beer bottles against undersized skulls, chains whipped against fleeing backs, and once Eddie's own dirt bike was snatched from his backyard in reprisal, his bedroom window smashed with a brick. They met the invading boys in night rumbles, in standoffs, and, at last, in one great and bloody melee in the house itself, each room filled with the shouts of skirmishing boys, the slapping and beating of little fists, until the police station dispatched two squad cars, and policemen came rushing through the front door of the dead woman's house, through the ruddy red parlor, up the carpeted stairs, dragging the South Phoenix boys out of the condemned house, lining them up before the bushes and the great white columns of the 51 Woodland porch for all the neighbors, looking on from dark stoops, to witness. Mama saw the commotion, ran over, and boxed Eddie's ear and smacked Turtle's face for letting Eddie out, knowing as she dragged the boys home they would sneak out the next night.

They ran out into the streets, across the park, seeking out boys to help them, came rapping at their windows at night, set up ambuscades, sharpened penknives, pumped BB guns full of air. They made twelve-hour truces, negotiated treaties in the moonlit cotton fields south beneath the jagged black mountaintops, where opposing lines of bastard boys stood upon the dirt. Before them, Turtle and Eddie stood face-to-face with the Maryvale boys (Adolpho at their flank). They would not give up the house, though Eddie did not know why, and Turtle did not seem to know why, only that this, the house, was all that mattered now, only that Daddy had run off and Eddie had wanted to scream but he could not scream, only that the neighbor woman had died, and there was no money, and they must now have something to compensate. The house must belong to them, and none of their enemies could claim it, because Turtle and Eddie had the advantage of logistics and blood desire.

They fought each night until the police no longer came to arrest them. Eddie could beat any boy down, boys fourteen and fifteen, their faces turning pink at sight of him lunging at them in the cramped rooms of the dead woman's house. He smiled in darkness. Fear and rage rushed into him; his arms stretched back; he beat them; there was the crack of his dry brown fists into the faces of the white boys, the sight of himself in Mrs. Walker's broken parlor mirror beating a stinking pimple-faced boy to the ground. Adolpho was always beside him, swinging his fists, Turtle howling like a dog from the top of the dead woman's staircase. Eddie had loathed Turtle, and now he almost loved him, needed him, in the same way Turtle needed him to claim the house, to beat the boys with his overlarge fists. Goddamn, Turtle was right, the house was theirs. Adolpho knew it, too. Adolpho said they could make some money off the house once they claimed it. And Eddie kept thinking about this, the money, the money, as he beat the Maryvale boys down . . . then Eddie wished the Maryvale boys would not give up, for he did not fear them now, and he wondered if Jesus had sent the Maryvale boys so that he might beat them, and bloody their faces against all fear. One night, after Eddie had beaten down two fourteen-year-old boys, Eddie, Adolpho, and Turtle ran across the street to the basketball court to wash the blood off their knuckles in the public rest room. Turtle turned to Eddie and he said, "Damn, Eddie, you fight, fight hard. You fight harder than me and Adolpho fucking put together, nigger!" And Eddie smiled at himself, smiled big, in the graffitoed mirror, and washed the pink blood of his hand in the sink. And Adolpho, nodding, gave Eddie's shoulder a slap.

One day the Maryvale boys ran off and they did not come back. Eddie watched the house from the bedroom window, waiting for the screeching of dirt bike chains, the shouts of boys in the darkness, but heard nothing but the recurrent sound of sirens racing up Van Buren beyond the park. They had won the house. That night Turtle snuck Eddie out of the bedroom and down the street to meet Adolpho, to watch the city of Phoenix above the rim of palm trees from the dead woman's balcony.

Eddie had never seen the city like this before, from so high, above the palmettos, at night. They ran through the house, Adolpho, Eddie, and Turtle, laughing in darkness, playing t-tag in Mrs. Walker's house. They found secret hiding places in her attic, a cubbyhole in the top-floor bedroom. Eddie had never seen Turtle so happy. The house was for them a blessing, the only good thing—Turtle confessed to Adolpho on the very staircase Mrs. Walker had toppled down—that had happened to them since Daddy ran off.

Eddie knew that Turtle could tell Adolpho and no one else. Adolpho was Turtle's nigger. Adolpho and Turtle had knocked about the South Phoenix streets together for as long as Eddie could remember. Adolpho had a year on Turtle, but they took the same remedial classes together until they dropped out.

The house belonged to Adolpho, too. He could have a share. Adolpho had been good to them. The second night after Daddy ran off, Turtle dragged Eddie from Nana's shouts and Mama's crying to Adolpho's house. "We needs to get y'all drunk tomorrow, what we needs to do," Adolpho said that night. "We needs to get you tore down." Adolpho stole beers from his uncle Balthazar's corner of the refrigerator and set them in his backpack, and they ran into the city to get drunk. Eddie did not understand why they needed to get themselves drunk until they'd wandered to the city the next afternoon, sat on a Van Buren curb before the Liquor Giant, and Eddie was buzzing off his second beer. Eddie felt good. Eddie felt nothing at all. Adolpho was right. The beer made you feel no hurt. Eddie no longer worried that Mama and Nana would lose Nana's house. And Turtle looked calm, too. They drank with Adolpho into the afternoon. Men in do rags, slouching men, the very men who Eddie sent Turtle on his errands, called Turtle "little nigger," and their hookers, emerged from the ten-dollar motels and Third Ward flophouses half asleep like walking zombies. Eddie watched Turtle watching the men. Turtle was drunk, his skinny body drunk on a couple beers, Turtle whispering, "Nigger, you is only scared. I will buy you toys, toys, toys, toys with the money I gets from Van Buren if you talk. You is only scared, Eddie. You is only scared. We don't need that no-

good son of a bitch." They sat on the curb with Adolpho that afternoon, drunk, watching the cars, taking solace in the familiar faces
of the pimps and whores, the waking hustlers, rising from a day's
sleep—like vampires, he thought, sleeping out the day—everyone
rising in concert, the men and women, wandering out of their motel
rooms, the men to sell the bodies of the women, the women to have
their bodies sold by men. And police cars slowed from the side
streets, cornered onto Van Buren, as if the cops inside too had slept
the day in preparation for this night. Eddie was high. Eddie had no
worries, only tomorrow, only tomorrow's beers to get. Daddy had
left them, but they could play in the house; it might could be a good
summer still.

Adolpho's uncle Balthazar liked to drink, drinking being his only
occupation, and though Uncle Balthazar possessed a forbearing dis-
position, he dragged Adolpho to the refrigerator when they returned
to the farmhouse that night, accused Adolpho of vicking his beers,
and beat Adolpho down right in front of Turtle, Eddie, and Adolpho's *familia* that evening, punched him closed-fisted. In the kitchen
before his cousins and his mama and his sister, the refrigerator
swung open, Adolpho confessed in Spanish, beneath his uncle's slapping fists, to thieving the beers, and Adolpho ran out of the kitchen,
Turtle and Eddie after him, into the red dust of twilight, Adolpho
panting, crouched on scattered chicken feed, and bleeding from the
face. Adolpho took the beating without complaint, his eye the next
hour swollen. Adolpho didn't make a fuss about it or fess on Turtle
and Eddie. Adolpho was like that. A boy will take a beating for you if
he is your nigger.

The three of them drank beers together each afternoon that first
week after Daddy left. Curbside beers seemed to lift Turtle's spirit,
his worries tapering after each sip, until he worried only for Eddie,
complaining to Adolpho that Eddie had not spoken. "Then, don't
you be beating on Eddie no more," Adolpho said. "That won't help

him now." And Adolpho took Turtle and Eddie back to the curb-side in front of the Liquor Giant each afternoon to buy liquor from crackheads, fairies who sold themselves on Roosevelt St., the white marks, executives in four-hundred-dollar suits who drifted into the ward to get their crack at lunch, Arizona State frat boys hunting for dime bags of weed.

One day, sitting at the curb, in front of Eddie, Adolpho made a confession to Turtle. "Turtle, Turtle," Adolpho said, "*mira*, there is something I gots to tell you, something I ain't never told you before. Sometimes, I fall out on my back. I got this epilepsy shit. I ain't told you on account of it gone away since I was eight, and it ain't come back since last month. Epilepsy make you fall out on your back and shake and spit and drool like a baby. I had a seizure last month I ain't tell you about. But it's cool cause I see the angels, nigger, and I get visions. I look into the future and shit. Uncle Balthazar took me to the doctor last month, and the doctor say I might fall out again on account of something he seen when he looked at a X ray of my brains." Beggars passed by above them. It was midday, sunny. It was hot, and they were drunk on the beers. Eddie felt so good. Eddie understood why Daddy had drunk beers so much. Turtle was staring at Adolpho. Eddie wondered why Adolpho had not told them this before.

"I, I," Turtle told Adolpho, nodding, stuttering.

Adolpho gave Turtle and Eddie an imploring look. "Somebody got to watch me. Y'all won't run from me when I fall out, when I is shaking on the ground?"

"Hell no . . . !" Stammering Turtle went silent; it was all he could say. Eddie shook his head. Of course not. He wouldn't run, not after everything Adolpho had done for them. Turtle said, "You, you, you ain't got no problem, Adolpho. You won't fall out, out nohow."

"You don't know that," Adolpho said. "I got epilepsy. My brain don't work. You got to deal with reality, Turtle. You can't pretend things ain't a certain way when they is. You got to deal. Your daddy run. You got to deal. Your little brother freak out, go quiet, and you want to beat him. I am telling you about my di-sease and you got to help me. You just look after me when I fall out. Put a twig in my mouth so I don't bite my fucking tongue off," Adolpho said.

"Your daddy run, boy, and you freaking, Eddie. It's okay. You ain't got to talk if you ain't want to. I know how you feel for the simple fact my daddy left me, too."

In the middle of that week Turtle met a funny man named Jules outside the Liquor Giant. Jules managed the mail boys in the basement of the Dial Corporation, up the street on Palm Lane. Adolpho made Jules out for a faggot first thing and told Eddie and Turtle this later that afternoon. Eddie had never met a faggot before, but Turtle said that one time on Roosevelt St. he had seen one of them dressed up like a woman in the back of a lease car with another one dressed like a regular dude. That was all Turtle knew about faggots except that they had AIDS and waved their wrists and said, "Woo-hoo."

Jules was removing a cigarette from a pack of Marlboro reds when Turtle propositioned him to buy him a six-pack of generic beers for Eddie and him (as Adolpho looked on from the alley across the street, in secret, in case the deal went bad) with $5.87 worth of loose change. Jules put a flame to his cigarette and shrieked in laughter. "You think," Jules told Turtle, "I want the money you stole from your mammy's purse?"

Turtle waited on the curb with Eddie for Jules to emerge from the Liquor Giant. He flashed the bottles of Mad Dog 20/20 before Turtle like scraps of meat before a dog. "Well, come on, boys," said Jules. "I ain't gonna give this to you out in the middle of the motherfucking street." Turtle followed Jules to his car. Adolpho was in the alley shaking his head. Turtle unlatched Jules's passenger door, climbed into the seat, Eddie after him, climbing into the back.

"I said beers," Turtle said.

Jules turned his head. "Beers stand out. You might be a little fucking snitch. These fit under your shirt. Oh, drama. What am I doing?" He looked at Eddie in the rearview. "What is you looking at, boy?" he shouted. "Say something." Eddie felt his face go red. He looked away.

"He don't talk," Turtle said.

"That is pitiful, and why? Don't tell me he big and stupid."

"No, our daddy left is why. He took it hard. He sensitive like that." Turtle arched his shoulders, pouring the change back into his pocket until his pocket had swollen. For show Turtle grabbed one of the bottles of Mad Dog, twisted off the cap, and took a swig before Jules, who covered his mouth, laughing, as Turtle took the bottles and went running out of the car to Adolpho.

Turtle and Eddie met Jules at the Liquor Giant the day after, brought Jules his lunch in the basement mail room of the Dial Building, riding their dirt bikes up Central to Palm Lane. In the basement Eddie found Jules in a collared shirt. Jules's desk was bigger than the desks of the other, white men. Jules had a good, indoor, air-conditioned office job, but Eddie knew the man hustled because Jules dressed too well for a man who pushed a mail cart.

Adolpho wouldn't come along. Watch out for Jules, Adolpho kept saying. Said, Watch your back, nigger. Turtle did not care. Jules had money. And Eddie was more curious of the man than he was afraid. Jules sent Turtle and Eddie on errands in the city: pick up Chinese takeout, pay the electric bill at the Checks Cashed, get cigarettes from the vending machine, seeming each time less surprised that the boys returned at all with a receipt, his change, with Chinese, his cigarettes. Jules had the manner of an elementary school teacher, of an aunt, always doting.

One night Jules met Turtle and Eddie at the Dial Corporation and drove them to 37 Woodland and, offering a business card, told Mama that he had an associate's degree in business administration from Florida International University, that he was a manager at the Dial Corporation, that he considered himself a Christian man.

"Want me to know they in good hands, what you wanted," said Mama, smiling, staring at the card. "You ain't got to say all that. Shoot, if you can handle them. These boys ain't been nothing but trouble since they daddy left."

*J*ules took the boys for the weekend. "I'll pick you up at the park," he told Turtle when he called. "You and Eddie be waiting there, little boy. Don't make me go looking." Jules loaded them into his car and drove them to the mall for errands, babied them, bought them comic books and candy. Jules would cut Turtle off when Turtle began to stutter. "Stop it! Just shush. We got to work on that."

At the end of the day Jules whisked Turtle and Eddie inside his town house, whisked Eddie and Turtle inside, shut the door, set down his bags, and took a sigh. The house was neat, decorated with fake African art. There was cable. Video games. Eddie's favorite breakfast cereal, Cap'n Crunch, and candy bars sat on the dining table. The man had been talking all day. The man would talk and Turtle would look out the car window. "You need to apply yourself. You is stupid and you don't listen. But I can teach you things." The man would talk about Eddie and again Turtle would look away. "Don't let me catch you slapping your little brother no more. Can't you see the little nigger be traumatized?"

Turtle listened to Jules ramble for the sake of the Burger King and Kool-Aid. "And don't give me none of that project-nigger sob-story shit," Jules kept saying. "I didn't have no daddy neither. I grew up in the ghetto, too, but you see my mama gave me home training." His voice was light and pitched and sometimes he laughed like a woman.

Eddie drank sugared Kool-Aid in Jules's living room and watched cable television. Pale fish swam in the aquarium. Jules set him on the sofa with fresh-smelling blankets and lay down with Turtle on the futon. On the futon beside Jules, Turtle blushed when Jules said, "Take off your jeans, boy. You won't be comfortable!" Jules smelled of the Marlboro he'd just smoked on the back porch.

"You think you can help him," said Turtle, "but can't nobody help, help him. Mama said he gonna be a mean buck nigger like his daddy. I only beat him to make him hard. He look big, big, and, and mean, but he soft inside like a little girl, Jules. You think I ain't worried. He my brother. I bought him doughnuts for breakfast with my own money. I could have bought me a *X-Men* comic book, I could have bought me a *New Mutants*." Turtle began to stutter. Jules giggled at his stutter. Jules was like Mama, Eddie thought, feeding you, touching your shoulders, until he was cruel, until he was laughing at your weakness. Eddie watched Turtle turn red. The room filled with silence. Eddie worried that Turtle would try to win Jules over with the dead woman's house, how they'd found out, battled for it, but Turtle kept quiet.

"You drink," Jules said. "You dropped out of school, you smoke weed, and you smoke my cigarettes! You stutter. A sad sight when I saw you on that curb, you little lush. You play it cool. I like that about you. Like last week when we talking to your mama, how you play it off about the booze, how you keep your mouth shut. That ain't something you can teach nobody, even if you stupid and you stutter," Jules shouted, the next moment laughing. "We'll take care of your little brother, Turtle." Jules looked at Eddie on the sofa. "Poor, Eddie," he said, squeezing Eddie's foot. Eddie watched him from the sofa and wondered what Jules could possibly do for him.

"You boys is going to church tomorrow. I told your mama I'd take y'all to church."

Eddie thought the man could only be joking because that night in the bathroom he'd found under the sink a triple-beam; a dime bag was taped to the back of the toilet. (And then when Turtle went to the bathroom to pee, Jules, drunk, took Eddie aside and in the darkness of the hallway said, "My daddy wasn't about shit neither, boy. You ain't got to be afraid of me. I won't hurt you. I told Turtle he best stop smacking you. Look at you. You is adorable. I won't let nobody hurt my little Eddie, you dig?") Turtle giggled as Eddie drifted. Jules had been slipping them Gentleman Jack, a liquor so smooth Eddie could not taste the alcohol beneath the raspberry Kool-Aid, sipping, sipping until he was drunk, lying on the sofa watching Turtle shirtless on the mauve futon below with Jules, the Movie Channel playing in the background. Slack-mouthed, in the shaking light of the television, Eddie watched Jules whip back the covers, stand, yank off his shirt, take down his underwear, and, sitting down, shift naked under the covers, grasping drunken Turtle in his skinny black arms, and sleep.

The next morning at ten Jules drove them to a JCPenney outlet, hurried inside, bought Turtle and Eddie church clothes, ill-fitting slacks, off-white oxfords, ugly matching blue ties, dressed them in the parking lot, racing back to South Phoenix in time for eleven o'clock service.

They sat in Jules's car, in the parking lot of a peeling matchbox-shaped Pentecostal church platted on the slope of a slanting industrial park of nine-foot chain-link and Porta Pottis and windblown garbage. Fat church matrons shouted inside the hollow church. Through the open back doors Eddie studied the old women in silhouette waving their arms in the air, holy shadows rocking in the pews. Jules removed from his pocket a small vial, which he uncapped, pressed to his nostril, sniffed, and laughed, leaning back.

In the distance mother and child climbed the stone steps, disappearing into darkness. "If I ever catch you snorting cocaine," Jules shouted. Eddie watched him, Turtle watched handing Jules his Bible from the glove compartment. Jules opened his door, wiped powder from his nose with his bony fingers, climbed out of the car into the blinding bright parking lot in his black suit, Jesus-happy, wing tips scraping against the gravel, Turtle and Eddie hurrying after him. "Our people have strayed from the church," Jules muttered. "Our people have gone astray with the out-of-wedlock and the drinking and the welfare and the drugs and the gangs and the killing and the homo-sexuality. Our people have forgotten Jesus, and it has been our ruination."

Inside the preacher sat on a beautiful wooden chair, fanning himself with the program. Behind him young men, a makeshift church band, strummed guitars, played the organ, beat on secondhand drums. Young black girls with cleavage, beautiful girls in beautiful summer skirts, sat along the third row, turned, watching Jules, Turtle, and Eddie enter. It was a church of women, save Jules and the band; it was a church of old haggard women, save the third row. The organ was out of tune. Turtle and Eddie stood next to Jules in the very middle of the dark church, parishioners in the midst of hymnal, Jules screaming louder than the women, clapping his slender hands, handsome in his dark suit, surrounded by the corpulent church matrons, everyone dancing, shouting praise at Jesus, at the old woman dancing before the altar in bouffant hairdo, impelled by the rhythm of drums and claps to stand before them all, the rows, a supplicant, shaking in half darkness, speaking in tongues . . . and there was that smell of church Eddie found familiar; it was the smell of sweat, which was the Anointing of the Lord, the funk of warm black bodies and Aqua Net hair spray and Right Guard aerosol deodorant, the smell of His Judgment, dime-store perfume, and warm oak wood, His Mercy. Eddie saw Jules sobbing, sobbing, salt tears streaming from both eyes, down his lips, into his open mouth. *A home in heav'n, what a joyful thought!* And Jules was clapping with spindly black fingers. *As the poor man toils in his weary lot.* Jules set a twenty and two fives, another twenty, and a ten into the basket, the old woman shouting, "Glory!" beside him, nodding at the wealthy stranger.

Church folk watched Jules take Turtle and Eddie outside into the parking lot after service—so tall he was, the wealthy man, so handsome . . . but funny, effeminate, that way. The church folk did not stop him to say hello, to court Jules, Eddie noticed, because they knew he would return, because they had seen him giving God His glory. They had seen Jules crying, the Holy Ghost possess his lean black body.

Jules walked Turtle and Eddie out to his car as the others, common folk, wandered home through the industrial park, figures lost behind the contractor chain-link. Jules was sweating. This was redemption. Jules smelled of church, of the Anointing . . . and there was a moment when Turtle had given himself to the Lord, as Eddie had seen him do before at Nana's hip, when the social security check did not come on time, when Nana gathered Eddie and Turtle into her bedroom, to pray, to kneel, to bow down before a wall cross, the room smelling of Nana's dying black flesh, and Eddie had himself prayed, and Eddie had himself felt the Holy Ghost flush into the stale room with them, only to sense the next morning, waking, that the Holy Ghost had run off like his daddy. Jules opened the car door.

Jules was okay, Eddie thought. *He only held Turtle naked. He ain't put his dick in Turtle's mouth like Adolpho worry about.* Church folk streamed out of the front door, shadows disappearing behind the defunct factory. Jules scanned the parking lot, removed from beneath his seat a package, a wallet-sized brick wound with electrical tape, and deposited the package into Turtle's weekend bag. It was the first time, Eddie thought. It was a test. Turtle was holding heat.

"They will come to my, to my, to my," Turtle whispered at Jules, almost crying, as the church mothers passed. Eddie watched him from the backseat. Eddie did not feel safe. He wanted to run out of the car but he did not know where he was. "The narc police," Turtle said, "point guns in my window, like the boy down the street."

"You is twelve years old."

"They will scare, scare, scare my little brother, and then he won't never talk."

"If you flap your lips, boy. If you get sloppy and stupid. You trying my last nerve. Shut your fucking mouth, you little bitch. That's what you is, a little bitch!" Jules reached into the bag and grasped the wound package. "If you be talking about how you is working for this man Jules. If you tell everybody what you be holding. You is just twelve year old. Ain't nobody going to mess with you. Shit, maybe I don't know you. Maybe you a little punk. Maybe I should send you back to your mama."

"No, no." Turtle touched his wrist. "I keep it for you. I got me a place up the street from my house. A house. It safe. It my house now. I claimed it."

Jules turned to Turtle. Turtle was not lying. Eddie watched. He wanted to scream. He'd known Turtle would tell Jules about the house. They'd fought so hard for it, and Jules would take it now.

"I found it, Jules. Ain't, ain't, ain't nobody live there! Nobody." Turtle withdrew his hand.

"But you keep it for now under your pillow. We'll talk about that house, Turtle. Don't let no other little niggers take it." Turtle nodded. He squeezed the package with his dirty fingers.

When they got back from church Nana said Detective Patricia was looking for Turtle again, and Eddie just knew Turtle was going to catch a beat-down. He spent the next three days watching Turtle climb out of the bedroom window, worried that he would come back with his face bruised from Detective Patricia's fists. Detective Patricia drove down Van Buren in an unmarked sedan. He oversaw half the Third Ward, but came to 37 Woodland at Nana's insistence. Detective Patricia had a nickname for everyone on the street, every hooker, every lookout, every crackhead. Detective Patricia gave Turtle his name when he caught him at nine with a nickel bag of weed in his pocket, and Turtle began to stutter, to speak in slow bursts of gibberish; and he was stupid; and his face was round and bland. He even looked like a turtle. Detective Patricia took the nickel bag from him, gave him his nickname, and let him run away. Turtle's name stuck. Turtle liked the name. A real street moniker. To him it sounded hard. And in a month, everyone, Mama, Daddy, Eddie, all the boys in the Third Ward—even Nana—was calling him Turtle and not his Christian name, Marcus. Detective Patricia called Adolpho Pirate because Adolpho liked to wear a bandanna around his head. Detective Patricia's name for Eddie was Bruno. *"Bruno, Bruno,"* he'd call to Eddie from the park, leaping behind the variety store, appearing from bushes like a child molester, shouting from his running car. Eddie hated the name; he hated Patricia. Eddie could not understand how Turtle could take his street name from Detective Patricia, the man who'd sent him to juvie.

Detective Patricia had appeared at 37 Woodland at Turtle's worst moments since Turtle was ten. If Detective Patricia intended surprise, he would park the unmarked car, hardly unmarked for everyone in the neighborhood knew it, behind the New State Variety Store and jaunt to the house in a mismatched suit, drinking instant coffee at the kitchen table with Nana, lying in wait for the unguessing Turtle, who never heard the low hissing of the Motorola radio on Detective Patricia's belt until it was too late, until Turtle had opened the screen door, crossed the welcome mat, stepped inside to find Detective Patricia waiting for him. It was pointless to run. After a while Turtle no longer turned pale at sight of him but strode to the kitchen table, suffered Detective Patricia's interrogations lest there be a confrontation in the street, a retaliation, a beating, or, worse yet, Detective Patricia lock Turtle in the basement holding cell of the Madison St. Jail for half a day, chained to the peeling lime green wall by a wrist. Patricia had done this twice. Turtle told Eddie that the chains, the cuff, the cell itself always caused him to imagine slavery days, and Turtle would turn and mention this to another scowling black boy. "Look at this, black," he would say. "Look. Our wrists, wrists, wrists chained, black, our wrists chained! Yes, just like how we come over here, my black, black, black brother, our wrists chained, at the bottom, bottom, bottom of a slave ship."

Once Detective Patricia yanked Turtle from Van Buren and dragged him into an alley behind a flashing police cruiser and took a belt to his back because Turtle had twice in one day run from Patricia, made Patricia chase after him in the three-digit heat, run when Turtle should have known better; Patricia took his belt to Turtle's back as the beat cops made Eddie and Adolpho watch, Eddie sobbing into his hands. Turtle had been beaten enough to know that he should march into Nana's kitchen when Detective Patricia came to visit and answer his questions. Turtle was not a reluctant snitch, and the Third Ward possessed no web of gang loyalties, intrigues. Turtle held no allegiance to anyone but Adolpho. In turn for small bits of information Detective Patricia would leave Turtle alone. In Nana's kitchen Detective Patricia had Turtle pore over photos of runaways, report on the gang activity of the ward though it was little and laughable, a caricature of Los Angeles.

Detective Patricia had come to apprehend him first as a beat cop, then as a city detective. He'd appeared at the door so many times that Nana called him "Turtle's cop." No one could fathom why Detective Patricia let Turtle survive at all, let Turtle canvass the block, feeding crackheads, running errands for the hustlers and the hookers, except that Turtle was ruled by Nana, who had herself called Detective Patricia from her porch, waved Detective Patricia inside, and offered up the evidence against Turtle, a dime bag of marijuana, a tiny orange case of Zig-Zag cigarette rolling paper. On that day Nana had offered Turtle to his antagonist, welcomed the squat, olive-complected Detective Patricia into the tepid corner house, into Turtle's filthy bedroom, where Turtle was napping on his bed in gym shorts and Reeboks after a pickup game in the Woodland basketball courts. Turtle woke with a start to find Detective Patricia above him, cuffing him, dragging him out before Nana and Mama, before Eddie, so that Turtle might be redeemed, sentenced to two weeks at the Apache Youth Corrections Center to be raped by boys, to spend his afternoons on the hot red clay beneath the red-rock mountains seen through chain-link, to read by court mandate the first chapters of *The Autobiography of Malcolm X* and *Native Son*, to write a court-mandated one-hundred-word composition on the first chapters of said books because the juvie judge was himself black and street born—the books, the report, which would take Turtle the whole of his two-week stay.

Detective Patricia came by the house for three straight days, looking for Turtle. One day he poked his head through the open bedroom window while Eddie was reading a comic book, and Eddie almost screamed in shock. "Hey, Bruno," Detective Patricia said from the front lawn, waving a manila folder, "where's your brother?" Eddie shook his head. Turtle, standing in the hallway, saw Patricia and ran out to meet him. Eddie heard them talking on the front lawn; they could only be talking about the dead woman's house, he thought, and he worried now that Turtle had lost the house to Patricia, but Patricia flashed a photograph to Turtle and said he was only looking for a man named Spider from Flagstaff, Arizona, and Turtle had never heard of a man who went by Spider before.

*B*y the time Tessa came down from California, Turtle claimed two blocks of Van Buren and ran streetwalkers twice his age. Turtle's girls paid him half what they paid a full-grown pimp, but Turtle didn't seem to care, as long as they were pretty, as long as they looked him in the eye and talked to him like he was a man. Like the others, Turtle found Tessa climbing off a Greyhound bus, in a sweat suit, hair pulled back. Turtle told Eddie and Adolpho he thought Tessa looked sixteen, seventeen, but never asked the girl herself. Even at twelve Turtle gave off a sense of purpose, and he could spot the girls coming off the buses, always lost-looking, sometimes pretty, carting suitcases or laundry bags, and he could cajole them back to the dead woman's house for a night. He could point out the mean pimps, the undercover vice cops, find the girls safe corners, his corners; and if the girls were broke—they were always broke—Turtle would put them up at 51 Woodland for a night, bedding them sometimes.

In the bus terminal Turtle told Tessa her hair looked nice pulled back, and she laughed at him, shaking her head, pointing. "Somebody pay you to talk to me?"

"Don't nobody pay me," said Turtle. "I pays people. People work for me."

"Look at you, then."

"You look tired, girl. I got a place for you. There a empty house down a ways," Turtle said. Tessa giggled. Turtle pointed south in the direction of the red mountains. "My house. I claim, claim, claim it. Keep you safe for tonight." Turtle introduced himself, introduced Adolpho, Eddie. Tessa panned the street for a lurking pimp. Turtle took her hand. "Come with us," Turtle said. Tessa let out a breath and shouldered her bag and followed the boys into the darkness of Central Ave. Followed them back to the house, and they shared a bucket of Kentucky Fried Chicken above a Coleman lamp in the cleared-out living room beneath framed portraits of the dead woman's sons.

"You, like, the first black people I seen since the bus got into Arizona," Tessa told them, folding a napkin across her lap.

"Lots of black people in Oakland?" Adolpho asked her. "Cause I gots people in Cali, East L.A., parts."

Eddie stared at her.

"Come on, now. Oakland gots mad black people," Tessa said. "A whole bunch of black folk."

"I gonna tell you this right now," Turtle said. "Niggers in Phoenix is weak, but you with some real niggers right now."

"Lucky for me, then." Tessa bowed her head, thanked Turtle for the chicken, laughing at his arrogance.

Soon she was standing at the windows, watching the streets.

Turtle watched Tessa watching the street. "I will take you to the strip," he said.

"I know where it is. My one friend told me. Van William."

"Van Buren," Turtle said. "I best take you."

"You is very pretty, mad pretty," said Adolpho.

"You might not never see me after tonight. I might not never come back."

"She scared," said Turtle.

Eddie stared at Tessa from the sofa with the intensity of an animal, an infant, staring at her in the darkness until she noticed him staring and smiled.

She shook her head at Turtle. "Don't think you can run no games on me," Tessa said. "Don't think I owe you nothing, and don't think I gonna lift up my shirt and let you see my titties so you let me sleep here. I got a man in Oakland, and I got a little baby son there."

"You'll be like the prettiest one," Adolpho said. "She scared," he said to Turtle.

"I ain't scared of nothing."

"She scared," Turtle said, "for the reason of she ain't done it before, for the reason of she don't know the area."

"I done it before. For two months. In Cali and New Mexico. Ain't nothing. How I heard of this." Tessa rubbed her cheek with her painted fingers, studied the mascara on her fingertips. "Can you watch my things here tomorrow till I get a room?"

Turtle nodded. A car passed, reflected lights yawing across the peeling walls.

"If y'all little thugs try and vick my shit . . . ," Tessa said.

"No, no," said Adolpho.

"Come on now," said Turtle, leaning forward in darkness. "It ain't like that."

Eddie began to drift to sleep on the couch. Tessa left the window, sat next to him. Eddie felt her set his head on her lap, rubbing his neck, applying to his ear, his forehead the same absent finger strokes used to check the condition of her mascara.

Tessa did not remove her makeup. Eddie wondered why she'd worn makeup at all on the bus ride down unless she did not have money for a room. The makeup was thick and stark white, coating her face and the pimples on her forehead, unneeded. Tessa stroked Eddie's head as he pretended to sleep on her thighs, fearing that if he opened his eyes she would stop. "This boy," she said. "I can't believe he ten years old. He is bigger than you. He so quiet. He don't shout or act up. This is good for his age. Gosh, he don't cause no trouble, talk back." She turned to Turtle.

"He ain't talk since our daddy run off," Turtle told her. "He ain't said a word."

"This is your little brother, Turtle. It's late. Maybe you best take him home now."

"My mama work, work, work late," Turtle said. "We live just up the street. Eddie sleep over here all the time with me."

"It's like"—Tessa coughed into her fist—"a feeling you get. I should be home. I should not be so far away from my baby." She turned to the windows, looking at the park and, beyond the park, at the now empty street. "Like bad things."

"Like bad things will happen. But won't nothing happen."

"Like you make a bad decision, like maybe I shouldn't be here. Look at me, confiding in some little boys." Tessa laughed at herself. She coughed. Even in darkness the room was hot, so hot, even now. One hundred degrees at night.

"You just scared for the simple fact you ain't know nobody," Adolpho said, dragging on a generic menthol.

"My grandmother know, I think, know I prostitute. I don't, you know, work in Oakland no more cause people talk about you. My sisters know. They will all be up in my face when I go back. They will be like, 'Stop, we will tell Bobby.' Bobby is my boyfriend. Cause like Bobby older than me by a lot, and he still have a stranged wife, and he said he would quote-quote leave her, and he don't help out with diapers and stuff. Oh, look at you!" Tessa whispered, smiling. "Little boys! You so lucky to be boys. I bet you wish you was grown. But you

don't want to be grown, trust me. I wish I was little like you, shit."
They looked at her in darkness; they realized she was strange. Tessa
noticed a framed picture of the dead woman's sons. "The people who
lived here, they got evicted?"

Adolpho turned to Turtle. Eddie opened his eyes.

"Right," said Turtle.

On the street a woman and her daughter were shouting, their
shouts slapping against the black windows of the row houses of the
street. Eddie heard the railroad bells. The 11:18 Southern Pacific
shoved across Grand Ave.

Tessa slept on the sofa in her street clothes, her arms wrapped
around Eddie. Adolpho and Turtle slept beneath them on blankets
on the floor.

Tessa stayed in the house for a week. Turtle liked her so much he
didn't ask her for rent money. Maybe, Eddie wondered, Turtle was
happy that Tessa didn't run off. Turtle had met hookers he liked. On
the back porch of the dead woman's house Turtle would sit next to
them in their too-tight shining dresses, cellulite hanging off their
thighs, sharing a blunt. Turtle would make his ugly dog face go
sweet. "I sort of like you. Can you be my, my, my girlfriend, tonight?"
he would ask them. And these women would, smacking their bubble
gum, eyes bloodshot, say, "Course, baby, ha, ha, ha, I'll be your little
girlfriend tonight." And Turtle, cocking his head, would say, "Adolpho sort of like you, too. Can you be Adolpho's girlfriend when I'm
done?" Then these hookers would be gone the next week to Lubbock
or Denver (a hooker would tell Turtle) and he might not see them
again for another couple months, if ever again, and he did not seem
to care—if they didn't owe him money—but Eddie thought Turtle
would care if Tessa ran off like that.

Turtle turned thirteen. Jules bought him some comic books and
taught him how to steal cars. Jules drove Turtle and Eddie into a
Central Phoenix parking garage where his man worked the gate and

passed Jules a gratis parking ticket. Jules inched the car up the curling cement path inside.

On the fourth floor they parked next to an Acura. "Get out," Jules
said. Turtle snuck over to the Acura, Jules behind him, pushing Turtle aside, removing from his pocket a thin aluminum bar to jimmy
the lock; and inside the car, he disabled the alarm with a pair of wire
cutters, inserted the lip of the wire cutters in a crevice, wrenched
open the neck of the steering column, cut wires, tied copper ends together, and, standing outside the car, waved Turtle into the driver's
seat, saying, "Obey the speed limit, signal." Turtle drove the car out
after Jules. They came back an hour later, and there was Turtle,
working the window with the aluminum bar, Jules crouching above
with constant instructions. Turtle was a quick study; he was inside
the next car in seconds, but popped a windowpane out with a screwdriver and left it on the garage floor with a fresh set of fingerprints,
which sent Jules shouting. Jules ran back to his car, patted Eddie on
the head, and followed Turtle back to Apache Junction, where a
dark-haired man met them outside a garage with a pale fist of cash,
and Jules counted into Turtle's hand more money than Eddie had
ever seen.

Eddie held out his hand, too, but Jules slapped it. "No," he said.
"This ain't for you."

They went to the Red Lobster for dinner. Jules sang happy birthday to Turtle. They drove home. Eddie felt stupid for holding out his
hand to Jules. He lay on Jules's sofa as Turtle opened his birthday
presents. Eddie wished he had not come. He imagined himself lying
next to Tessa in the torn-up sofa in the dead woman's house. "The
Club, the Club. The Club ain't shit," Jules was saying, hovering over
a bubbling aquarium, feeding his fish. Jules was in one of his pleasant moods. Eddie waited for Turtle to mention Tessa to him, but he
did not. "All you need is a little Freon and a hammer," Jules went on,
"a hacksaw. Auto-theft protection! Shit, can't nobody stop you when

you get your hustle on. Now they got the Club, Turtle, but once they realize niggers already found a way around that, they will come up with something else."

Jules and Eddie and Turtle ate Turtle's birthday cake. Jules seemed happy, but Turtle did not tell him about Tessa. Turtle told Eddie he thought Jules might like Tessa if he met her, but Jules didn't like strangers in the house, and Jules did not trust women. Jules said you had to keep people out of the house unless they paid. Jules was funny about the house. Jules said Turtle had not put the dead woman's house to good use. And once, coked up, in his anger, he'd beaten Turtle for this reason. Turtle had Adolpho escort Tessa out every other week on the night when Jules appeared to check on the condition of the house. Once Jules had come unexpected on a Tuesday when Tessa had just run out to get some condoms at the Circle K. It was getting difficult. Eddie would hear Turtle and Adolpho worrying about what to do about her. Turtle decided pimping Tessa himself was the best way to keep her safe while she stayed in the city, but he would not ask Tessa until the end of summer, when she'd grown to trust him. They slept those hot nights in the living room; they fell asleep to the sound of sirens and shouts, and barking dogs and cars racing down Van Buren.

The roar of garbage trucks roused them on an August morning, rubber trash cans crashing against the sidewalk, the shouts of city workers, boots upon the concrete startled them, lulled them back to sleep.

Eddie woke to the squeaky voices of teenage boys. The storm door smacked against the doorjamb three times, and the front door burst open. Eddie rubbed his eyes. The Maryvale boys, some six, nine, in total scurried through the house; they were shouting at Adolpho and Tessa, beating Turtle with fists, smacking Adolpho's baseball bat against Turtle's skinny legs, ranging through the house in twos, without order, without reason, a barking confusion, breaking windows, pissing in corners, slapping Tessa's doll face. A white boy in a hoody kicked Eddie in the ribs. "Beat him good," said another, and four boys were atop him, kicking his ribs, beating him with sticks, bats, kicking his stomach until Eddie's mouth was filled with blood. "This is the one, the big one." The boys, twelve and thirteen, who'd cowered under him the weeks before as he fought them in the very same house, circled above him, kicked his face with Nikes, and baseball bats—*Here, nigger, here, take it, nigger!*—and beat him until he was ten seconds unconscious. He woke again, bleeding on the dead woman's floor, the boys having left him, to the wild shouts in every room; he crawled to his feet and ran up the stairs to hide.

Three boys encircled Turtle and beat and kicked him where he lay, spat upon his face, cussed at him. Eddie watched the mayhem from atop the staircase, crouched, his mouth, his throat filled with blood. A tall boy cornered Adolpho in the kitchen, knocked him down, stomped upon his knees, beat Adolpho until he broke away, sliding across the linoleum, running out the back door. A nameless acned boy, the eldest, dragged Tessa by her long curly hair from the sofa, where she lay, across the red velvet parlor, to the staircase; others, knowing, ran after him.

Eddie ran into the dead woman's bedroom and hid in her closet. Eddie heard Tessa screaming. Through the narrow crack of the closet door Eddie saw the Maryvale boys drag Tessa into the bedroom and cut her shirt open with long knives. They snatched off her jeans, her panties. Climbed atop her and beat her down, her gangly brown arms rising above the mattress, swatting and repelling. Tessa was shoving them away, screaming—it was a mangled scream—and Eddie was screaming into his own palm until the salt of his skin lined his tongue, until the boys almost heard him screaming, as he watched through the crack of the closet door, the Maryvale boys raping Tessa, waving their tattooed arms, slapping her face as the garbage trucks made their rounds on the streets outside, workers, shirtless, hanging from the rushing garbage trucks, tossing rubber cans against the curbs as the Maryvale boys stabbed themselves into Tessa, causing the bed coils to whine, the springs inside to quicken, the acned boys shoving themselves inside Tessa to the chortled laughter of the others from the doorway.

The boys raped her, one after the other, and did not stop until Adolpho appeared at the back door with his uncle Balthazar's .38 and ran through the kitchen and up the stairs to the bedroom, where he three times shot the gun, hitting one boy in the arm, another in his left foot; the last bullet passed through the bedroom ceiling. The popping sound of exploding gunpowder, bullets, winging then lodging into wood, beat against the thin walls, shaking the window glass . . . it was a hollow sound, like plywood slapping against concrete. Tessa went silent. Eddie saw the last boy scramble, naked, barefoot, pale back bleeding, off the harried girl, dragging his jeans in one hand, past Adolpho and out of the room. Other boys came flushing down the red velvet stairs, the last shot boy trailing blood from a shoulder, leaving faint streaks of red blood across the peeling red wallpaper, on doorknobs, and the Maryvale boys ran out of the red velvet parlor, taking their parked bikes from the front yard, pedaling home, another limping on bloody sneakers down the street.

The closet door swung open. Eddie appeared before Tessa, his face covered in blood. She looked at him as if he should have saved her when he could not save her. Her face was bruised, her lip bleeding. Tessa screamed at him now, as if Eddie were a stranger to her. Tessa crouched naked and bleeding before him on the bed, her dough-colored legs and arms folded as she cried at him, then covering herself with a sheet of torn cardboard from the floor, staring, silent. Then he felt it, like the blood in his throat, coming out of him, like vomit, and he could not stop it, and he could not keep it in anymore, and he was shouting in the narrow space. "Run," Eddie screamed, "run, girl, run now."

Tessa looked at him in shock, sobbing behind the cardboard sheet. Eddie stared at her until he realized Tessa was naked, and he turned from her and left her crying, hurrying down the ruddy red stairs. All the Maryvale boys were gone. Turtle found him in the kitchen. "They raped her," Eddie shouted at Turtle. Eddie was crying. Turtle's face was bruised and bleeding. Everyone was bleeding. "They beat on her, Turtle, and they raped her. They cutted her clothes off with they knives. She gonna leave us now!"

Sirens raced down Van Buren. Soon the police car would turn onto Woodland Ave., park before the dead woman's house.

There was no time. "Come on," Adolpho said. "We best hide." And he took Eddie up the stairs, Turtle following after.

A pad car turned into Woodland, rushing. The four of them, Adolpho, Eddie, Turtle, and Tessa, sat in the tepid darkness, waiting on the mattress of spotted blood for the beat cops to abandon the call (for there was no time, and Tessa was too frantic, to conceal themselves into the cubbyhole in the dead woman's bedroom), to abandon the front yard of yellowed grass and overgrown weeds. Tessa sobbed into a dirty pillow, the room smelling of her blood, of the dirty teenage bodies of acne-faced boys, of sex and mold. It was 111 degrees outside. The policemen went to the front door but did not enter. The policemen orbited the dead woman's house, peered into windows. Twenty minutes passed. The policemen would not stop knocking at the door, circling the house, their black boots crunching blanched grass, calling to one another above their radios; they did not come inside.

The odd, suffering girl did not for three days move from the upstairs mattress in the dead woman's house. Turtle and Adolpho brought Tessa food and liquids. In compensation for the ordeal, the horror, the rape, the valuables ripped from her Samsonite, all in reliance upon Turtle's promise that the house was safe, Turtle fed Tessa, and at Tessa's request furnished her enough liquor to maintain a numbing three-day drunkenness, enough to blunt the pain; he sent Eddie into the hot, stinking room to lie with Tessa on the mattress, so that Tessa might squeeze Eddie like a baby doll, so that the shrill sobs from upstairs would cease, so that Tessa would not leave them.

On the fourth day Tessa could stand, keep a semblance of composure. Tessa descended the stairs. Turtle and Adolpho and Eddie stared at her from the parlor. She went out onto the porch of squeaking wood boards, swearing to them that never again would she sleep in the dead woman's house, as she wandered down the stoop to the front gate. Turtle watched Tessa journey from Woodland Ave. to Van Buren, returning the very same night when she'd spent her hotel money on liquor and junk food, clean undergarments.

But the house was a horror for her, filled with memories of the rape. Tessa woke crying in the mornings. Turtle bought her doughnuts. Tessa suffered little panics. She wanted to go back home to Oakland, she told the boys, but she could not go back now. "I need to see my baby. I didn't mean to stay this long. Them boys raped me, ruined me. My grandma will look at me and she will know. I can't tell her how they done me!" Eddie, Adolpho, Turtle looked at her, puzzled. Tessa did not feel safe in the house alone. No one did. For Tessa's sanity Turtle watched—or had Eddie watch—from the cracks of motel closet doors Tessa dating the men, the fat white, balding men, groaning atop her, so that Tessa would not in a horror revert to the shrieking naked woman raped by the Maryvale boys. And later they would walk her back to 51 Woodland, but she would not sleep in the dead woman's house without one of them beside her.

Turtle found Tessa a motel room at the Coral Reef on Van Buren and 27th Ave., where she could recuperate far away from the dead woman's house, from the madness of Woodland Ave.—Woodland Ave. being just a park's width from the Van Buren strip. Each night, after Tessa had completed her rounds, Turtle would visit her at her

Coral Reef motel room with Snickers and M&M's, leftovers from Adolpho's house, which Tessa swallowed down like a welfare child, demanding Turtle sleep next to her in her motel bed, if only so that she might have something to hold, something in which to take solace, stroking Turtle's cheek, drifting to sleep to the sound of sixteen-wheelers thundering up the I–17.

*T*he Maryvale boys did not come back, but no one felt safe in the house again. The doors of 51 Woodland did not lock. Too often Turtle found strangers at the door in the night, vagrants, men who were insane. Eddie and Adolpho felt it, too. There was the upstairs and downstairs to search, the cubbyhole, under the bed; board the kitchen door before you lay down for the night. Eddie did not trust the house, but went each night to check on Tessa. He could not let Tessa sleep there alone.

In Turtle's mind the dead woman's house belonged to him, but Eddie knew Turtle now kept the house for Jules. When vagrants appeared at the back door, snuck through the window, Turtle evicted them on Jules's authority. When roving gangs spotted it, Turtle shot at them from the balcony with a BB gun, and reported to Jules. Jules himself checked the dead woman's house on Wednesdays and Sundays. Turtle held small weekend gatherings with girls in the dead woman's house Thursday through Friday, would-be sex parties, midnight games of spin the bottle, truth or dare, where once Eddie was forced to kiss a fat mulatto girl named Beatrice, whom Turtle called "Beastrice." Turtle would send Tessa to the flophouses, and walk the gaggles of pubescent giggling girls down the dark street to the front of the giant house. Adolpho would blow out the candles and Turtle would whisper ghost stories, his square face hovering above the flashlight, to the young girls coupled or lying in sleeping bags on the carpet: it was then that Eddie and the others would stare up from the floor at the pictures and portraits and certificates of accomplishment on the walls and imagine the dead woman's life, Eddie thrilled and frightened at once, on the brink of fleeing home and sleeping next to Mama. Turtle described the look on the dead woman's face, how he could hear the blood thickening in her veins, Eddie and the once giggling girls watching the staircase in silence, in the periphery, its upper half dark, as if any moment Mrs. Walker's spirit would come rushing down the stairs.

Later, love music blasting, new couples fondled in the various rooms, in corners of the parlor. Advanced lovers, the young harlots who even at thirteen had reputations, would leave with Turtle or Adolpho to the separate bedrooms as others, Eddie and the neglected sisters and girlfriends, the perpetual third wheels, those too fat or too ugly or too plain or too Christian to be taken into one of the functional bedrooms, lay on the parlor carpet, everyone smoking menthol cigarettes and listening to hip-hop on the boom box.

If a vagrant did not appear at the back door and frighten the girls, if Jules did not come storming through the front door unexpected with errands for Turtle, the upstairs floorboards would soon be heard through the hard music to creak, Eddie imagining the soft and wondrous violence of the act, his brother and Adolpho naked with naked girls, an act that Eddie thought so poisonous, so dangerous, so forever out of grasp and impossible and horrible; or, on other nights, a john's car would park right then outside the great dead woman's house, and Eddie would remember the sound of sex heard through his own bedroom window at night when the prostitutes of Van Buren and their johns would, against all complaints of Mama and the neighbors, park their cars and commit the act before Eddie's very window, and Eddie from his bed could hear through the car windows of the johns the sound of the screeching black voices of the prostitutes commanding and hurrying the act, calling out, "Shoot that hot cum out, shoot that hot juicy cum out, shoot that hot juicy cum out, baby," the voices of the prostitutes tinged with such fear that Eddie would forever associate sex with a kind of hurry, a desperation, a transaction, the shaking of expensive lease cars or taxis, of condoms strewn out in arrogance on the dark sidewalk, Tessa bleeding on the foul mattress.

One night Jules caught Eddie sleeping next to Tessa. He swung by the house looking for Turtle and found Eddie on the cut-up sofa with the teenage prostitute. Jules ran out and came across Turtle on the corner of 18th and Van Buren, coaxing a runaway teen from Nogales into prostitution, and smacked him before the startled runaway. Turtle went back to the dead woman's house and, as Tessa slept, yanked Eddie from Tessa's lap, slapped Tessa across the face, walked Eddie home, forbade him to sleep in the house, in Tessa's arms anymore, only to find him lying against her the next night.

It was no place for a little boy to sleep. Turtle bought a small pistol from a forty-year-old burnout in a Kmart parking lot and now refused to go into the house unless Adolpho was beside him or the pistol was creasing his back pocket. Turtle sent Tessa to the Coral Reef.

That summer a South Phoenix boy named Michael Carbajal qualified for the United States Olympic boxing team in Seoul. He'd made the team without management, only his big brother training him in their backyard. And for this reason, and because Eddie was so big, Turtle took Eddie to the boxing gym up the street to keep him away from Tessa.

Bumpy's was enormous inside; it sat just across Woodland Park, on Van Buren, a slanted line from Nana's house. Above the sharp, practiced breaths of the fighters, Marvin Gaye sang "Sexual Healing" on a clock radio. Every three minutes the report of the wall buzzer punctuated the chaos of the Saturday morning workouts, two sets of shifting, shouting, jabbing, grown Hispanic men in blue jeans, sparring in two rings. Eddie noticed fight posters on the walls: the Golden Gloves semifinals at the Arizona State Fairgrounds, the USA/Arizona box-offs, the Tyson/Mitch "Blood" Green fight. Little Chicana girls ran the steps of the mezzanine. Two rings dominated the gym floor. Small crowds of regulars formed pockets about the northern ring, watching the fights.

The manager, Kell, appeared before Turtle and Eddie. He smelled of liquor and coffee. He was a short, silver-haired Jewish man of sixty or seventy. He called Eddie over to the empty ring, and Eddie straightened as Kell waved him up the scaffold and inside, grabbing him by the wrist, measuring Eddie's arms. "Long arms," Kell announced. "He'll be an outside fighter."

Now Turtle removed his baseball cap and began a small soliloquy. "I figure Eddie age ten now, almost eleven, and they say age ten be a good age to start at."

"Ten is good. Eleven is good. Under ten is too young in my opinion."

"He a big boy," Turtle went on, "a tall, tall, tall, tall one. I seen him beat up dudes who was twelve and fourteen. He fight better than anybody I know. I seen him beating on a dude and I seen him smiling. He like it. He ain't got no daddy, Mr. Kellner. No, no, no daddy, no masculine role model and such to teach, teach, teach Eddie how to be a man and shit. Already, already, already, already taught myself how to be a man, you see, and I can't be teaching him how to be a man. Can't have him following me around all the time, time, time."

"I understand," said Kell. Turtle had stumbled on his words, but Kell had not interrupted. "Now, I won't be anybody's daddy, you understand. I am not a baby-sitter," said Kell, removing from his worn brown clipboard a tattered Xeroxed permission form. Turtle nodded. "This is a hard place, a hard place," Kell went on. "The boy will find it trying. My boys follow directions. My boys keep up their grades. He will earn his spot."

Kell took Eddie over to a heavy bag hung from the longest chain and, standing above Eddie, leaned over, took Eddie's hands, like molds of brown clay, formed them into fists, pressed Eddie's thumbs under his fingers, Kell leaning and staring, breathing, molding, considering. "Hold out your arms! Out! Now make a fist," and he dragged Eddie closer to the Everlast heavy bag and now stood behind him, pale fingers wrapped about Eddie's brown wrists like calipers, directing Eddie's malformed fists into the heavy bag wound with duct tape until the long gray ceiling chain shook. "Breathe, breathe," Kell whispered. "You must always watch your breathing, you must not forget to breathe, but it is the first thing you'll do. No, no. Snap, snap! Do it again to one—two—three! One—two—three! I told you, do it again," he shouted. Turtle was watching. Eddie beat the bag. The bag shook on the long chain. Eddie breathed out with every punch. Kell watched him in contented silence. Again, Eddie beat his naked fists against the red bag leather, letting out a breath with each shot, breathing, until Kell returned Eddie to his brother. Turtle took the permission form and nodded at Kell, leading Eddie out into the frenzied street, where a prostitute recognized him, whistling at him, shouting, "Turtle, Turtle!" high heels clicking against the pocked sidewalk as she ambled to them through a swirl of red dust.

Part Two

Eddie

*A*t the sound of the wall buzzer Eddie climbed through the ropes, a Chicano boy's sixteen-ounce gloves flailing his cheeks. The entire gym began to reel, Kell watching from the floor with the other boys, little Chicana girls looking on him with pity from the mezzanine, brown fingers curled about the banister in the whirling backdrop. *Tss! Tss! Tss!* And his feet were flat and he did not snap his punches, and he had no form. And he did not know a single combination. Eddie could think of nothing but the stench, the heft, of the black sixteen-ounce gloves, the dingy mop-water light of the gym, the sour smell of his own body, the varicoselike splinters across the wall mirrors, Kell looking on from the concrete floor without concern or sympathy as the young boy beat him down—right glove at your ear, left snapping out. Explode in a second and return to form.

Eddie languished for ninety seconds until his arms hung at his sides. Don't hold your breath, a boy told him before he stepped into the ring. You can faint, and the stomach shots hurt more. Eddie could not make the *tss-tss* sound like the boy. *Tss-tss* for speed. *Tuh-tuh* for power. The Chicano boy hounded him across the springy apron. Eddie fled, jogging backward. The whole gym was watch-ing, the whole Chicano gym, indifferent. The boy struck Eddie and struck him again; before Eddie could process the first blow, there was a second and a third, until some part of him wanted to scream out, "Stop, stop!" but Eddie could not stop the fight; no one could stop it but Kell. When the little bout was over Eddie was bleeding from the nose. Kell guided him to the industrial sink in the broom closet, where Eddie's nose blood purled down the black drain hole. Kell put Kleenex in Eddie's nostrils. Eddie could say nothing be-cause he was bleeding into the sink, his fingers wrapped about the rusting porcelain. The bloody nose seemed only an inconvenience, an emblem of failure. It did not even throb. Kell stepped out of the closet and waved at the cocky Chicano boy, and the small boy spat into the tin bucket, climbed through the ropes, and sauntered down the scaffold to the water fountain. When Eddie emerged from the broom closet the gym had forgotten him, and he was glad of this; the gym was a dark, cruel place. He would come back, suffer another month; he would spar with the Chicano boy again and beat him down, and then he would not come back.

The next time he fought the Chicano boy he beat him, in forty-nine seconds, knocked him on his back, and the Chicana girls on the mezzanine went silent, and Kell came into the ring (the Chicano boy lay blinking on the worn mat), patted Eddie's head. Kell's assistant, Tommy, a stringy-haired eighteen-year-old boy from Apache Junc-tion and the 1986 state Gloves middleweight champion, woke the Chicano boy with ammonia. Kell took Eddie into his makeshift of-fice, a converted boiler room adorned with trophies, faded Kodaks, a folding table covered in graph paper, a slide rule, and miniature he-licopters, plastic model helicopters hung from the ceiling of rusting pipes. Kell sat him on the sofa. He leaned back on his desk, sipping a warm beer.

"I've run this gym for fifteen years," he said. "Never seen a boy knock another boy down flat in forty-nine seconds. You stick around."

Then Kell seemed to have forgotten him and he screamed at him the way he screamed at the other boys in the afternoons, at Tommy. He kept to his routine. He did not lag between the rest buzzer and the fight buzzer. He did not sacrifice form at the heavy bag. He fought all the boys and knocked them down until there was no one three-fourths his size to fight, and Kell farmed him out to the Scottsdale clubs and the North Phoenix clubs, so that Eddie might not think too highly of himself, so that boys five years older and fifty pounds heavier might bloody his nose, offer perspective. Sixty/forty. Kell taught Eddie sixty/forty before the wall mirror, staring at Eddie's reflection: "Stand sixty percent forward and forty percent back, thumbs tucked inside your fingers." How the tight-wound hand wraps made Eddie feel like a real prizefighter, like Tyson on the wall posters. It was a diversion, a distraction from Tessa; he knew this, but he liked it. He peered at himself in the mirror each afternoon, at his reflection skating across the mirror cracks. *Tss, tss, tuh! Tuh, tss, tuh! Tss, tss, tss!*

He wondered if he would see Tessa again. Turtle had kept Tessa from him, shuffling her amongst flophouses. Tessa got herself a room at the Copa, on 32nd, in the middle of the strip. She appeared at 37 Woodland and stole Eddie from the bedroom window—though Turtle forbade, his cardinal rule, that any prostitute appear at his bedroom window—kept him in her motel room at the Copa, and twice Turtle had caught her and walked Eddie home. Then Eddie went without sight of Tessa for a month, though he could, in the midst of practice, jabbing, skipping rope, shut his eyes and think of her, recall the perfume Tessa wore on their last encounter in the dead woman's house the month before, the feel of her scented blouse, her T-shirt brushing against his arm, his cheek, the tangy scented skin beneath cotton blouse, the signature pinch of her chin into his shoulder when at last Tessa embraced him, held him, kissed, kissed, kissed him, Eddie clinging always longer than the last time or, if nothing else, making his right cheek available for her kisses, so that the last time as Tessa had spoken to Eddie in the darkness of her motel room lined with stuffed animals, as they lay upon Tessa's bed and a burst of happiness overcame her, some manic and impossible vision of claiming her son in California, Eddie was nearby when in her mania Tessa climbed atop him and pressed her lips against his cheeks, kissing his nose, his laughing, laughing mouth.

Turtle was not keen on Tessa's affection for Eddie. While before Turtle was happy to have Tessa in the dead woman's house, now her constant need to dote on Eddie worried him, and though Tessa had not once cheated Turtle of his take, Turtle distrusted her in the way Turtle distrusted all women. Eddie asked Turtle why he didn't like Tessa anymore; Turtle told him only that it no longer mattered why, for the awkard, bright-skinned girl had run off to Albuquerque with a new boyfriend on the simple promise of cocaine and Eddie would never see her again, which was good, Turtle claimed, because Tessa was odd, odd, odd—but Eddie knew she was odd—because Tessa filled her Samsonite with stuffed bears, headless baby dolls, pressed daffodils in motel phone books, because Tessa the whole day slept, stranger still because Tessa's daffodils, the headless baby dolls, could not be explained by crack or horse or speed, an abusive pimp; and how she covered her face in white powder, the whitest powder, so much powder, Turtle complained, that when he saw her from across the street Tessa resembled a ghost haunting Van Buren, haunting the white men in the passing cars, who saw Tessa's pale, powdered face and wrenched their necks, and then stopped only because Tessa was so beautiful, the pale makeup being an offense, for which once again, Turtle pointed out, he did not beat her.

Turtle rarely beat Tessa, and on a good week would not press her for his take, if only in remembrance of the Maryvale boys, the mob

rape in the dead woman's house that had brought Eddie out of his silence. It was odd, Turtle would say, that after everything, all she'd
been through, Tessa was short of the hard edge of the other girls—
this only caused Turtle to distrust her all the more and to demand
that Eddie keep away from her.

That night Turtle ran out, and Eddie called Adolpho in a panic at
his farmhouse. Eddie was crying when Adolpho came to the phone.
Tessa had run off after all.

Adolpho spoke above the shouts of his adolescent cousins. "Chill
out, Eddie." Adolpho began to laugh. "She right here, Eddie Eagle,
in the city." Adolpho went silent, and Eddie knew that what Adolpho
would tell him came from one of his visions, but this was not a vision, for Adolpho had just seen Tessa at the Circle K. Eddie's face
went flush, and he took a sigh, but Adolpho did not sound relieved.
"Tessa," Adolpho said, "crazy from when they raped her, Eddie. All
right? That rape done drove Tessa crazy. Turtle don't understand,
and he ride her too much. Maybe I talk to him, Eddie Eagle. Maybe
Turtle stop choking her up."

"You talk to him," Eddie said, wiping his eyes. "You tell Turtle I
box like he want, but he let me see Tessa. I know how to make her
feel okay."

Then he saw her from the back of Kell's conversion van, just like
Adolpho promised. Tessa had not left the city. The other boys caught
sight of her from their windows, her lank body, her tilted half-naked
brown hips, and stood on their seats, voices breaking. "Look, look,
Eddie. Do you got them where you live at?" Eddie's friend Woscar
whispered. "We got them. My mama hate them. Look at her. My
mama say they is nasty, no-good bitches." Woscar pointed. It was
Tessa standing on Van Buren and 24th St. She stood before a patch
of blanched grass in her brightest Lycra pants, her round face the
second before turned in an absent moment to the wild curls of graffiti on the side of a bone-colored warehouse. Eddie watched her eyes

pass across the van until she saw him staring at her from his seat. And by instinct, without a thought to Woscar, the other boys, he waved at her from his window, and from the corner, drawing away from him, Tessa lifted a hand and waved back. The boys looked at him in shock, laughing, and he did not care. Leaning upon his folded arms, he smiled at her, staring at her, and Tessa staring back. The boys teased him, mocked him, but he did not mind them now as he from the window gazed at her, his Tessa; he could only smile because he had after so long seen her, because she'd not left the city, and this, a chance sighting, the knowledge that she had not abandoned him, was enough to sustain him through the horror of the Club S.A.R. bout and the sting of the black gloves into his face and lips, and Kell's scolding that afternoon, at the completion of which Kell grabbed Eddie by the shoulders, shook him in the darkness of the empty gym, as if to teach him, as if to make him stronger, as if Eddie needed to have been beaten in front of strangers by a boy five years older, and now, the other boys gone home for dinner, when it was enough that he'd lost, Kell was shouting at him, red-faced, full-on drunk. "You think I am your daddy here, you little son of a bitch? You think I am your fucking friend? You think I am a fucking social worker, here to improve your self-esteem?"

"Let me go!"

Kell let him go. Eddie stared into the old man's shaking, wrinkled, puffed face. Eddie began to walk away, walk backward out of the boiler room of clanking pipes, watching Kell as he walked backward. The man was crazy. The man was white and he lived in the hood. The man had been an engineer and he now lived in the boiler room of a broke-down gym. Kell shook his head. Eddie felt as if any moment the squat old man would lurch at him. "Where are you going?" Kell shouted.

"I going home now. I tired and my face be hurting."

"No, you ain't. Don't you go nowhere." Kell pointed. His fingers were pudgy. "I've got an errand for you. And you show up tomorrow. You are my new assistant."

"But I don't want to be your assistant!"

"Come here, boy. I am making you a man. I am going to make you a champion. I am going to save you from these streets. I am going to impart my wisdom to you. I am going to channel that talent of yours and save you from your brother's fate. I am going to teach you things I don't teach the other boys because they don't listen and because they are stupid, because they are not humble to it, the boxing; they have no, no deference to it. I've done it before. It's just a diversion program for the other boys, but it could be different for you. The way you knocked Giancarlo down like that." Eddie stopped. "What, you want money?" Kell went on. "That's what all of you want, little black boys. Can't see nothing but what's in front of your face. You can have money. We can get you lots of money. You are so lucky to have found me. You best win the Gloves. I won the Gloves when I was a little bit older than you. I won the Gloves in the nineteen forties, that's how antiquated I am, in New York, in Brooklyn. I was the bantam Golden Gloves champ of New York! I boxed in the army. I boxed in college when the war was over. I will show you things, Eddie. But you have to listen to what I tell you. You have to be disciplined. Discipline means doing what I tell you." Kell thought for a moment. "Boxing is like a good woman. She can make your life so good. But you must take it seriously like a craft, like it is your job. I don't need to help you, but I will. I'm an engineer by training, you understand, but I know the sport." Eddie gave Kell a look of shock. The old man waved his finger. "From now on, you do what I tell you."

"I will mop the floors, you need me. I'll run your errands. I'll do extra jackhammers. Be on time."

"You be on time. No excuses. None of this street nigger bullshit," and Kell waved his hand at the front door, at the street outside.

Eddie stared at him.

"Hey, look, you are my assistant now, Eddie. You run the errands like I tell you. I mean, this is serious responsibility. I don't want to be left in a lurch. Come here," Kell shouted. Eddie was shaking his head. "Come here and take off your right shoe. Do it."

A horror flashed through Eddie as he came forward, staring at the pink, wrinkled face. Eddie stared at the man, kicked off his shoe. He took in the odor of Kell's stale clothing, his unwashed polo shirt, the liquor on his skin. Kell sat up on the sofa and took Eddie's socked foot and squeezed it, Eddie balancing himself on a foot, Kell pressing his white thumb against the inside of his socked foot, saying, "This is what you watch, boy: the left shoe if he leads right, the right shoe if he leads left, watch the inside of the boot. You'd have beaten that boy today if you had known this. I don't care how much older he was. You should have beaten him. I am sixty-four, Eddie, and I am a student of the sport, and I have never seen a heavyweight flurry that fast coming off an uppercut the way you did that day you knocked Giancarlo on his ass. You could have beat that Mexican boy today. You grow a little bit and you learn to snap your punches, you could be a mean fucker."

Eddie was staring at the inside of his socked foot; he smiled. Kell let go of his hand. *Mean fucker.* No two words had ever seemed so pleasant to him. "Mean" suggested that he would survive it, the ward, the street, the pink corner house of his grandmother. "Fucker" was another story altogether, something all the more beautiful, for it signified abundance, more wealth than Eddie could imagine, more money than Jules had counted into Turtle's hand. He could buy Mama a house. He would be rich like Tyson. "Fucker" meant Kell would be his daddy, would love him like the managers loved their best boys, their best fighters . . . how he'd said it, "fucker," his voice for once gentle, his eyes that moment soft, the pitiful old man.

Kell squeezed Eddie's shoulder and gave his cheek a light slap with his age-spotted hand. And he was not so drunk when he said this, not so drunk. He was not lying, Eddie told himself. "Don't think I'm gonna give you a light load because you are my assistant, when you lost to that punk at the S.A.R.!" Kell rubbed his own stubbled cheek with the back of his hand; he reached into his pocket, passed Eddie fifteen dollars in clean, brand-new five-dollar bills. "Don't you be telling Tommy about this," Kell said. "Tommy is a tight-ass. Tommy thinks I drink too much. Tommy won't run errands for me anymore, so you are my assistant now. Now, go get the old man some wine coolers and some potato chips at the Liquor Giant around the corner."

Eddie stared at the money. Eddie left Kell on his red leather sofa and passed between the giant empty rings in darkness, into the lobby, where old Mexican men still sat at a table next to the arcade machine, smoking clove cigarettes. He ran to the liquor store, told the bearded clerk the wine coolers were for a prostitute across the street, came out with pint bottles in a brown bag, Lay's potato chips, which Eddie set down on the cement floor before the napping old man, counting the change in his pocket with the fingers of his left hand, as the television flashed light against Kell's cheek. Eddie ran home, wishing Tessa might find him now as he rushed across the park so that he might tell her that if he learned to snap his punches he would be a mean fucker.

Tessa had found him that day, and she would find him again. He could not remember being so happy. The hot wind brushed across his cheeks. He wanted to seek Tessa out, but he would wait. He ran home, $6 change in his hand. Six dollars. He'd never held on to so much before. It would be a secret, his errand, like watching Tessa from the closet.

He lay in his bed and thought of how soon he would see Tessa . . . how he was most eager to lie near Tessa when Tessa's grandmother sent a letter and a picture of her son from Oakland, when Tessa would jump on her motel bed and peer into the picture, saying, "Oh, look at him, Eddie. And now he look just like me!" And she would kiss Eddie's cheeks. Then, on another night, Tessa's pager would go off while Eddie lay beside her, in summer, watching the television snow. Tessa would pick up the phone and dial the number, whispering into the receiver, the other voice being the voice of a dark stranger, a regular, and Eddie would clasp his arm around Tessa's waist as she spoke into the phone, Eddie fearing that this dark voice would take Tessa from him; or when it was hot and the afternoon of walking and riding buses with Tessa through the city had fatigued him, Eddie might allow himself to sleep, but never so much so that he lost consciousness, only enough that he remained aware of Tessa's presence, her soft breathing and shifting; or in his favorite juxtaposition of their sleeping bodies, he lay in Tessa's motel room enveloped by her, her arms cresting around his shoulders, the brush of her lollipop breath gliding against his neck as Tessa stroked his hair to the rhythm of the soupy songs of the bedside radio; then—a horror worse than the dark voice on the telephone or even someone kicking at the door—the realization that he'd allowed himself to drift so far into sleep that he'd lost all sense of her presence, the absent strokes of her fingers across his head, and now it was dark, eight o'clock, and Tessa was telling him, "Eddie, I best get you back to your mama," Eddie wishing that he might remain with her and at last sleep the night next to her, how this would equal a thousand of their little naps . . . though he sometimes enjoyed the daily separation if only because it meant that Tessa would squeeze him harder than before, her voice piqued, whispering, "Oh, my baby doll, my little doll, I don't want you to never leave me," he now standing, readying himself to leave the motel room, but not with such hurry that Tessa might think he did not love her and not so as to hang back so long in the dirty motel room that he might cause Tessa to feel more abandoned than she was.

If Turtle was not running up and down the strip, Tessa would escort him as far as Van Buren and 14th St. and not farther, so that she could watch him walk home in safety but remain undetected by Mama or Nana watching from the kitchen window. If in the darkness of 14th St. no one except the slowing cars could see them, Eddie would not feel embarrassed if Tessa bent down on her dogged sneakers to hug him and to kiss his forehead before he strode into darkness, waving at her, happy, smiling because Tessa's perfume clung to his neck, because he might, if he did not wash for bed, call her memory to his mind in the morning when on his pillow he lingered between sleep and waking, when his powers of imagination were such that he could, inspired by the remains of her perfume, recall her image, and replaying her image in his mind, press his face, his lips, into his pillow, imagining her dark mouth kissing his own mouth, recalling for himself the graze of her slinky arms when they enveloped him just the night before, the texture of her curly brown hair when in her embrace he stole a touch of it, even the scent of her freckled skin, which was like a secret divulged only to him, for he had noticed it, for her johns did not bother to remember Tessa's perfume or the texture of her freckled skin . . . Yet despite the growing powers of his morning imagination, his thoughts did not progress any further than the thought of sitting naked in a room with his weird and wonderful lover (and in his first dream of Tessa, his first dream of any woman, they had been naked in a forest, sitting naked on a fallen tree, though in fact he'd never been to a forest nor seen a fallen tree, and the only forest he'd ever seen had been in a *Scholastic* magazine), and always this foreshadowed a vision of Tessa standing in the midnight crowds in Vegas or Jersey, watching him, her hair brushed back or braided, Tessa in her blue dress, his favorite dress, cheering for him, and Kell cheering from the corner, Eddie being now a mean fucker . . . being a grown man, a prizefighter, his once lumbering arms hung beside him, seeking out Tessa's face in the crowd.

The next week Turtle found him staring out of a dark bedroom window at midnight, his face bruised from sparring. Turtle came into the room, shutting the bedroom door behind him. Eddie watched Turtle's face. Turtle knew that Eddie had found Tessa, for Eddie no longer complained of the gym, of the bruises, his scraped knuckles, which Turtle had always taken as signs of his loneliness, the strange girl's absence. "I know she done found you," Turtle said. "Stay away from her. She crazy. On the streets, Eddie, you meet people who is, is, is, is just off. You know, a little bit crazy. That is Tessa. I know you and Tessa is tight, and that's cool. I know you and Tessa see each other soon, no matter what I say, if you ain't already. I won't tell Mama, but you know what Tessa is, right? You know what 'prostitute' mean?"

"A prostitute," Eddie said, "somebody lay down with the man, and the man give her money." He did not turn from the window.

"Well, then, that's what Tessa do."

"I know."

"I ain't saying you shouldn't like her. Shoot, my girl is nice, and pretty, a pretty girl, but that ain't got nothing to do with the price of tea in China, Eddie. I mean, don't be all getting attached to her, don't be love, love, love, loving her and stuff. Goddamn. That is one crazy bitch."

"I know she crazy. Your fault she got raped. Your fault if she gone crazy."

Turtle shook his head. "She messing with your mind, Eddie, making you feel sorry for her, making you catch feelings for the simple fact she got raped. Now, I told, told, told, told you what she about. You don't be catching no feelings for no hooker." Turtle climbed into a T-shirt and went to sleep.

In the morning Eddie woke and ran the access road to watch the red mountains at dawn.

Tessa sauntered past the front door of Bumpy's that afternoon, up and down Van Buren, until, carting the spit bucket, Eddie noticed her. He went to the door, and from the Laundromat across the street, she pointed to the lee side of a Levitz factory building one block east, where, after practice, Eddie found her sitting on concrete steps. Tessa held him a moment. The wind blew against her hair. They watched the street. They went into the city. Tessa bought blue ICEEs from a street vendor, and Eddie followed her a block in the direction of the state capitol to a green bench. On the green bench Eddie told her what Turtle had told him. She looked as if she was about to cry. "I guess," Tessa said, crying, "Turtle fixing to take you away from me now, and I'd best respect that. I guess maybe you don't think I'm such a nice person, neither."

"No, no," Eddie said. He'd never made a girl cry before.

Tessa began to sob. Men in dark suits passed from the capitol to their cars, turned to look, ties flipped up in the wind, watching Eddie touch Tessa's hand. "Sometimes, Eddie, I just can't wait to go back to Oakland. I gots friends in Oakland. I gots family in Oakland, my son, my son, my son be there. I ain't mean to be here but for a little while nohow, and I might have my son right now if I had just gone back right then, or never come at all, and never met no Turtle and never met no Adolpho and never met you, Eddie!"

"I wanted you to know Turtle wrong."

"One thing about being somebody's friend, Eddie, is to think about they feelings." Tessa turned to him and wiped her blue lips. She gave him her ICEE and removed a crumpled Kleenex from her purse. Eddie took the ICEEs in both hands. Tessa turned her back to him, wiped the mascara from her cheeks. "We don't see each other enough, sometimes, you know, enough quality time, and it's not like I can call your house or come to your windows—oh, no, your brother don't allow that! And you know, I thought we'd do something different today, Eddie. I thought we'd get away from Van Buren and all that this afternoon, because we ain't seen each other in so long, because I need a vacation from Van Buren, and you been working so hard at that gym, and we always go to that same old Baskin-Robbins, and you always get mint chocolate and I always get orange sherbet, and it's like, gee whiz, the state capitol building ain't but a hop, skip, and a jump from the strip, and I wanted to take you to the Heard Museum and do, you know, something educational for you, so maybe if your mama ever find out and come yelling at me, I can say, 'I'm sorry, Mrs. Bloodpath, I didn't intend on nothing bad, and I took him to museums, and I took care of him and bought him ice cream, and we did educational stuff.'" Tessa folded over, sobbing into her hands—and it caused Eddie to feel hollow, helpless, her sobbing, until he took the ICEEs in one hand and pressed his other hand against the flat of her shoulder.

"I ain't mean to say nothing bad about you. Turtle just talk."

"I ain't like the other ones." Tessa sat up in the bench, checking the condition of her mascara with her finger. "Do you think I ain't got feelings, Eddie? Do you think I just a robot? I told you I sensitive about the stuff people say about me. I ain't like the other girls. I don't even hang around with the other girls. I don't mess with none of them hard drugs or nothing."

"I know you ain't like the other ones."

"I don't even smoke. Do you know where the other ones is? They in Vegas working the Tyson fight. They spent all their money on plane tickets and bar clothes at Dillard's so they could fly down to Vegas. I ain't like that. Dag, your mama ever met me at the Laundromat, and I was dressed in my normal clothes, she probably think I was just a regular person. And when we together"—Tessa turned to Eddie, and in a moment her voice was high and light, and she was smiling—"what do we talk about, boy? We talk about kiddy stuff, silly things. Now look at me, boy, crying at you, like you a grown man already and you done broke my heart." Tessa laughed. She adjusted her bright nylon leggings. "We ain't spent no quality time in a while. And then I think of what your mama would say if she ever found out you was hanging out with the likes of me, and I just feel like someone is trying to take you from me. Then, I feel like I a burden on you. Tell me I ain't no burden on you. Tell me you like to spend time with me, too."

"Course I do," Eddie whispered, nodding. Tessa took her ICEE back and licked it.

Mother and child passed them, the child's helium balloons tilting in the wind.

"Do you remember when that thing happened to me back in that house? And do you remember how you helped me out when I was laying up in that nasty bed? Well, you really helped me out there, Eddie, letting me squeeze on you, and gosh, it just hard to think about someone or something coming in between us and busting us up now when we is already so close, and when I scared, Eddie, so scared. I want to go home and I want my son back, but every couple months I fixing to leave, raising up a stash, and along come Turtle, take it."

Eddie walked with Tessa down Central Ave. to the Heard Museum, to the entrance, where, beneath the awning, Tessa stared at a wall. Children hurried inside, into cool darkness. Inside, along a wooden perimeter walk beneath long figurines and grand horses on canvases suspended from wires, Eddie followed her until they had walked through the museum, Tessa squeezing his hand because they were inside, away from the watching street, Tessa whispering, "Look, look!" And after the museum Tessa took Eddie north until they came to Washington St., and she brought him a fish stick dinner at Pete's Fish & Chips, which they consumed on paper plates in her motel room, on the edge of her bed, staring at the snow on the television screen, and Eddie slept against her back until dark. "Sleep," Tessa breathed in his ear. "Don't you ever just love to sleep, Eddie? I never miss my sleep. Don't it make all your problems disappear? Don't you just sometimes wish you could just lay up in your bed, child, and all your problems disappear, just, just lay up? Ain't got to worry about nothing." She turned, wrapping her arms around him, tighter than ever before, tighter than any memory, squeezing him and he squeezing her hand until, as Tessa promised, sleep overcame him; and he turned his back to her and slept under her arm, and now as if by habit he found that he could lose himself in sleep and yet remain conscious of the feeling of Tessa's arm wrapped around him, her breasts tucked against his shoulder, her breath wisping across his ear. Eddie thought to himself, We worked things out. I love you. And she loved him, he knew it. It was in her silence as she watched him sleep, Eddie sensing, even as he slept, that Tessa was the whole time watching; and she felt it, too, and could for this reason allow him to leave her tonight without her customary "Oh, my Eddie." She'd only rubbed his head, watched him trot down the street through her window because there was now the certainty that they would, each workday evening at six-thirty, meet at the eastern wall of the Levitz factory, where Eddie might for Tessa's sake allow himself to belong to her.

Now Eddie kept himself late at the gym to see Tessa, until a quarter after six, until he was alone with Kell, until Eddie caught sight of Tessa walking past the front door. Eddie would keep an eye on the front doors as he mopped or ran back to the gym from the liquor store with Winston cigarettes or liquor, the liquor that made Kell placid, the cigarettes pensive, that a booster of whiskey might cause Kell to say in the afternoon, "You are a good boy," as Eddie swept the floor, or pressed his fingers against the plastic model helicopters on Kell's desk. Or Kell might say, "Boy, let me tell you. I have this sense about you. Not like some of these boys. Some of these boys are doomed, I know." Or, at worst, upon his third glass, Kell might say, "You don't lag. And you can be a good listener when you want to be. Yes, I tell you something once. Like today with the hook and step out." And Eddie could not understand why Tommy had refused to buy liquor and cigarettes for Kell when liquor and cigarettes brought out the best aspects of Kell's personality, all wisdom and kindness. Or, in the best of all possible conditions, Kell was passed out, and to his slumbering body, his bloated face, Eddie might whisper whatever thoughts filled his mind. Each week to the inebriated old man Eddie would, in the narrow window of time in which they found themselves alone, when Kell was drunk and Tessa had not yet walked past the front door, implore the sleeping old man, "Tell me how important I gonna be one day." Or once, after a school yard fight, Eddie told him, "This one nigger at school be talking shit about me. And I beat on him, and he said I ain't got no daddy, and I beat him down." Kell's eyes popped open.

"Well, did you beat up this boy, the boy who talked shit about your daddy?"

"Yeah."

"And were you watching the inside of his shoe?"

"Yeah."

"Well, then, what are you worried about?"

The man talked without end of his ex-wife, who had left him fifteen years ago for his drinking. Eddie sat with Kell in his office while he spoke, until it was too much to hear again, verbatim, the stories of Kell's ex-wife, who had ruined him, though Kell never explained how, of his children, now grown, living in Connecticut, whom the same evil woman had turned against him. He found Kell most amenable when he was sleeping or half sleeping, even more amenable than when Kell was drunk or merely passed out. He found Kell to be in this condition most approachable, that he could, if he wished, ask any advice, or confide in him his worries of Turtle, for the man without exception never remembered the conversations; of Detective Patricia, who poked his head through Eddie's bedroom window, who beat his brother with nightsticks; of Tessa, who'd lost her mind and might now any day abandon him like his daddy.

One day Eddie asked Tommy as Tommy was coming down the stairs from his mezzanine loft what had caused Kell to become so miserable. Tommy bent down and stared at Eddie. "He was driving drunk, Eddie." Eddie gave Tommy a look. "He was drinking all the time and his family got tired of it, and his boss got tired of it and he lost his job. They took his driver's license away. That's why he can't drive the van. That's why I told you don't be buying no booze for him. You been buying booze for him, Eddie? You buying liquor for him? Tell me now, and I won't get mad."

"No, no," Eddie said. "Just some cigarettes is all from the vending machine at the Page 4 Lounge."

"I hope you ain't getting him booze." Tommy searched Eddie's face. "Listen to me, Eddie, you might think you're doing Kell a favor by running errands, letting him bawl on about the past, but the things Kell tells you are the same things he told me when I was little."

Eddie told no one of the secret arrangement, of the drunken praise.

In the morning Kell would forget whatever promise he'd seen in Eddie and trudge out of his boiler office to rant through the gym, lining the boys in a row to lecture, shouting spittle into their grimacing faces, to cuss at them in broken attempts at Spanish. He'd have finished three quarters of the whiskey the night before and the rest in the morning, reeking of the surplus, snapping up report cards from the boys' brown hands. He shouted at the sobbing faces of the Chicano boys, slapping the ones who did not bring their report cards, barking at the rest, running his soiled finger along the duo-colored lines of each transcript as Tommy jotted the GPA on a clipboard, Kell shouting *"Estupido!"* or "Adequate," shaking his bloated red face.

Eddie stood next to Woscar, happy that Woscar's transcript was a string of D's and F's. Kell dismissed the two boys. Kell shoved another to the ground. Tommy followed him, taking notes on a clip-board, assigning push-ups. Kell came to Woscar. He took his report card, running his chubby white finger along the duo-colored lines. "Hey, this is suboptimal, boy!" Tommy ordered Woscar to perform some jackhammers in the corner. Kell straightened his watch on his tattooed wrist and peered at Eddie. He wore an awful drunken mask of a face. He snatched Eddie's report card from his hand, looked at it, drew back his arm, and slapped Eddie's cheek, to the shock of the Chicano boys, laughing into their palms. Eddie stared at him. "Go tell your mama I slapped you," Kell shouted.

Tommy grabbed the drunken old man by the shoulders. Eddie ran out, Chicana girls staring on from the mezzanine, Eddie running now through the blight, a hatred welling for Kell, whose dark image lurked in his memory as he hurried home to tell Mama. No doubt the police would come, no doubt take Kell in cuffs out of the gym. It was Saturday morning, Mama at work, and Nana would be napping. Eddie turned around, raced east across the park. He ran down Van Buren.

Eddie found Tessa at the corner of 32nd in dark mascara, face painted stark white. Tessa noticed his red cheeks, took him by the hand three blocks to the Baskin-Robbins, wobbling on her high heels. Men, horny johns from the passing cars, watched the strange girl take Eddie to the ice cream store. They passed a patch of blip-ping orange waist-level construction blinkers, an open manhole.

Outside the Thirty-one Flavors, Tessa knelt down and kissed the bridge of Eddie's nose. Tessa opened the front door; bells shook; Eddie took comfort in the air-conditioning. The attendant noticed Tessa, stood from a chair. Tessa sat Eddie at a booth and returned five minutes later with a tray of ice cream.

"I told you he would," Eddie said, sobbing. "I told you that crazy old white man would hit me!" Tessa watched him. Eddie had hoped that, in the least, Tessa might sit beside him on the cushion, hug him again, plant kisses upon his nose, but Tessa's reaction was only to smile, to squeeze Eddie's hand from across the table until he fell silent. A hooptie paused at a stoplight and the young black man inside gawked at Tessa through the window. "He got me buying him liquor. Tessa, I told you he crazy. What a white man doing living on Nineteenth and Van Buren? I'm gonna call the po-lice."

Tessa looked at him. "Pretty soon you won't like me no more. Pretty soon you won't want to be seen with me."

"Why come? What is you talking about?"

"Cause you be getting old, cause you getting at that age where you care what people think. I don't know. I know you'll leave me, boy." Tessa grabbed his wrist and squeezed it. He noticed that Tessa's mascara made her expression seem dark. Eddie wanted to ask her why she wore so much powder at work; he wanted to tell her that at night sometimes, when he saw her from Jules's passenger seat, from the balcony of the dead woman's house, she resembled a ghost. Now sun through the window made the freckles stand out on the bridge of Tessa's nose. "A time will come when you don't like girls, but you think about them all the time. Don't you never have no sex dreams about girls, Eddie?" Tessa rubbed the white plastic spoon against her tongue, smiling. "Like, don't you never have no sex dreams about me?" She stared at him in a way that made his face go red, scraping her spoon along the edge of her ice cream cup as Eddie watched her staring at him, his ears burning. "Why, I told that cashier we was on a date, that you was my man, my daddy." The spoon went into her mouth.

"Shut up!"

Tessa pointed out the window. "All the people passing by in them cars, Eddie, all them johns, they think you is my man, my boyfriend." This caused Eddie to look through the window, through the diaphanous paint, at the street outside. "Because you're getting to be a man."

"Shut up."

"Things change, boy." Eddie looked at her. "You will be grown up and one day you won't want to be seen with me, and one day, you can't sleep next to me no more, and I won't be able to hold you in my arms no more," she said. Eddie looked at her. He wondered what she could mean. "Know what I done today?" she went on. "I went to the Bank of America and I transferred thirty dollars from my checking to my savings and yesterday I transferred eight dollars from my savings to my checking, but I ain't need all that money, so I transferred thirty dollars back for the simple fact that I making interest off that money, Eddie. And I'm moving into the Copa for good. I ain't never sleeping in that stank old house again, no more. It ain't worth the money I save. Do you like girls, Eddie?"

"Shut up."

"Is you talking to girls? Is you talking to little girls at school?" Tessa made a silly face. "I can teach you secrets about girls, stuff make them go, 'Oh, Eddie. Oh, Eddie. Oh, Eddie.'"

"Stop it."

"My grandmother put a order out on me, from the state. You know what that is? A order say like you ain't nothing. My order say I am a quote-quote known prostitute. Ain't good enough to raise my son. Well, I'm fixing to raise me a stash of bills off the interest I earn in this Bank of America savings account, okay, get me a lawyer for when I go back to Oakland, okay." Tessa nodded her head. "You see, I gots real problems. You need to grow up, Eddie. You need to go back to that gym. What is you, almost eleven now? This means you gots to act grown, like when them boys raped me. I going to tell you what. I think, seeing that you is a man now, Eddie, seeing as this old white man ain't mean to hurt you from what you be telling me about him, maybe you shouldn't tell the po-lice about this quote-quote incident, maybe you ain't snitch just yet, because I think this old white man ain't mean to hurt you."

"Then how come he smacked me for the simple fact that I got one C when Woscar got F's and he ain't smack him?"

"Maybe Woscar is a dumb motherfucker, boy, and F's is the best a dumb motherfucker like Woscar can do. I don't know. Don't squash a good situation. This man like knows you can do much better, Eddie. This old white man needs you to keep your grades up so you can box for him. And since you got something on him, you ain't need to act right away. So what he needs some liquor? Sometimes people be hurting and they need a drink, boy. I think he likes you. Now, you be a man. You go back there tomorrow and act like ain't nothing happened." Tessa held Eddie's hands and leaned across the table to him, and Eddie thought for a moment that he should lean to her, as if she might kiss him now, kiss him across the table, for this is what he most wanted of her, and he loved her and he wondered why she had not gone back to Oakland, why she felt ruined, why she thought the Maryvale boys, anyone, could ruin her, but then Tessa did not, as in his fantasy, kiss him, but set her chin upon the flat of her hand, staring forward across the linoleum table, and he realized that he was a child and not the man in his mind's eye who had just kissed her freckled nose, her red, now ice-cream–covered lips. Tessa breathed. She sat up and looked at him. "Do you know what I would do, if I was you, Eddie? Go home and don't you worry about it no more. Gee whiz. A sunny day like this. Go sit on your porch, little boy, and watch the cars," Tessa said, coming around to him, sitting next to him in the seat, kissing his forehead, pressing her cheek against the crown of his head, until by instinct Eddie found himself wrapping his arms around her, pressing his face into her blouse as he always did when she held him, comparing the feel of Tessa's small frame to his previous and now receding memory, the feeling of squeezing Tessa the week before, as if he could add to this memory, now supplanted by the sensation of squeezing her now, her smell, the small pressure of her painted fingers into his shoulder, the warm rush of her breath against his forehead when Tessa sighed and then whispered, until Eddie was too long squeezing her, causing Tessa to let out a laugh from deep within and then once again to kiss him. Then there was a vibration from Tessa's hip, as Eddie took in her scent, that terrible and wondrous odor of her, a woman's odor, into his nostrils as Tessa leaned back all of a sudden and again stared at him and stood and looked at her pager, saying, "Oh, child, I must go."

Then, as she promised, Tessa took a room at the Copa. Tessa did not like the Copa. She did not like the sirens along the street outside, the constant traffic, the bleating horns and angry shouts of hookers barking across chain-link, the midnight knocks at her door. But after a while, the manager offered Tessa the best room, let her pay by the week and not the day, and took her mail at the office. Eddie stole utensils from Nana's drawers, plates, napkins, gobs of aluminum foil, cups, a clock radio from the pantry for her. And he met her at the Copa, a boy each night running to her through the warm darkness, down Van Buren to her motel, his tawny body stinking of glove leather from Bumpy's. He sat with Tessa in her motel room, watching, silent, the black street through her dusty window, and for seven years he did this, until he was grown.

Book Two

Bow Down

Part One

Tessa

The month before Eddie turned eighteen, a skinny, redheaded man in wire-rim glasses chased Tessa out of her Copa motel room, shoved her across the hard dirt in the back lot under the twenty-foot neon Copa sign, and strangled her in the darkness until Tessa kicked him, clawed at his pale cheeks with her painted fingers, and ran to a busy corner of Van Buren, sobbing. She flagged down a police cruiser, and a cop applied Neosporin to her lip while his partner went back to the dirt lot behind the Copa with the Copa manager, finding only the imprint of the man's leather shoe, the torn strap of Tessa's purse. The cop returned with Tessa's purse strap. Tessa, sitting in the back of the cruiser, and her hands for once uncuffed, said that if the man was ever found she intended to press charges. The cops looked at each other and smirked.

The next day Tessa left her room at the Copa, where she'd lived for the past seven years, and fled up the street to the Coral Reef. At the Coral Reef she unpacked her suitcases, arranged her dolls, her stuffed bears, and stared at Van Buren through the dusty slats of her window blinds.

Turtle could not have rescued Tessa that night; he was sitting in a Madison St. Jail processing room, charged with assaulting a sheriff's deputy. Turtle called Adolpho from the Madison St. Jail the next morning, and Adolpho took Eddie to the visiting room, where Turtle related the incident to them. Turtle had been spending all his free time at his two-hundred-and-sixty-pound baby's mama's trailer home in Maryvale, playing with his newborn daughter. Turtle was driving back from the trailer park the night before when a sheriff's deputy pulled him over on 59th Ave., on the pretext of expired tags, to which Turtle took personal offense (though his tags were indeed expired) because Turtle had been returning from a visit with his baby, and his car happened to be this night clean of drugs. Turtle found himself shouting at the deputy until he was stuttering, cussing, the deputy dragging Turtle out of his car, beating his skinny legs with a nightstick. Turtle, roiling in pain on the dark gravel, struck the deputy's thighs with his tiny fists. More deputies arrived, beat Turtle again, arrested him, and impounded his car. The deputies kept Turtle chained by one wrist the whole night (without coffee) to the peeling lime green wall of the Madison St. Jail, and at an hour to four, cleared out the black drug arrests, beat Turtle with hoses, at the very moment Turtle was tired enough to sleep with his wrist chained to a wall. This was Turtle's version.

The next morning the public defender pled Turtle guilty without his consultation. The judge sent Turtle along with seventeen black drug arrests to the Tent, a newly constructed jail, a small city of moldy canopy army tents platted out on the hot dry dirt beneath the mountains up north. Prisoners were starved of coffee, pornography, forced to wear pink uniforms, eat only bologna sandwiches, sit in the three-digit heat on bunks without air-conditioning, clean the sides of the I-10 highway in chain gangs.

Adolpho and Eddie went back to the sheriff's building to find out what Turtle got. His public defender told them Turtle got eighteen months, but he'd be out in six or nine. Adolpho said nothing. Adolpho was furious. Outside, smoking on the steps of the sheriff's building, Adolpho blamed the whole incident on Turtle's two-hundred-sixty-pound baby's mama, who made Turtle drive out to Maryvale to visit the baby. "Stupid fucking Turtle," he said. Now, said Adolpho, Jules would make him pick up Turtle's slack.

Jules made Adolpho look after the dead woman's house. This came in addition to Adolpho's other work. Jules now owned half of a nude cabaret in Goodyear called the Tropicana Club, where Adolpho bounced and Turtle tended bar, two slum liquor stores in South Phoenix, and a food mart in Glendale, each with months of back rent to be collected for Jules. And there was Van Buren, Turtle's prostitutes to look after.

Tessa called Eddie the next week and asked him to bring her some paper plates from Nana's kitchen, a plastic fork, knife, and spoon for her new motel room.

Eddie took the plastic silverware from Nana's cupboard and trekked down to the Coral Reef. He found Tessa sulking in her motel window. She let him in. Tessa sat on the bed and turned her back to him. She rubbed her neck. She claimed that the man had left marks on her, but Eddie could not find them. "Can you see them?" she kept whispering, pointing. "Turtle should have been there for all the money I be paying him. Right there. Look."

He searched her neck for bruises. Tessa kept pointing with her fingers, pressing into the freckled flesh where the marks should be. "I don't see them, Tessa."

"How can't you? Right there! See? God, he almost killed me, that crazy fucking white man."

Then Eddie told her, in a moment, because he had to tell her. "Turtle got eighteen months. Turtle pled, Tessa. He be out in six or nine months."

"Goddamn it," Tessa said. "Who gonna watch for me? Who look out for me with all these crazy motherfuckers running around?"

*A*dolpho did not watch the dead woman's house so good. Jules looked after it himself, driving down Woodland Ave. in his car every other week, to check the face of the dead woman's house, to stand on the squeaky front porch and listen for squatters. Sometimes from his stoop Eddie would catch sight of Jules unlatching the front gate of the dead woman's house; or Jules would appear at Eddie's bedroom window, having just come from the house, his leased car running at the curb, and take Eddie to a Mexican restaurant up the street, where he smoked and bitched about Turtle. Jules would now drive Eddie to his town house in Scottsdale, his town house of parrots. Eddie would hear them from downstairs in the makeshift bedroom aviary of wire cages stacked to the ceiling, filthy, neurotic parrots in cages, squawking at him when he entered the room drunk, only to be confronted with the odor of bird dung and sawed wood as Jules conversed on his cordless upstairs. Jules's voice could be corporate, each word enunciated, with the appropriate "were's" and "aren't's" (which Eddie took to be signs of proper grammar), and in the same breath ghetto and raw, but no one would ever mistake him for a common thug.

He loved Eddie to no end. When Eddie made the regionals in Golden Gloves the year before, Jules drove down to Tucson in a Lexus to see Eddie compete, Jules standing in his sharp, hip-length Andrew Marc leather jacket amidst the drunken Mexican laborers in cowboy hats and Wrangler jeans, their shirts marked with sweat, Jules smoking his Marlboro reds, only to witness Eddie's knock-out loss to the regional champion, a hulking Mormon boy named Roman Medford. Roman Medford was a twenty-two-year-old air force private, stationed at the White Sands Missile Range, in New Mexico. He'd once been disqualified in a bout for putting colloid on a face wound and he was slow, but Eddie could not beat him. Jules emerged from the crowd and found Eddie moping in a corner, still dressed in his trunks. "Now," Jules said, "don't you be feeling sorry for yourself." Jules motioned at Kell, who was standing with Tommy at the other side of the auditorium. "Go change. Tell your coach I'm taking you home," Jules said. "This place is *che* low class, and I ain't fond of spics."

Jules whisked Eddie out of the cold gymnasium away from Kell and Eddie's stable brothers and fed him at the nearest steak house, in the shadow of the University of Arizona, a little basement restaurant staffed by pretty coeds in checkerboard aprons. Eddie ate a T-bone steak, two potatoes, some fries, and a bit of salad, chomping the food mouth open, licking the steak sauce off his fingers, holding the fork with his fist. Jules ate nothing; he watched Eddie swallow down his dinner and smoked. "Damn, boy," he said, "don't hold your fork like that."

He drove Eddie back to Scottsdale, to his town house. The town house was for Eddie like a dark circus of liquor and video games, of fast food and cable television, gifts. Eddie walked into the kitchen to find a pair of designer jeans in his size waiting for him on a wooden stool, CDs, comic books. Eddie thanked Jules for the jeans and washed his face in the bathroom sink. He'd almost won in Tucson. His cheeks were marked, his forehead. His temples throbbed. He would feel defeated until the next year. He wished he could spend the whole weekend, the whole summer in Jules's beautiful Scottsdale town house. In the kitchen he put an ice compress to his head and finished off some day-old Kung Pao chicken. Jules was rolling a joint in the den. Eddie sat down next to him and looked at television. Jules lit the joint and inhaled. "This will help the pain," Jules said.

"I don't smoke that," Eddie said. "I'm in training."

"You a liar like your brother. You drink. Shit. Don't you know that all the prophets smoked weed? It was in the Bible before the white man took it out. Maccabees," Jules said, inhaling. Eddie sat closer to him, to the smoldering joint, took it from Jules, eyes widening, and set the joint to his lips for the first time.

"Hold it, hold! Hold it in!" Jules screamed. "Took me a month to get a buzz the first time." Eddie took in the smoke, let it funnel out of his mouth, passed the joint back. The smoke burned his throat. He wanted to feel high for Jules's sake. He felt nothing. Jules was saying something to him now. Eddie watched the ice melt in his compress. He felt warm. He felt no more pain in his cheeks, his temples, his shoulders. He looked at the flat pictures on the television screen. He fell asleep. Later he wandered into Jules's makeshift aviary of squeaking parrots, into the study of shelved junior college texts, dime-store novels.

That night he slept beside Jules on a mauve futon in the den beneath the television. After a silence Jules reached up and turned off the television. Frog fish raced in a bubbling tank. "Thank you," Eddie told him in the now black room, "for the jeans and stuff."

"Shut up, boy," Jules whispered. "Ain't nothing." Jules was staring at the ceiling. For a long time he said nothing. "Do you know what I

wanted to be when I grew up?" he asked Eddie. "A nuclear physicist."

"What?"

"A nuclear physicist, until my second semester of junior college.
Numbers, they always come to me." Eddie wondered why Jules
spoiled him so much. Jules was speaking to him now. The words
took on colors and sensations in Eddie's mind, the darkness seeming
viscous . . . he was high; so high he forgot the pain in his face and
neck and chest and knuckles; he could taste the steak in his throat,
the leftover Kung Pao; he could taste even the sallow skin of the
pretty, white coed server in checkerboard apron, as in a fantasy he
kissed her, she smiling, smiling as they made love in the back of her
1982 Datsun, Eddie, in the dream, pressing her brittle, stringy black
hair against his face; he could taste her red lips, taste the red and
tawny glove leather, the glove Roman Medford had one hundred
times beaten into his face—his mouth blood coating it—his own
mouth blood beaten back into his mouth; he kissed the coed's lips.
He'd lost today. You lost and you wanted to cry. Jules ran his pinky
across Eddie's forearm, Eddie thinking that moment of Tessa, Tessa
somewhere in the city, climbing into a car because it was Friday, as
now Jules kissed Eddie's forehead, caressed his face with his spindly
black fingers until Eddie froze upon the pillow—*No, no, please,
please, I ain't no punk. Don't . . . I will hit you if you touch me, no matter what you done for me*—and Jules lay down again.

"Do you know what they make?" Jules said. "Do you know what
they make per year, the nuclear physicists? A hundred thou a year. I
bet you think that's a lot," and Jules began to laugh, to shriek in the
dark room.

Jules was rich. Once Turtle had seen Jules count $1.2 million on
his dining room table. A million dollars hard cash, Turtle said. Into
the busy Tropicana cabaret Jules strode each night, so tall in the fit-
ted suits, keeping cool in the face of the occasional white man who

mistook him for a mere bar back or a bouncer, who asked him where and from whom one might score some coke. Eddie had followed him every other weekend since Jules had opened the club in 1989. If Jules arrived at midnight, by one he was socializing with the affluent white men in the VIP lounge. Unlike the topless coquettes who escorted the men up the stairs and into the gaudy velvet room, who could only look pretty and make innuendo, Jules could talk with the lawyers and executives, the land developers. Eddie studied the men from the cabaret: the way they breezed up the VIP staircase and through the swinging doors of the swanky room, girls on their arms, how they tipped the lap dancers, could beneath the music mouth sums of money sufficient to coax a dancer into onetime prostitution, how they stroked their ties, mounted the high bar stools, and stirred their drinks. Eddie memorized the drinks they ordered. They talked to him; they called him "kid," passed him money in the darkness, folded bills from money clips. Eddie had their expensive lease cars waiting at the entrance at the end of the night.

Jules could be vengeful and Jules could sympathize. He could shout the strippers down. The cabaret girls, the out-call escorts bitched about Jules behind his back, forever beholden to him the instant a customer refused to pay an out-call in full for services rendered, or a drunk dared fondle a cabaret girl. A red-faced stripper would appear at Jules's office door. An escort would call the cabaret on her cell phone, screaming, looking for Jules. To the stripper Jules would say, "Keep the man there. I'll be right down"; to the out-call, "Relax. I'm sending Adolpho."

Not once had Jules ever slept with an out-call or a lap dancer, and yet he went after a beautiful woman when he saw one. In trendy bars, it was said, Jules could approach the most stunning woman in the house, entertain her for hours until last call without once requesting the customary dance, buying a drink. Adolpho told Eddie he had seen this. The slender man standing with the loveliest woman in the house, her head bobbing back in laughter. Jules sometimes talked to Eddie of a distant black woman in San Diego to whom he was engaged, but whom no one had ever seen in the flesh. "She ain't fly," he would say. "I've been with fly. But she's thorough. Got a master's degree. That's what I need." Eddie could not understand why Jules did not simply date his strippers now and again. "You really think I'm going to fuck some booby dancer? Please. Firstly, they're strippers. I don't care how the bitches look. They're booby dancers. Secondly, sex is never such a simple equation, boooky. Sex is expensive. Not financially, but it always has a cost."

Jules's office sat across from the dressing room, on the balcony, above the ruckus of the cabaret. Each night the man would rush up the stairs to his desk, crunching numbers on the adding machine, tearing off stark white curls of accounting paper, Eddie right behind him on weekends, carting drinks up from the bar, sitting with Jules in the office as Jules ran payroll or processed applications, Eddie's chair in full view of the dressing room, a lovely box of fluorescent light through which women rushed in and out the whole night, dressing and undressing, standing absolutely naked, making up their faces and smoking before, and speaking into, the letter-box mirror. Jules had removed the dressing room door to prevent theft and excessive on-the-job drinking, offering Eddie an open view of the strippers removing dollar tips from G-strings, straightening bustiers, toweling baby oil off breasts. From the office Eddie would gaze at the lazy belly flesh and thighs, heart-shaped buttocks exposed in the fluorescent light, breasts foreshortened and reflected in the mirror, cabaret girls applying or swabbing makeup off their cheeks, combing dark curls, unaware of the peeping boy. How easily Eddie could have fucked any of them, Jules promised. "I could make you a player, boy, I could teach you," though Jules ignored them, even when they strolled topless into his office, the constant nakedness. "That's why I don't want you running around with some booby dancer," Jules would say. "Just to get your dick wet. Get some bitch pregnant like Turtle. You don't need that. This is the black man's pathology. Always got to prove his manhood with some hood rat. Oh, Christ, take me now! Save this damnable country from the niggers. That boy turned me Republican."

Inside the Tropicana, Eddie never left Jules's side unless Jules requested, needing the office to himself or when his partner came by, a lapsed Mormon in a bolo tie and snakeskin boots. In this case strong drinks were ordered, carried up the stairs by a topless waitress, whom Jules's partner tipped, fondled, and then asked to shut the door behind her. In the cabaret Eddie would sit, eyes to the stage, a procession of twisting, gyrating oiled bodies, high heels clicking against the polished wood, sitting so close he could hear the tiny bulbs inside the stage lamps clacking on and off. The blasting go-go music and rising cigar smoke made the dancers seem more glamorous, more exotic than they were in full light. Bursts of dry ice drew out the contours of their legs, gave dimension to their twisting thighs. Destiny or Ecstasy would sit next to Eddie as men of importance entered through a purple draw curtain in the back and sat before the stage and drank. They stroked Eddie's head and whispered to him. They said, "Oh, cutie, if you had a little bit of cash flow and a ride, I might could put you on."

*T*he next week Adolpho had a grand mal and he could not look after the house anymore. Eddie and Adolpho were standing alone in Eddie's bedroom when Adolpho turned from the bedroom window to say something to Eddie, and in midsentence he collapsed and lay convulsing on the bedroom floor. Eddie shoved the bed away to give Adolpho space, moved the clutter, Turtle's cassettes and comic books. Eddie had never seen Adolpho seizure before. Adolpho looked so frightened, and his eyes went blank; his thighs beat the thin carpet, and he grasped Eddie's hand so hard that Eddie screamed. There they were, alone in the house, Adolpho without power of his limbs, his arms and legs flopping against the floor, Eddie kneeling helpless above him. When the spasms broke off Adolpho whispered, "I love you, Eddie," and lay half an hour catatonic on the dusty carpet. Eddie could only hold Adolpho's hand and stare at him, wondering now if Adolpho would have said such a thing to Turtle, to anyone but him. *I love you, Eddie.*

The next day Adolpho appeared at Eddie's stoop, and Eddie followed him down the street, beneath the drooping palmettos, to check on the dead woman's house at 51 Woodland. Adolpho stopped him. "Eddie, Eddie," he said. "I got something to tell you. You is very psychic, Eddie. You is, but you don't know it."

"You a bug-out, Adolpho."

"No, I'm serious, Eddie. You is in touch with a whole different level of life. I knowed this about you for a long time. I can read people's thoughts. But you block me out whenever I touch your hand. I seen Mary yesterday. Mary the Mother of God. *Dios*, I seen her. I swear. I went to the St. Pius X this morning. I prayed because I seen Mary as clear as I be seeing you right now."

This was Adolpho's way of explaining what he'd said. *I love you.* The next week Adolpho had another seizure in the dirt lot behind the tilting farmhouse, another seizure in four days, convulsing atop the chicken feed. Juanita and Adolpho's cousins ran out to take care of him—Juanita stuck a wooden spoon in Adolpho's mouth—but the seizure lasted so long they could do nothing but shade Adolpho's eyes, watch his brown body shake upon the ground.

Adolpho did not take Eddie's calls. For two weeks, Adolpho's sister Elvira told Eddie, Adolpho stared at the pierced Jesus figurine on his mama's coffee table. Adolpho was in no condition to check on the dead woman's house. Eddie found himself looking after the dead woman's house from his stoop for Adolpho's sake, checking the condition of the boards.

On his first inspection Eddie found a morbidly obese prostitute named Milly breaking into the front door. He opened the gate and went to her on the path, crunching leaves along the walk. The woman turned to him in shock, her chubby hands twisting at the doorknob.

"It's okay," Eddie told her, standing on the steps. He did not trust her. Turtle and Jules would get on him for letting a fat prostitute inside, but she was already at the door, and he felt sorry for her. She smelled sour as vinegar. She was the ugliest woman Eddie had ever seen, but he would let her stay the week because she looked like somebody's mama.

In his bedroom that night he heard Milly shouting from the balcony of the dead woman's house, high on crack, barking like a drunken dog.

Milly would be gone after a while, he thought. He described Milly to Tessa and told Tessa to look out for her; and soon he saw the two of them sharing a corner.

On his second inspection of the house Jules caught him. Eddie had crossed the park and stood at the front gate about to go in. Jules was calling to him from the porch. "Eddie! Come here, boooky." Jules waved at Eddie with his long fingers. Eddie unlatched the gate, strode to Jules. Jules rubbed his head. "You must be traumatized about Adolpho," he said. "Adolpho gonna be all right. Look at me in these leather shoes all creeping up into a nasty crack house. Lord!"

"I can do it," Eddie told him. "I can watch it for you. I found a woman. Told her she could stay till Turtle get out."

"No," Jules said, "I don't want you coming by this house. That's your brother's job. Turtle will deal with the woman when he gets out. Now, go! And don't you never come back up in this house."

"Adolpho had a seizure. I was just looking out for you."

"This house ain't for you, boy. And I want you to stop messing with hos. Don't play, boy. I seen you coming out of Tessa's motel room," Jules shouted. "I know you fucking that crazy, high yellow heifer," and Jules giggled, but he was furious. He smacked Eddie in the face.

Eddie quailed back. "No, I was just looking out for her."

"Looking out, looking out. Shit. After all the time I spent teaching you how to dress, how to talk, how to carry yourself like a civilized man, to find you dealing with a common ho. A hooch, a stank bitch! Don't lie to me, boy. I don't want you getting hoes for your brother and I don't want you fucking them. Look, the Tessa situation is tired. You is eighteen now. You don't need to be fucking around with no prostitute." Jules peered at Eddie as no one had ever peered at him before, not Kell, not Detective Patricia. "I'm about to ostracize your black ass! Next you gonna tell me she pregnant! I should take off my belt and tan your hide. I thought we had a little program going for you. This is why I set myself before you as an example, but this is privilege that can be revoked." Jules turned from Eddie and smoked his long cigarette. "Oh, drama! Oh, scandal! This is scandalous. . . . After all our talks. Just go home. I am banishing you. Go, you is banished! I'm through."

Eddie went home, cussing Jules under his breath. Jules appeared at his window the next hour, as if he'd been driving around the block, and drove him to the Tropicana. "I've given you a reprieve," he whispered inside the club after he'd crunched numbers for an hour upstairs in his office. "That means you get one more chance." He had a drink in his hand, and his brown forehead was beading with sweat, and he was speaking above the house music, indifferent to the beautiful naked Chicana jiggling in the smoke and purple lights. One more chance, Eddie thought. Jules could be so petty, but it frightened Eddie, just the thought of losing him now when Turtle was locked down and Adolpho had spooked out. "But you leave Tessa alone and you leave that house alone and you keep your grades up, my little boooky." Eddie nodded. He wondered if he could cut Tessa off. Jules was foul. Eddie'd gone to see Tessa almost every day for seven years; Jules had known this and never said a word. Now, he could not see her no more.

He let a week pass without calling Tessa. The second week of school he found her loitering at the corner of Van Buren and 7th St. as he slipped down the other side of the street. Tessa appeared at his bedroom window that night, as Mama and Nana slept, Tessa stoned and drunk on lime-flavored wine coolers. "I seen you today," she whispered through the window screen. Tessa went silent. She stared at him. Her face was impassive. Eddie sensed her disappointment in him. He stared at her moonlit cheeks. Tessa begged $40 from Turtle's secret closet stash without a hint of shame, as if he had not snubbed her that afternoon.

The next day Tessa darted out of a Van Buren alleyway as he was walking home from school with his boys. "Hi, Eddie," she said. She stood in a bright, shining Lycra outfit before him now, his boys staring at her body, ogling her.

Eddie blushed. His boys stopped on the concrete, turning to him.

"Eddie," said one of them, chuckling, "you be messing with your brother's hookers?" And the others jumped, laughing into their hands.

They waited for Eddie to say something to Tessa, but he said nothing. This was her revenge. Eddie stared at her, his friends laughing louder as he stopped, crossed the street, and took another street home. Now he understood why Turtle could smack Tessa on the street.

He went home and slept until dark. The phone rang four times and stopped. Eddie thought it was Turtle calling collect from the jail. Nana came into his bedroom with the cordless, and it was Tessa; Tessa was screaming at him, her voice low and panicked. She said the white men in the room next to hers had banged on her door, called her out. He could be there in two minutes; he could bring a baseball bat; he wanted to call Adolpho, so Adolpho could back him up, but there was no time, and Adolpho was still haunted by the seizures, locked in his dirty bedroom. "Please, please come!" Tessa was crying. "They won't hurt me if you come. They bang on my door. They call me names, they called me a whore, Eddie! They'll kill me, choke me dead. Please help me! They catch sight of you, and they won't bother me no more!" Her sobs were like little punctures in his side, like the unending signals of pain the Club S.A.R. boys each other week sent into his face, his side. "You hate me," Tessa cried. "You hate me! I know I made you look bad! I know what I done!"

"No, it don't matter now. Hold tight. I'm coming."

Mothers on stoops, their children watched him cross Woodland Park in darkness, sauntering up the hill to Van Buren. He imagined himself beating the men down for Tessa . . . of course, of course, how frightened she was, frightened they would rape her in the room next to the room she'd stayed in seven years ago, black-eyed and bruised, still reeling from the Maryvale boys, the rape! Poor thing. He would punish the men, pound his fists into their pleading faces as he'd done ten thousand times to the heavy bag. He would run the men out of the hotel, out of the city. Tessa would make love to him that night, as if she had not humiliated him that afternoon, he thought, clowned him before his friends, as if she were not a whore. He ran to her motel room now to save her, but really only to lie beside her, only for the chance late that night to hold her in darkness, a fantasy of her burning in him. This was the last time. He would save her tonight and he would never talk to her again. He did not have time for this. Regionals was coming, Roman Medford.

He came to the front of the Coral Reef and zipped past the empty manager's window, his sneakers squeaking across the moonlit cement. Tessa saw him from the side of her window as he sprinted to the door next to hers and banged on it.

The door opened, the two white men inside gaping at him in drunken horror . . . how large he was, how tall, their reckoning, a buck nigger come to beat them down. They stared at him in silence. For a moment Eddie said nothing. They got guns, he thought, buck knives. He saw the men stabbing him in the side, cutting up his hands so that he could not box, so that he would, like Tessa, have nothing.

Now Tessa opened her door, stood barefoot on the concrete behind him, smoking a menthol.

Cans of paint, folded spill plastic lined the floors, a ladder, tool belts. The men were painters. They smelled of liquor and turpentine. "We didn't mean nothing," said one of the men, in paint-splotched denim, sitting at the desk. The other wore a baseball cap and kept patting the side of his leather varsity football jacket.

On the walk Tessa let out a long funnel of smoke from her lips.

"We ain't mean nothing. She is a pretty girl," said the first man, chewing a toothpick, his neck covered in white paint splatter. The man sat in a chair. Eddie walked up to him.

"There is misunderstandings," Eddie said.

"There is," said the first man, leaning back in his chair.

"Jimmy scared her," said the other, tapping his foot on the spill plastic. "We is leaving in the morning."

The man in the leather varsity stared at Eddie.

"That Jimmy fucking drink too much! Ha! Ha! We ain't mean to put a scare in her. We like her," said the first one. "She pretty."

"No," Tessa whispered from the walk.

"And now that you're here."

"She's a darling."

"For both of us if she's up for it. I expect we pay you."

Eddie went out to the walk. On the walk Tessa cussed at the men in darkness, a hand on her side. Eddie watched the door a moment, turned and went to her. A rage flashed through him, and his cheeks grew hot. He should beat the men down in front of her, but he might sprain his hand. Not now. Not with regionals coming. Tessa was looking at him. She took the cigarette from her mouth, the cigarette the manager had given her. The manager was waiting, too, a small gay white man, waiting on the walk. The manager wanted the men gone. "They are out of here tomorrow," he shouted so the painters could hear him.

Tessa was angry. Now the door shut, the painters laughing inside. It occurred to Eddie that he was tired, though he'd slept from six until nine, a boxer's nap. How ironical, he thought. To have gotten in a boxer's nap only to have wasted his night, a night of sleep, on Tessa, to have run to her when he was the next week competing, when he most needed rest. God, he loved her. At least she is safe now, he thought. Tessa stepped through a patch of darkness and held Eddie on the walk. The manager smoked a cigarette and walked away. Eddie wished this little crisis might finally cause Tessa to leave the city, go to California; then he wished he might go with her, somewhere together, to another city, another state, but that was impossible.

"Here," the manager said, returning, and left Tessa with a pint bottle of liquor, which Tessa began to sip, ambling into her open room, waving Eddie inside, shutting the door and bolting it and bolting it again and checking the bolt.

"I'm leaving," Tessa said above the hum of the air-conditioning.

"You ain't got to leave. They is just painters from out of town, drunk. They is leaving in the morning. They won't bother you."

"I'm leaving the Coral Reef. I'm leaving Phoenix. First the Copa, now the Coral Reef. You can't be safe fucking nowhere." Tessa rubbed her bare shoulders. Eddie took comfort in the chilled motel room air. After a long while Tessa said, "I made you look bad today."

"It don't matter now."

"I know I be stressing you. You don't come around no more."

"Got my mind wrapped around regionals."

"I know you got your fights. But don't stop talking to me. I don't know nobody in Phoenix. You want me to go away!" Tessa drank. "But you won't say it. Your friends was laughing at me. They think I know you from Turtle. They didn't know. I didn't mean it! I'm sorry! You're all I got, Eddie," she whispered.

"What about when Turtle come out and start beating on you and taking your money again?"

"I don't care. He don't do it that much. He don't take so much." Tessa looked at him. "You want me to leave! Tell me you don't want me to leave, I'm sorry about today. Tell me I ain't lost you!"

"It just ain't right for Turtle to be hitting on you how he do. It just ain't right for you not to have something a little bit more than this, Tessa."

"You know I can't go to Oakland now. You know my grandma adopted my baby legal! You know I been gone too long to claim my baby." She took a sigh. "Stay with me, Eddie. Don't leave me tonight. The men will come back and they will rape me and kill me."

Eddie watched Tessa turn to the window, sipping the liquor, watching the street through the curtains. He stared at her naked brown shoulders, wishing she could belong to him in a way she could not, wishing she might never abandon the city. She had embarrassed him in the afternoon, and he loathed her, but he could not let her leave. He would never see her again. He wiped the sweat from his neck, his heart still thudding from the confrontation with the painters in the room next door. He sensed her sorrow. The men in the room next door would be gone by morning, and still Tessa was frantic; she was lonely. Eddie felt it, too . . . a perfect loneliness, paradoxical and insuperable, a loneliness without Turtle. He was fighting the champion, the big Mormon boy, Roman Medford, arms as big as Tessa's waist. Roman Medford was sleeping now. The Mormon boy had no worries, nothing to prove. Eddie would be too tired to do his roadwork in the morning and doubtless he'd sleep in Tessa's room tonight and he did not have his running shoes.

It was ten o'clock now. It seemed later. Eddie sat at her desk of baby pictures and scribbled-out love songs, as Tessa drank, watching the beat cops march down Van Buren through her window. Eddie woke in his clothes atop her, seized by an unconscious desire to be inside her, kissing her sad lips, breathing into her drunken, pouting mouth, kissing, kissing her until she pushed him away, her reaction neither annoyance, nor excitement, nor surprise, only a stoic indifference to the weight of a man's body upon her. He lay beside her, listening to her breathe as she stared at the black wall. He slept and woke that night to find Tessa atop him, staring at his face, Tessa naked to the waist, stroking him, her little breasts jiggling, even as Eddie whispered, "No, no, Tessa, you ain't got to," for it was not necessary, Tessa stroking him anyway, whispering in the dark motel room, "I told you if you stay . . . come, come, boo, come, child, come, child, come for me," stroking Eddie now until it was too late, her pretty, desperate, freckled face above him in the darkness, the peal of her tiny voice as she stroked him with her warm brown fingers . . . God, God, God!

Eddie hurried out of her motel room the next morning, Tessa still passed out on her bed, curly brown hair splayed out on the pillow like magnolia petals. He washed his face in the motel sink, and, smelling of her drunken, willow body, hurried to school.

And then to his surprise Tessa left the next week to claim her son in Oakland, cleared out her motel room, left without a word, and he did not see her again for a long time.

*B*y habit he found himself searching for Tessa on the street, at the Coral Reef, peering through the dusty window of Tessa's old motel room, only to find it cleared out, her favorite corner empty. He lost himself in training. He forgot her and he did nothing but train and skip rope and stare at himself in the Bumpy's wall mirror, lie unsleeping in his bed each night.

At the state fair, beneath carnival lights, he beat the piss out of Roman Medford. He beat the hulking Mormon boy on the springy apron of an old wrestling ring on a few hours' sleep. Tommy was jumping. Kell kept slapping his clipboard against his thigh. After the fight Tommy called Eddie over to the doctor, and the doctor shined a penlight into Eddie's eyes and made him recite the alphabet.

People stood from the folding chairs and the crowds split apart, drifting across the grass, the blinking park rides swirling in the backdrop. Strangers took Eddie's picture with pocket cameras. Then Roman waved him aside, and they wandered together through the

fairgrounds in their club robes and beyond the fairgrounds into a
7-Eleven.

"This ain't sore talk or nothing, Eddie," Roman told him in the
store, his hands wrapped in gauze tape, "but I didn't want to be
champion no more." Eddie looked at Roman and decided that he
was not talking shit. They had fought twice before. You went four
rounds with a man, beating his skull with your fists until you were
too worn-out to vomit, and you trusted this man more than your
own mama. Roman squeezed on a package of powdered doughnuts.
"I knew you'd take it this year, and you can have it. There ain't no
money in the sport for regular dudes like you and me. I best get back
before Father leaves me here in the ghetto!" Eddie rolled his eyes.
"You know this is the first time I seen Father in a month, Eddie. He
only come to drive me to the fight. He stopped training me. I quit the
air force and Mother kicked me out of the house because I dissoci-
ated myself from the Mormon religion, because I drink coffee and I
fuck Indian girls, and because I wouldn't go professional. I been log-
ging in Surprise, man. I been chasing after this pretty little squaw."
Roman got a Pepsi and the doughnuts and paid the cashier through
the bullet-proof cubbyhole with a five-dollar bill and poured the
change into his robe pocket. "God, I ain't felt this happy since I quit
the air force. I expect Father will smack me around for falling to you,
but I don't care. I'm a grown man now. Today was my last fight, Eddie. You come visit me up in Surprise, Eddie. We can chase after
squaw together."

"I got nationals to think about."

"Oh, yeah." Roman cracked open the Pepsi and sipped it. "It's all
corrupt, Eddie, the profession of boxing. Father took me to Vegas
for a month last year to meet this promoter. It's lonely there. It's
dirty. They made me stand naked in the ring in my jockstrap. I felt
dirty. Then Father took me home because it was against our religion
to live in such an ungodly environment, with the drinking and the

smoking, and then the next month Mother kicked me out the house because I wouldn't go on mission to Venezuela, and I'd quit the air force, so I ran to Surprise to log and chase after squaw. They got all kinds of pretty squaw up there, Eddie, and more trees than you ever seen, and fucking robins wake you in the morning." Roman sipped his Pepsi. Eddie left him outside the 7-Eleven.

He wore his Golden Gloves jacket to school the next day, the regionals jacket, a leather varsity, purple and old gold, his name stitched in the right sleeve. In the hallway heads turned, girls in lipstick and mascara noticed him sauntering in his jacket—no one had a jacket like this; everyone, the cheerleaders and the gangbangers and the football players in oversized jerseys and the teachers, noticed.

That afternoon in chemistry a senior girl in a pink sweater in the lab behind Eddie pointed a Bunsen burner at herself, the blue flame hissing at her chest, the girl setting up a low peal until Eddie came running to her table to turn off the flame. In the hallway after class she asked Eddie for his phone number. He looked behind him to see if she was talking to another boy. Princess stood an inch taller than Tessa, but she was not so lank. Princess smiled at Eddie in the hallway as he whispered his phone number to her, Princess scribbling it on the back of her chemistry notebook.

After school, as the cars inched out of the parking lot and the underclassmen began to ride their bikes or walk home in packs, or huddle at the edge of the campus to light cigarettes, Princess stopped him.

"Someone told me you is Turtle's little brother."

"Yeah."

"He locked down, ain't he? I heard."

"Yeah." Eddie stared at Princess's lips.

"Turtle funny. I used to watch him dance at parties. You saved my life back there. This sweater be cashmere, you know," she said, looking at it. "Hey, is you going home right now? I need a ride. You got a car?"

He shook his head. Boys passed behind her on bicycles.

Princess gave him a look. They stared at the parking lot. A sweet-faced black girl in denim, riding an antiquated blue Schwinn Phantom, her books in a wooden basket fastened to the handlebars, went sailing across the walk before them, a serene look on her face like, Eddie thought, the Oriental monks praying on rugs in gray flowing clothes he'd seen on television once, contented as if listening to music, pretty, pretty, a little brown-skinned girl with a ponytail on an antique bicycle with a basket filled with books, and Eddie watched her gliding across the walk until the wheels of the Schwinn ran over a broken pencil, and the little brown-skinned girl went tumbling to the ground, her books flying out across the walk to the laughter of students who stopped on the walk, in the parking lot, to laugh at her.

"Silly ho," said Princess, laughing. The little brown-skinned girl wiped her jeans and went picking her books up off the cold cement. Princess pointed to the parking lot, at a car. "There go my girlfriend," she said. "Let me beg a ride off her. I'll call you tonight, Eddie. Ciao."

Princess asked him about the boxing. She asked him if the punches hurt. Everything about her seemed easy and sexy, as when she broke her nail and shouted, "Fuck, fuck, fuck," on the phone in her sugar voice, and he knew he could have her if he wanted. He imagined Princess's bed, her bedroom, as pink as her sweater, her pink bed, pink room, pink bears. She cussed like a gangbanger. He imagined lying beside her as she called his name in her slutty voice. After a silence Princess said, "I'm talking to Turtle's little brother," and she giggled. Eddie thanked God she'd failed chemistry, failed it twice, that the blue Bunsen flame had whipped at her abundant chest, poor Princess waving her painted fingers until he ran over to her lab in his Golden Gloves jacket and turned the little hissing demon off.

Princess said on Saturday she was going shopping for some shoes. Said on three occasions she'd gone to Dillard's with her girlfriend to look at a particular pair of Steve Madden shoes, and each time the same shoes had been twenty percent off. "Fuck around," said Princess. "I'm saying. Three times in a row is like destiny."

That night Adolpho came out of his funk, and they rode the streets together in Adolpho's hooptie, Adolpho drunk and quiet; they went chasing after girls together, at the video arcades, the dollar theaters, smoking weed and watching, weeded, the airplanes ascend from the Burger King parking lot behind the airport, as if Adolpho had not seizured at all. Adolpho had grown a beard, and he kept playing with rosary beads. Adolpho drew angels with a blue Bic pen on his left hand, the shining bellies of airplanes descending above them, and he said nothing when Eddie told him, "Tessa run away."

Princess called him the next afternoon, a cable fashion show in the background. "I want to be rich," Princess said. "Why can't I be rich? Can I ask you a financial question? Does they pay you money when they give you that jacket?"

"No."

"All that work for a jacket. I'm saying."

"I'm going to be rich," Eddie told her. "I'm going to be a prizefighter. I'm going to be the nationals champ and then I will go to the Olympics in ninety-six and then I will be a pro."

"Step back." She smacked her lips. "I'm talking to a serious young man."

Eddie watched children in the park from his window. He'd said too much. He was boring her. She could care less about Vegas. Princess did not even see the money in him. She was listening to an R&B song, now humming to it. Eddie imagined her climbing out of her pink underclothes, lying naked in his bed, imagined her shopping at the mall. She was not so easily impressed, he thought; it was better for him. She would not let him get by with ghetto dreams, watching the train tracks with her from the back of the Levitz factory.

Eddie hung up the phone. He would not call her back. He did not care if she was easy. He needed a car for a girl like Princess. Turtle's car had been impounded. Needed money. He went to the closet, reached under the closet floorboard, counting the money in Turtle's stash.

Mama came to the door, and Eddie wondered if she'd seen him counting Turtle's money. Mama sat on the bed, eyes red. "I told Turtle you won your fight. He happy for you." Mama looked at him. "They letting him out early," she cried. "Turtle coming out. Two weeks. The man say maybe ten days."

"That's early."

"You know how them jails get overcrowded. I think Turtle depressed, Eddie. That Tent ain't no jail. They don't give you no coffee, no television. I stood at the gate after I seen him last month, and it was out in the middle of nothing, that Tent, and there was all that dust and big rocky hills, and they make them wear them pink jumpsuits to embarrass them, and what did he do but call the cop a name, grab at his knee? How you gonna assault on a cop when he beating you with a nightstick?"

The next weekend Adolpho took Eddie to the Good Times. At the Good Times a plump South Mountain High School girl named Sherice swept back her braids, strode up to Eddie at the Mortal Kombat, and pulled Eddie aside. She was seventy pounds overweight and proud, a second-year senior barking at him in the blinking lights of the arcade. He'd seen her before at house parties in Chandler. She'd gone to grammar school with Turtle, bought weed from him sometimes. "Eddie," she said, girls in makeup giggling behind her. "I'm sorry, but I just had to stop you. My girl think you fine.

She wants to talk to you, but she is shy. But life is short, I'm saying. Is you talking to anybody right now?"

"Stop! You're embarrassing him," whispered a small girl under her fingers.

"Look, she think you all that," Sherice said, pointing to the small girl in a ponytail at a table, enveloped by others girls giggling into their hands. "The pretty one over there. That's Marchalina Canister. She's a junior. Look, boy, I barely know you from Adam, but life is short, and that pretty little girl over there wants to talk to you," and Sherice dragged Eddie by the hand over to the table where the little brown-skinned girl sat, cheeks growing hot. "Eddie," said Sherice, "meet Marchalina. Marchalina, meet Eddie." He stared at Marchalina until he remembered her, her bike careening, her books sliding across the walk, falling onto her hands.

he little brown-skinned girl with the gap in her teeth. The little brown-skinned girl with the gap in her teeth. The little brown-skinned girl with the gap in her teeth. How she'd crashed her Schwinn Phantom after school in the South Mountain parking lot, little palms smacking against the white concrete; how everyone had turned and laughed at her, everyone, the football players, all the juniors and seniors walking to their cars, freshmen even, wandering home across the football fields, everyone laughing, shouting laughter, pointing at her, as she dusted off her jeans and climbed to her feet, the whole time serene.

He called her from his bedroom. Her mother picked up the phone, called to Marchalina in her bedroom. A moment passed on the telephone, and Eddie could think of nothing to tell her, nothing. "Sherice said you were quiet," Marchalina said. "Sherice said you were kind of funny, not funny funny or weird funny, but mysterious. Yes, I think you are dark and mysterious. I think you have an edge. I think you are brooding. You have secrets." Through his window he heard a ragged-out hooptie racing across Van Buren. Marchalina had heard the noises, bleating radios, ghetto children screaming from the park, street noises on his end of the phone, and she had known that he was poor. Eddie palmed the phone and shut the window.

On the first date she wore a black cross the size of his hand outstretched. He took her to the Coffee Plantation on Mill Ave., in Tempe. "Sometimes," Marchalina told him, "I go by myself just to watch the people. Sherice said you wouldn't like it, the Coffee Plantation. Sherice said you weren't the type. I have a surprise for you," she told him.

At noon he waited for her at the bus stop. Marchalina appeared a miniature body strolling to him across the sunny walk. She'd lopped off her ponytail and washed out the perm, her hair cut in tight nappy black curls. This was the surprise, a natural. Eddie's mouth hung open. She might at least have warned him in advance, he thought. It was too much. He would not hold her hand. He would not hold her hand even if she offered it to him, pressed it against his hip on the bus ride to Tempe.

They sat at the bus stop. "You get so tired," Marchalina said as they waited, patting the back of her hair, "of the processors, you know? All these ugly chemicals. Getting a perm every six weeks. And David, my hairdresser, says I'm pretty enough to wear a natural."

She wanted a compliment. He wouldn't give it. The bus was late. He peeked down the road to see if it was coming.

"Sherice said you would hate it, the natural. Sherice thinks you're this I-don't-know-what. I told Sherice she has you all wrong. But then, Sherice thinks I'm a bourgeois black girl from North Phoenix. And now you're taking me to the Coffee Plantation. Don't you love college towns? I love Tempe, all the bookstores. Wilma, that's my mother, says I read too much. Says it's a wonder I don't need glasses.

I love books, Eddie, the way they feel, they smell. And I keep a jour-
nal. Do you think that makes me bourgeois? Do you think that
makes me, you know, a white girl? Sherice says I talk like a white
girl. But I don't care what she says. I have a confession for you, Eddie. I know it's very very soon for confessions. I love to sniff the
pages."

Eddie stared at her. Marchalina realized he was mystified, covered
her mouth in laughter. "It's not that you can get high or anything. I
don't know why I do it. It's my little idiosyncrasy. I can't believe I just
told you that I like to sniff the pages. You must think I'm a straight
fool!"

The bus came halting before them now, and they climbed inside,
sitting in the very back on teal, sun-worn cushions. She told him
she'd written a poem about Newport cigarettes, an ode dedicated
to her mother and Sherice, who smoked them. "You don't smoke
them, do you? These are the worst kind, Newports. Menthols. Com-
posed of fiberglass. Residue. Sits in your lungs, the fiberglass. Why
have black people claimed them, Eddie? Why, Eddie, are Newport
cig-arettes the *black* cigarette?" Sherice had consulted on the outfit.
Marchalina sat next to him on the bus in faded jeans a bit too tight,
with cloth flowers sewn on the pockets, small yellow daffodils, and
leather loafers. The loafers did not match the belt, but this, like the
slight gap in her teeth, only made her seem all the more attainable,
and he would remember only that each foot, shoe and all, could fit
into one of Nana's mason jars, the black cross staring at him from
her chest, drawing his eyes from her face, a mild oval face, a face so
small as to be enveloped in his hand, and it seemed to be forming before him, as though Marchalina was trapped between adolescence
and womanhood, so that, yes, yes, he could imagine her, a little black
girl wandering through the aisles of some bookstore, removing some
book, splaying it before her face, sniffing the pages when no one
looked. She'd seemed so out of place with the likes of Sherice in that
dirty arcade. Perhaps he should save her from Sherice. Sherice was

no good for her. Two kids. And Sherice would tell her about Turtle. He would save her from Sherice. It was the least he could do. The ponytail cut off. Yes, he decided, Marchalina was pretty enough to wear a natural.

At the Coffee Plantation he ordered an American and Marchalina ordered an espresso. Eddie didn't know what an espresso was, only that it cost $3. "High school is bullshit," Marchalina said, sipping the espresso, and it was odd to hear her swear. "Don't you think? I wish I was a senior like you."

They abandoned the café and strolled down Mill Ave. Passing down the cobbled sunlit walks he worried again she might expect lunch, at one of the Mill Ave. restaurants he could not afford. They passed kiosks littered with multicolored notes. ROOMMATE WANTED, said the Xeroxes flapping from the kiosks. FREE TIBET. W/UTILITIES. SUBLET. FUTON. SUBLET. FUTON. FREE TIBET. FUTON. FUTON. FUTON. FREE TIBET. Who is Tibet? he wondered. No doubt Marchalina knew, but he could not ask her. There it was, her favorite bookstore, the Changing Hands, stood three stories high, a windowless brick edifice. They entered through the back, down stairs.

"Do you want to see my all-time favorite book?" Marchalina whispered and waved Eddie to the very center wall, to a low shelf. She bent over and ran her fingers across the glossy spines and removed a slender paperback entitled *Spy in the House of Love*.

"It's about love, Eddie, love and . . . it's a naughty book."

"A sex book?" Eddie whispered. "A nasty book?" He leaned toward her so that no one could hear him. "You read nasty books?"

"Erotic," Marchalina said, straightening her cross. He did not know the word. "There's a difference. It's about life. And the woman who wrote it lived in Paris, and one day I will live in Paris, Eddie. That's why I take French. I've read it four times. I read it each summer when I stay with Elroy in Scottsdale, in August. Elroy, that's my father. Elroy and Wilma. That's what I call them, my parents. I mean, why do we have to call our parents Mom and Dad? That's an arbi-

trary worldview to which I refuse to subscribe." She left the shelf
and went outside through the back door. He followed her.

"Because it's your mama."

"It's a cultural construct. You've only been conditioned to think
that way."

"That's bugged out."

She was silly in a way that drew him to her. The words he did not
understand. Half an hour passed, and Eddie could say nothing to
her that did not sound vulgar and simple, that was not, like himself,
beneath her.

Marchalina watched Eddie now, smiling. Too little time had
passed to go home yet, to bring the date to an end. They had gone
to the café and they could not go back to the bookstore.

"Would you," Marchalina asked, walking beside him, "like to hear
the poem I wrote, an ode to Newport cigarettes? It's in my bedroom."
He nodded.

They got on the bus. The bus stopped in North Phoenix. They
walked down a street of pretty lawns, into her complex. She lived
in an upscale town house with her mother. Marchalina opened the
door. The walls inside were high, beautiful furniture. He followed
her into her bedroom. A low shelf held her books, countless paperbacks.

Slow jams. Kiss, kiss, grind on the bed. The big fat black cock-
blocking cross, he thought. The telephone, the first time he'd called.
She'd heard the ghetto children shouting in the park outside his window and she'd known he was poor . . . but today, at the bus stop, how
unaware she'd been, of the beggars, the pocked streets, the graffiti,
and Eddie in the same moment feeling responsible for the beggars,
the condition of the streets, as if he had himself applied graffiti to the
walls, broken the high windows of the abandoned factories.

"I can't read it to you, not yet," Marchalina said. She shook her
head. "The poem. It's like revealing myself to you when I don't know
you. I'm sorry. We can play cards instead."

"No, no." Eddie smiled at her. He touched her hand. "You ain't got to read me nothing. I wrote a poem one time in English class," he told her. "It was a rap song. Ice Cube. I told the teacher I wrote it, and she thought I was a genius. I was goofing off."

"You could be a rapper, Eddie." Marchalina sighed, eyes widening, as if she'd considered this before. She tilted her head, squeezing a deck of Bicycle playing cards in her ringed fingers, until she was laughing. "You have a deep voice. You have a commanding presence. That's what they tell you when you join Drama Club. You have a commanding presence. Tupac has a commanding presence, Biggie has a commanding presence, see? All good rappers have it. And the best rappers are touched with tragedy, like Tupac. With irony and sadness, Eddie. Though I think Tupac is absolutely morbid. I think he's a manic-depressive. Here," Marchalina said, reaching for a pack of Newports from under her pillow. Marchalina took out a cigarette and a ceramic ashtray from the shelf above her bed and lit the cigarette. "Now, I've got to smoke a cigarette. I can't talk about Tupac without smoking. Here, I stole it from Wilma's purse."

"But I thought you said black people should stop smoking Newports."

"I'm being ironic." Marchalina frowned at him, letting out smoke. "Of course, you don't smoke. You're a boxer," Marchalina said, nodding, inhaling. She kept the cigarette in her mouth while she shuffled the playing cards. "Big champ. I wanted to do a feature on you in the school newspaper, an in-depth—the boxer, dark and brooding—but I quit the paper over an editorial matter, which I won't discuss with you. High school is bullshit, man," said the little brown-skinned girl, turning her face to blow smoke. "Take me to Homecoming."

"Okay."

"Think carefully. I am not your only choice. A lot of girls are after you now. You could take Princess. She's a certified freak. Big boobs. She gave head to one of my friends one time. But I think she's too surface for you, Eddie. You're brooding, Eddie. You have a darkness to you. The way you kept looking out the window on the bus like you were haunted by something."

"Brooding."

"Haunted. Like Tupac. Now everyone is judging him, the media, because he went to prison. People think Tupac is wild because he's a young black man, but of course he's wild. He's an artist. Wilma doesn't like Tupac because she's old, because she has hang-ups. Wilma doesn't even date black men anymore after Elroy. She has that whole suburban self-hatred thing going on. But," Marchalina whispered, ashing her cigarette, "I think black men are the shit." Eddie gave her a look. "Tupac is the shit. Tupac is suffering inside. Tupac feels the pain of our generation, but he is conflicted. One half of him is beautiful and conscious and positive, but he raps about the ghetto and the ghetto is raw and ugly and real and brutal. Wilma hates Tupac. I hate Wilma sometimes. Wilma is a sellout. I hate anyone who hates Tupac. Tupac is searching, like you."

He laughed at her.

"That's why Princess went after you, Eddie. That's why girls like you when you don't have a car. It's the Golden Gloves jacket, true, but it's something more. I knew Princess wasn't your type. You're way too deep for her. I can look at you and know that you have secrets, that you are haunted by things. You think I'm riding your jock right now, but I'm not." Marchalina's little face went long. "You look at me like I'm crazy. Like I'll get in your way, distract you from your competitions—tempt you with sex. But I am the perfect person to understand you because," Marchalina said, sighing, "I am an artist. Sherice thinks that that is corny. But a boxer is like an artist. I can prove it. After I met you I bought a book from the Changing Hands. I've never done that for a boy before. The book is called *On Boxing*, by this famous writer named Joyce Carol Oates, and it talks about how the boxer must work alone, like the writer, must go into seclusion before each performance."

"You met me and you bought a book?"

"It reminded me of you. Here," Marchalina said, removing a copy of the very same book from a plastic bag under her bed, passing it to him. "You can take it. You can tell me if it's true what this book says, because you would know."

"No, no," he said, looking at the cover. "I can't read this now. I ain't even won nationals yet."

"Maybe you will read it, this book, and you will realize why you do it, see yourself in the book. Know yourself better than the others. It's a psychological advantage." The little brown-skinned girl set the book in Eddie's hand. He looked at her and realized how naive she was. He stared at the book. Now he would have to read it. "You think I like you too much, but I don't," she whispered. "I know you like me, too."

"You all right," Eddie said. "You kind of kooky."

"But you still like me, even though I'm kooky. It's in your eyes, boy. God, your lips are beautiful," said the little brown-skinned girl. "I want to kiss them. They are dark and serious like you. Kiss me now." Marchalina, leaning back against the wall, shut her eyes, waiting for her kiss. They sat beneath a framed Romare Bearden montage, *High in Cotton*, of slave women in cotton fields. Eddie leaned forward to kiss her, cards shifting, slipping on the comforter into the impressions made by their hands.

Then he kissed Marchalina's lips, pressed his face softly into hers. Her kissing expression was, like the black cross, so serious, so practiced, so purposeful, as if everything must be momentous. Like a book. Her lips were dry, her cigarette breath wretched, but he continued to kiss her nonetheless. He pressed his cheeks to hers, drew his hand across the pink comforter, clasping her tiny hand, imagining the canary yellow flowers sewn into the pockets of her jeans.

Eddie felt the cross against his chest as she pressed herself into him. No doubt the little girl felt guilty messing with him on the bed, and if she did, he thought, he would not push her. "I imagine you is really Christian," he said. A good Christian girl. It was okay, he thought. He could be patient.

"I'm an agnostic. I am nothing. Here." Marchalina lifted the cross from her chest and set it beside them on the bed. She sat down next to Eddie, closer, her thighs rubbing against his.

Eddie sat back. "What, you don't believe in God? I ain't never met a black person who don't believe in God."

"I wear the cross in the city when I want people to leave me alone." Eddie shook his head. Marchalina squeezed his folded leg. Marchalina unbuttoned three buttons of her dark blouse, pressing his hand against her breast. He stopped her. It frightened him. He did not want her to be a kooky tease. She pressed Eddie's right hand of scarred knuckles against her soft tweaked nipple. "Agnostic means you don't know if there is a God. Atheist means you know there isn't." He was staring at her breasts. "I'm not as big as Princess," she said. "I'm just a B-cup. Is that okay?"

"Yeah," Eddie said. "I don't care."

Marchalina took his hand, pressing, pressing, looking at the ceiling while he kissed her breasts, her nipples. Now it was dusk, the light through her window, the light settling on her manicured North Phoenix street, pink and orange at once.

"There is one thing you must accept about me, Eddie. I don't believe in conventions, in arbitrary worldviews. You must let me have that," and she spoke, he thought, as if she were herself the heroine of a book, a kooky book, of a book she'd doubtless three times read, sniffing the pages, inserting her round scrunched nose inside and drawing in deep the ink smell. How disappointing, he thought it, her unbuttoning. At the front door Eddie kissed her, knowing that he could, if he wanted, ignore her on Monday, never call her again.

Returning from the access roads, his morning run, the fields of hedgehog plants, Eddie saw Tessa walking to the Coral Reef from the direction of the Greyhound bus terminal, carting her suitcase, just come back from Oakland.

Eddie found her in the afternoon. A building was going up across the street on the empty lot. Behind a chain-link fence construction workers hammered nails into wood. A concrete truck hovered at the corner. Tessa opened her door and let Eddie in. Her suitcase sat on the floor. She was unpacking it. Tessa kissed Eddie's cheek and for a long time held him.

"Who that girl I seen you walking with last week? I came down for a weekend to work, and I seen you walking together from school. You afraid to tell me?" Tessa shook her head. "Like I ain't got real problems."

"She ain't nobody."

"Eddie," Tessa said, sighing. "Don't never tell me to go back to California. I got a bank account here in Phoenix at the Bank of America. They gave me my old room back. The Coral Reef is my permanent address, where I take my mail at. I done gone to Oakland for the last time. They won't let me see Wendell unsupervised. So you can't be telling me to go back there no more." Tessa smiled at him. "She pretty, that girl."

"She ain't nobody. We going to Homecoming."

"Homecoming," Tessa said, setting a stuffed bear on the television. "Eddie's going to the Homecoming." She looked at the wall. "Well, if you ever need to know stuff," and she watched his face, unpacking a headless doll.

"What kind of stuff?"

"What to say and shit, I don't know." The room smelled of stale cigar smoke. "Eddie is going to get him some! Shoot, somebody just grew up!" Tessa turned to him with a pair of nylons in her hand, staring into his eyes. "You want to freak her, don't you? My little Eddie grown now and he want some ass. Shit." She stared at him until his face went red. "No, no," Tessa said, pointing. "You sweet on her. And you want to make love to her, Eddie." Tessa covered her mouth. "Wait a minute. I just thought of something. You ever gone up in a woman, Eddie?"

"Shut up. That ain't none of your concern." He turned his head.

"Yeah, you is sweet on this girl and you want to make love to her. My little Eddie." She giggled. She came to him now. "Maybe this is why you come to visit me, to ask me things to make her love you."

"I seen you was back. Why you got to be twisting things?"

A hooker and her john passed by the window. Cars with sirens, riot lights, raced down the street. Tessa went to the window. "Now, I want you to be good to this girl. And when you kiss on her I want you to really kiss on her. Girls liked to be kissed proper." Tessa came to him and sat him down on the bed. Eddie watched Tessa touch his cheek with her fingers.

"Shut up," Eddie said. "Shut up. Stop it."

Tessa rubbed Eddie's shoulders with her soft brown hands. Construction workers hammered their nails across the street, set the wooden frames of walls upon the concrete foundation. "First off," Tessa whispered, shutting the blinds, "you must be tender and slow."

"Like do not rush the situation. Let it happen."

"It ain't a quote-quote situation! With boys everything got to be rush, rush, like that porno." She pointed at the television. "And you must think about tender things in your mind, like a lake or a pond, or a hillside." Tessa straightened her legs, took a long sigh, shut her eyes, and drew her hand over her face and chest. "Pretend I is this girl. And now we at her house, Eddie, after the Homecoming, and I is her and you is you, and the slow jams be all playing and we be sitting on her sofa. And you snuck you some beers and now you want her, you really want her. You want to hit it real bad. I want to see what you do."

"I know what to do."

"Now we chitchat some. This is of critical importance. Tell her something, boy, before you make her nervous."

"You, you look nice."

"No. You either say that at the front door when you give her the flowers, or you say it after you kissed her on the lips one time. Do you even know about the flowers? You too far away for that now. She thinks you don't like her. And don't say something corny. Say, 'Damn, girl, you know, I never realized how pretty your eyes was until just now, in this light.' Dag, come here, boy. Now sit up close and put your arm around her."

"I was waiting for the moment."

"You done waited too long, fool." Tessa sat Eddie closer to her until their thighs touched. She put his arm across her shoulder, and her curly hair brushed against his lips. The construction workers shouted from high raised wood beams to the ground below and back. Tessa watched Eddie touch her cheek with his bruised knuckles. How odd she was. She stared at him. Eddie curled his arm around her shoulder. All women were odd, he decided. Tessa let out a breath. "Good. When they sigh like that, means you broke the ice. Now is when you kiss, but your kiss must not come when she don't expect it or else she will blink at you and pull back; so you cannot talk for too long or too short—and don't go for too long without gassing her up about how pretty she look."

"Then I won't know when."

"Tell her about the good feeling you get. Tell her how happy you is to be spending time with her. Now give her shoulder a little squeeze," Tessa said, sighing when he did. Eddie stared at her and he whispered her name. He thought of the little brown-skinned girl for a moment and wondered how it was that, looking at Tessa now, she could seem in a moment so unimportant. "Yes, yes," Tessa whispered back, "a little jolt just ran up her spine, and she tingles, this girl. Now kiss her slow and soft, Eddie, look into her eyes, and do not look away, not even at her lips, until the final, final moment when her eyes is closed and she leans into you, and then at that final, final moment you may look at her lips just once, and her soft face, just once, yes." Eddie leaned forward as Tessa closed her eyes, and pressed his lips against Tessa's lips to the sound of sirens in the distance, watching her face in soft focus, the freckles on her nose, the contours of her cheeks the hillsides he imagined, her eyelashes curling willows sprouting up from the pond, and they sat upon a warm blanket on grass. Now some memory of the citrus perfume, some memory of the scent of her brown skin, mixed with the reality of her scent now, and Eddie squeezed Tessa's waist, dreading the moment she would push him away, when he would feel no longer her warm presence, the little exercise completed, but Tessa did not push him away. Eddie kissed her ear, her neck, wondering if—surely now—he should tell her he loved her, but his desire to complete the exercise and his fear that Tessa would laugh at him were greater than his need to confess anything to her, and so he did nothing more than whisper in the faintest breath her name, her name, her name, kissing the somber lips, thinking to himself that her mouth tasted like Coke, Cherry Coke, and liquor underneath. Then, when the little exercise had gone forward, and his fear that Tessa would any second cut it short vanished, he realized that he could, in the moment, compare the memory of Tessa's perfume to the reality of the sweet scent on her neck, her chest, her arms, compare the memory of the scent of her skin when he was a boy and she had brushed against him in the Baskin-Robbins, or when he was the youngest child and Tessa held him, that the memory of once touching her curly brown hair in the booth of an ice cream parlor resembled nothing of the feeling of pushing his own fingers through her hair, the memory of her soft brown hands against his ten-year-old back resembled nothing of reality of the pressure against his back now as he lay now atop her, grown, a man.

Tessa stopped him with the slightest pressure of her painted fingers into his back. "Very good."

"Tessa."

"Shush, shush. Kiss her here."

Eddie leaned over and grabbed Tessa's waist, sticking his thumbs into the loops of her jeans. He breathed upon her neck where she'd directed him with her painted fingers, kissing, chewing upon the ginger flesh, tugging the flesh with his teeth. He kissed her mouth until Tessa stopped him at last with a push of her finger into his shoulder. "By now," Tessa whispered, though it was unnecessary, "she will probably take off her shirt and stuff." Eddie called Tessa's name again. In one movement Tessa pushed him away, tugged off her T-shirt, pressed his face against her breasts until he was kissing, and in another moment—too soon—Tessa reached back with both hands at once and then, staring at the ceiling, unclasped her bra.

Eddie kissed her nipples, her nipples to her neck, and then, as if Tessa had been testing him, Tessa stopped him and began climbing out of her clothes.

"Now," Tessa breathed, "she take off her clothes." Tessa climbed out of her jeans. He remembered watching her go naked with men from the motel room closets as a boy. She lay beside him now, stripped to the waist, then slipping out of her panties so that she was naked, sitting, her arms behind her, until he found that he had grown hard and his cheeks grew hot, his reflex to turn from her in the waning light.

He squeezed her shoulder. She was for some reason angry at him. "You looking at me," he said, "like I done something wrong."

"Will you love her?" Tessa whispered. "You don't love her."

"No." He shook his head. He coughed. "I got love for you, Tessa."

"What did you just say?"

"I said, I got love for you."

"Don't ever tell a girl you *got love* for her. That's what you tell your nigger. Say, 'I love you.'"

"I love you, then, I love you. You know it." He lay atop her, her body smaller than his memory of it. Tessa went silent. Eddie kissed her Cherry Coke lips, breathed into her mouth of liquor. He kissed Tessa again. It occurred to him she'd been drinking, drinking on the bus ride down. He imagined Tessa's hateful visit to Oakland, the long bus ride home. There was no staying there. She would never get custody of her boy. He could not blame her for drinking. He kissed her again. He nestled his face into the nape of her neck, kissing until her silly dime-store perfume lined his tongue.

"I don't care about the girl," Eddie said. "Just tell me what to say."

"Touch her," Tessa said, all his weight upon her, staring at the water stains on the ceiling.

"She nice, but you is all I think about," Eddie whispered, and he wanted her to smile, but Tessa was pouting. "I love you," Eddie told her, gazing at her pretty, pouting face. She was staring at the ceiling, her expression void. Eddie watched the freckles on her nose. He should not love her. A stuffed bear fell off the radiator.

"This is the hardest part," Tessa whispered. "You must be delicate, gentle, gentle." She took Eddie's hand, molded his fingers, and drew them down, the whole time staring at the ceiling.

"I won't touch you if you look at the ceiling."

"Touch her, touch her, touch her. And bite, bite, bite on her neck while you touch."

Eddie squeezed her waist, fought the urge to stare at her body now, to examine her nude body in the afternoon light in the way he looked at the naked girls in dirty magazines, at girls dancing on the Tropicana stage. Tessa looked off. Eddie grabbed her chin and turned her face to his. He kissed her dark lips until she turned away, as if she'd found his lips sour. The sirens in the distance reminded him of the children crying in the park across the street from his window. He froze, and when Tessa did nothing, he squeezed the little fat of her thigh and in a moment touched her, looking, looking, until Tessa's neck loosened. "Rub, rub, *ummmm*," Tessa said, and she was happy. "She be thinking of hillsides, she be thinking of pretty things."

"You is crazy."

"She be thinking of a hillside, of a meadow. She like it."

"You is so beautiful. I love you, Tessa, like I love you for real, but you keep looking at the ceiling. I feel like we should be doing it, doing it right now but, you is looking at the ceiling."

Tessa grabbed his wrist and pushed him away and climbed off the bed, and he watched her. "You think I'll just fuck you like that? Cause I ho?" Tessa stared at him, pouting.

"No, cause, cause we love each other."

"We ain't love each other, Eddie. I'm a ho, Eddie. I ain't never loved nobody in my life. Nobody never loved me for real. But now you want to fuck me, but I can't say hi to you on the street when you with your boys!" Tessa pushed him away with her little hands, and he watched her dressing, the fleeting memory of her naked body a sort of punishment, Tessa climbing into her clothes, waiting for him to leave her, imperious that he do it now. Eddie called her name, and she stared at him for a moment and turned to look through the window at the construction outside.

Eddie climbed off her bed, wishing he might not have to leave her now, forcing himself to stand, to put on his clothes, his shoes. And he was shouting at her. "You played me!" he said. "You played me for the last time! You is crazy like my brother say, you crazy trick bitch! I'm gonna fuck that other girl then!"

"Good. Hope you catch something."

"Fuck you, you trick! I ain't never loved you! Why you even come back?"

"Fuck you for saying that to me right now, Eddie. That was mean. Go on, I hate you! I hate you like I hate Turtle."

Eddie watched her. He stood at the door. God, he was sorry, and, God, he loved her. She peered at him from across the room. He realized he must leave now; there was nothing else he could say. He was sorry, but it was too late; she was waiting for him to leave, waiting to shut the door behind him, tears in her eyes. It was hopeless now. Because she would leave him, because there was nothing he could say, he ran out, shouting, "Fuck you, fuck you, Tessa!"

He hurried through his afternoon workout, silent, lump-throated, and wandered home; then he realized Homecoming was coming— the Friday after Turtle got out of jail—and he did not have a tux. Adolpho's cousin was a tailor. He called Adolpho's house. "Yeah, he can get you a deal on a tux," Adolpho told him. "My cousin Georgie, he just relocated on Adams St. next to that U-Haul."

"But not a blue one, Adolpho, not an ugly one. A black one."

"A black one, Eddie. A few bucks. Come by tomorrow, and we'll check him."

In the morning he wandered in the shadow of the mountains until he saw Adolpho's house slanting on the hill. Juanita was feeding the chickens in the yard. Elvira stood at the porch, waiting for Eddie. Elvira had lupus, and the drugs she took made her carry extra weight; she'd always been heavyset but her face was beautiful and delicate. Elvira worked in the hospital with Mama, on the floor below. "Adolpho sleeping," Elvira said at the porch. She took Eddie into the house, splitting the hanging door beads of the living room with her plump fingers. They sat down on the sofa, the statue of Pierced Jesus watching Eddie from the coffee table. "I got something important to tell you," Elvira said. "I think Adolpho shooting heroin. There is a man," she whispered, "near the Texaco on Sixteenth St. He seen me filling my car with gas, Eddie, and he recognized me from Adolpho, and he said Adolpho owe him money, and he told me it was for horse."

"No, Elvira, it's just some crazy addict."

"I know, but what he said, Eddie."

"Adolpho ain't doing no horse, Elvira. Have you seen a kit, have you seen tracks in his arms?"

"No, I ain't seen no tracks. I think Adolpho shooting up to stop the seizures. I want you to tell me if you see something, some tracks, a kit. Adolpho don't even take his shirt off in front of us no more. I'm saying. He be locking his bedroom door at night."

Elvira went silent. Then Adolpho emerged from his bedroom in a full beard, saying, "Eddie, Eddie Eagle, come to visit me. Let's get your tuxedo, nigger."

He skipped school on Thursday and took the number 86 bus north, watching the mountains from his window. The bus, filled with mamas and babies' mamas and the babies of prisoners, hurtled forward. The Tent sat in flat, red-rock desert. Eddie saw the forms of the massive bodies of the prisoners in the distance cleaning trash by the highway as the bus approached. Christ, he thought, Turtle was five seven and hardly 150 pounds. No doubt they'd raped him again in the Tent. The bus stopped; people filed out. He could not bear to go inside. He waited at the perimeter fence with the mamas and the babies, imagining Turtle striding out of the front doors, tent canvas flapping in the backdrop, Turtle grinning, knowing that Mama was making pancakes for him, that Adolpho would be waiting for him that evening with brew and weed and prophetic dreams to be deciphered as they rode Van Buren hard.

Deputies patrolled the Tent with shotguns. A sixteen-foot barbwire fence ran around the perimeter. Prisoners in pink jumpsuits shuffled around inside. Eddie stood at the gates in his street clothes. The front gate deputy sensed his fear, slapped a clipboard against his forearm, stared at Eddie. The deputy made a call, and Turtle appeared in a T-shirt, his hair tied in cornrows, a duffel bag on his shoulder, in a pair of obnoxious wire-frame sunglasses Turtle had bartered from a purse snatcher.

Turtle took a few steps across the hard dirt away from the Tent, as if to see if it were real, his manumission, as if the deputy should not overhear the first free words he spoke to Eddie.

"I need to go by the house," Turtle said. "Adolpho said you brung a woman up in there." Turtle was shaking his head. "That's my property, boy, I'll have to meet her. She got to pay me rent or ho." Turtle looked around some more. "Mama fixing me pancakes?" Turtle asked.

"Yeah."

"I'll, I'll, need to get my car out the impound, take a shower," he said; his body stank. He was smiling at Eddie. "Adolpho said you gots yourself a little girlfriend now."

They climbed onto the bus. Turtle gave Eddie a dark look; and then he was humming to himself, taking in the view, red rocks rushing past, the road curling. They returned to South Phoenix by noon, Turtle striding through the front gate, into the dead woman's house. Turtle went, seeking out the prostitute, the squatter, but he found only Milly's pillow, hamburger wrappers, traces of her obnoxious perfume on the soiled mattress, to which Turtle took offense, for it was his house, and Milly was his guest, and Milly should be waiting for him on his first day out.

*O*n Homecoming night, they shared a limousine with Sherice and Sherice's boyfriend, a twenty-four-year-old serviceman who worked at Williams Air Force Base, who Sherice called her "big, ugly boyfriend." The limousine dropped them off in front of Sherice's apartment. Eddie paid his share of the limousine tab with the money Adolpho had given him and the money he'd borrowed from Turtle's secret closet stash. He passed the money to Marchalina, who passed it to Sherice, who paid the limousine driver in the front, and he left them in front of the apartment Sherice shared with her sisters and her boyfriend, in Chandler, the house filled already with cigarette smoke and blasting music, young people in tuxedos and dresses, Sherice's older sisters, and her crying babies. In the kitchen Sherice's boyfriend produced a bottle of vodka, and Marchalina poured the vodka into a blender with orange juice, emptied a tray of ice. "I've got a secret for you," Marchalina whispered to Eddie, as drunk high school boys in tuxedos funneled in and out of the kitchen shouting the music, and Eddie knew it was something terrible and sexual, something to be whispered, something to make him worry about her and want her at the same time. He felt acid in his stomach. The blender whirled, splattering orange juice, vodka, ice chunks across Marchalina's smooth brown face. Eddie stood on Sherice's dirty floor laughing and Marchalina laughing, the boys in tuxedos, Sherice's older sisters, her big, ugly boyfriend. Then Eddie saw a big fat food stamp tucked under a box of Cheerios on Sherice's counter and started laughing harder because the sight of oversize food stamps always made him laugh, even when it shouldn't. Marchalina ran barefoot to Sherice's bathroom, giggling. Eddie followed her and shut the door behind her, still laughing, and then he thought of Sherice's little children, and he stopped. A sophomore boy and girl were messing around in the shower. The shower curtain zipped back, and the boy pulled up his pants and hurried out after the girl. Marchalina ran the faucet, the top of her dress yanked down, washing the pulp from her face. She unfastened her bra and let it plop to the floor.

"I met your brother."

"Where?"

"Here, at Sherice's, last night when Sherice was fixing my gown. He told me about you. Sherice heard Turtle was out of jail and she called his cell, and he came by with his baby and his girlfriend and they played with Sherice's children."

"No," Eddie said, shaking his head. Turtle had not told him. Turtle had not been out a week and already he'd caused him trouble. "You stay away from him!" It was worse than he'd imagined. Sherice had gotten to her, ruined her, his sweet little girl. He wanted to be furious at her, but she was laughing again, and her top was down; he lurched forward in his drunkenness and touched her breast. A fist banged on the door outside. Marchalina put on her top.

"He's so proud of you. He must really love you. He asked me a thousand questions, he grilled me. He doesn't look anything like you." Marchalina dried herself with a towel and zipped up her gown.

She went to her pocketbook and took out a nickel bag, a box of Phillies blunts. "He gave me this for free, for us, for tonight."

"No." There was another bang on the door. "You stay away from him. I told you to stay away from Sherice." He peered at her and grabbed her shoulders. He shook her like he shook Tessa when she would not listen to him when she'd done something stupid, when she was frantic. Marchalina pushed him away. Marchalina was not like Tessa. She was not shaken and beaten and hugged and fucked for money, left on the bed like a doll. Marchalina slapped his chest as the faucet ran.

"Don't you ever touch me like that! I'll do what I want," she said, and she was giggling again. "Roll it for me, I've never smoked it before."

"No. You is a good girl. You shouldn't be doing shit like that."

"You're only mad because I met your brother, because that was the one person I was never supposed to meet. Turtle is one of your secrets. Sherice told me about him when I met you. That's why you hate Sherice, because Sherice knows Turtle."

"He's dirty," he said. He wanted to kick the door. "Sherice is dirty. Sherice got two kids with two different daddies. You shouldn't be hanging around with her. Turtle ain't nothing but a thug." And he ran out of the bathroom. Boys stood at the door, ties hung loose around their collars, staring at Marchalina. Eddie rushed through the dark room of music, out into the hall, and down the stairs and outside. He sat on the front porch.

He sat on the porch for an hour, love music pulsating above him. The little brown-skinned girl did not run after him like she was supposed to. She did nothing like she was supposed to. Black boys played catch with a Nerf football in the dark street, stopping a car cornered into the street. He thought she looked pretty when she was drunk.

Marchalina sat down beside him on the porch and patted his head.

"Turtle said you hate him. He said you're embarrassed about him. Why?"

He turned to her, frowning. "You is a fucking kook."

"You're so judgmental, Eddie, so old-fashioned. Angry. Turtle said you were the angriest person he'd ever known." She was patting his head. "Roll it for me," she whispered, setting Turtle's nickel bag beside him. "I want to see what it feels like."

He shook his head and opened the box of Phillies blunts for her. Marchalina sipped from her plastic cup and sat next to him to watch him make a blunt like the Asian kids watched the chemistry teacher setting up lab. Eddie made the blunt the way Turtle did, slicing it open with his fingernails, gutting it, flinging the cigar leaf on the concrete step. He took bits of dried marijuana leaf in his fingers, squeezing them, sprinkling them across the cigar shaft, squeezing the shaft together. Marchalina sipped her vodka, mesmerized. He took the drink from her hand and set it down. He held the blunt in front of her mouth. "Spit," he said. She shook her head. "Spit, you bourgeois black girl."

"No, that's disgusting."

"Ain't you never spit before? Spit, spit, spit." She spat. She spat again. He took a lighter and held the blunt over the lighter. A cop car went down the street. He held the blunt on his lap until it passed. Then he lit it and passed it to Marchalina and she looked at it for a moment and put the smoldering blunt to her lips and sucked in, coughing, her eyes going wide as she did. She looked at him, little mouth filled with smoke, half choking, waiting to feel high.

"Well, then, there you is," he said, laughing. "Happy now? I bet you feel like a real ghetto nigger now, don't you?"

Marchalina let out smoke. "I don't feel anything," said Marchalina, staring at the blunt. "Now, I do. I do, I do." She smoked until she was choking on the smoke, until Eddie thought, That is enough, and took the blunt from her, put it out, and threw it in the bushes.

Part Two

Edward Bloodpath Sr.

The next week it monsooned, rained so hard that Nana had Eddie shut all the windows in the house. After the rain tapered off, Turtle ran across the street to the variety store and bought dollar bags of ice, and they strode to the park, Eddie, Turtle, and Adolpho, set the swollen bags on the summit, and skimmed down the hills like old times. Eddie went down the hill, his head gonging from the marijuana, Adolpho at his heels, screaming, "Hurry, hurry," until they crashed, and their bags imploded across the grassy bowel of Woodland Park.

"*Mira*, Eddie," Adolpho said, "we gots to use Turtle's bag." The remains of their bags sat at the bottom of the park, plastic skins stretched out like jellyfish desiccating on a beach. Adolpho waved his hand at Turtle, seated already on his bag. "Raise up, boy."

"Yeah, you gave us the busted bags," Eddie said. Turtle stood. Adolpho climbed atop Turtle's bag like he was test-driving a new car, and kicking off, slid down the hill.

"Don't even talk to me, Eddie," Turtle said. "You ain't even popped your cherry! Niggers who ain't popped they cherry can't talk to me."

Turtle laughed. Adolpho laughed. "Don't sleep on Eddie," Adolpho said, rushing up the hill. "Eddie be the mack daddy one day. Put us all to shame. There, take it, Eddie." Adolpho passed him Turtle's ice bag. Eddie sat square on the moist bag, folding up his legs, and Adolpho gave him a hard shove. Eddie slid down across the pebbles and down the bank, where he smashed into a tree and careened on his side, Turtle's laughter tumbling down the hill to him as he climbed to his feet. "Come on, then, pretty boy," Adolpho shouted in darkness, "we gonna get you a *heina* tonight."

Adolpho opened the windows. It was Saturday night, Turtle's getting-out-of-jail party. Turtle was free. Eddie waited in the den for the crush of dark, perfumed bodies. Adolpho stood on the kitchen floor, mixing the jungle juice. There was music. The room swelled. Eddie could not dance. His feet were too big. He was notoriously clumsy. He knew only enough moves to abide. He needed the heavy bass lines. Eddie studied the hustlers and imitated them. A hustler did not dance, but only rocked his shoulders to the music. A hustler did not smile or acknowledge his joy but stared forward, unmoved. But Turtle could dance, could twist his arms and legs into the most precise and funky angles, could ride the music and defeat it. In the press of sweaty, drunk people there was Turtle free and stoned, freestyling, spinning beneath the drunken hoods, the cheering, tramped-out South Phoenix girls. They were watching him now, the *heinas*, comparing him to his brother, pretty Latina faces watching him in darkness, the overgrown virgin, knowing it, giggling.

People filled the house. For a moment Turtle's friends wavered on the stoop outside, malt liquor jingling inside their bottles like coins, the next moment rushing inside, searching for Turtle.

Turtle sat down on Adolpho's sofa and sent Eddie into the kitchen, where the old people (the *tíos*, the *tías*, and the neighbors) had sequestered themselves with Juanita and the troubadours were belting out old-fashioned Tejano serenades on the radio. Eddie took beers from the fridge and returned to Turtle with long-necks of Guinness Stout, which he distributed to Turtle and Adolpho, lying on the sofa with them, sipping his own Guinness. Adolpho was smoking another blunt on the sofa, and the blunt smoke went into Eddie's nostrils. He felt hazy. "Between the Sheets" glided across the front lawn from the window. Neighborhood boys outside raced through the streets and through the park, playing freeze tag.

The back storm door opened and slammed shut. The figure of a woman waved at Turtle from the harsh fluorescent light of the kitchen. The figure shouted, "Turtle, come dance with me! This is my song."

"Eddie, go dance with that old welfare bitch from nineteen fifty-nine!" Turtle whispered. "Eddie gonna dance with you, Lovie," he told the woman.

It was Lovie Ward, Mama's girlfriend from the towers, who was always borrowing money. She stood in the kitchen with Juanita and the *tíos* and the *tías*. Lovie came to the parties uninvited, but managed always to appear at the front door, to drink the booze and eat the food, alone in corners. "Hurry," Lovie shouted at Eddie, and stripped out of a sherbet orange Nautica sailing jacket, which she plopped on a love seat, grabbing him at the waist, positioning his hands on her waist, pressing her face into his chest, forcing him into her rhythm. She rocked him to the music, Eddie's back to Turtle and Adolpho catcalling from the sofa. The fluorescent light from the kitchen was hard on her face, and he thought she wore too much makeup. She stank of menthol cigarettes, impostor perfume. She lingered after the song, arms wrapped about his waist, the pretty South Phoenix girls watching them, giggling.

"Eddie, what are you now? I know you ain't eighteen because your mama baby-sat for me last year," Lovie said, smacking bubble gum, "and you was, what, fourteen then?"

"Eighteen. The song is finished."

"Eighteen, yum. God. When did you get to be such a nice-looking young man?" She gave him a look and pumped his hand. Eddie blushed in the dark room. Her breath smelled of watermelon bubble gum and Newport cigarettes. She removed the blinding bright jacket from the love seat, her beer, and sensing his embarrassment, jaunted back into the kitchen to drink some more.

At two the *tíos* and the *tías* usurped Turtle's party, swaggering sarcastically through the diminishing crowd, blasting their music from the stereo, dancing with exaggerated movements as Turtle's friends funneled out onto the wet, windy street. The next hour the house was quiet, each room flooded with grainy darkness; the cousins and uncles, the aunts, Adolpho, and Turtle had filled beds or laid out blankets on the wooden floors; Eddie lay unsleeping on the sofa, staring at the swaying door beads. Now and then Adolpho's cousins, his nephews rose from the floor, spreading the beads apart with their somnolent bodies, startling Eddie on the sofa as he slept.

In the morning Eddie and Turtle and Adolpho ate *fritas* cooked in corn oil, spiced with Adobo, and Adolpho's house was alive with so many voices. Turtle kissed Juanita on the cheek, called Eddie from the table, and the two of them left Adolpho and Juanita, the cousins, the uncles, and the nephews in the kitchen of Spanish and tramped down a hill of hot blinding dust, scattering chickens with their boots, making their way home across a paddock of weeds and strewn trash.

*A*t 37 Woodland they found an unfamiliar Cadillac parked in the driveway, and inside, through the storm door, his face obscured by the window screen, the figure of a rotund man, their estranged father, Edward Bloodpath Sr., reclining on the sofa.

Turtle walked into his den, nodding at his father. "Hey, Pops," Turtle said. "Long time no fucking see."

Pops gave Turtle a look. Turtle ran to the bedroom and slammed the door. The man sat before the television in a gray polyester suit, eating pancakes from a plate, pads of his fingers glistening with syrup and bacon grease. The house had that fleshy odor of sausage and bacon. Nana watched Eddie from the pantry.

Pops smiled at Eddie from the plate of pancakes. Pops set the plate on the floor, stood, wrapping his bloated arms around Eddie's shoulders; Nana grinned from the pantry.

"A stranger come to see him from his past, Mama," said Pops. "He ain't know what to say."

"We wanted to surprise you, boy." Nana smiled, shelving the Bisquick, her back crooked as a twig. "Well, your daddy and me wanted to surprise you."

Eddie wandered down the hallway. Turtle opened the bedroom door, waved Eddie inside, and slammed the door behind him. "Let's just be out, Eddie. I just come out the Tent. I don't need this, shit. I ain't, ain't, ain't. I ain't got no words for that motherfucker." Eddie watched Turtle strut back to his bed, slip a CD in his boom box, jack up the volume. Now the music from the boom box could only recall for Turtle the freedom of Adolpho's party, the lost freedom of the night before. In the jolting music Eddie stared at his brother, at the scowl on his thuggish face, his thinning, almost blondish hair tied into cornrows, Turtle lost in music as if he had not just seen Pops, as if Pops would not now appear at the door.

A hurried knock. The portly man entered in the middle of the song, a chubby index finger stretched out at Turtle. "I drive all this way, and you ain't got nothing to say?"

"We ain't got no words for you," said Turtle.

"Least one of you turn out okay. Where you get that stereo, boy?"

Turtle sulked. "At the getting place, at the store."

"Turtle work at a nightclub," Eddie said.

"Yeah. Unlike you, I got a job."

"I got family, though," Pops said.

"Not this family," said Turtle.

"I got family in Amarillo, and I got family in Oklahoma," said Edward Bloodpath Sr. "I got family in Phoenix. I got my mama and I got Eddie. I got this house."

"Your mama's house," said Turtle.

"My mama's house is my house. And when I was in Texas that was my house because I had family there. Oklahoma. My family, my house. And this is my house, and now I must ask you to leave, son, for your nana informed me about what you do, and the jail time, and how you got that stereo, and that fancy Acura parked outside, and I cannot tolerate that as a Christian. This will not be acceptable. You may not respect me as a man. Maybe I ain't got no job, but I got a place in the Body of Christ, and I walk the path of Christ—oh, Lord!—and it ain't Christian to live with a certified drug dealer, a convicted thug! Maybe your mama couldn't do it, but I can ask you to leave. Cause your nana and me decided this will be a Christian house."

Nana lurked in the hallway, frowning at Turtle. She waited for Turtle to take up his belongings and go. Nana and Pops had executed a coup, planned in secret, via letters and late night phone calls over the months. Pops returned unannounced, born again, unemployed, some three hundred pounds, to his long-forsaken sons, and now Turtle would have to leave. It was almost funny. Turtle managed to smile at Pops and Nana. Turtle waited for Eddie to follow him out of the house, but Eddie did not. Turtle peered at him from the hallway, tossed his clothing, his most precious comic books, into a cardboard box and, box in hand, traipsed out of the bedroom down the hallway with only a muttered "Fuck you" to Pops and Nana.

Eddie looked at Pops, trying to bring forth all of the anger, but he could only feel sorry for the man. There would be Bible talk in the house, Sunday service. Turtle had been banished. Nana left Eddie in the bedroom with Pops, who was staring at him from a wooden desk chair. Turtle was gone. Pops seemed almost disappointed at the outcome. "I wrote you from Amarillo. You get the letter I sent? I ain't mean for it to happen like this." Pops spoke above the stereo, the music seeming inappropriate now. "Your brother said some things. Your brother ain't got such a high opinion of me, it seem. You see, Eddie, you down, and people count you out. This is me right now, huh? But I still live a Christian life. Did two tours for this country in Vietnam. A good country. Never lost my hope. What's that? Huh? Huh? Come again. What you say? What? What? It's a hard world, boy. They make you pay for everything twice. You'll learn that, huh? You a big boy, Eddie. They got you playing football? That's all they talk about in Texas, son. Huh? Huh? What? People be killing each other over some football down in Texas. Ha! Ha!"

Eddie looked up from the floor. Nana had not told him. "I am a boxer. Golden Gloves. A heavyweight. I'm the regional champ."

"Well, good Lord. A boxer." And Pops was laughing—it was a gutty country laugh.

By evening the bedroom was so hot that Pops knocked on the door, waved Eddie outside. "Come on, boy, you ain't seen the Cadillac yet." Eddie followed Pops outside. A burgundy '83 Cadillac with a sloping, bunted trunk sat in the driveway, the backseat cluttered with blankets and piled clothes, a coffeemaker. "I just wanted to get you out of the house, huh, so maybe we could talk man-to-man. Talk to you, huh, find out about you, what you all about, like maybe you real popular at school, like maybe you got a little girlfriend." Eddie sat with his fingers pressed against the dashboard and looked out the window. "Only ninety-seven thousand miles," Pops said. "Well, I shouldn't say 'only,' but that ain't bad for a eighty-three. I guess I say that cause it run so good. I love this car, Eddie, I love it, huh? Very comfortable, plush, plush. My feet is barely touching the pedal right now. I could drive forever in this car, huh? I used to drive a very important Christian man about Amarillo in this car, a retired preacher he was. Not a black preacher, but a white one, deacon of the First Baptist Church, because my brother, your uncle, is one of the few black parishioners of First Baptist. Not so much spirit maybe— that's what your mama would say. Ha! Ha! Ha! For your mama, a church better have spirit. Huh? Huh? But the people nice and the preacher himself invited your uncle and me, huh? Got your license yet? You must be what, sixteen? What you say?"

"Eighteen."

"Eighteen, you say. I am his unofficial chauffeur. He, the deacon, the preacher, has advanced emphysema from the smoking. I need a job and your uncle gets me the job, and when last month I left Amarillo, that very important and pious man gives me the Cadillac for a flat three thousand on account of my service and that I am his brother in Christ."

Pops stopped the car, wrenched his hips, and removed a leather wallet from his back pocket. "I gave my heart to a Mexican lady, son. In Amarillo. Huh, huh, what you say?" Pops offered Eddie a three-by-five-inch dog-eared picture. Eddie looked at the picture. The woman's features were hard, hair uncombed. "We lost her in the spring, son, to the cancer. Maybe I did not leave you all under the best of circumstances, did I? Huh? Huh? Well, this is for real, Eddie. Your daddy here to stay, can you believe it? Returned to take responsibility for his family. Now I don't think your mama will take me back. That ain't the point. And your daddy ain't as thin and handsome as he used to be. Ha! Ha! Ha! Tell me, Eddie, tell your father the God's honest truth here. What's her situation? She a attractive woman, Eddie. A woman that fine must have male companionship."

"I wouldn't know about that."

"What? What? Your nana say she might be seeing one of the deacons at the church. Just tell me that."

"I don't, don't know. You'd have to ask her."

"He can neither confirm nor deny! He can neither confirm nor deny! My boy."

Mama had been seeing one of the deacons, Deacon Hill, but this had not gone on for more than a couple months. Really, she had been seeing no one at all because no man could offer her anything. And she'd been too busy compiling her visions in a green wire-bound composition book, the beatific visions that possessed her since the age of eleven. Just the month before, the Holy Spirit commanded Mama to self-publish a book of her visions entitled *Can the Things I See Be Real?* In it she sketched out drawings and expositions of her symbolic dream images, images like *Black Hands Praying* or *The Lamb,* daunting visions that she believed to be signs of the coming of the end of the world. For a month Mama had gone about town selling her self-published book amongst church friends and Christian bookstores. Mama had self-published two hundred of these small yellow books in all, quit her selling at sixty, the week before Turtle got out of prison. A plastic Albertson's bag of 140 remainders sat beneath her bed. And Mama believed herself to be a manic-depressive, and for this reason took the Zoloft pills and sometimes Paxil, samples offered in charity by a hematologist who worked her floor at Phoenix Memorial when Turtle had been sent to the Madison St. Jail on assault the months before; once the year before, in an inexplicable rage, Mama had taken the flat end of a carving knife and with it whapped Turtle's forearm until Eddie pulled her away.

Pops turned the car left. "I knew you'd turn out okay, Eddie. Oh, Eddie, I'm doing this all wrong! Huh? Huh? What you say? Took a week of driving just to get up the courage to face you. Spent half my money on motels because I was fearing this moment. And now maybe I'm saying this all wrong, like you don't have no say, like this ain't your house, too. That's what family all about, having a say. I ain't been a very good father to you, Eddie, but sometimes we would talk on the phone, and do you remember what I would tell you, Eddie?" Pops asked, hand cupped around his ear.

"There ain't nobody like me before me, and there ain't be nobody like me after."

"That's right, that's right! Look at you, Eddie. Look at what you do with what little you've been given in this world. Why, Eddie, anyone can see that you is a unique and special individual. What's that? Huh? I been wanting to tell you this to your face all these years. Your daddy here to stay. He happy you walked the straight line in life. Do you have a girlfriend, Eddie?" Eddie shook his head. "Kids your nana don't know about?" Eddie shook his head. "I'm not trying to be

up in your business, but always use a rubber. I'm not saying to forni-
cate outside the bounds of holy matrimony, but always use a rubber.
I'm sure you know all about sex, but sex and love ain't the same
thing. Just always use a rubber. Huh? What's that? What you say?

"And don't never follow the crowds in life, huh? Even if this mean
standing out on your own. Leader stand out alone. You watch. Just
always be yourself. Give a good day's work. Uh, say your prayers.
Your word is your bond. Huh? And stay away from the bad crowds.
Like Turtle, huh? Let's see. Do you got a criminal record of any sort?
That's just asking for trouble. And, and, good things come to those
who wait. Ain't trying to be up in your business, son, about your girlfriends and your life. I'm sure you're very popular with the girls,
huh, and of course you're welcome now to use your father's car to
take one of your girlfriends on a date. Church girls is the best. Met
your mama up in church. And I want you to stay in school, huh? A
boxer, huh? Maybe Eddie will let his daddy see one of his bouts.
Huh? Huh? What's that?" Pops parked the Cadillac behind a Mexican restaurant. "Before we go any further, I want you to understand
something. You is a fair person, Eddie. So before I ask of you and
beseech of you this second chance, I want you to understand, my,
my namesake, that I have sincerely and with all my human, earthly
faculties whatsoever accepted Jesus Christ as my personal savior.
Therefore and so on, I ain't the man who left and abandoned you,
huh? Huh? Yet and still, that was not a man but rather a boy, a boy
who spoke the Word, but who did not live the Word, who did not
stand upon the Word!

"Why, I was only about the Flesh! My mind was all about the
Flesh, all my business, son, was about the Flesh, about sin and adul-
tery. My son, my namesake, I want you to reach into that glove compartment there for me. Don't worry, it ain't locked. Reach in there for
me now, that's it." Eddie pressed a button, and the glove compartment fell open, revealing the ribbed black leather spine of a Holy

Bible, which he passed to the man. Pops leaned back in the billowy seat cushion, stared up with a great echoing sigh, set the Bible upon his knee, grimacing as if in the utmost pain, and squeezed shut his eyes. "Oh, Eddie! Oh, my son! My son, my namesake! I swear with all my heart and sinew as if the Lord Jesus Christ is sitting with us in this Cadillac right now"—his eyes watered—"that I shall from this point forward in life be a good and upright Christian father to you forever, so help me God." The pudgy man clasped Eddie's fingers. "So help me God! Jesus. Oh, God!" With this Pops let out a sniffle and a vacant, whelping cry. Eddie stared through the window at the patrons of the Mexican restaurant, wondering if they could see him through the window tint in the front seat of the '83 Cadillac with the fat, sobbing man, who removed a handkerchief from his breast pocket to wipe his eyes. "Eddie, do you know what a covenant is? I just made a covenant with you. I made a covenant with the Lord three years ago, and now I making a covenant with you."

The lights of 37 Woodland were out when they pulled into the driveway. The stifled applause of a game show murmured from inside, jiggling blue lights of a television refracted through the windows. At the porch Pops squeezed Eddie's shoulder and stared forward as if about to meet his Christian judgment. Nana was watching television from the sofa with Mama, who sat, knees pressed together, on the piano stool and who did not return Eddie's hello. There was an awkward moment where Eddie stood next to Pops, both of them looking at Mama, who did not turn her gaze from the television, Nana watching them from the side of her bifocals until Pops went quietly to the kitchen and removed a soda from the refrigerator, sipping it alone at the kitchen table. Across the dully lit room Eddie gazed at Mama crouched on the narrow piano stool, rolling a glass of iced tea in her palms. Mama turned in an instant from the television (the whole time she'd been watching him from the side of her pretty, pouting face) and then screwed her face into its most ill-spirited form, stood, straightened the hem of her blue summer print dress, which glowed like neon in the dull blue light, and marched to the kitchen in her stocking feet, past her husband, where the contents of her drinking glass were dumped into the sink, and stomped to her bedroom. From the sofa Nana stared at Eddie through her tinted bifocals, grabbing his wrist. "This won't work if we don't give your daddy a chance."

*H*e made a point of leaving early, however little he slept the night before. After seven he found his neighbors rising for work, staring at him from kitchen windows, hurrying off, packing children into the cars whose engines roared in the darkness. But at dawn the city was silent.

He ran two or three miles to the city and back, slow, trodding miles, to the edge of Phoenix, to cotton fields bounded by giant red mountains, red rocks jutting out from the baked, broken earth. Long stretched-out nothingness. The clouds at morning made dense black shadows on the mountaintops. The fields were peppered with spiny mescals, chubby hedgehog plants. It was only here that he could allow himself to worry about Turtle, and only for the length of the access road. There was the afternoon's exhibition, the unknown boy in Guadalupe. Kell knew only that the boy had a Mexican surname, but he could not locate an official record. The boy was a tune-up for nationals. The boy had not fought five times, for no dot-matrix printout had arrived in the mail from the State Boxing Commission, no videotape. Do not think of the boy, Eddie thought. Do not think of the boy. The boy meant nothing now. He should not be afraid, but he was. Doubt is the secret desire to fail, Kell told him. At the moment of fatigue Eddie let out a protracted sigh, turned on the balls of his feet. In the city he brushed past hurried executives shocked by the sight of his lumbering brown arms and legs laboring through the morning crowd, the once sober expressions dissolving before him. He had fought the state tournament circuits, the exhibitions at the Club S.A.R. in Scottsdale, the two-week youth-enrichment boxing summer camps at the Tocco in Las Vegas. At the Tocco, Roy Jones Jr. presented him with a certificate for most improved. He'd met Hagler and once saw from across a gym Burt Sugar, the famed sportswriter. The year before that, Eddie appeared in a crowd of disadvantaged boys in a wide-angle photo of the very boxing retreat featured in the May 1990 issue of *KO* magazine, of which he was given a complimentary subscription. In Vegas once Eddie spotted Rock Newman reading a paperback in the dim fluorescent light of a back office at the Tocco gym, waiting for an afternoon flight—a light-skinned black man, so light Eddie wouldn't have guessed he was black had he not been wearing a Morehouse sweatshirt. His record was a mixed bag. Until the age of fourteen the record propelled him forward because it was so bad, twenty-nine and seventeen, and so he fought to have won enough times to make the number seventeen seem smaller than it was; the next year he fought thirteen times in a new weight class, losing eleven times. Then he learned to counterpunch, to drop his head and snap his punches, and the next year he was eleven and two and twelve and one; and this last year, his best, all wins.

He turned onto Van Buren and followed it to 7th Ave., past the red-brick tenement flats of Woodland Park. Project towers stabbed into the sky. By habit he kept his hands above his head, excepting this last stretch through the projects, when he pumped his arms and tilted his head forward like a bull, a rose-cheeked Chicana girl watching from a project window, tapping a naked Barbie doll against the screen to the rhythm of the Tejano music trumpeting inside. Slow jams and love songs bleated from tower windows. Teenage girls inside taunted him as he strode past. Then stairwell doors burst open, children spilling like marbles across the hot black gravel, down from the busy rooms, from the rooftops, from the stolid Section 8 apartments, the kitchens of gossip.

A whole week and Turtle had not returned for the rest of his belongings; he had not called. This was Nana's report. Eddie came in from the morning run, into the dark kitchen, still panting, and found Nana sitting before the table, her small back to the window. The kettle was on the burner. "Your brother don't come by for his things," Nana said. Eddie washed his face in the sink and through the kitchen window watched a phalanx of bandy-legged boys jaunt down the sidewalk to the open doors of a waiting school bus. "Called over at Adolpho's house, but he ain't there. Juanita didn't know."

"You ain't kicked him out a week," said Eddie.

"Don't say that." When the kettle went off Nana strode to the stove top, presenting her diminished body before him.

"I don't know. Maybe he slept in his car someplace, Nana. Out in the cotton fields near South Mountain."

"Or maybe he stayed with his baby's mama," Nana said. She considered this for a moment, taking solace in the possibility, though she did not like the girl. Said Turtle's baby's mother wore too much mascara and cussed too much, did not give a good accounting of herself, but really Nana disliked her because she was poor and fat and white and lived in a Maryvale trailer park. Nana stirred her tea; she made Eddie some eggs and toast and instant coffee.

Eddie showered and slept a fighter's long sleep in his bedroom, waking at noon to the sound of Pops's barking laughter, running out with his gym bag.

Boys piling into the back of the van. Through the back Eddie saw them piling into the side of Kell's conversion van, the stable boys. The engine was running, and Kell was closing up the gym. Eddie hurried through the hollow gym, late, rushing between the rings, to the back door, to the van. Kell climbed into the front seat with keys and gloves. Tommy took the back farm roads to Guadalupe. At the edge of Phoenix the van halted because ranchers from way up north had driven pure Arabian horses down from the black mountains, down the dry plain to the street, stopping midday traffic. The boys pointed. Proud horse bodies flushed across the road tar, sweeping up plumes of red dust thick as plasma.

In Guadalupe, Tommy found a back kitchen and Eddie undressed and for a moment stood naked upon the cold kitchen tile. He put on his jockstrap, his trunks, and lay on a mat, and Tommy rubbed his shoulders. He tried to think of Turtle again, of the cloistered Woodland Ave. house, Pops, the coup, so that he might extract but a portion of this to unleash upon the nameless boy, but lying on his belly, his body separated by a thin piece of nylon from the filth of the kitchen floor, he panicked. In his mind he was rising, rising from the floor of the kitchen, taking flight from the auditorium, sprinting through the muck streets of Guadalupe.

But he got sweet angles on the boy from the start, knocked him off his rhythm. The boy was a year older than Eddie but unseasoned. Eddie slapped the boy's pocked cheeks with his ruby gloves, Kell watching from the corner. He had reach on the boy. It was not a violent sport, not in the amateurs. Doubt is the secret desire to fail. Today it would be like working the peanut bag. He would not let the boy put one combination together. Catholic nuns watched the bout from the floor, priests, the people of Guadalupe. Twice Eddie caught him on the jowl, and there was that sudden rise in the crowd across the auditorium, each time more profound. Hush. You could tell a boy was unseasoned by the way he took his shots. The boy had cotton mouth. The boy was getting his cherry popped tonight. It was the worst feeling; Eddie knew it. You got hit once and you were running all night because you were young, because you hadn't taught yourself to suffer. Eddie could look into the boy's eyes and know he had not studied the tapes. The nuns started shouting the boy's name with a feminine exasperation that only defeated the boy in advance. The nuns did not understand that the boy must lose because the boy was soft, that doubt is the secret desire to fail. Nuns were sobbing because it was imminent. You fight like you are already bleeding. The bruises and the after pains were the worst. They reminded you of your own desire to fail. Everybody thought they looked tough on the heavy bag, thought it was all heavy bags and speed bags and shadow boxing, and they didn't know, the baseline hurt. . . . Eddie beat the boy's stomach until he dropped the guard, and . . . like pressing a button, the chin. Worst feeling when you drop, he thought. Arms wrench up like your body is in free fall. Thighs shake and give. The sense that you are being shoved, that your boots are not flat on the canvas. Your eyes shoot down. And then that moment always, a kind of prescience, when you know in advance that you will fall, must fall, surrender to it, when, in the moment you see yourself falling, you are falling.

Walking home beneath the trees of Woodland that night Eddie imagined the pipeheads basing on the floors of 51 Woodland, sleeping out the day like vampires. The park was black. Eddie crossed the empty street to the sidewalk opposite the giant house, tucking his neck chain under his shirt, watching the wild overgrown bushes, letting his hands swing about his sides as he neared the house, the dead woman's house, until a thought struck him, and he stopped. He opened the gate, striding up the stone path, where he found Turtle standing barefoot at the bottom of the front porch smoking a blunt.

"Eddie," said Turtle. "Is that you? Is that my long-lost, pie-back brother? *Indeed,* it is! My dear brother come to see me after a week."

"Don't tell me you stayed here? Why didn't you go to Adolpho's?"

"Come on, now. A hustler don't be camping out at his homey's house cause his daddy kick him out."

"So, you slept in a crack house?"

"Come on. It's just for, for a couple days, my brother, my pie-back brother. Going to, to Adolpho's house tonight after work, after the club. Come. Come with me. I was hoping you would check me out. I don't hate you no more, not tonight, Eddie. I don't hate nobody on payday. You got your gym bag, and your nose is bruised up a little bit. Well, did, did, did you win? I knew you would. I got a surprise for you. We'll celebrate, we'll get drunk at the go-go club, and your brother will forgive you your transgressions as you forgive those who have transgressed against you."

"You got Nana worried."

Turtle took another drag of the joint. "And what, dear brother, did Mama do?"

"Mama start her screaming. She won't come out her room except for work."

Milly coughed inside the house. Turtle's squatter. They turned and looked into the dark face of the crack house, Turtle's house. "That bitch owe me rent," Turtle muttered, waving his fist at the house. "Jules say give her a few weeks to get out, or evict her. She got to go. Tessa up in there right now talking nice to her, make her leave." Eddie looked at the house again. Turtle was drunk and weeded out. Turtle looked at his bare callused feet on the porch, his ugly black feet, sighing. "Jail fucked up my feet, Eddie," he said all of a sudden. "That Tent. You know, athlete's foot and shit. I don't know. Niggers be jerking off in the shower, and I think they clean the floors with some kind of harsh abrasive and the, the, the, the harsh abrasive mess up your feet. I need some cash flow, brother." Turtle peeked at the carport to see if his Acura was still there. "Well, you best look after Mama until I get her a place, since you can stand the man. I need a crib, Eddie, a place, a tip."

"What about your baby's mama?"

"Come on, now, a hustler don't be camping at his baby's mama's place cause his daddy kick him out." Turtle took a final drag from the blunt and offered the smoldering wad of moist cigar paper, the premium chronic California weed, to Eddie. Eddie shook his head.

Turtle went silent for a moment, staring at Eddie. "How can you live with yourself? How? How? How? How, my brother, can you stay in the same house with that man, that phony? Don't you hate him for running out on us? Come back now we fucking grown. That Bible thumper! They all a bunch of stuffed shirts, Eddie. I'd rather live in the fucking gutter than deal with that phony. I don't know how you can stand him, how you can forget how he done us. It don't matter now. I'm gonna kill him, Eddie. Adolpho dreamed I would. I'm going to kill our daddy, brother, my brother, my brother, my brother."

Eddie looked at Turtle with a disbelief that only caused Turtle to shout. "You think I wouldn't? That's the problem. Everybody sleeps on Turtle! Everybody think they can come up and just claim Turtle's house, house, house, choke a nigger up! I guess everybody think Turtle soft right now." Turtle tossed the blunt against the stone walk, set a bare foot upon the first step, stopped. He began to giggle. "Hey, boy, you, you want to go up in Tessa tonight?" He chuckled. "She owe me money." Turtle was laughing. Turtle ran down the steps and got into his car. Eddie followed him. Turtle pulled out, stereo blasting, shaking his tiny torso to the music as the car pulled out of the carport. "Come on, boy, let's go find Adolpho."

Turtle drove down 16th St. to the edge of the city, calling out to the girls with bamboo earrings along the sidewalk, who looked at the car with fear and excitement both, the mountains of morning now black hulking forms against the night sky. Young men leaned against

cars, gawked at Turtle's Acura as it hummed down the street. Turtle
raced to the mountains, to the fields of weeds and dirt, to piles of
strewn trash that lay like a moat around Adolpho's slanting farmhouse, past a gathering of Mexican youths with pads of jet black hair
and sagging jeans traipsing up the hill to girls dressed in spaghetti-
string tank tops, who gave looks of trepidation at Turtle's rushing
black car. The car rushed across the dark field to Adolpho's house, to
the house angled on a hill. A distant streetlamp lit the tilting house in
a bright penumbra.

Behind a tall chain-link fence hedged with barbed wire Juanita
peered into the darkness of a chicken pen. Juanita was throwing a
party. Adolpho's uncles were loading cases of beer and kegs into the
house from the back of a rusty pickup truck. Juanita wore a sleeve-
less nightshirt and held a long-neck bottle of Guinness.

"Where Adolpho at, *mujer bonita?*" Turtle shouted.

"Gone to work. Hey, call your mama, Turtle. Tell her where you
staying at. Why you worry your mama?" Juanita said. "Why you
worry me? Call your mama, man."

Turtle shook his head and got back into the car and drove the
car down the hill through the overgrown weeds, spreading dust
across the field, and the headlights caught a black Labrador standing on three legs, defecating in the dark of night on a rock, and Turtle laughed as the dog went scurrying. *"Run. Run, run, run, dog!
Thought, thought cause you was black you could hide in the dark. Ha!
Ha! You know you black, dog!"*

Turtle drove down the fields to Baseline Rd., where he spotted a
working phone booth at the Texaco and cornered inside, passing a
short brunette waiting on the curb with her mulatto daughter. She
stood on Eddie's side, and Turtle slowed the car, leaning over Eddie's
lap to wave her down. "Can I get to know you?" Turtle shouted. The
woman took a sigh, nodded. She grabbed the mulatto girl by the
hand and followed Turtle's Acura to the phone booth, where Turtle

fished a quarter from his pocket as the reflection of the woman's body grew in the rearview mirror. Turtle turned to Eddie. "Get me some orange juice, nigger."

When Eddie came back to the car with the orange juice the woman was letting her daughter into the backseat of Turtle's car. Eddie climbed into Turtle's car, passed the orange juice to Turtle, who looked at the woman through the rearview as Tupac chanted from the back woofers. The woman leaned forward and asked Turtle, "You know Levon?"

"No, but I'm trying to get to know you."

The woman looked at Eddie in the rearview. She was barely five feet tall, petite, a brunette, and, oddly for Turtle, a beauty. The woman looked twenty-five or thirty. Eddie wondered what Turtle could have said to make such a woman climb into the backseat of his car. She did not look like an addict. Her eyes were clear. Dressed too good, Eddie thought. It could only be meth. She'd seemed so out of place standing on that corner outside the Texaco with the mulatto girl. She looked as striking and as sharp, as put together as one of the most expensive out-call escorts at the Tropicana, the beautiful ones, running out to meet a date. The bangs were short, so that she resembled a flapper, like the pictures of the Roaring Twenties Eddie had seen in his history book, but the purse clutched to her side was cheap, the strap frayed, its gray cloth as dirty as the billowy blue dress of the mulatto girl, whose cheeks were stained with catsup.

Eddie watched the woman's eyes in the rearview. "Just that," the woman said, "you look like a friend of Levon. My husband, my soon to be ex-husband. Man, I can't deal with marriage no more."

"Lose that zero and get with this hero."

The child was crying now, crying at the music. Eddie reached for the knob. Turtle slapped his hand.

"I said, 'Lose that zero and get with this hero.'"

"I don't even know you."

"The name is Turtle, otherwise known as Marcus Bloodpath." Turtle waved his fingers at her in the rearview. "Now you know me. This is Eddie Bloodpath, my brother."

"You're crazy!"

Turtle parked the Acura in front of the nearest Albertson's, and the woman searched her purse for her ATM card, and when she was gone, Turtle glanced in the rearview mirror at the little mulatto child, who sat on the edge of the backseat, a finger in her mouth, peering out the window.

"She want to fuck us both, brother," Turtle whispered. "I'm saying."

Eddie stared at the mulatto girl in the rearview mirror. The woman came striding out of the Albertson's looking happy, expectant. She climbed into the backseat. They would drive back to the woman's place, be let into some strange apartment, the mulatto girl quickly put to bed, the woman undressing before them both in an unkempt bedroom before an unmade bed, and Turtle undressing, slipping out of his tank top, his sagging jeans, the skinny torso, the splotch birthmark on his right chest. So gaunt you could count every rib. No kissing, just the woman crawling back on the unmade bed, her petite body, white fleshy thighs. Eddie would for a moment gaze at the naked woman, little breasts, belly, contrast of black V against pale skin, and he undressing with them, the whole time thinking of the poor mulatto girl sobbing in the darkness of her bedroom.

The woman flashed Turtle forty dollars. "Meth money," Eddie thought.

"Who said nothing about no money?"

"So, what are you saying?" Her arms were folded. "Turn here."

"I'm saying we want to get to know you, me and my brother. Don't you think he look good? Women be sweating my brother."

"What are you saying?"

"What are you saying? What are you saying?"

"I don't like this."

"We trying to get to know you is all I'm talking about. Now, don't worry. Turtle take you wherever you want to go, regardless, because you and me is friends now. Ghetto bastards live by a code. But I see a pretty girl and I'm trying to get to know her. Do you gots a job?"

There was silence, the woman considering. The mulatto girl looked at Eddie in the rearview mirror. Her hair was done in pony-tails, plastic barrettes. The woman sat behind Eddie. She set one hand on his headrest, letting out a sigh that kissed the back of his neck.

"I don't want a job. I ain't no prostitute."

"Nobody's saying you a *prostitute*. Did you say this fine young lady was a prostitute, Eddie? I'm just being real. I'm a real nigger, know what I'm saying? I believe in keeping it real. Maybe that's why you riffing with your husband. Maybe he don't keep it real. Maybe he don't be hitting it right. Maybe he a stuffed shirt. Turtle ain't no stuffed shirt."

"This shit better be good."

"Oh, this shit will get you fucked up, baby. Turtle believe in high quality. You gots the, the, the, slamming body. Can you dance? I manage a go-go club, you know. Sun City, fourteen miles east of that. We was headed there before we seen, seen, seen, seen you. Good money."

"You said that already. I don't want no job."

Tupac shouted. Turtle drove east to a complex, which sat beneath the now black mountains and facing the cotton fields. The woman scanned the parking lot for her husband's car. "He probably won't come back tonight. After the way we was going at it! Wait here a sec-ond," and she pulled her little girl out of the car and to the stairwell and they climbed to the second floor.

Eddie stared at the stone face of the apartment building until a single window was lit, the woman's miniature silhouette darting from window to window, turning on lights. The mulatto girl was sent to bed; a light was turned on and then off. The silhouette paced back to the den. For ten minutes the woman was hurrying through her apartment as they watched the stone unconscious walls of the building. Turtle turned to Eddie and smiled. "Don't hate me, brother, but we hired your girl, Princess. Stripping at the club tonight. That bitch be wanting to dance at my club since her freshman year," Turtle said, waiting for the shock to fan out across Eddie's face. This was the surprise. This was Turtle's vengeance, because Eddie had not run out with him when Pops came home and kicked him out. He'd called Princess once. He could care less if she stripped for Turtle. How stupid Turtle was, how petty even now, his revenge, like everything he did, a failure. Eddie wanted to laugh. Turtle was foul. In the Tent, they'd raped him, and he was twisted now. Eddie stared at the dark lot. It should not bother him, Turtle's stunt, but it did. He imagined Princess running in and out, under the black lights of the Paris Room. It thrilled him, the thought of seeing her go naked in blinking lights and smoke; and the woman pacing in the apartment above had confessed, Turtle said, to wanting him, and this thrilled him too, even if Turtle was lying. Marchalina, he'd forgotten to call. Poor thing. Princess was straddling him somewhere, in a thought, in the dank, graffitoed bathroom stall at the Tropicana between lap dances to throbbing house music. He'd find Princess, sweet-talk her, bone her to spite Turtle.

"Eddie," Turtle was saying, "I, I, I was only teaching you a lesson. How you be catching feelings for no-good tricks. You wave a little bit of money in they face, and boo-yah! I'm just looking out. I don't want to see my brother going out like a buster. Bitches is, is, is incorrigible. Can't be trusted. That goes for the little short-haired one, too."

Eddie punched Turtle in the jaw. The cigarette went flying out of Turtle's mouth. "You leave Marchalina alone. You don't be talking to her no more or giving her no weed!"

Turtle examined his jaw in the rearview. He smiled at himself, put another cigarette to his mouth, and lit it. A rusting, wheat-colored sedan pulled up on the other side of the parking lot, and a tall black man in a striped rugby got out, eyeing them, two suspicious black boys in the late-model Acura, noticed the light in the second-floor apartment, removing with a look of worry some cardboard boxes from his trunk.

The man and the woman screamed at each other on the stairs; they whispered; they shouted again, the woman with her arms akimbo, the man shaking his head, the woman pointing to the car, the man peering at Turtle, the street tough below hanging out the window of his car, smoking a cigarette, at the car enveloped in a bubble of violent music.

"What is that?" Turtle shouted.

The woman rubbed her face with the flat of her hand. "We just want a little bud, a dime bag."

"We? Which *we*? I told you I don't need no money. I ain't got no weed. What happened to the meth you was telling me about at the gas station?" Turtle leaned forward. "Damn, woman, me and my brother is trying to get with you. What up?"

"Uh, this is my husband that just walked up them stairs if you ain't notice."

"What's that got to do with the price of apples? I told you, 'Lose that zero and get with this hero.'"

"With my fucking daughter upstairs asleep? With my husband just come home? We just want weed. I'm off meth. You almost made me slip."

"So, that ain't stopping you from getting high up in that house with your little baby girl up in there, woman, ain't stopping you from bringing meth up in that motherfucker? What up? Two buck niggers is trying to get up in your drawers, baby. Tell that sucker-nigger ex-husband of yours you gots to go for a ride. How about that, two buck niggers up inside you?" Turtle swatted at the woman's chest.

The woman leapt back. "You're fucking wicked!" She wrenched her neck to see if her husband was still spying from the window. "That's sick! You're sick! Do you know that you're sick? You're fucking wicked. You must think I'm some kind of fucking whore!" Her voice was low. She pointed to a window, to her husband's silhouette. "Levon is back," she whispered.

"We got a backseat, ain't we? Tell him you gots to come with us to get the weed."

The woman looked at Turtle in disbelief. Her expression was Eddie's own. Turtle was nasty. He wanted only to get Turtle back. Turtle smoked his cigarette. "I told you, girl, I keep it real," Turtle said. "Your body is dope and we trying to get up in it."

"Jesus," said the woman. "You make it sound so sweet. I bet all the girls just love the way you sweet-talk them. You almost made me slip. Now, you gonna get us a dime bag, or what?"

Turtle looked offended, as if selling dime bags was now beneath him. "You coming with?"

"With my husband watching from the window?"

"All right, all right," Turtle said. "And I'll be driving dirty for you, too." He tossed his cigarette on the gravel; he snatched the woman's ten-dollar bill from her pale hand.

Turtle drove to Scottsdale and knocked on Jules's back door. Jules came to the door in a monogrammed bathrobe, a cordless to his ear, a look of celebration flitting across his thin face at sight of Eddie. Turtle lingered in the kitchen for payment. "You keep quiet," Turtle whispered to Eddie.

Jules went to Eddie and touched his shoulder; he looked at Eddie's face and said, "Turtle, what did you do to this boy? He looks traumatized."

"I ain't traumatized," said Eddie.

"You know Eddie," said Turtle. "He don't understand females. He busted up over Princess, the new girl." Turtle was staring at Eddie. "Come on, Eddie, let's ride."

"And you got the boy riding around with you?" Jules said. "No." Jules went to his pantry and removed a money box. It was customary that Turtle be paid on Friday nights in cash. Jules counted the money into Turtle's palm, and Turtle re-counted the money in front of Jules. Jules pushed him to the door. "Go on to the club, fool, you're late. Your brother can ride with me."

Turtle shook his head at Eddie and went out the back door. Jules went to a cabinet, poured a drink, and removed a pillbox. "Here," he said, handing Eddie a shot of scotch and a Valium. "Don't you worry," said Jules. "This will make you feel better." Eddie swallowed the pill with the shot of scotch. Jules took him into the living room and sat him down on his patterned sofa beneath the twenty-gallon bubbling aquarium and started ironing his slacks. "Lay down and relax," he said. "I ain't going to the club for a minute."

Eddie lay on his back. He heard Jules's parrots squawking in a room below—how long it had been, how long since he'd spent the night at Jules's town house.

"Antidepressants. Don't you feel better? I always wondered why white people be walking around so fucking chipper all the time, and then my doctor prescribed me these." Jules ironed his slacks for the club. "Poor Eddie, busted up over a hoochie-hoo. At least you is done with hookers." He laughed. "Love is a bitch. Well, ain't nobody worth catching a lump throat over." Jules stopped ironing and poured himself another drink. "We didn't know you had a history with the girl when we hired her, boooky." Jules stopped ironing and poured himself a drink. "Well, I cannot say that I am surprised that mean old Turtle would try to turn your girl out. Fuck her, then. She cute, but she ain't half of that."

"It don't matter. I don't care about Princess."

"Eddie, I disowned a brother once. What is a brother? What is a family? You love a woman and you marry her, and this is your family—it's even a fucking religious sacrament. Bitch step out on you with some other dude, and you drop her. Bitch ain't your family no more." Jules sipped his drink. "There's something wrong with that Turtle. He's been stealing from me since he got out, Eddie. Don't even have the sense to hide it. Oh, drama, and hiring your girl like that. That was cold."

"Turtle just trying to get back at me. Pops come home after all these years and he kicked Turtle out first thing, and I wouldn't leave with Turtle."

"In a way, you are like a brother to me, Eddie," Jules said. A glass of whiskey was at his lips, and he'd uttered these words and looked off, like a man who had just professed his love to a woman who said nothing in return. "Do you believe that? I've never wanted you to end up like some cheap hoodlum like your brother." A cloud of smoke dispersed from Jules's thin lips and glided to the fish tank. "That is to say, I have adopted you as my own. That's why I had to step in with the Tessa situation, boooky. And don't pretend like you wasn't stank at me for ending that foolishness, but I love you. You have, for all intents and purposes, replaced the brother who I disowned because you are a very sincere, even gullible young man. While your brother, who I lifted up from nothing, be punking me right now. He's been robbing me blind since he got out of jail, and you know I'm not one to sit idly by. But it ain't in Turtle's nature to think things out because your brother is a thug. Now, why would he steal from the register right under my nose unless he was about to do something foul? And I can't just kill him, Eddie, if only for your sake. I mean, I ain't no thug, Eddie. I pay nine-forties and nine-forty-ones. These are tax forms. I file them. I am an eleven-twenty-S corporation. I'm a Promise Keeper. Is your brother trying to kill me?"

Eddie looked up from the carpet. "No. No. Come on, Jules."

"Don't you lie! That boy gone crazy. I caught a bad vibe tonight."

"No." Eddie sat up. "I wouldn't lie to you, Jules. You been real good to me."

"I want to believe that."

"I would tell you."

"Yes, you would, boooky. Then, you could sit here, drink my booze, and lie to my face. Maybe that's what you *got on your mind*." Jules dressed, straightened his tie, and turned off the lights. They went out the back door. Jules stopped to smoke a cigarette on his porch and scanned the night stars. Jules hurried down the stairs to the Land Rover, which he drove on four shots of whiskey.

The Tropicana sat on the edge of Goodyear, a tiny village a few miles outside of Sun City West. Jules parked. The club music could be heard from a great distance. Eddie followed him inside. A line of old men, retirees escaped from Sun City, was forming before the entrance. Adolpho and one of the cooks were hunkered under the open hood of a broken-down limousine. Jules examined his face in a pocket mirror and passed Eddie some cash, and they cut through the line of old men.

Eddie followed bikini-clad girls into the Paris Room, searching for Princess. Turtle was tending bar, smiling at Eddie under a blue light. Now a girl Eddie had never seen before danced naked on the stage. Eddie found an empty corner of the cabaret and sat down on a black recliner. At the stage a balding man in a green suit danced before the rim, waving his fingers, a dollar bill balanced on his nose. A short dancer, a brunette named Melody, saw Eddie on the recliner and took him by the hand. "Follow me," Melody said, pinching Eddie's cheek. In a moment Princess appeared before him.

"Hey, Eddie," Princess told him. Her face was made up and she wore a black teddy. She was buzzing, a drink in her hand. "How you doing? I'm just telling Melody I was hoping you would come by one of these days. I missed you." Princess hugged him. Eddie looked behind Princess into the secret room behind the black wall, looked down a narrow corridor at naked legs reclining on folding chairs in the low orange light.

"You think I should be embarrassed."

"No," Eddie said.

"Whatever. I know how you think. How come you don't call me no more? Eddie's cute," Princess told Melody. Princess watched Eddie. He'd never called her back, but she wasn't as salty as he thought she'd be. Melody put her fingers to her lips. "Can I beg a cigarette off you, Princess?"

"In my purse," Princess said, looking Eddie up and down in his busted sneakers, his dirty jeans.

"Hey, girl, want a drink?" Eddie flashed the money Jules had given him. He waved down a bikini girl.

"I gots me a drink, silly." Princess raised her glass of rum and sipped it. She leaned closer to him and for a moment he was certain she would, as in his fantasy, kiss him there in the club, Turtle watching from the bar, and this would be his revenge. Princess sniffed him and jumped back, shouting, "Hey, boy, you stink!" She giggled under her hand. "I'm sorry, but you funky."

"I fought today. At an exhibition. I knocked this boy out cold."

"Um, that's nice. Ain't they got showers where you fought at?"

"I was headed home from the competition to take one, and then I come across Turtle. There wasn't no time."

"No time for a shower?" Princess looked into her glass. The bikini girl came up to Eddie to take his order. He waved her off.

"We got showers upstairs in the changing room, you know. I can get you in."

"I'm cool."

Princess scrunched her nose. Melody came back, smoking a cigarette. Princess leaned over and whispered something to her, giggling, until Melody was giggling too.

Princess looked at the floor. Eddie could think of nothing to say to the silly, sleepy-looking girl to make her drag him into the bathroom as in his fantasy. Old men stared at Princess from the seats. Eddie felt them watching. He wanted to run out of the club, but he didn't have a ride. He was stuck in Goodyear.

"Hey, I colored my hair red," Princess said after a while. "You feeling it?"

"It's tight."

"I'm getting a whole new wardrobe practically. The Tropicana rounded me off. I'm getting a brand new car, Eddie, an IROC! Melody and me looked at it today. Tropicana be paying good money."

A stripper called to Princess from a dark corner of the room, and Princess turned and began to hurry away. "Yeah, Eddie," Princess said, "maybe I'll come see you after my show. Let me know if you need to use the shower."

He watched her disappear into the black door. Melody led Eddie back to the recliner, to his corner of the room. Eddie watched the drunken suit now stand again and raise a glass to the stage. Princess entered the stage from the side. Smoke rose from the blinking floor. From the balcony the DJ introduced her by her cabaret name, Eva. Eddie watched Princess dance naked before the drunken man; he wanted almost to cry at the sight of her beautiful naked golden body on the stage. For two minutes she pranced along the back of the stage, letting down too soon the straps of her teddy, and went to the brass pole, swinging around it, one leg kicked up, her sleepy face going blank. The drunken man danced at the stage, called at her, a dollar balanced on his nose. He waved his finger at Princess. Others watched the man, laughing, smoking their cigars from their tables. The bouncer and Adolpho waited behind the draw curtain. The drunken man squeezed her leg, and Adolpho and the bouncer rushed in to beat him.

Princess ran off. Men cleared out of the cabaret. "The police is coming," a dancer named Lola kept shouting from the balcony. "Somebody just called them!" In an hour the lights had gone out, the cabaret closed. The four-story neon NUDE GIRLS sign, which could be seen from I-10, blinked off, the kitchen door shut and locked. Jules ordered the busboys and dishwashers to rush through the dark cabaret, the VIP lounge, the private rooms, straightening up, shutting off lights, locking the doors of the adult video room. In ten minutes they had done this, rushing through each room, riding home on their bicycles. The bouncer was paid $200 to drive the strippers and the escorts and the hostesses home. Women gathered in the blinking lobby, half-naked girls, girls in robes, bikini girls now dressed in street clothes, Princess and Melody with them. Eddie watched Princess climb into the back of the limousine. He wanted still to follow her a moment, to follow the limousine, to tell her again that he would be rich, though he did not know why, but the police were coming and Adolpho was pulling him outside, where Turtle was waiting in his car.

Laughter and Spanish and Tejano music wafted like clouds of marijuana smoke from the black windows of Adolpho's leaning house. Adolpho and Turtle sipped beers in Adolpho's room with neighborhood girls. Eddie went into the living room to find a patch of floor on which to sleep for the night, but it was filled with a bunch of Juanita's friends and Uncle Balthazar. Everyone was smoking marijuana and watching *Sábado Gigante* on the television. Eddie found a space on the sofa and sat down. A woman squeezed his arm.

"What's the good word?" said Lovie. The perfume, the smell of watermelon bubble gum. Eddie shook his head. "I said, 'What's the good word?' I say, 'What's the good word?' And you tell me a good word. Tell me a good word."

"What up?"

"No. You can't say, 'What up?' You can't tell me, 'Hi.' Tell me a good word. I'm so fucking drunk right now. I'm so fucking drunk and I want a menthol." Lovie reached into her purse and removed a crush-proof pack of Kools. "You ain't my friend cause you ain't tell me a good word."

"I couldn't think of one."

"Say what? The music."

"I said, I couldn't think of one."

"Don't you want to be my friend?"

"I guess so."

"I offer him friendship, and he says, 'I guess so.'"

"Yes, I want to be your friend."

"Then walk me home, boy. I'm feeling my drinks."

They cut through the empty dirt fields toward the project towers. "Stop walking, boy. You walk too fast." In the morning he would call Marchalina and tell her Turtle had dragged him out. He'd borrow Pops's car and take her to the movies. Lovie yanked his arm. She leaned against a fence and lit another cigarette. "Rush, rush, rush. Is this how you go through life? I love the fall. Don't you feel safe in the darkness on a night like this?"

"I don't know. I guess."

"You guess, you guess! Listen how everybody outside, whispering in the darkness. Children, mothers, daddies, teenyboppers—*lovers*. I love this street at night, this park. Peaceful. I want a house. Look at the windows. Look how all the windows done turn blue cause everyone be watching television. Little children be sleeping in they beds. Look at how the blue lights of the television wiggle against the walls inside. Look at the shadows of people on the porch, watching us. I like that park across from your house. I take my son to that park. You got kids?"

"No." He remembered the cool eel skin of her back through blouse cotton when they'd danced before, at Turtle's getting-out-of-jail party. He thought of the little brown-skinned girl for a moment. Lovie was muttering something about her baby's daddy. Damn, he was a son of a bitch, Lovie was saying. Damn, he was a son of a bitch. Lovie could not speak the man's name without adding that he was a damned son of a bitch. "Am I your friend now?" Eddie asked her.

"Walking me home, ain't you?"

They passed Bumpy's. The light in Tommy's loft was on. Eddie

wanted to stop right there and see Tommy. Lovie was saying something to him now, but he did not hear her. He wanted to see Tommy,
wanted Tommy to tell him he would win the regionals and nationals
and that he would be rich, but not so that Princess would sleep with
him—he'd forgotten her already—but only so that he might move
somewhere and never see Turtle again. He wished the little brown-
skinned girl was not so kooky. He kept thinking this. If he slept
with this woman from the projects, she had only herself to blame,
he thought. They passed Bumpy's, a few blocks from the woman's
apartment, and he realized he could not stop himself. The project
towers seemed foreign to him now. He had not been here in so long
and could recognize none of the slouching black boys who leered at
him now from the courtyard. "You need," Lovie said, "to walk me to
my door. Niggers is foul around here."

Hers was the third tower. He followed her, heat rising in his chest.
Lovie swung open the heavy wooden door of her section. A collection of boys at the bottom of the stairwell shouted insults to their
backs to which they dared not respond, outnumbered at night.

"I got to teach you how to be my friend," Lovie said, opening her
door. "I need more friends, Eddie. I need friends who real, count-on
friends." She opened the door. Shut the door and pulled from her
purse a fresh pack of watermelon-flavored bubble gum. He smiled,
erection rubbing against the cotton of his underwear.

He stood in her tiny apartment. "Nice," Lovie said. "Subsidized.
Lots of room. Just me and my son here," she said, cracking a bedroom door open to look in on the sleeping boy.

Lovie tossed her orange sailing jacket on the sofa and waved him
into the kitchenette. "Hungry? Want a drink?" Eddie stared at a box
of Froot Loops atop her refrigerator, and Lovie noticed. "Help yourself. Damn. *Mi casa, su casa,* and shit."

"All them old people was smoking weed at Adolpho's," Eddie said.
"Contact high. Munchies."

"Shoot, I feel you. I was one of them." Lovie placed a bowl and spoon on the kitchen table before him and poured two-percent milk for him and told him to say when.

"So, little boy eating all my Froot Loops," said Lovie, sitting beside him, "what you want out of life?"

"What I want out of life?"

"We friends now. I must know about you. You gonna turn pro and buy your mama a house? You gonna remember our friendship when you the champ?"

"I'm going to be a pro. I'm going to Vegas. But it's a industry, my trainer says, but he says I could make some money on account of my solid size, you know, and my defensive skills, but you got to understand what you're getting into, you got to think about the extra punishment to your head."

"They hit you harder. Mess up your brain. Like Muhammad Ali?"

"No." Eddie made a fist. "The padding in the gloves makes your brain shake in your skull. Somebody hit you bare knuckle, and the bones absorb all the force, but padded gloves spread the force out, shakes your brain." Kell had told him this.

The woman gave a sickened look at the thought of brains shaking in a skull. "Muhammad Ali ain't punch-drunk," Lovie said. "I heard the government gave him a lobotomy because he was a righteous black man. The CIA. That's what they do to all the righteous black folk when they don't kill them. Snip, snip. Give them lobotomies. And if you become a righteous black man, they give you one, too. Cut your head up, make you retarded." She giggled.

"What you want out of life?"

"What anyone want out of life, boy? A million dollars hard cash. Just basic things, shit. Be fucking happy. Find a nigger that ain't bullshit, raise a family. Now you make me depressed. You got any bud on you, boy?"

"No."

"Like you would tell me if you did?" Lovie sipped, laughing. "They don't give us no money for liquor, cigarettes. Bud. But you know nig-gers. Niggers got to get they drink on, they weed on. So then you ex-change the stamps on the street—at a discounted value—if you want liquor or cigarettes, some bud. End up wasting the money they give you in the first place. They might as well just give us the money for liquor and cigarettes to begin with, you know."

Lovie wanted to listen to music. He followed her to the bedroom. The bedroom, like Lovie's blouse, her breath, smelled of menthol cigarettes and the bubble gum. Lovie set her drink on her dresser and set the radio to 88.9 FM, Friday night slow jams. Eddie stood at the door, hands in his pockets, while she turned her back to him and fiddled with the radio, then stood, turned to him, spat her gum into her hands. "Do you like my room?" Lovie asked, flicked off the light, and thrust her tongue, her watermelon-flavored tongue, into his mouth. The slivers of her braces were cold from the chilly walk to the projects. Lovie unbuttoned her blouse. Manicured fingers tugged at his shirt. He laced his arms about her waist, feeling the cold leather of her belt against his wrists. He caressed her neck. "Your hands is cold!" She giggled. His fingers brushed against the cotton of her bra. Lovie was kissing him and pushing him away at once; she felt the erection and said, "Woo!" Lovie stopped herself, pushed Ed-die away, staring at him in the dark room. "God, if your mama find out. You don't," she asked, "be running your lip, do you?"

Eddie shook his head, offered Lovie a look of emphatic sincerity. The blinds were half drawn. She sat down on the edge of the twin-sized bed that reeked of tobacco. The room was level with the street-lamp, and in the harsh light Lovie crawled to the center of her bed, inching back to the wall, now supine, navel dancing in the win-dow light. In the silence between love songs Lovie unclasped her bra, got naked. The light gave Lovie's body an oblong look. In the window light he could see her spongy body. He unbuttoned his jeans, climbed naked onto the bed. Lovie was humming the lyrics of the slow jam. He kneeled on the bed before her, on the edge. In an odd moment she drew her fingertips along her own thighs, her belly, her nipples, to her shoulders, sighing. Too soon there was a terrible wondrous welling in his groin, and too soon the abandon, too soon the sudden release, and he was shouting into the pillow. Lovie pushed him away, and he lay on his back and she walked to the closet to get a towel. Lovie returned, lying next to him. He wanted to run out of the Section 8 apartment, but it was bad manners to leave. Lovie put a wad of bubble gum in her mouth. Her son was sleeping in the next room. No doubt the child had heard the squeaking bed. He'd grow up twisted and stupid and foul like Turtle because he'd heard his mama's bed squeaking at night, his mama sleeping with strange men. "The next time you hook up with somebody," Lovie was saying, "you better wear a jimmy, boy. With spermicide on it. How do you know I'm on anything? Lucky I'm on the pill, boy. I could have AIDS, herpes, the clap, you don't know." Lovie pulled him close, giggled. They made you lie with them and hug up on them after. He stared at the ceiling; his expression was the expression of the johns after they had finished with Tessa, of guilt and release; he'd seen this expression watching from the crack of a motel room closet. Lovie touched his shoulder. "People think I'm easy," she said. "But I'm just sensual. You know, sensual. In touch with my body and shit. Sensual."

The next week he woke to the sensation of a thousand insects nibbling at his genitals. Lovie! he thought and climbed out of bed, almost shouting into the darkness of his bedroom; he leapt to the floor, turned on the light, yanked down his underwear. He discovered a legion of crablike beings festering across his pubic hair, his thighs. There were a hundred of them, each nesting, breeding, multiplying, sucking the blood out of his skin. He stood in the center of his bedroom, examining himself, sickened—to look at them was to know their presence, the crabs, to know that they were that moment gnawing at him, incubating, his own blood feeding their tiny articulated bodies. Eddie slipped into his jeans. He picked up the phone and called Turtle's cell phone three times. He called Adolpho. Tommy would know what to do.

He stood before Bumpy's for twenty minutes, hurling pebbles at Tommy's window until the light went on. Tommy came to the door in his underwear, led Eddie inside. Kell was sleeping in the boiler room. Tommy snuck him in behind the second ring, and Eddie told him in a whisper of his condition.

"Gasoline," said Tommy, nodding. "Kerosene. There's some kerosene in the closet."

"You mean like burn the—my hairs?"

"No, no, rub it on the hairs, and the kerosene kills them." Tommy picked up a bottle of whiskey from the floor. "I find this tonight," he whispered. "I want to pour it out."

"You want to, but you don't."

"I want to but I don't want the old man to start hollering at me in the morning. This is the man who taught me how to fight. This is the man gives me a place to live while I study for the police officer exam." Tommy fingered his stringy dirt blond hair. "Eddie," he said. "You the one buying liquor for Kell when I told you not to?"

"He needed it. He is miserable, Tommy. Look at him. He won't never stop. But I watch him. But I check on him every day."

"Because you believe all that bullshit he is telling you. Eddie, you're a smart kid. I hope you ain't taking the old man serious," Tommy whispered. Eddie looked at him in shock. "I'm your friend here, Eddie. The drunk talk of a seventy-year-old burnout won't get you nowhere in the pros." Tommy was frowning and laughing at once. Eddie shoved the stringy-haired man, tackled him to the ground, and they were wrestling, Tommy squeezing his neck, tussling on the warm concrete floor.

Kell appeared out of the boiler room before them both, in his liquor, beating the concrete floor with the ten-second cane, laughing, laughing, dancing on his corned, callused feet. "Both you boys shut the fuck up! Stop it!"

"Come on, Eddie," Tommy said. "Let's put him back to bed." Eddie stared at Tommy for a moment and followed him into Kell's office, to the couch, where they lay the old man down. Eddie took the ten-second cane from Kell's hand and set it against the wall. The office was dark and smelled of vomit. Eddie turned on the light. Kell had vomited in his trash can, across the floor. The model helicopters swung from wires as Eddie and Tommy went cleaning up the dark room. Kell puked on the sofa. Eddie turned on the light. Kell's face was covered in vomit. "Oh, shit," Tommy said.

"Oh, shit," said Eddie.

Tommy wiped Kell's mouth with an old Burger King napkin, set the napkin in the trash can, passed the trash can to Eddie. "Wash that in the sink, Eddie," Tommy said. "Get the Lysol." Eddie took the trash can and washed it in the industrial sink in the utility closet; he went back to Kell's office with Lysol, set the trash can next to Kell's sofa. Tommy was sitting on his knees, washing Kell's face with a wet rag. Eddie set the trash can next to Kell's head. Then Kell sat up and leaned over the trash can, spat into it, but his stomach was empty.

"Come on," Tommy said, touching Eddie's shoulder. "Maybe you stop feeding him liquor so much, is all." He looked at Kell. "Let's take care of you." Tommy went to the utility closet, Eddie after him. Tommy searched in the soft light amongst industrial cleaning supplies, bleach, oil, ammonia, for an aluminum canister of kerosene. Eddie wiped his eyes. He stood in the utility closet with Tommy in the muted light, frowning, a knot in his throat. Tommy was right. He'd leave the old man tomorrow, let him choke on his vomit. Eddie stared at the faded girlie poster on the wall as Tommy found the canister of kerosene. Tommy doused an old handkerchief and instructed Eddie to rub it across his pubic hair, and turned and himself looked at the girlie poster while Eddie did. But I can't stay in Phoenix, he thought. I'll go crazy. Eddie rubbed the burning kerosene across his pubic hairs, indifferent to the sting. "Then, Eddie, and listen good," Tommy said, "take all your clothes, whites and coloreds, all your blankets and sheets, and wash them, hot, hot, hot water. They nest, Eddie, they breed."

He went home at three in the morning, high from the fatigue, the inhalation of the kerosene fumes in the cramped utility closet. He crossed Van Buren and once again cut through the little park to Woodland, stopping before the giant dead woman's house. There were shouts inside, shuffling noises, like a couch being shoved across a wood-panel floor. Milly was being evicted tonight. Eddie heard Tessa coaxing her out, saying, "Come on, girl, you can't stay here no more." A beer bottle smashed against the wall somewhere inside. Eddie heard Turtle and Adolpho grunting from inside the living room, grunting as they pushed Milly out. Milly—they'd gotten her good and drunk and slathered her legs and feet with baby oil—was barking, panting as she shoved back.

Jules stood on the porch, smoking a cigarette. "Shit," he called to Eddie, "I should make you come up in here and help these fools," and he began to laugh at the sight of Milly's bare foot at the doorway nudging back as she struggled; and Eddie laughed. Eddie did not mean to laugh—it was so mean, so cruel—but he could not help it; it was the funniest thing he'd ever seen. "I told you not be bringing stragglers up into this house. Look at this. Look at me standing in this nasty house like I'm some cheap hoodlum."

He snuck back into his bedroom through his window, brushed his teeth in the bathroom, stared at himself in the mirror, slept hard on the naked mattress. He dreamt, waking to gunshots. The kerosene infused his dream with the wildest colors. It was night in this dream. Eddie was the next moment chasing Turtle across night dirt under South Mountain, Turtle himself chasing a black Labrador beneath the mountains across the dry cotton fields and Eddie after him, through the red rock dust, Turtle's black boots crunching the field dirt. Then Turtle chased the black Labrador to the back brick wall of a strip mall, cornered it before a Dumpster, and there beneath a bare sixty-watt lightbulb Turtle beat the wailing dog with two solid whacks against the curl of its fleeing twisting back.

"Did you hear them, boy?" Mama stood in the hallway. His door was open. Pops stood behind her.

"Down the street," Pops said. "The shots."

"He count nine. I counted six," Mama said, without looking at Pops. She loathed him. The man was a fool to come back to get her. "Everybody heard them. What happened to your sheets, boy?" Eddie lay on a naked mattress; he'd thrown his sheets in a corner. Mama shut the door. Eddie's phone rang three times and stopped. He went to the phone, but the caller hung up. Someone rapped at his window. He crouched beneath the window, expecting Adolpho and Turtle to start cackling at him from the bushes, but when he let the blinds up, it was Milly panting in the darkness, drunk and stinking of the house.

"Eddie, I needs your help." Her face shook in the streetlight. "They gonna kill me!" Milly whispered. "Somebody already got killed. Killed some dude. Tessa seen it. Tessa running down the street. Please, Eddie, let me in."

"No. Where Tessa?"

"Open the window."

"Go away."

"Please, Eddie. I'm a witness. Come after me. Cold shot him dead, Turtle and Adolpho! Please let me through the window before Turtle see me crouched outside his fucking house."

"Who?"

"Turtle done it. Turtle killed that dark-skinned dude."

"Ain't nobody killed nobody."

"Please." She was crying now, crouching in the darkness before his house, pulling back her hair, hiding in his bushes. "Your brother and Adolpho killed some dude, the dark-skin one. I seen it. They looking for me on the street. I need to get off the street tonight. They won't look here tonight. Please! Christ Jesus, let me in your house."

"Shut up."

"You got a dog? I sleep in your backyard." A car passed, reflected headlights streaking across the bedroom walls. Milly whispered a drunken prayer. "I hate Phoenix. Phoenix is too hot right now. Just let me sleep in your backyard and I'll be in Albuquerque tomorrow."

"Who got killed?"

"I told you. The dark-skin man, the tall one. They kicked me out, Adolpho and Turtle. Please, boy."

"Jules?"

"Your brother done it."

"Shut up." ,

"Yes he did, your brother. Your brother cold shot that man. God, it was foul! Help me."

"Shut up. Fuck you, you crazy ho. Go away. You know hookers ain't allowed to come to the window."

She thrust her head at him like a rabid dog. "Your brother, boy! Your brother, your brother, your brother! They was fucking mad. Ain't let me get my shit, my suitcase. Just shoved me and Tessa out the backyard. Then Adolpho cracks Tessa on the head, push us down the back stairs. Me and Tessa stand out in the backyard, in the weeds, cause we ain't got no place to go. We hide out back in the weeds if stuff gets hot. And the dark-skinned dude shouting. And the shooting. The shooting, the shooting, shooting, shooting! Adolpho open the back door and seeing us in the light, in the weeds. Tessa break, I break. Adolpho shooting. I'm running for my life, Eddie, through the grass, over the fence, I don't look behind me. My feet be covered in blood!"

"I seen them kicking you out." It could only be a lie. Adolpho and Turtle had kicked her out, and she wanted to play him for a little money.

"Your brother, he foul. He straight killed that dude."

"Shut up. Shut up."

"Your brother, your brother, your brother!"

"Fuck you. Step off. I ain't got no money for you."

"I appeal to you in the name of Jesus," Milly cried. Eddie let down the blinds as the mad woman ran off, her bare feet clapping against the street tar.

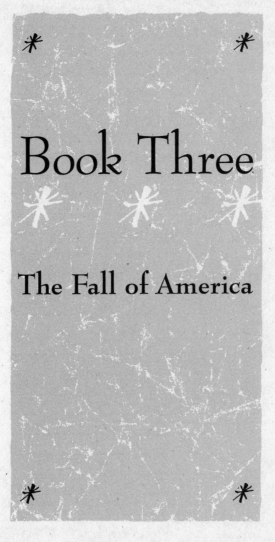

Book Three

The Fall of America

Part One

Fugitives

He found Turtle's prostitutes working their corners unsupervised, his old back-corner haunts vacant. Turtle had taken flight. He could not search for him anymore, not even to tell him Milly had violated his single rule—appearing at 37 Woodland in a fix. He could know nothing when the police came by. He forbade himself even to pass the looming house the next week, to search its dreary face for new boards, police tape.

He put his brother out of his thoughts, bought roses and love cards for the little brown-skinned girl, jewelry from street addicts, borrowed varying sums from Turtle's secret closet stash, leaving IOUs scribbled on college-ruled paper in the black hole under the floorboard.

Marchalina asked him why he got so quiet on the phone. He told her he was thinking about his brother; he told her Turtle was in trouble. He told her this and nothing more. She did not ask what trouble meant.

After a week he realized Jules was dead and there was nothing he could do. He did not feel safe. He almost panicked when in the space of an hour three girls from the Tropicana called him at the house one afternoon, asking for Turtle, asking if he'd seen Jules. Jules's partner, the Mormon, was looking for him now. "He might give you a call, Eddie," said one of the girls. "Just to figure out where Jules could be." The girls who called, Ecstasy, Destiny, Melody, let out thin worried laughs when Eddie told them he did not know where Jules had gone. It was rumored that Jules was running from bad debts. It was rumored that Jules had gone to live with a man in San Diego. The Mormon partner had killed him. When Melody called again two girls had quit. "I mean, did he fall in a ditch and die? Someone should call the police." Eddie hung up the phone and fell asleep on his bed. He woke and almost screamed at Adolpho, who was standing in the bushes, tapping at the window. "*Mira*, Eddie, Turtle run off last night, Eddie. I gave him all the money I had. My mama packed his bags. Say he running off to Show Low when he get some more funds. The po-lice be stressing him about these guns. . . . These guns, these guns have murders on them, old murders. They ain't Turtle's murders, but the guns was stolen and they got murders on them, I think, and Turtle left them in the dead woman's house."

Eddie did not understand. "But Milly said you shot Jules."

"Turtle left dirty guns in the house. Turtle fucked up."

"But what about Jules? Is he okay?"

Adolpho looked at him and said, "I'm trooping out to California, boy. Hold tight, Eddie Eagle." This was Adolpho's "yes." Yes, Turtle had shot Jules, and no, Adolpho did not know why. "They will come looking for you, Detective Patricia and these cops, at school, at the gym," he said. Funny, Eddie thought, he'd been dreaming of Detective Patricia, too. "They will come. They will interrogate you and shit. Don't you tell them nothing, Eddie! I'll call you when I get set up in California."

He skipped four days of school. Marchalina called him on Friday morning, frantic. "God, Eddie, where have you been? Why won't you talk to me?" she said. "You don't like me. Are you dropping out? I've got a math quiz first period," and then hung up.

He met her at her doorstep after school.

They made love on her bedroom floor. Marchalina turned on her boom box.

"I went up into the city this morning," he told her, "to the Bank of America building on Central, where all the businessmen work at. I thought of you and I sat on the front steps and watched the people. I watched the people smoke cigarettes and eat hot dogs. I listened to them talk. I watched these men carry a Christmas tree through the front door."

"I tore up the note I wrote for you. I failed my quiz. You're bored with me."

"No, I ain't."

"Look, I won't bother you now just because we did it. I don't want anything from you."

He waited to feel regret, the impulse to stand and leave—it was a cruelty to the little brown-skinned girl to bone her on her rug when he loved Tessa, but he felt no guilt, only the stillness of North Phoenix, the suburban quiet of her development. Marchalina took a piece of carpet lint off her thigh with her little fingers and, absent, stared at her own naked body.

"I don't understand," she said, "what you think you can't tell me. If it's your brother, Turtle, I know. I know he's in trouble. Sherice told me he was always like that." He wondered if he was for her a phase, like her natural, if she liked it that Turtle was a thug. Turtle was a murderer. Turtle had killed a man for no reason, and he'd run. The moment he told her this, all her love for him would vanish. He felt dirty. He did not belong with her. She lay on his chest; she was waiting for a story, an explanation. It was electric, her need to know his secrets, and he could tell her nothing. He wished, Marchalina's warm body atop him, that she could be his Tessa, broken and ruined, worthless like himself. He lay naked under her, her tiny body, new and wondrous to him, like marijuana the first time he'd smoked it on Jules's sofa, knowing only as he inhaled that he wanted to smoke it again. He stared at her naked body until he grew hard again and went, sighing softly, into her.

Now he was overcome with a terrible emptiness, something worse than the realization that Adolpho was gone, that Turtle had for no good reason shot Jules to death in the dead woman's house, that Kell was a worthless drunk and could take him nowhere. It was a loneliness, a longing, even now, for Tessa. To sleep on the stank wooden floor of the dead woman's house, a mucus-mouthed child on Tessa's lap in 1987, in a tepid second-floor bedroom, lying atop her sobbing body, in a bed stinking of her blood, a miserable child, seemed better than this, the emptiness he now felt.

"I love you."

"I am poor."

"You are poor. You are poor. I don't care."

She'd lopped off her ponytail to feel black. "I know it's high school. This isn't one of those stupid high school things." She was seventeen. She thought she loved him. Next year she would think she loved another boy. He stood, silent, climbing into his clothes, and left her.

He found two yellow Post-its Nana had left for him on his bedroom door. *Mr. Patrisha call.* He went into Nana's room to ask when Detective Patricia had called, but the old woman was napping. Nana caught him the next morning on his way to school, grabbed Eddie's wrist, and peered at him. "You know," Nana said, Mama behind her sobbing at the kitchen table, "the cops looking for Turtle. He done something serious. You best call Mr. Patricia back."

"I will, Nana," Eddie told her, walking out. But he couldn't. If he called back today he'd seem too eager. If he waited another day he'd look guilty. He did nothing. The next day, catching sight of Detective Patricia's blue Taurus shoving down Woodland Ave., Eddie ducked into an alley. When the Taurus rushed off he ran up E. Monroe and entered Bumpy's through the back. Kell caught him climbing the mezzanine stairs to look out the high, fogged windows at Van Buren with the adolescent Chicana girls. Kell waved at him, and Eddie ran down to him. Eddie could not remember the last time he'd seen Kell sober.

"I take it you don't have health insurance," Kell said in his office. The pipes began to clank. Kell waited for them to stop. "And where you been? Got nationals in a little while."

"I been coming by. I been leaving you beers behind the sofa."

"I see that look you give me, like the old man will let you down, Eddie, but he won't. When we go out to nationals, I won't touch a drop, okay. It's all business. We're gonna surprise some people. Tommy told me you, ha, borrowed some of my kerosene from the utility closet. We can't have you running around with a VD, son. Now," Kell whispered, "there's nothing to be embarrassed about if it's just crabs, but don't be stupid. We need you at your best. Christ, Eddie, do you know how sick a piece of ass can make you these days?" Kell shook his head. "I once caught a case myself on tour in the Pacific. Pubic lice is a lesson in discretion." Kell stepped close to him and stared into his eyes. "Can you still, ha, piss straight?" The kerosene had worked, but Kell laughed anyway until his pink, bloated face went serious. "Tommy's a fucking idiot. You can't rub fucking kerosene on your balls and call it a day. Now, this doctor is an old Rotary friend. I should have him give you a fucking HIV test, but I won't." Kell passed Eddie the doctor's business card and $35 for the prescription.

Eddie shook his head. "You ain't got money to be giving me. We took care of it."

"Not with kerosene! I got some money. Don't worry about my

money. Some money came in the mail, a little extra for nationals. In fact, you can walk the rent check up to the people tomorrow. But right now, you just go up that street and drop your pants for the doctor and get the prescription filled tonight. And don't come back and tell me the doctor wasn't there."

Eddie wandered up 16th St. to Washington St. He came to a block of professional buildings, saw the brownstone, the doctor's name embossed on a wooden sign, climbed the steps, and opened the door. It was 5:40, the receptionist breezing out as he stepped inside. Through the lobby window he saw the doctor, a gentle, full-bearded man signing standardized forms at the counter. The doctor noticed Eddie standing at the lobby window. "Kell's boy," he said. The doctor went around and came through the lobby door. "Some floozy gave you the crabs, eh?" He removed a pair of latex exam gloves from his lab coat pocket, asked Eddie to drop his jeans, and, squinting, gave Eddie's crotch a cursory inspection in the lobby. Then he tossed the latex gloves in a trash bin, took out a small pad, and scribbled out a prescription.

Eddie turned in his prescription at the nearest pharmacy in a dark strip mall on E. Washington St. and drank a Sprite outside as the prescription was being filled. The shampoo had an odious clinical name and cost $23. With the change Eddie bought two supreme burritos at the all-night Filiberto's down the street, and a six-pack of Keystone for Kell at a corner liquor store. A six-pack was the least he could do, he thought, Kell squaring away the nationals money. Two blocks west he wandered past an inconspicuous two-story mosque, a gathering of bodies in shadow talking under the red crescent awning. A chubby young man almost yanked Eddie off the sidewalk. Eddie waited for others to attack him, men from every side, black Muslims in a flash of suits and bow ties, but the chubby young man was shaking Eddie's hand. "Hey, brother," he told Eddie. "You in my history class. I want you to meet somebody. I want you to meet this brother Bilal. This brother Bilal got crazy knowledge. Me and Bilal here was just pontificating about history."

A service of sorts was letting out, unsmiling young men, and, distinguished by their suits and regulation bow ties, black Muslims in uniform gathering on the dark walk beneath the awning. "You should come join us sometime," said the chubby young man. "In the basement. Study group." He stood in the darkness, a composition book tucked under his arm; he turned to a Muslim preacher in a natty ocher suit and maize yellow bow tie. "You see, Bilal? I'm bringing them in already."

The young minister turned his body, his full attention, to Eddie. "Forgive this crazy Negro," he said. "My name is Bilal Al-Jallal. I've seen you passing sometimes." He waved up to the mosque, to a window that looked down upon the street. The mosque resembled a converted funeral home, elevated above the storefronts, the Laundromats, and the antiques shops, prominent for the white crescent moon sewn into the red awning and a church marquee of block letters. "You go to South Mountain High School with this character?" Bilal asked him. The delicate young minister stood hardly an inch above five feet and he was svelte to the point of looking undernourished, as though he'd just endured a prolonged fast. His hands and fingernails were manicured, his shining cheeks smelled of musk oil.

"I just playing with you, homey," the chubby young man said to Eddie. "My name is Cyprus. That's my street name, too. Cyprus. I just rolled down to the A-Z from Cali. They don't even got one paragraph on Malcolm, like I was telling my man Bilal here. Not one paragraph in our history book."

"What do you expect?" Bilal scoffed. He turned to Eddie once more. "What, brother, is your name?"

"Eddie."

Bilal straightened his bow tie. "Well, forgive Cyprus for being so crude, but how glad I am to meet you." The front door cracked open,

revealing a dark lobby inside, and another believer in dark suit and
bow tie summoned Bilal. "We must close up shop, brothers," Bilal
explained to the modest crowd of would-be Muslims. "We have,
Brother Eddie, a study group each Friday night open to the community at seven-thirty sharp. You're welcome to attend." Bilal went up
the sinuous stone steps, under the awning to the front door, and
slipped in behind the believer who'd called him. With that Bilal took
a breath and announced to the scattered crowd of young men gathered on the dark path below:

> *This is the place, and you know the time! Come, my lost black
> brothers, come when you are ready to be real, civilized black
> men, strong black men. Come when you are ready to walk
> with your chest held out, when you are ready to walk like a
> man, when you are ready to save our poor, lost, stubborn,
> stiff-necked people from all this foolishness, in this Babylon
> we call the wilderness of America, come when you are ready
> to subscribe to the teachings of the Honorable Elijah Muham-
> mad, who taught us what we did not know. Now be humble,
> and may Allah bless us and enlighten us all. As-salaam.
> alaikum!*

The fat wooden doors of the little mosque folded shut; the porch
lights blinked off; a dead bolt was heard to slide and to lock from
within. Eddie was left with Cyprus. The other young men scattered
in every dark direction. Cyprus hustled to the nearest stop sign, waving good-bye to them, pausing to light his cigarette. A convert, Eddie
thought, smoking a cigarette not a block from the mosque, and he
left him.

He could miss no more school and went back the next day. Cyprus
tracked him down the next afternoon after school and offered him a
ride home. "I got the car today," he said. "My baby's mama and me,

we share it. Just an Escort, but it runs." Eddie followed Cyprus to the parking lot. "But watch out! I'm getting me an Impala pretty soon, a sixty-two." In the car Cyprus told him he'd been a bona fide Crip in South Central Los Angeles. Then his mama died of colon cancer the year before, and Cyprus came into $60,000 in life insurance, enough to get out of L.A. So, Cyprus hopped out to Phoenix with his baby's mama and his baby.

Cyprus walked Eddie into his apartment. The apartment was empty. In the center of the living room sat a toddler's playpen. There was the odor of dirty diapers. Polished thousand-dollar Dayton rims sat in a row against the wall. Atop the television a detailed miniature '67 Dodge Coronet 440. Another miniature, a burgundy '66 Mercury Cougar, sat unfinished on the kitchen table. Cyprus was a regular at the car shows, of which there were faded color pictures on the walls, pictures of the California shows, Cyprus's old car club, Cyprus and some Mexicans, a white boy profiling before this ivory '85 Buick, revamped, lowered with hydraulics, three wheels down, one up, so that the front rake arched into the sky like an arrow! Pictures of Honda Civics with ground effects and OEM-style rear wings, hoopties with hundred-spoke Roadsters, Players, gold-and-silver-plated Konigs, Primas, Spectrums, Platinums, custom interiors, and bikini girls, smiling, smiling, the ubiquitous bikini girls posing, too much mascara, too much hair, tattoos on their shoulders, black and Hispanic, posing, posing, posing.

The next Friday afternoon Eddie skipped class with Cyprus to look at this Impala Cyprus had been sweating in Scottsdale. The whole bus ride Cyprus was humming, rhyming, looking out the bus window, pointing at cars.

The car did not look like much when the salesman walked them over, a rusting '62 primer gray Chevy Impala Super Sport, but Cyprus plopped down in the bucket seat, caressed the steering wheel. "I could do a lot with this car," he said. "I could do beautiful things." The salesman was nodding. Cyprus made the down payment in cash.

Riding back on the bus Cyprus told Eddie that the Nation made you fill out an application form and take introductory classes before you converted. Eddie ignored him. "I'm processing next month," Cyprus said. The old white woman in the seat before them was listening. "The apocalypse is coming, nigger," Cyprus went on. Eddie turned to him. "All these funny hurricanes in Florida, the riots in L.A. Minister Farrakhan be talking about them. Says they is Bible signs. You know," Cyprus said, whispering so the woman in the seat before them could not hear, "it's a conspiracy, a setup like Tupac say. All us niggers up in the jail. I used to slang rock for the Crips, man. I ran away from all that when my mama died. My mama ain't die and leave me life insurance, I'd be doing that right now."

Eddie looked out the window behind Cyprus at the passing storefronts. Cyprus was taking him back to the mosque, to convert him, and he did not care. The bus came teetering down E. Washington St., until the mosque appeared atop the grassy sweep, a small chain of black men and women filing up the concrete steps.

In the mosque basement two teenage girls in head scarves, a gold-toothed junior high school boy sat in a semicircle of folding chairs on the thinning carpet. An old black man in a polyester suit trodded down the basement stairs to them. In a moment Bilal was marching down the stairs, past the folded accordion-like wall divider, carting a pile of books and handouts. Behind Bilal a striking Muslima, twenty-something like Bilal, descended the stairs, covered in a blue patterned head scarf and ankle-length dress.

Bilal greeted the class, smiled to his small audience, draped his jacket with delicate movements over his chair, and sat down. The slender Muslima sat across from Eddie and the old black man in the polyester suit. Bilal was a captain in the mosque. Eddie imagined having to salute the skinny boy. There were introductions: the sisters, the young boy, the old black man in the polyester suit, Cyprus, and the Muslima, whose name was Uzma.

She was half black and half Malaysian, brown-skinned with Asian features, so beautiful that Eddie found himself staring at her as Bilal lectured, as Uzma turned her full attention to the young captain, smiling, unaffected by the condition of the makeshift classroom, the peeling carpets, blank concrete walls, water-stained ceilings, the moldy odor of the room only slightly improved by the fragrance of generations of burned incense. Uzma's hair, which Eddie imagined to be jet black, was hidden under the head scarf, unlike that of her plain-looking sisters, whose scarves barely hung from the backs of their heads. Patterned with auburn leaves, Uzma's head scarf seemed both as stiff as a nun's habit at the brow, then loose as satin at the long, invisible neck. Eddie had never sat so close to a Muslim woman, close enough to look into her eyes, and the women seemed, when he encountered them, the meek women, black and Arab, in cloth, traipsing down the street with children or sitting alone on the bus, never happy, and he did not know if this was because they were toiling away at city errands or if they felt the eyes of a thousand strangers on them, or if the dour looks betrayed what Mama called their "oppression," because Uzma, like her sister believers, had been forced to wear the head scarf, the loose-fitting body garment that announced to the streets, the shops, the city buses filled with unbelievers, her religion. But not once had Eddie seen a Muslim woman accosted on the street by even the hardest of thugs, who lowered their eyes when they passed. . . . He imagined Tessa dressed like Uzma, covering herself in all the cloth, all her sins forgiven, unbothered in the street.

Like Bilal, her captain, Uzma sat with a practiced, perfect posture. Uzma had carried with her into the classroom a stiff straw satchel and set it against her leg. It looked expensive, and Eddie imagined Uzma purchasing the satchel at one of those posh Mill Ave.

stores that sold wheat bar soaps, natural toothpaste, and natural perfumes that had not been tested on animals, and there was indeed the scent of some natural perfume, something like henna, a body oil, an aloe smelling as fresh as if just squeezed from the stem. ("Four hundred years of oppression," Bilal was saying.) Eddie imagined Uzma buying the satchel, the oils, rubbing the oils into her forbidden body, and then donning the head scarf, which drew out the most striking features of her face, tweezed eyebrows, the brown eyes, the head scarf, which somehow made her seem doubly feminine. In his mind Eddie had already married the beautiful Muslima, forgotten Tessa, forgotten Marchalina, converted, explained his conversion to his sobbing, born-again mama, to his Jewish manager, though sight of his fine-looking wife was explanation enough. Eddie pronounced her name in his mind, wanting her to look back at him; and if Uzma would look at him, she might love him and she might save him from his lowest self, his drinking and weed smoking, his now blossoming hatred of Turtle, but Uzma did not look back. Eddie followed the patterns of the cloth, which matched Uzma's head scarf, as she looked to Bilal, the cloth being the deepest green against brown autumn leaves, framing the long face, lying then in ambiguous folds about the body, a series of distended brown leaves that stretched and collapsed across the shapeless figure as they pleased, matching the brown clogs, and even the tiny satchel, until Eddie found himself too long staring, as if profaning her, knowing that even were he to join at this moment, to rise in the Nation, she would always look down upon him because he was poor and street born, never loving him except as a brother in a struggle that was not quite her own.

Photocopies of an article from *The Final Call* circulated, and one of the young Muslimas read an excerpt entitled "Three Year Economic Plan."

"If only," said the old black man in the polyester suit, and he spoke as if he was himself, at seventy, on the verge of a conversion. "If only we would follow the three-year economic plan the Honorable Elijah Muhammad so long ago outlined for us, we could use our collective fiscal monetary power to do for self. But we, the lost-found Negro in the savage wilderness of America, been too busy spending our money on cigarettes and liquor and Air Jordans, spending the money we don't have on these Visa credit cards, spending our way into poverty."

"Thank you," said Bilal.

"Like who gonna spend fifteen dollars on shoes, mister?" said the gold-toothed junior high school boy, pointing at the Xerox.

"That why black folks is in the position we in," said the old man in the polyester suit. "But the Honorable Elijah Muhammad in his wisdom has removed the cigarettes from our fingers, yes, and promised us good homes, good cars, financial security if we just follow this simple plan."

"This is why we must get Cyprus to stop smoking cigarettes," Bilal said. The circle laughed. "Brother, you are paying that Philip Morris Corporation to kill you."

"But I smoke Newports."

Laughter. The young Muslimas looked at the floor. The old man in the polyester suit said, "Don't smoke."

"Be that as it may. Newports or Marlboros. You're still paying that wicked company to kill you. Just imagine if you put that two dollars a day into a bank account like the Honorable Elijah Muhammad would have you do, imagine what you could with that. We're not picking on Cyprus anymore, but the point is made."

"Come on now, Cyprus," said Uzma. "Imagine if all the Cypruses of the world stopped buying Newport cigarettes, well you know that *trifling* Newport Company would be in big trouble."

The class dispersed. Cyprus ran outside to smoke a cigarette. Eddie watched Bilal walk Uzma up the steps. He sensed an attraction between them. Bilal seemed to want to give Uzma a hug good-bye, but this, a hug, was not permitted in the religion. Uzma left Bilal at the bottom of the steps. Bilal noticed Eddie following the others upstairs and stopped him.

"Well, what did you think of our little discussion group?" he asked after a frantic silence. "I'm afraid we got a tad off the mark tonight. I didn't really get to my lesson, but I always find that study group is the essence of what we're trying to do."

"Don't smoke, don't eat pork."

"Between you and me, Brother Eddie, I had a hunch you might be coming back. Tell me something. What do you think of me?"

"I'm sorry."

"What do you think of me?" Bilal waved him over to the side of the wall. "Sometimes I feel like the other brothers in the mosque are better equipped to connect with the people, given their experiences. They have street credibility. I think it comes across in class. But I just want to connect with the people. Like you and Cyprus. Look at Cyprus. Where he's been, catching hell, a Crip. He's the real thing, Eddie. Look at me. All the blessings of the suburbs, a two-parent home, college, all the things brothers like you and Cyprus deserve. I sometimes feel like a pretender in the Nation." Bilal put a hand to his cheek. "Oh, listen to me. It's your spirit. It makes me want to tell you everything. Yes, you have a very open spirit. This is a good thing. And now I've made you nervous. If you ever have questions about the Nation . . ."

"You seem all right to me."

Bilal clapped his hands. "Then tell me at least what you thought of me when you first met me last week—when that crazy Cyprus pulled you off the street like a damned fool!" Bilal giggled.

"You're straight, the mosque is straight."

"People like me and Uzma, you must understand, are the last to join the struggle. We have the easy lives. You heard Uzma. I am a self-confessed bourgeois Negro, Eddie. Ha! Ha! But now, I've told you too much already. Well, haven't I made you nervous!" Now Bilal frowned at himself, as though he'd said too much. "Well, I hope you'll come back. Well, *as-salaam alaikum* now."

Cyprus drove him home. Detective Patricia's Taurus was cinched in the narrow driveway next to Pops's Cadillac. Eddie stood at his front door and cussed under his breath.

Detective Patricia sat at the kitchen table, whispering to Mama beneath the whine of the air-conditioning. Pops sat at the other end. Detective Patricia noticed Eddie first, saying nothing. Mama looked up from the table. Nana stood at the counter, pouring hot water for Detective Patricia's tea, turned, saw Eddie, and set a cup of tea down before the city detective.

"Look," she said, "how much Eddie grow, Mr. Patricia."

Detective Patricia nodded. "He grew. He shot up, all right."

Eddie shook his head. "Why would y'all let him in here?"

"We need to finish this, Eddie," said Detective Patricia, sipping his tea.

Nana said, "Mr. Patricia just come to clear you, to ask if you seen Turtle."

"But I ain't," Eddie said. The Motorola radio on Detective Patricia's lap made a low moan, and he adjusted the volume. Nana sat down.

"Just tell the man what he want to know and be done with it," Mama whispered, fiddling with a plastic fork on the kitchen table.

"Eddie," said Detective Patricia, "we don't suspect you. You've got nothing to fear. I've known you since you were this tall." He took another sip of tea. "The shooting last month. We realize you had no involvement in it. I know you're a good kid, Eddie, so I came over to talk to you. Because this is your brother, because we all know this is Turtle's house we're talking about. Fifty-one Woodland. This is no big secret, right? Because, hey, we all know about Turtle."

"This is serious, Eddie," said Pops, a hand to his ear. "What you say? Say that again. What that?"

"Somebody put your brother at the scene of a shooting last

month," Detective Patricia went on. "There's a volley of shots fired, half the street calls us, and the next week somebody places your brother at the scene, at the house, and they tell us two young black men were seen driving off in a black Acura, women fleeing from the house. We search the house. We don't find a body, but there are signs of a homicide." Detective Patricia's gray eyes shot up. "Blood on the mattress, on the den floor and so on, bullet holes."

"Lord," said Mama and she began to cry into her hands.

"Eddie, has Turtle contacted you recently?"

"No."

"You haven't seen your brother once in the last few weeks?"

"What?" said Pops. "Speak up, boy."

"Eddie," Nana shouted, waving her hands, "what's gotten into you! The shots come from Mrs. Walker's house, Turtle's house. You heard them. Everybody on the street heard them. Now, can't nobody find him. Tell us where Turtle is."

"I ain't seen nothing. Pops kicked him out."

Detective Patricia touched Nana's arm. He looked at Eddie. "Nobody's calling you a liar, Eddie. We just want to talk to your brother. Let him explain. We think he's still in the area. He hasn't been working Van Buren. He'll run out of money. He'll come back. The guns we found stashed in a cubbyhole, in the old Walker house, the twenty-five and the thirty-eight snub-nosed revolver. These are Turtle's guns, guns with his prints. The good news is that these guns do not match the bullets lodged in the walls, the sofa, the floors, et cetera. The bad news is that we run ballistics, a trace on the guns, and the guns have murders on them, old murders from up the street. They are connected to two unsolved robbery-homicides up north from two years ago."

"Turtle killed two old ladies," Nana said, and she was stammering.

"They got evidence," Nana shouted, "the guns, boy, ballistics they call it. There ain't nothing you can do for Turtle, Eddie, so tell Mr. Patricia what you know."

"These guns could very well be stolen," Detective Patricia told Eddie. "I wouldn't be surprised if they weren't. But don't you think Turtle's acting a little suspicious? I drive these streets every day, Eddie, for the past ten years, Turtle is like a fixture. Now, Turtle is AWOL."

"I don't know nothing," Eddie said. "I don't know nothing. He just ran off. I don't know where."

"Hey, your dad told me that you're going to nationals," said Detective Patricia. "That's a major accomplishment. I know you keep your nose clean. I made a special trip tonight. We got history. I've known you since you were this big. Turtle is connected to two homicides, maybe another. You don't return my phone calls."

"I don't know nothing. Why should I return your fucking calls if I don't know nothing?"

"Eddie!" said Pops. "Mr. Patricia, I'm sorry."

"It's okay, Mr. Bloodpath," said Detective Patricia, holding out his hand. "Eddie, this isn't a game. I'm going to leave your house right now. If you know where your brother is, you need tell me now."

"Tell him, boy," said Pops. "Goddamn, be happy he ain't drag you down to the station."

"I told you," Eddie shouted, shaking his finger at him. "You act like you doing me some favor by waiting for me up in my kitchen instead of stopping me on the street, you son of a bitch!" Detective Patricia glared at him.

"Eddie," Mama shouted. Nana and Pops looked at him in shock.

He went out the front door, across the cold park and beyond. Detective Patricia would be in his car and on the street in five minutes. Eddie ran west. He could sleep in the gym, but Detective Patricia would look there first. He stopped. He wandered into the dusk, down Van Buren, its west side, toward the highway, the gym, all sanctuary behind him, wishing he might simply confront Detective Patricia and be done with him. He rushed forward across the dirty sidewalk, then turned and wandered home. The Taurus was gone.

He found it hovering before the South Mountain football field

Monday morning. The marching band drilled across a wet field, beating drums, blaring horns. Girls loitered outside a 7-Eleven across the street, sharing long cigarettes, applying makeup, lipstick, squinting one eye open into compacts. Detective Patricia spotted Eddie, started the car, wrenched the steering wheel. Between lights Detective Patricia hurtled the car across the four-lane street, pulling up beside Eddie. "Bruno," Detective Patricia called, "fucking get in now."

Eddie stopped on the sidewalk. He felt acid in his stomach. He opened the door and took a seat beside Detective Patricia. "I told you I don't know where he at," Eddie said. Detective Patricia broke at a light, smacked Eddie across the cheek, made a left.

On the radio the dispatch blurted out something incomprehensible. Detective Patricia stopped at Van Buren and Twelfth. White patrolmen lurked in the alley. "Please, you know my mama and my nana," Eddie told him, voice breaking. "My nana make you coffee when you come." Detective Patricia smacked him. The police cruiser hovered at the other end of the alley, its front doors spread out like wings, the officer inside speaking into a radio, the other waiting on the hood. Detective Patricia unlocked the car doors and shoved Eddie out. Eddie fell out, clutching his books, a beefy blond-haired cop marching to him, belt leather stretching. The blond-haired cop looked about and kicked Eddie in the buttocks. Detective Patricia climbed out and knocked the schoolbooks out of Eddie's hand. There was laughter, riot lights. "This is the perp? This is Turtle?"

"This is Turtle's little brother, Bruno," said Detective Patricia. "The one gives me grief." Detective Patricia stood before Eddie now, shoving him, smacking his face. The cop stood behind Eddie, choking his neck. He shoved Eddie's face to the ground, until Eddie was staring at his scuffed wing tips. A police radio chirped. A cop yanked Eddie to his knees. "Where's your brother at?" asked the other cop, squeezing Eddie's throat until Eddie felt his tongue protrude. "I don't know, Officer," he whispered, little breaths squeaking out of his throat. "I told Mr. Patricia."

"He lies? He's a big gorilla. You got any sharpies on you, Bruno?"

"Don't get pricked, Lou. Bruno might have needles."

Patricia, the beat cops made Eddie spread his legs before the wall of broken cement. Fingers stabbed into his pockets, dumped his keys to the ground, needled down his chest, his back. They waved their batons behind him, unholstered their guns, their voices dark as they paced.

"He runs that crack house at Fifty-one Woodland with his brother," Detective Patricia told them.

"Your brother fucking raped and killed these little old ladies up the street a couple years ago. We know he did. We know you slang rock with him. We got reports."

"I don't sell nothing."

"What if we found some on you right now, what if you got pinched with some rock? Don't you resist me, don't you move, you big monkey! I'll taze your monkey ass! I ain't done searching you! Take off your Jordans, motherfucker. You got rock in your Nikes? Take them off!"

"I ain't done nothing, Officer." Eddie unlaced his shoes. The cop slapped his neck. The other yanked off his sneakers. Detective Patricia was screaming into Eddie's ear. He took the sneakers and shook them, tossed them against the brick wall. Eddie felt the cold wood of a nightstick against the skin of his neck. His hands shook. They made him bark like a dog. They shoved his face into the wall. He lay on his stomach, a boot against his neck. Their radios screamed in the narrow space, and they six times beat his shoulders with nightsticks until he roiled upon the gravel, little gravel rocks cutting against his cheeks. Now they were jogging to their cars, racing off in opposite directions, Patricia and the cops. Eddie stood, wiping the pebbles off his cheeks; he ran after Detective Patricia's car in socked feet, snatched his schoolbooks from the ground, and tossed them at Detective Patricia's fleeing car. The arcing, flapping books spun in midair, slapping against the windshield. Detective Patricia did not stop the car. Eddie caught his breath, took up his keys, stepped into his shoes, and hurried down Van Buren in the direction of the projects, past more beat cops and hovering patrol cars, the liquor stores, the Laundromats, the walls of slouching drunkards, bent knees thrust out like daggers, through that hateful gauntlet of prostitutes and pimps in Jheri Curls.

He ran home. He sat on his bed and flipped through the attorney section of the yellow pages, calling instead by memory the 800 number of a billboard lawyer who advertised in the neighborhood in Spanish. The receptionist told him the lawyer handled accident and injury cases only. No lawyer would believe him anyway. No lawyer would sue for him: the bruises, the welts, the beating itself, did not seem sufficient. He could not go to a court and speak against Detective Patricia. It was laughable. He opened the top drawer of the small bureau next to his bed, and went through the things Turtle had forgotten: two expired LifeStyles non-lubricated condoms, four paper clips bent into odd shapes, two welfare ID cards held as collateral on small-sum welfare loans, a lone food stamp, topless pictures of his obese girlfriend, a folded, unread copy of *The Watchtower*, on the margins of which Turtle had scribbled the names and phone numbers of various project girls, three stale Kool Mild 100s, four .22 bullets. Army green Velcro wallet.

Eddie left the house at noon. He took the alley. In the shadow of St. Pius X, Chicano boys leaned against the redbrick walls in loose T-shirts. A patrol car hovered at the opposite corner, its windows open, the man inside, the officer—the *overseer!* Eddie thought— waving the boys over to interrogate them. Crossing the street, Eddie passed before the patrol car, glowering at the cop inside. The summoned project boys saw this and let their mouths hang open in joy as they jogged over to the squad car.

He wandered to Cyprus's apartment and found him under his hood in the covered parking lot, working on his '62 Super Sport. Cyprus looked up and noticed the bruises on Eddie's face and wiped the grease off his hands with a rag.

"The cops beat me down," Eddie told him.

"What?"

"Look, I got to find my brother quick. I need a ride." Cyprus started the Super Sport and Eddie got in. Eddie told Cyprus the story of the shooting, of Detective Patricia, of the beating. Eddie did not feel relieved afterward, but Cyprus took the account with little shock, and this increased Eddie's fondness for him.

On Van Buren white johns peered at them through the window tint of leased cars, pimps in running suits from the blackness of every dark dirt field and dark lot, from the myriad dark spaces between condemned buildings, the curb of every liquor store. A blond-haired black girl, underage, climbed into the leather passenger seat of a green Ford F150 pickup. And he'd kept silent for nothing. He'd hidden for nothing, avoided Detective Patricia. Eddie told Cyprus to drive him back to Woodland Ave., and he walked straight to 51 Woodland, into the dead woman's house. The police had come and gone, yellow tape torn away by vagrants.

Eddie spoke to the squatters. "You seen a dude named Turtle?"

A wrinkled face glowed in the orange light of a joint. "We ain't seen nobody. We was headed to Albuquerque until we come across this."

Eddie stood in the perfect darkness of the porch, the squatters behind him, with Cyprus. He followed Cyprus to his car, and Cyprus drove. They made another run down Van Buren until Eddie saw someone he recognized, a redheaded prostitute named Jenna, walking from 16th St.

Eddie tried to flag her down, but she only quickened her pace at the sight of two black men in the low-rider coasting beside her and would not stop until her name was called. Jenna paused before the old Airport Motel, fenced and abandoned now, and stared into the car and saw Eddie.

"Jenna," Eddie shouted. Jenna looked about for cop cars and waved them to the nearest corner. Cyprus cornered at 18th, where other hookers stood, obese and drunken black girls in spandex, hooting at the slowing cars. Cyprus parked blocks down the street away from them before a factory of high, painted windows, and they waited for Jenna to come to them. Jenna wandered to them, looking over her shoulder, shouting something to the prostitutes collected at the corner. She came to them and went to Eddie's window, taking solace in the darkness.

"You a pimp?" Jenna looked over her shoulder. "I ain't supposed to talk to you."

"It's Eddie. Turtle's little brother. I'm looking for him."

"Eddie! Hey. Damn, I don't know where Turtle at." Jenna called through the darkness to the far end of the street to the drunken girls. "Wanda," Jenna shouted. "Where Turtle at? Turtle." The other girl shouted something back. A car pulled up at the end of the street. One of the girls climbed inside. A hush fell on the block. Jenna turned to Eddie. "Wanda seen him yesterday. He must be at one of the flophouses on Madison, or if he got a little more cash, the St. James. I can't go there as a female. All them crusty old men, you know, knocking at your door. It's right across from the Madison St. Jail. Where you go to visit people."

Eddie knew the place. Cyprus drove him there, the St. James, five blocks west. Turtle had been hiding out in the very shadow of the downtown police station. They parked on Madison St. and stared into the lobby window. Old men sat before a ceiling-mounted television set locked in a wire cage.

The St. James attendant had a bush of orange hair. "He's upstairs if he's your brother," he told Eddie. "Ten minutes." Eddie nodded, and the attendant buzzed him in. He went up the stairs of peeling carpet to the second floor. Transients, drifters stood before their doors, talking. Eddie came to the end of the hallway, to room 17C, knocked. The door cracked. Turtle let him in and went back to the open window, where he'd been looking down upon the street. Eddie shut the door.

"The cops," said Eddie, shutting the door. "They beat me. They come looking for you. Detective Patricia." Turtle did not speak. "They say you killed other people. They say they found guns. The guns had murders on them or something. Detective Patricia told me hisself. He came to the house like when we was little. I called him a son of a bitch in front of Pops and Nana, Mama. He bum-rushed me this morning on my way to school."

Turtle chuckled. He turned from the window, a mild shock. "You done that?" He turned back to the window. He'd been smoking. A box of Newports and a lighter sat on the very edge of the windowsill.

"Detective Patricia come into the house. He said you killed these two other ladies."

"What is Patricia talking about? I ain't kill no old white ladies up north." Turtle shouted, smiling. "But, they ain't found Jules! They ain't found old Jules! I told, told, told Adolpho they'd never find where we put, put, put him at." And he began to laugh, to laugh, head hanging out of the open window, smoking, laughing.

"They made me get to my knees, bark like a dog. They beat me down."

Turtle looked back at the bed, at the walls, and pressed a cigarette to his lips and lit it. "This, this, this, this place is straight," he said. "They don't ask no questions. They don't snitch. But it cost fucking twelve dollars a night! Down the street be seven, seven, seven but it's all crackheads and crystal addicts. And the rooms. I walk in the place and the rooms is like the Tent, like a fucking cramped jail cell. They must have taken each room and divided it into three. They build little bunks into the walls. I can't believe it!" Turtle looked at

Eddie. "They want, want, want to bust me on some shit I ain't never done. Ha! Well, they won't never find that Jules. Look at you, nigger. It's funny. You know it is. You act like you ain't never been roughed up before."

"I threw my schoolbooks away. I threw my books at Patricia's car. I left them on the street."

Turtle peered out the window at the Madison St. Jail below. He took a drag of his cigarette. I don't owe you nothing now, Eddie thought. He hated Detective Patricia; he hated the white cops who'd beaten him; but he hated Turtle most of all. He watched Turtle staring out of the window. He spat on the floor and left Turtle in his room.

Eddie climbed into Cyprus's car. Cyprus turned down his radio. "I found him," Eddie told him. "But I don't know why I bothered looking. I can't go home right now."

"I'm taking you to see Bilal," Cyprus said. "Bilal will know what to do." Eddie looked at his face in the side mirror. "I don't care," he said. Cyprus called Bilal on his Motorola and drove Eddie north, down Central Ave. Cyprus drove between the mountains, into the suburbs of Moon Valley.

Bilal answered the door in blue jeans, a T-shirt. A brown kitten scurried before them under Bilal's legs. Eddie had never seen Bilal out of uniform. How skinny he was. Bilal waved Cyprus and him into the foyer and shut the door behind them. Long rugs ran into the family room, the kitchen, where Bilal's mother stood in a head scarf, a handsome black woman. She came to them after a moment through the dark hallway of wall rugs, introducing herself, noticed Eddie's bruised face, but said nothing, offering to warm up dinner for Bilal's guests. "Oh, Mother," Bilal whispered. "Not right now, please." Bilal's father sat in his study, working an equation on a scientific calculator with his long black fingers, his back to them, rubbing his beard. Bilal's younger sister stood atop the staircase, in an

Abercrombie sweatshirt, a head scarf thrown the last minute atop her head, peering down at the foyer to see who had come to the door; she was gossiping into a cordless phone. "Please, if you would," Bilal said, "take off your shoes, brothers, and we can talk in my bedroom." Cyprus and Eddie looked at each other, took off their shoes, and followed Bilal in socked feet up the carpeted staircase.

Bilal's bedroom was as neat and ascetic, as monastic, as Eddie had imagined. There was a made bed and a desk, a computer into which the young minister had been typing his master's thesis. The walls were bare, white, excepting the third wall, where the young minister had hung a portrait of the Honorable Elijah Muhammad wearing a crescent fez. Bilal sat Eddie and Cyprus down on his bed and took a seat on his desk chair. "Cyprus told me something happened," he said.

"The cops beat him," Cyprus said. "For real."

Bilal sat back.

"I brought it on my own self," Eddie told him. "It's over. They come looking for my brother, and I cussed this cop."

"Stop it." Bilal was frowning. "How can you bring a beating on yourself, Eddie?" He was shuffling on his chair, outrage on his face. "This is very serious. You can file a complaint. I'll call the director of our mosque, Minister Don Muhammad."

"No," Eddie said. "I don't want to file no complaint. I ain't going in no court."

"Go on tell it, Eddie," Cyprus said. "Tell him what happened." Eddie looked to Bilal and for the second time recounted the story, demeaned by it, the outcome seeming, like all things, inevitable, but now so inevitable, so inescapable that he wondered if he'd not brought it all down upon himself, wondered if he should not take the rest of Turtle's stash, pack his gym bag, and catch the Greyhound to Vegas, make his own way. Now Bilal was peering at him with such intensity that Eddie found himself looking down at the floor, feeling vulgar in the beautiful house, an enormous house of spices and incense, and prayers, of ornate rugs, a house in which one removed one's shoes at the door. He wondered why Bilal had ever joined the Nation when he lived in such a beautiful house, a college boy. Bilal seemed so incensed at the story of Detective Patricia, the cops in the alley, that it caused Eddie to wonder if perhaps he himself was not incensed enough. He told Bilal the story and repeated it for him until it was midnight, and Bilal was walking them to his front door. "I wish I could tell you," he said, "that you were the first young man to come to me with such a story."

Part Two

NOI

He stole into the mosque every day, reading the books along the library shelves, each with CONGREGATION stamped in red block letters, gazing out the second-floor window at the workaday people traipsing along E. Washington St. After five the little mosque would swell with evening parishioners, working-class men and women, filing up the stone path. At the ringing of a bell the believers gathered into a musty room for prayer, Bilal in his suit and cherry red bow tie leading prayers in the cloistered room of red dust, men cordoned off from women by a mere square of flapping white cloth. From the doorway, from the margin of the room of prayers and cloth, Eddie spied upon them, their backs to him, unknowing, prostrating, whispering, standing, genuflecting. These were the successive motions of belief. Stand. Bow down. Prostrate. Rise again.

Eddie bought NOI books from a top-floor glass display in the mosque, and Bilal gave him pamphlets to read. Bilal kept a library of pamphlets. For every black pathology, for every crisis, Bilal could produce a pamphlet. *Birth Control = Genocide. The AIDS Conspiracy.* Popeyes fried chicken made black men impotent. Eddie would read the pamphlets in wonder. How silly they seemed, no different from Turtle's comic books, until he missed the number 88 bus, or caught sight of grown black men in ranks, arms slung beside them, loitering at the 40th St. Job Corps station.

On Tuesdays, on folding chairs, Cyprus beside him, Eddie watched pretty-boy ministers practice their sermons before Minister Don Muhammad and old heads visiting from California. "The young black man is like a bullet," said a handsome young minister one evening to applause from folding chairs, from unregistered young men and women, old women in head scarves, unreformed gangsters in puffy goose jackets, "without the barrel to deliver it, concentrate its rage, give it trajectory, to unleash it—a vector of force." Eddie was clapping, clapping from his chair, for nothing he'd ever heard had ever made him feel so purposeful. He was a bullet. The young black man was a bullet, and Allah would save him, lift him from his degradation, the pretty-boy minister promised him from the rostrum.

Bilal drove Cyprus and Eddie home in his station wagon that night, pulling out from the mosque parking lot. They passed dour black men in beards, Sunni Muslims, coming out of a storefront mosque, in long foreign-looking robes, kufis on their heads, men who'd left the Nation years before. "Look at them," Bilal said from his steering wheel, "dressed like Arabs. We save them, we get them out of prison. We teach them how to bathe and eat. We teach them pride. We raise them up, and they leave us for the 'true Islam.' They cannot tell the difference between religion and culture. Some of them even speak with affected foreign accents. A black man will do anything to run from himself." Bilal took a breath. "Brothers, understand they may approach you."

"Don't say nothing to them," offered Cyprus.

"Give them the greetings and be polite. Do not engage in violence. They are lost, but they are our brothers. We never give up hope on our people. Maybe they will come around the next time the police stop them for driving while black." This was Bilal's joke. Cyprus laughed.

The young black man was like a bullet. He ran to Marchalina that night to tell her the young black man was like a bullet, but instead made love to her on her floor with muted groans and cautious thrusts so that Wilma could not hear them.

He marched up 16th St. to the mosque at eight-thirty the next morning, panting, wondering why he was walking up 16th St. to join the Nation of Islam except that Turtle had killed a man for no reason, excepting that Detective Patricia had beaten him like a dog. He found Cyprus sitting with two other teenage processees in a moldy basement corner room, everyone anxious and sleep-deprived, dressed in his best church suit. Bilal came in the room with paper and pens, and everyone sat down in antiquated grammar school desks. He scribbled HYGIENE on the blackboard with orange chalk. "Who knows what this means? It's our first lesson after you fill out your applications."

The processees looked at each other. Cyprus looked thrilled, as if "hygiene" were like the code word, a secret handshake. Bilal made him look up and recite the definition from a Funk & Wagnall's pocket dictionary. With great effort Cyprus found the definition, reciting it to the others. "Hy-giene: the science of health," he read. "Hy-gien-ic: sanitary." Cyprus put down the dictionary. He looked frustrated, all the buildup for this.

"The first thing we teach you in the Nation," Bilal told the class, "is how to wash yourself." With that he circulated a mimeograph entitled "General Civilization Class Lesson #1: Keeping Clean." In exacting detail the mimeograph instructed each processee to take at least one shower per day in the manner prescribed. A shower was required if one had defiled oneself from sexual intercourse (with one's lawful spouse). "Hair is cropped neat and short," Bilal said. "You must be a witness to your civilization, an example of the Original Man. We expect clean fingernails. Not a speck. The uniform"— Bilal straightened Cyprus's bow tie—"is a dark suit, dark bow tie, and a white shirt with matching handkerchief square in the jacket pocket. It doesn't matter if you only have one church suit. Keep it clean. Keep your body clean. You want to know something?" Bilal said. "They say when the coroner examined Malcolm's body in the morgue, he said he'd never seen a body so clean."

Eddie nodded at Bilal; the class was nodding, everyone proud that Malcolm X had been so clean on the day of his assassination, as if it were a secret known only to the initiated. "Hygiene will be our first lesson after you send in your applications to national headquarters," Bilal said.

Bilal circulated another dog-eared mimeograph, the application mimeograph, to the small squad, pens and blank paper, instructing each young man to copy the mimeograph verbatim, everyone in his own cursive hand, before the end of class, without consultation. "Word for word," he said, stern. "No mistakes, misspellings. Sign it in your legal name. No nicknames, no street names." And Bilal left them, the squad of young men mouthing out words at grammar school desks too small for their thighs.

Dear Savior Allah, Our Deliverer:

I have been attending the teachings of Islam by one of your Ministers, two or three times. I believe in It, and I bear witness that there is no God but Thee, and that Muhammad is Thy Servant and Apostle. I desire to reclaim my Own. Please give me my Original Name. My slave name is as follows:

Name
   Address
   City and State

But sitting amongst his fellow recruits, reading aloud the words of the mimeograph, a sense of the occasion struck him. The one-paragraph application letter seemed inadequate. "Dear Minister Farrakhan," Eddie wrote.

All my life I been searching for something. I been looking for something definite. I been looking for a place where my endividuality can be appreciated. In the Church (Baptist) my spiritual background I never felt nothing like I feel about this Islam.

Maybe I tell you a little more about myself this will explain my desire to be a registered Muslim.

Just a few months ago, I was taken into a alley by the wicked police and savagely beaten like a "run away slave" if you will for no reason other than the reason that the cops was looking for my brother. They called me racial names of course as South Phoenix cops is want to do, and almost planted something on me. (This really happened). Before that, I never looked at things racial besides the simple fact that I was a black man in America and sometimes the cops would mess with me and my brother.

After the cops beat me, I looked into the situation on a national level. I realized that everything was systematical and basically designed to keep the black man down. I read some of your literature and pamphlets about the wickedness of America, of which I now agree. And the prediction of THE FALL OF AMERICA by the Honorable Elijah Muhammad.

In addition, I am a boxer. I am the state and regional

heavyweight Golden Gloves champion. (I might could be of some service in the bodyguard department). I box out a gym called the Madison in South Phoenix under the mgmt. of Gene "Bumpy" Kellner.

Sincerely and Most Respectful,

Edward Shabazz,
formly known as Edward Bloodpath
37 Woodland Avenue
Phoenix, Arizona 85007

Eddie hurried to Bilal's office and passed his application into his hand. Bilal gave him a pile of *Final Call* newspapers to sell.

Mama was crying on the sofa when he came home. Some beat cops had caught Turtle at the Greyhound bus terminal, sitting on a plastic chair watching cartoons at a pay television. Turtle had called Mama from the Madison St. Jail this afternoon. Now Mama was waiting for Pops to come home from work so they could drive over to visit him.

Nana was in the kitchen baking yams for Turtle to eat in jail. She'd called the church saints and started a prayer chain.

Eddie set his unsold papers down on the sofa. "Now," Mama cried from the sofa, "they want to send him away on a double murder charge! But at least Turtle is somewhere safe for now, Eddie. At least, I don't have to worry after him no more. Your daddy and me is going to the jail soon as he comes home. Come with us, boy."

"No," Eddie said, and he went to his room to sleep.

The next morning, walking out to the mosque in his uniform, Eddie heard Pops taking a collect call from Turtle.

Now it was time to meet Minister Don himself, whom Eddie had only seen twice in passing, hurrying in and out of the mosque in his glorious suits and brim hats, on business errands, darting out in shined wing tips. Bilal escorted Eddie up the stairs to the minister's office.

Bilal left them and shut the door. Minister Don Muhammad offered Eddie a salaam and waved him in. The minister stood before his desk, a seventy-year-old man, a pair of half glasses on his skinny nose. He was, Bilal had told Eddie, of the first generation of converts in Detroit, what the old heads called the First Resurrection of the Nation. It was said Minister Don could speak fluent Arabic, once a month reading the Qur'an from beginning to end, that he'd indeed been a confidant of Minister Farrakhan from the old days, accompanied him to Libya in the eighties, that he'd known Malcolm X and the Honorable Elijah Muhammad both. The tall man waved Eddie into his office and took a seat at his desk, pushing aside some papers, opening a manila folder with BLOODPATH typed out on a file tab. Eddie took a seat before Minister Don and recognized his own handwriting, his letter to national headquarters atop the manila folder, beneath a little memo in Bilal's elegant cursive.

"We can't have you send your letter, son. It would be immediately rejected."

Eddie checked his posture.

"All application letters," Minister Don went on, "must be written in the traditional format, hand-copied in cursive, neat, without error. I'm sure you want to write the same letter Muhammad Ali wrote, don't you, the same letter Minister Farrakhan, Malcolm X, and I wrote? Bilal tells me you've been going through some trials of late. Your brother was arrested yesterday on some very serious charges," he said, staring at Eddie through his glasses.

"The cops found him. Yes sir."

"You've had problems, Bilal tells me. Your letter suggests you've had some terrible events foisted on you. You are angry, and your application letter is filled with your anger. Anger is not a bad thing if it is channeled properly. Why, the Honorable Elijah Muhammad taught us that only our dissatisfaction would make us change our condition.

"You've made the most important decision of your life, son. But slow down. I've been in this Nation for over thirty years. I've seen many a young man come to the Nation in his anger and burn himself right out. You must pace yourself. Islam is the religion of peace. So, never let anyone take your peace. When you find yourself distressed, read the Qur'an. And try to learn seven new things every day. Read the newspaper. Know what the heck is going on in this crazy world. And don't curse. Never curse. This is baby talk.

"I run a tight ship. Keep yourself busy. I don't stand for foolishness. Read, read, read. The Qur'an teaches us to seek knowledge from the cradle to the grave. There are twenty-four hours in each day. Keep a cool head always, and submit to the teachings. Follow the Honorable Elijah Muhammad's advice for healthy eating, and you'll live as long as Methuselah! Would you believe I haven't had a hamburger or chewed a stick of gum in thirty years? And be patient. Patience is half the religion.

"Bilal tells me you may have already changed your name. I applaud your initiative if that's the case, and I won't have you change it back if you've already gone to the trouble. They make it an ordeal, don't they? The county government. Once they hear you want to get rid of your slave name, they make you go through hell and high water. However, you're still an X. This is how the process works. I was an X. Farrakhan was an X. Malcolm was an X. Therefore, you will be an X. In fact," he said, peeking at a dot matrix printout, "you'll be Eddie 92X."

"Ninety-two, sir?"

"If you pass orientation. Be glad we're in a small region. Don't worry, in the mosque you can be just Eddie X."

"Thank, thank you, sir."

"Now, it won't be easy. This country is following the footsteps of

Satan himself, and our job is to resurrect our people from their mental and spiritual death. So just remember when you keep a fast, you're keeping it for them, and when you pray, you're praying for them. And so on. Yes, we must lift our stiff-necked people from all this liquor and promiscuity, this self-destruction, dependency. It will seem hopeless at times, but this is the path Allah has chosen for you.

"I read a book once called *The Magic of Thinking Big,*" Minister Don continued. "Our Mr. Schwartz, the author, suggests that one of the first steps to self-improvement is to walk twenty-five percent faster, as if you have a purpose. Isn't that an odd piece of advice? Odd but true. Now that I think about it, Malcolm used to do this back in Boston, you know, walk so fast we could barely keep up with the brother—before we, ha, ha, had our falling-out, that is. This is what I want you to do, my ambitious young brother, yes, yes, yes. Walk twenty-five percent faster because you have a purpose. Because Allah has given you a purpose."

"Yes sir."

"I understand you're something of a pugilist, with big competitions on the horizon. All praises be to Allah. Suffice it to say, your academics and the Nation must come first. And 'Read profusely' is my motto—promiscuously. Don't be *promiscuous,* but read *promiscuously*! Ha! Ha! Ha! Learn seven new words a day. Leaders are readers, yes? Study elocution, this is the art of public speaking. Read at my desk if need be, but don't fool with the stereo. I'm always out doing the Nation's business. Now, did I tell you about learning seven new words? Did I tell you to listen twice as much as you speak? Did I tell you to walk quickly? Yes, yes, I did. And no cursing. And never laugh uncontrollably. This is bad etiquette. Now, I must get back to work."

Eddie 92X, he thought. A small setback. Will of Allah. He would take the news in stride. He stood and almost bowed his head before the elderly man, wishing only that he were a registered Muslim so he might offer Minister Don a brisk salute.

"And walk quickly," the minister said. "I want to see you walking quickly. Twenty-five percent faster."

"With purpose, Minister," Eddie told the old man and hurried out of the room, leaving Minister Don to his papers.

r. Chestnut, a neighbor man who'd been trying to find temp work for Pops at Sky Harbor, called the house on the morning of Turtle's first day of trial. One of the skycaps had suffered a heart attack, and Mr. Chestnut needed someone to fill out his shift at the United Airlines curbside. Pops came into Eddie's bedroom that morning. "It's only the first day of trial," he said. "You tell Turtle I didn't mean nothing by it. You tell him I'll be there next week if I can."

Eddie found Mama drinking coffee in the kitchen. "Come on, Mama," he told her. But Detective Patricia would be there. He could not see him now, not until he was a registered Muslim, and he would not fear him anymore. He'd walk Mama to the steps there and not inside. Nana walked them to the stoop and waved good-bye.

Mama wore a bright red suit, her interview suit, under a Levi's denim jacket. He walked her to the courthouse that morning, dressed in Fruit of Islam regulation uniform, drawing looks of awe from thugged-out boys on stoops, young women pushing babies in strollers along the walk. He searched for Detective Patricia in the parking lot, in the sunny arcade across the street.

He found Mama at four-thirty, after school, before the court-house, and walked her home. Mama was flustered. "Detective Patri-cia didn't even show up to testify. He was testifying in another case. The judge rescheduled his testimony. The public defender didn't even object, Eddie. He just sat there. He don't like Turtle, Eddie."

Another case, Eddie thought. He imagined Patricia testifying in the trial of another thug, another Turtle, and he realized that this was what Detective Patricia did, locking up black boys and testifying against them. He'd never thought of this before, as if Detective Patri-cia's job had only been to hassle Turtle. "Turtle need to plead," Mama said. "The jury didn't take to him in his cornrows."

"What you want me to do about it?"

"Eddie, you talk to Turtle tomorrow morning," Mama told him, "tell him to get another public defender or plead out." Mama looked at her reflection in the window of a parked car. She breathed in the bitter winter air. She'd begged the public defender to get Turtle to plead during a recess, but Turtle was stubborn, and the public de-fender was too harried to care. Mama was certain the public de-fender disliked Turtle, but she could not figure out why. They took the back way home. The same lollipop song poured from every ra-dio, from every cracked window, from every passing car; it chased them through the back streets. Mama stuck her hands in the pockets of her denim jacket. Eddie always thought she looked so pretty for a woman her age. "This is your brother," Mama said, cutting between parked cars. "Maybe he done some things, but your brother ain't kill and rape no old ladies." Eddie shrugged. Mama swatted his arm. "Turtle might never see the light of day, and you is fine with that?" Mama stopped in the middle of the street and touched Eddie's hand. "The public defender said Turtle will get sixty years. He might could

get fourteen if he plead. I know you is angry, Eddie. I know you is going through changes, baby, but I want you stay close to me through
this. I want you to do what I say, please, please, before I just lose my
mind, Eddie, and they put me in the loony bin. I want you to go to
your brother tomorrow and make him plead."

"I can't, Mama. I hate him."

Mama began to sob. Eddie walked her home and showered while
Mama sat sobbing at the kitchen table with Nana. He went to his
bedroom. Pops came home after a while. Through the door he heard
them all going on about Turtle in the kitchen.

He hurried up 7th St. to visit Turtle at the Madison St. Jail in the
morning, dressed in uniform, to beg Turtle to plead, wading through
rooms of mothers and children and black men dressed in sagging
jeans, beneath public service posters, rooms reeking of diapers, cigarettes, hair spray. Eddie sat down and stared into the glass. The
smell of industrial disinfectant spray went into his nose. Turtle appeared behind the glass in a moment in an orange jumpsuit.

"Mama be crying, Eddie?" Turtle asked.

"That's the only reason I come. You could get sixty years, all I
care."

Turtle looked at Eddie's bow tie. "Well," Turtle whispered into the
telephone receiver, "if my brother ain't a Black Muslim now, another
stuffed, stuffed, stuffed shirt. Mama must be bugged." Turtle was
staring at Eddie through the glass. "Surprised Pops ain't kick you
out for going Muslim. Who knows, maybe in the pen I'll become a
stuffed shirt like my little brother and get me some religion."

"Mama said the jury don't like you. Mama said if you plead, you
can get fourteen years, maybe seven with good behavior." Eddie
heard Turtle tapping his slippers on the tile floor, thinking, counting
out the years in his head.

Turtle shook his head. Turtle was untying his cornrows. This is
how he spent his time, tying and untying his hair. What a waste

Turtle would make of prison. Turtle would get the sixty years and never pick up a book.

"Look, don't be stupid," Eddie told him.

"I ain't gonna plead," Turtle said, "for something I ain't done. It ain't like I killed them old white ladies. I might plead if they found Jules," he whispered, giggling, peeking at the guard stationed at the door, "but they, ha, ain't never gonna find him."

"Mama said the public defender don't like you. If you don't plead, Mama said you'll get sixty years."

"I know I ain't brought you nothing but trouble, so let me do you this favor. Tessa will, will, will come back. You stay away from her is all I'm saying. Get your mind right. You keep riding this Islam gig, if it keeps the po-lice off your back. Maybe you fight pro. You come into money, give a little bit to Mama, I'm saying, a little bit to my baby daughter for me. But don't give nothing to Pops, nothing, no matter how he make you feel sorry. And, and, and, and, don't go chasing after Tessa," Turtle whispered into the phone. He leaned into the glass. He stared at Eddie.

"Well, don't worry about that. You scared her off good when you done what you done."

"Jules," Turtle whispered, looking at the guard, "he was always fucking with me, fucking with my head since I was a shorty. Calling me stupid, touching up on me. He thought he was my fucking daddy. I didn't owe him shit." Turtle looked at his fingernails.

In the hallway outside the waiting room Eddie removed from his jacket his NOI regulation steno notepad, a pen, scribbling in a kind of release a somber note about Turtle. A processee should record his thoughts, Bilal said. *So blind*, Eddie wrote. *His whole life was like a prison*. Then walking home he stopped again, on the concrete, writing: *I notice how the county jail is only 4 minutes from my own house. This is no co-encidence*. And he hurried forward, angry, in his suit, looking down upon the hustlers on the corner, grown men dressed like boys because they did not own a suit, because they had not studied general civilization in a mosque basement, had not memorized the circumference of the Earth.

Conspiracy Secret No. 44: The Egyptians had wings, were black. Napoleon defaced the Sphinx's black nose. Conspiracy Secret No. 33: The Ku Klux Klan owns the Snapple Corporation. Conspiracy Secret No. 14: The U.S. government sold crack to the South Central gangs on consignment for Pharaoh Reagan and Pharaoh Bush. It was all true. Crack cocaine, mandatory minimums, a conspiracy. The beauty of swirling Arabic kufic symbols of his Qur'an, of words he could not pronounce, testified to this. But he prayed upon his prayer rug that Turtle would plead, though he could not say why, because he wanted never to see him again, because Turtle was a dog, a savage, unredeemable, *because I suffered for him too many times*.

The next afternoon Mama appeared at Eddie's door. "Turtle pled at trial today," she told him, smiling. Turtle had pled to the rape—felony murder of Mrs. Eloise Lingley of 44 Harvard St., to having shot her with one of the stolen guns, one of the guns with murders on them, shot another woman named Delphina Carcey, a block down. Turtle pled to someone else's murders while Jules lay dead in a trunk, buried somewhere in dirt. Eddie went out into the kitchen and he found Nana and Pops in joyful prayer. Calls came in from the prayerful old women of the church. Turtle got fourteen years as promised; the plea agreement would not be finalized until the morning, but everyone in the house took a sigh. "They'll send him to Florence in six weeks, Eddie," Mama told him, "but you must come to see him off, Turtle say. That's what Turtle wants."

"No, Mama."

"I know you is mad at him, but Turtle made me promise you would see him off if he pled. He'll be there so long in that prison. He's scared," Mama whispered. "There was fear in his voice when he told me he pled. They is shipping him to Florence County Prison.

Turtle ain't never been to a big prison before. He is a little man. You know," she whispered, "they probably raped him at the Tent. They will beat him in Florence; they will mess with him because he little. You hear me, Eddie? He want you to see him off. He pled like you asked him. Come see your brother off, boy. Come see him. Make your peace."

Part Three

Chicago

*T*here was no peace to be made with Turtle, not now. Turtle sat in the Tent for a month, awaiting transfer to Florence. On Turtle's last day at the Tent, Eddie slipped out of the house in the morning and slept on the north ring at Bumpy's, avoided the pink corner house until nine o'clock that night, when he found Nana, Pops, and Mama just returned from the Tent, dressed in their church clothes, peering at him from the kitchen table.

Minister Don called Eddie into his office two days before he was to fly to Chicago for nationals. Bilal found Eddie in the basement and escorted him into Minister Don's office. The minister had just come in from his downtown print shop, and there was the faint odor of ink about him. He removed his blazer, hung it on the coatrack, sat. Eddie offered him a salute. "Sit down. All praises be to Allah, Bilal tells me you are flying to Chicago to attend the Golden Gloves championships. Why didn't you tell me you were this good? This is quite an achievement, and you'll be in Chicago." A nine-by-eleven-inch manila package sat on Minister Don's desk. "You'll be flying to Chicago and now you may do me a personal favor, a favor of the utmost importance. How long is your stay?"

"Five days, sir, depending. It's a three-day elimination, sir, a couple days of information sessions before that."

"Elimination. And you'll make it to national headquarters?"

"Yes, Minister, I planned to visit, and Captain Bilal called ahead, contacted some brothers in Chicago for me."

"Perfect. Of course, this is very serious. You will take this package to national headquarters for me. I could send it through the mail, but I don't trust the mail—even now. This way I know it gets the leader's immediate attention. If only you knew how important this was. Tell me, do you knock them out, or beat them on points?"

"Points, Minister Don. Mostly."

"That is what I hear. Good. You cannot fail me. I want to know that he gets it. They're so busy up there. Doing the people's work. Wait until you see it, Mosque Maryam. Knock your socks off. But, there's no room for error. Bilal and I see great promise in you, and what better way for you to make a few connections in Chicago? This could be a giant step for you. Mosque Maryam is filled with talented young brothers and sisters just like you. They're all committed to the Nation. Meet them, Eddie. Meet as many as you can. So, my advice to you is this. Be humble. If they correct you on some small point, a speck on your shoes, your greetings, or what have you, it's only because they expect perfection. Take their criticisms with all humility, and be patient. The men and women who rise furthest in the Nation understand patience." With that Minister Don leaned forward and pushed the package across his desk. It was a slender package, firm, smelling of ink from his print shop. The envelope was addressed to Minister Farrakhan. Eddie pressed his fingers against the package, grasped it with both hands. He could only imagine.

He took a United Airlines nonstop flight to Chicago with Tommy and Kell. He'd never been on an airplane before. He spent the flight with his nose pressed against the window.

He studied the skyscrapers of Michigan Ave. from the backseat of a Yellow Cab, Kell and Tommy beside him on the worn cushions.

The taxi let them off at the Hilton and Towers. Already the curb before the Hilton was filled with out-of-state conversion vans from Baltimore and New Jersey, Wisconsin, taxis, the lobby crammed with Golden Gloves officials in loungewear, fighters from every state, teenage boys dragging suitcases across the light, hexagon-patterned rugs, joyriding elevators.

For a day and a half Eddie worked out at the Club 10 down the street. Kell and Tommy sat at a small, round table in a conference room of the Chicago Hilton and Towers as the Gloves director ran through the regulations, plain-faced temps in skirts circulating the paperwork, the releases, the agreements, the accumulating minutiae, which Kell stuffed in an old FedEx mailer.

Eddie would return from the Club 10 to find the Hilton bar filled with celebrities and boxing types, with seventeen-year-old boys, watching ESPN from lounge seats. Big-haired East Coast boxing chieftains in black suits, wrinkled men with name tags worked the room, shook hands, slapped shoulders. There was Sean O'Grady. Hector Camacho. On the second night Eddie caught sight of Johnny Tapia, the Baby-Faced Assassin, at the end of the hotel bar, his hair cut army short. Tapia looked serene. His suspension—word circulated—had been lifted. Ugly as a bulldog, skinny as a cockroach, Tapia was beautiful, beautiful . . . . Eddie heard him talking to a reporter, Tapia's voice like Spanish when it was sung. Flat-faced officials from every sanctioning body, men in striped polo shirts and gold neck chains, spread across the room like thrown dice; a dim, middle-aged black man with a certified case of TBI, the president of the Retired Boxers Federation, took small-bill donations for a fighter named Bubba Lewis in a Chicago Hilton and Towers envelope;

Bubba had the week before lost his house to the IRS. The Fraternal Order of Police. Boys Clubs of America. YMCA. There were fighters known and unknown, men with model-type girlfriends and dog-faced babies' mamas; there were flat-nosed, encephalopathic men who could not afford the cab fare over to the Hilton, third-tier, fourth-tier pros, everyone dressed in obnoxious suits and loud button-downs . . . blond girlfriends, overweight, doll-faced Mexican *mamacitas* wearing REST IN PEACE, TINY in gothic font across base-ball caps and black T-shirts, wary-looking sportswriters in tweed jackets, unregistered boys from the Chicago gyms, boys too young, onlookers in Raiders jackets, orbiting like the obese mamas, black and Hispanic, in extra large T-shirts, their baby boys' boxing medals hung around their double necks. Someone saw Buddy McGirt in the lobby bathroom. Someone saw Mills Lane signing an autograph. Someone saw the actor Mickey Rourke talking to Riddick Bowe.

Tommy took Eddie and walked him through the people to a tall dark-skinned boy in a button-down oxford, leaning against a wall. "Eddie," said Tommy, "this is Kevin, the dude you're going to fight."

The boy smiled. He was plain and soft-spoken, corny, Eddie thought. He was from Kansas City. He had the manner of a farm boy. Eddie nodded at him.

The boy from Kansas City did not give ugly looks. He did not talk street. "Hello," he said, shaking Eddie's hand. He spoke slowly. "I seen your tapes, Eddie. You fight real good. I met your trainer, Kell, last night. Did he adopt you? My trainer adopted me. You is from Phoenix. My cousin lives in Phoenix. God bless you. My cousin say the churches in Phoenix got spirit."

Eddie left Tommy and the boy from Kansas City and changed into his Fruit of Islam uniform. Walking out of the Chicago Hilton and Towers to deliver the package to national headquarters, a middle-aged bald black man in a suit tapped him on the shoulder.

"Eddie Bloodpath," Akbar said. "*As-salaam alaikum*. I looked your name up at the Club 10 register this morning. My name is Akbar

Muhammad, from Las Vegas, Nevada." Akbar had approached Eddie the very moment Eddie's back was turned. Akbar smelled of a pungent musk and he wore the most beautiful suit Eddie had ever seen. He was tall, thin-necked, but striking. He seemed to be angry even when he was smiling, which was always. Eddie took him for a retired welterweight, but his nose was not flattened, like O'Grady's or Tapia's. O'Grady! He'd seen him talking with Tommy the night before at the hotel bar!

"Eddie Bloodpath," Akbar said. "Kell's boy." He was rubbing his hands, wincing as he did, as if they hurt him. "I seen you sparring this morning," Akbar said. "I was spying on you. You got a tight left straight jab, that's a nice staple punch; you got a hook, but you need to work on your defenses. Cats in these ranks will sting you."

"Thank you, sir."

"This here," Akbar said, "is damn near the pinnacle of the game. At this level you need to perfect your defenses," and Eddie had been nodding, and had he thought of it, would have scribbled down each word Akbar said, but he was too nervous, for Akbar had seen him training that morning and found something lacking. "But I ain't seen you take a punch, or come back after a whupping. I'd have liked to see you go more than four rounds, but Gloves is kindergarten. Thumb attachments!" he laughed. "Twelve-ounce gloves! What is that? Boxing is a blood sport."

"I gone nine, sir, in an exhibition at the Club S.A.R., in Phoenix, unofficial, against a pro one time. He had a twenty-two/eleven record in the pros, sir. I train five-minute rounds. I could go twelve rounds, too."

"You think cause you a young buck you can wreck shop. But what you know? In the pros, we bust balls every round. And then you got the card girls coming round while you bleeding, so pretty make you want to cry. It's a different story." Akbar was laughing, stroking his lapel with his manicured fingers.

Akbar was management. All management was rich, Tommy told

him. Akbar looked rich, richer than Jules even, than the white men in the VIP room of the Tropicana Club. The cloth of his beautiful suit dripped off his shoulders. Boys standing before the elevator listening to Walkmans stared at Akbar, others, clerks at the front desk, bellboys shuttling piled American Tourister suitcases in brass rolling carts along the floor, even the cocky New York fighters, boys from Gleason's, from the Twenty-third, to whom an Olympic tryout slot was almost a sure bet. And Akbar had approached him when the New York boys stood on the other side of the hallway, slapping hands in the lounge, watching ESPN on the wall-mounted televisions.

"I got a second, Mr. Akbar." Eddie was spitting out the words. "I mean, maybe he could come with me if I go to Vegas."

Akbar rubbed his bald head and began to laugh. Seventeen-year-old boys in Kronk windbreakers saw Akbar laughing at Eddie and smirked. "I said, I seen you working out at the Club 10. That's all I said."

Akbar leaned close. "We're building in Vegas, a place for regular niggers like you and me, niggers that don't want to be hoodwinked all the time." Akbar nodded at the Kronk boys. "Look at these little black monkeys running around with the Walkmans their white trainers bought them." Akbar leaned forward, pointing at Kronk boys, headphones on their ears, blank-faced, absent. Eddie stared at them. Akbar was the angriest black man Eddie had ever met. "Look at that boy from Detroit," Akbar said, "and I do mean *boy*." He pointed at a Kronk middleweight with a patchy goatee, sitting in the lounge, nodding his head to the music. "All these black boys with talent, half of them can't barely read, running around with headphones on, shucking and jiving like some little bare-ass monkeys! And then you look at who is signing them, who is managing them, who is thieving fifty, sixty, seventy-five percent of their purse, reading the contracts to them, the white man, brother, keeping them ignorant, leaving them with crumbs. The white man can make you a champion, but he can't make you a man. This is our predicament. Look at Cus D'Amato. Taught Tyson how to be the youngest heavyweight champion in history. Fucking unify the belt. Where is Tyson now? Rotting away in some Indiana prison. You remember that next time Kellner tells you you are like a son to him," Akbar whispered, staring at the trainers, thirtyish white men like Tommy, harried men rushing out for the conference room double doors, gathering their teenage fighters, rounding them up like day care workers collecting children, shouting at them across the patterned carpet. The ceiling lights bounced off Akbar's angry face; his eyes were like tiny BBs. How Akbar's breath, his angry words smelled of sliced honeydew and cantaloupe of the Hilton continental breakfast. "You get to the point," Akbar said. "I like that. You're hungry. I'm building an empire in Nevada. Maybe you can come fight for me someday, fight pro. Shoot, you come this far, I might could snap you up now. Course, we don't have no openings now. Life is all about timing, Eddie. You remember that. When the time is right. When you come, I'll take care of your spirit and your wallet, but first, you best jump out of that Nation of Flimflam! Ha! Ha! I used to be in that Nation, too. Bunch of no-good crooks."

Eddie said nothing to this. He remembered how Bilal had warned him about ex-NOI, how bitter they could be. A cream-colored business card appeared in Akbar's fingers. Eddie stared at the card and took it. Akbar leaned forward and again whispered, "Room four-oh-one-two. I'm collecting all the conscious brothers like you and inviting them to a little powwow in my presidential suite while the slave masters go to that administrative meeting, you dig. We're planning a little, ha, slave revolt! I'll give you a free piece of advice, son."

"Yes sir."

"Drop that Jew," Akbar whispered. Eddie's ears went red. "It's not like I don't like Kell on the personal side, but he don't know nothing about the fight game. Tried to take this Phoenix heavyweight named Andre Green into the I.B.F. in eighty-two, you know, and messed him up real good, drank up all his money. They were on a streak for a hot minute till Kell fucked him up. I saw that Andre Green sweeping floors outside the MGM last week. I gave him a hundred dollars for old times' sake."

Eddie offered Akbar his salaam, and ran out of the Hilton.

And he was late. He ran out through the lobby onto Michigan Ave., clutching the envelope under his copy of *Message to the Blackman*, searching for the nearest El.

The El was streaming in the direction of Mosque No. 2.

7351 South Stoney Island Avenue. He'd memorized it in the library of Mosque No. 32, at the window in Phoenix. He learned everything in the library, everything by rote. The leader's birth date, circumference of the Earth.

He climbed two stories of wrought iron staircase to the platform, bought a token, shoved through a turnstile. Slouching black boys in loose fluttering T-shirts noticed the uniform and stared. The train came sliding in.

The platform scarred with graffiti, the slouching black boys reminded him of what he had always imagined the East to be. He pressed the package to his side like a woman clutching her purse on a dark and notorious street. The boys stared at him, laughed when the bright manila package smacked across on the station concrete. It spilled on the shoe-scuffed floor, bright white papers flushing out. Eddie read it. The letter was CONFIDENTIAL, a letter of the utmost importance, top-secret, and he, a nobody, a lowly processee, had read it. He lurched forward, snatched up the papers with a shout, brushing off the dirt, stuffing the bright papers back inside, examined its front, its back, like a spy. All praises be to Allah. A million! The folder looked acceptable. The flap had opened; it had not been sealed. Should he seal it? Should he send it at all? Could say he lost it. No.

Perhaps it was a test. He was staring still, the fluorescent lights above bouncing against the papers and reflecting on his peeking face. Oh. Eddie looked, swallowed, ignored the flood of anonymous people enveloping him. He almost shouted at the departing El, folded the flap, bent the clasp, sat. Boys laughed, pointed. Slouching black boys. One million. One million. He inserted the papers and shut the clasp. It looked okay. He would deliver it. Another El train arrived, and Eddie boarded. The leader would not know. The compartment shook, lights flickered. HAND DELIVERED. He should meet the secretary himself, take a receipt.

He could not fail. He discovered a twirling motorized crescent moon twisting atop the national headquarters building from half a mile through the El window. He had forgotten his opponent, the polite country boy from Kansas City. Minister Farrakhan was out of town, his assistant. These were busy men. On the move, making decisions. We don't have time for your games, your useless talk. The black men and women inside this building do not slouch. We don't have time for your booze and your pork and your cigarettes. We don't have time for your shouting and clapping and getting happy up in the church when black people are catching hell. Slouching men could not have built such an edifice. Eddie was facing the mosque, the package clutched to his side.

Mosque Maryam. Young black men patrolled the building, peered from various windows as the motorized hilal moon twirled atop. Like the headquarters of a small corporation. The guards stopped him. The bow tie was not enough. What if they want the package opened? The package must go directly to Minister Farrakhan's executive secretary. As per Bilal's note Eddie requested a man named Mansoor and through the shaded glass watched the figures of young laborers, women and men, hurrying across the lobby floor with manila folders, stacks of papers. The sight of such busy, diligent sisters and brothers!

Mansoor appeared behind the glass in a flawless olive suit. His face was leonine; he wore a dark, trimmed mustache. His skin was bright. Mansoor waved at the guards, who buzzed the door open for Eddie. Mansoor vouched for him, okayed the package. "This brother came all the way from Phoenix," he said, "to deliver this package to the leader's desk." The guards gave Eddie a second look, waved him inside after Mansoor. Eddie followed Mansoor across the ornate lobby, examining the high walls, the pictures. Here was a young man on the rise. Assistant to the youth minister at twenty-two. Eddie wondered if Mansoor knew about the Million Man March, if there were rumors already. He was handsome, an inch taller than Eddie. Eddie followed him to the end of the great lobby. They rode an elevator, ventured through another security post, and down a hallway to an open door of typing. Mansoor ducked inside the office. There was an easiness, a certainty to everything that Mansoor did, something corporate, winning. Mansoor passed the package to the secretary, a busy young head-scarfed woman, into her hands so Eddie could see the chain of custody for himself. The secretary locked the package in her desk and ran out to catch the El train home.

A million! Eddie thought. It was odd, young sisters and brothers now working, here, inside, backs straightened, a military order imposed, proud.

This busy room a million times multiplied. He imagined it. Yes, he would go to Washington, stand in uniform. He would take Adolpho. He would run across Woodland Park to the basketball courts and collect black boys and he would take them to the march, as many as he could, and save them, for he had been this moment saved. He stood now in the giant lobby of clacking leather-sole shoes, of men in suits and women in modest dress, walking in every direction with papers and errands. It was like watching E. Washington St. from the library window of Mosque No. 32, the months before, looking out on the people, bustling through the cold wind, believing everyone he saw, the prostitute and the beggar, the hoody, the white cop even, to

be redeemable, saved from the Fall of America, everyone redeemable excepting Turtle . . . and the package—to the leader!—that
most important package had smacked against the cement floor and
spit out elegant paper, the watermarked paper, made him privy to
the most beautiful secret, a sign from Allah—a million!—and now in
the National House, he was among believers.

"Have you heard of Cabrini-Green?" Mansoor asked, taking a Motorola radio from the charge base, glancing at a corkboard. "Because
this is where the schedule puts us tonight." They sat in Mansoor's office. Mansoor leaned forward, smiling. "I like you, brother. I want
you to meet Minister Farrakhan." And what would it mean for the
Nation if tomorrow he won, if he took nationals? Eddie thought. "If
only you were staying a week longer," Mansoor said. "I could show
you Chicago. Isn't fair, is it? I could introduce you to some very beautiful and quite marriageable sisters. I love our Nation. We take care
of our own. I feel like you haven't seen enough. I want you to return
to Phoenix with good things to report."

"I've already got good things to report, brother."

"The Nation is a family. Did you notice how I made certain you delivered the package to the minister's secretary yourself?"

"Yes."

"Whereas some brothers would have taken advantage, dropping
that package off themselves to get a little face time with the leader,
but I say you are my brother and you've come this far. Too bad the
leader is out of town."

"I can't thank you enough."

Mansoor had his own office, a telephone, computer, cherry-wood
desk. Eddie wondered how he could ever compete with such a handsome, charming young man like Mansoor. A college boy. "There's too
much naked ambition in our Nation," Mansoor said. "I don't believe
in that, and I like you, Eddie, I really do. I must say I'm fond of you.
If only there were a thousand brothers like yourself."

"Like me, brother?"

"Of course," said Mansoor.

Down the hall there was the noise, and clapping of hands, camera flashes. Mansoor frowned. "That's MC Ghetto Fabulous out there in the hall," Mansoor whispered. "He's a gangsta rapper. You probably haven't heard of him yet."

"A gangsta rapper? What's he doing here, brother?"

"A convert. Excellent publicity. But problematic as far as I'm concerned. You probably haven't heard of him yet. He gets a lot of airplay on the local underground college rap stations like eighty-eight-point-five. Lots of rehashed 'keeping it real' thugged-out nonsense. Of course, I have mixed feelings about hip-hop, brother. Of all of the beautiful art we black folk have given this no-good country, it is the most dynamic, original, the most ingenious—all the talent, all that entrepreneurial drive—but like everything with us, so much self-hatred. I'm from the old school, I don't think the Nation needs the endorsement of someone who calls a black woman a bitch. And don't tell me I'm talking censorship."

"Right," said Eddie, nodding, though he didn't know the word.

"But now we're engaging in gossip. It's a mulatto thing, you ask me," said Mansoor. "My man grew up in the suburbs. He's a mulatto, you know. The whole militant mulatto phenomenon. Nat Turner. Always trying to prove something. You're half black, but only half, so you have white privilege, consider yourself special. The rules don't apply. It's a real issue in the Nation, all these mulattos." Mansoor leaned across the desk now and began to whisper. "Why do you think we won't let white boys in? I mean, there are the obvious reasons. But they'd probably work harder just for the privilege of being blacker than black. Personally, I think this is the solution to our so-called dwindling numbers problem. I say, let the white boys join the Nation if they want, the wannabes! Think of all those lost white boys searching for something. Indoctrinate them with our beliefs, grafted white devil, blah, blah, blah. No doubt, they'd work hard in the Nation, harder than us. You're just a baby Muslim. You'll see it after a few years. It's like when we pick up Minister Farrakhan at the airport, Eddie. All these white folks want to shake his hand. A black nationalist! The big anti-Semite! A so-called racist!"

There was a knock at Mansoor's door. Eddie turned his head. The others came inside, Mansoor's security patrol, awkward nineteen- and twenty-year-olds, college boys, their sleeves too long for their arms, with walkie-talkies, red crescent armbands wrapped around the arms of their jackets. They saluted Mansoor.

Outside Mosque Maryam they piled into Mansoor's car and drove to the edge of Cabrini-Green. It looked as if a great violence had been done to the streets, the lots, the swaths of grass surrounding Cabrini-Green: concrete walls torn down; potholes dotted the roads before the countless buildings, the concrete sidewalks buckled, the windows of the little food marts broken.

Mansoor had parked several blocks from Cabrini-Green, turned on and tested their walkie-talkies, once encountered another FOI squad marching in the opposite direction, patrolling the adjoining streets. His method, Mansoor explained, was to orbit the streets surrounding the target (here, Cabrini) once or twice before going into the target itself, to avoid surprise confrontations.

They began at a series of row houses along a dumpy side street called Larabee. A cop had been sniped at in the 1970s, Mansoor told him as they walked. Girl X. They went two blocks forward, saw inscribed in an open, wrought-iron fence, ABR NI-GR EN. The fence shook in the wind. Behind the fence, in socked feet on the grass, a ten-year-old girl, hair uncombed, watched the patrol in a hooded purple jacket, her older brother behind her in darkness, dragging her back across the low grass to their home in the red project building behind them.

The noises did not stop, noises rising above noises, shouts, laughter, music blaring, sirens . . . but distant, shouts, shouts at the patrol!

He should not be running around the night before a competition. He imagined Tommy sitting at the managers' meeting with Kell in the conference room under the fluorescent light, taking down the instructions. Eddie could get back by eight, call Marchalina. Could get his sleep and Tommy would prep him in the morning and his muscles would be loose and his shots would rip. Now the squad passed beggars, sitting against a metal fence . . . black boys in hoodies, jogging down the street, a jangle of limbs and arms and sneakers. Someone must save them, something, some religion—was it this? Yes, yes. A million! The wind blew trash across the street.

There was a spirit here . . . even in Cabrini, in the language, in the way the boys walked and patted fists, embraced on a corner, the words they used, the slang; he'd never heard it before; he felt as country as the boy from Kansas City. It was eastern, and bold and cool.

A boy appearing out of the darkness held his twin brother's hand and asked the little patrol to look after him as he climbed the stairs to his apartment. Mansoor stopped, Eddie after him, the squad. They stood on tossed crack vials, on the broken cement, and waited for the boy and his brother to climb the stairs of his apartment until he had gone inside and was waving at them from the window, from behind green curtains of the fourth of five floors, and it was a moment so simple that Eddie wondered if Mansoor had scripted it. They marched past a stoop of black girls in denim cutoffs, bustiers.

Gunshots from the north! The girls screamed. A young black boy, not fourteen, pick in his hair, hands tucked in the front pocket of a black hoody sweatshirt, ran down the other side of the street. *We have been turned into savages,* Bilal had told him. *It is painful when you realize. But we must not give up on our people.* Mansoor held out his long arms like wings before the squad; everyone stopped. "Wait, wait. I will call dispatch." Mansoor whispered into his walkie-talkie; they waited in darkness for dispatch to relay a command to them.

When the command came, a relayed message from a police scanner, Mansoor said, "They are looking for that poor, lost brother who robbed a convenience store, the boy we saw. Let's go." The squad hurried. "We have to be careful, Eddie," said Mansoor. "I'm afraid there are nights like this," Mansoor said. They were running now, and Eddie did not want to run; they should not run, not in suits, not now, when they were dignified men, reformed.

They stopped running and began again to patrol the street. The sirens stopped. Eddie caught his breath. Never had his uniform aroused such respect from the people he passed on the street; never had he felt of such significance. Mothers waved from windows. Children approached them, touching their hands, calling them by name. Slouching boys on stoops even crushed out their blunts at sight of the patrol. "Have you ever noticed, brother, how the attendance fluctuates?" Mansoor asked him. A walkie-talkie went off. "The minister makes a speech or something, a black boy gets shot in the back by some wicked cop, and all of a sudden there's a rise in attendance. They come for a bit, and then they go back to their ignorance."

"They come into the mosque and they ask about Malcolm," another said. "Malcolm, Malcolm, Malcolm."

"Yes," Eddie said. Yes, yes, it was true. It was Malcolm, calling you to the mosque, even now. The coroner examined his body on the day of his assassination. How clean it was, Bilal said. Never seen a body so clean. It made you proud. "What do you tell them when they ask?"

Mansoor sighed. "You tell them don't believe everything you hear. You tell them in our opinion—if they have the spiritual maturity to handle it—that he turned against his own teacher, the man who raised him up from nothing. Everything ain't like he lays it down in that stupid book."

"By any means necessary."

Laughter.

"Malcolm was too busy chilling with the goddamn crackers," Mansoor said. "Too busy trying to impress his mortal enemy. My dear brother, I'm afraid he loved the white man more than he loved his own people. One of the old heads told me that that hajj business was a big publicity stunt."

"Tell him the story, Mansoor."

"Have you heard the story, brother? It's real." Mansoor poked his shoulder with the antenna of his walkie-talkie. Eddie shook his head. The projects loomed before them now, in every direction, dark towers of chaos, noise. Looking faces in the windows behind wrought iron, graffiti, shouting children. The street smelled raw, of garbage. "You're still a baby Muslim, brother," said Mansoor, "and I mean this in the best way, and so I bet you haven't heard the story yet.

"The leader was on vacation in Mexico with his family back in the eighties, and there was this earthquake, and the Most Honorable Elijah Muhammad appeared before his bed in a vision and then raised him through the sky to the Motherwheel, you know, where the minister saw all the prophets of the Bible and the Qur'an. So, of course the minister made prayer with them on board the spaceship, by which I mean, the Motherwheel, a plane where all the prophets exist, as you know, and of course Elijah Muhammad himself, the Messiah."

"Motherwheel?" Eddie asked.

"Motherwheel," said Mansoor.

"Of course. After they made prayer, the Most Honorable Elijah Muhammad escorted Minister Farrakhan around the Motherwheel, and told him he'd been bestowed with the title of prophet. Then he took Minister Farrakhan to the brig—and do you know who he saw in the brig, brother? Malcolm X behind bars! His hair all gray, an old man now, the big sellout. Behind bars, where that backstabbing bastard belongs!" They laughed at this behind their hands; their shoulders shook.

Eddie gave a weak smile. "I have not heard that one." He hid his face so that they would not see his anger. That anyone could believe this. He was competing in twelve hours. He'd wasted the night running around with them, dodging bullets, to uplift the ghetto, when they believed this! Now they were at Mansoor's car.

At the end of the little patrol Mansoor reported to his superior at Mosque Maryam, disbanded the patrol of tired college boys, and drove Eddie back to the Hilton. Riding back, Eddie felt his time with Mansoor slipping away. He wanted to go somewhere to talk to him alone. Motherwheel. Mansoor would say something else, would explain it, and Eddie would have a laugh with him.

"*As-salaam alaikum,*" Mansoor told him, leaning over the stick shift, watching Eddie through the window as Eddie leaned forward, staring at Mansoor from the busy Hilton curb. "You have a contact in Chicago now. I pray that you win tomorrow." Eddie nodded and leaned forward and shook Mansoor's hand. The words felt hollow now. What a flake Mansoor was, he thought, what a phony. Then guilt washed over him, and he wondered if it was only a test of his faith, for surely there was a meaning to the story, a deeper spiritual meaning that he'd missed, surely he was weak. Mansoor sped off and went inside. It was eight o'clock. He should call back home. Tommy had bought him a prepaid phone card. But he was too scared now. The minute he called Phoenix, his nerves would go. He needed to be alone. A Hilton attendant in an apron stood before the closed door. Tommy and Kell would be coming out soon. He rode the elevator to the fortieth floor.

The foyer was marble. Akbar had rented the presidential suite. Boys sat on sofas inside. Akbar sat alone on a sofa. The main lights were off. There was a balcony, Eddie realized. Two! The boys next to him shook to the beat. An old Tupac song blasted from a boom box on the floor in the center of the giant living room; a boy held a brass desk lamp as a spotlight, under which another boy from Idaho, in the 125-pound weight class, was, for Akbar's edification, dancing, shouting the lyrics to the Tupac song.

"What? This ain't music," Akbar said, leaning back on a chocolate Huaweimei sofa.

"It's music," said two boys in tandem, laughing from a love seat, others repeating after them.

"I know the words! It's Tupac. I know all his lyrics," said the dancing boy. He turned the volume down and began to rap, dancing on socked feet:

They hate it when a real nigga bust
They hate when I cuss, they threaten to bust

"Dance, Idaho!" Akbar screamed. Akbar climbed off the chocolate leather sofa and started tossing fifty-dollar bills on the rug, at the dancing boy's feet, bills, bills, boys in nylon windbreakers scrambled from the sofa, the doorway, to grab them, the dancing boy himself, grasping for money, arms stretched out, the sound of rubbing nylon as the boys snatched money from the beautiful carpet. "Dance, boy, dance," Akbar shouted, and the boy picked up four fifty-dollar bills—four, four!—he'd never held so many, and danced some more.

"This how you dance for your white cracker trainer, Idaho?" Akbar shouted at the boy dancing in socked feet. "The one who wants to steal all your money! What is you about, boy?"

"Making dollars, Akbar."

"That's right, and who gonna make all y'all niggers some money in Vegas?"

"Akbar Muhammad!"

"Who gonna keep it real? Who gonna keep it realer than real!"

"Akbar Muhammad."

"Who gonna keep it in the community?"

"Akbar Muhammad."

"Who give a damn about the young black man?" he chanted. The boys called his name. "Now run, run on, boys," Akbar shouted, "and go back to your slave masters, and get your sleep for tomorrow, and remember who give you that money, run back before your—ha, ha—they come back to the room and find out we done plotted a slave revolt!" With that the lights went on, the dancing boy stopped dancing, unplugged his boom box. Akbar saw Eddie and waved him in. He looked as if he had something to tell him. Eddie sat down next to him on the sofa and then he noticed a beautiful blond woman who'd been watching the boys dance from the bedroom door. She smiled at Eddie. "Speak of the devil!" she said.

"Speak of the devil," said Akbar, shaking his head at Eddie. "Well, ain't that funny?" he told the woman. "And we were just talking about him." The woman nodded. Akbar turned to Eddie. "I just called my people in Vegas. Good news is we lined up a multimillion-dollar cable contract. Bad news is we had a guy, a heavyweight, quit tonight over a personal issue, one of those family things, you know. My man wants out of his contract," said Akbar. "I'm a compassion-ate brother. These situations, they creep into the sport." Akbar had a blue folder sitting for Eddie on a desk. He scribbled his Vegas phone number down on the front. "It's decision time, brother. When can you be in Vegas?"

"Vegas," Eddie said.

"I want to scoop you. I like what I saw. These other little kids. They need time to mature. You seen them, dancing on the floor like fools. That was just a sociological experiment for her." He pointed to the woman. "She grew up in Carmel, California. I was giving her a little lesson in *ghettonomics*. Drag a dollar through the ghetto and so forth." He slapped Eddie's leg. "Let's talk dates, Eddie."

"But you ain't seen me fight yet."

"I seen you train. I got hold of your record. You can fly back with us in the Piper after the competition if you want, or you can take your time and tell Kell slow. I understand either way. Shoot, trainers are like women," Akbar said, eyeing the woman. "You got to let them down with a little syrup." Akbar laughed.

Eddie laughed. He imagined a somber Muslim life with Akbar in Vegas, working and praying together, lowering their eyes at sight of the leggy Vegas women, stopping his workouts at the noon and afternoon prayers, when there would be no distinction between his boxing life and his spiritual life. He would never be able to repay him for this. He could lie on his bed now and sleep tonight without a worry of tomorrow, but of course he would be too excited to sleep. He felt in a moment separated from all the poor boys in the Hilton. He pitied them for dancing for money.

"What do I do now?" He looked at the folder again. The contract was in it. Malcolm in the brig. There was clarity now. He saw Vegas. It would be simple. He wondered how soon he could fly home and be in Vegas, a day, ten hours? He couldn't wait to see Tommy's face when he told him a manager had approached him with a contract.

"You're in a situation right now with Kell. It ain't doing nothing for you. I would have had you up here at nationals last year, Eddie, I would have had you fighting pro by now. I would have fixed your weaknesses. They're blatant. It's a sign of bad training. It's a waste of potential. You want to do right by your Jew. How he took you in, was like your daddy."

"What I tell him?"

"Nothing." He leaned forward, whispering. "The ghetto is filled with sentimental motherfuckers. You don't owe nobody nothing. When I saw you I knew you had heart, Eddie, I knew you was a real Muslim. I said, Akbar, teach this boy the true Islam, guide him. Get him away from the Nation of Flimflam. Make him rich. How'd you like to spend Ramadan in Mecca? This can all be arranged."

"Yes," said Eddie. His face lit up. He imagined walking across the sands of Mecca. "I need that." The blond woman stood at the bed-

room door, listening. He did not trust her. What was she, a secretary? Didn't she know to leave them alone? He was too happy to
care. "My life, my life is filled with, with negativities. I want to live a
clean life. That's all I ever wanted. I am haunted by things. I seen too
many things I shouldn't have. I want to say the things that happened
to me is the will of Allah, like a good Muslim, and leave it at that, but
still I be looking back. I am a hypocrite sometimes, Akbar. With sex."

Akbar leaned back. He smiled. "I rode in an elevator with Malcolm
once."

"With Malcolm X?"

"That brother was about business. I was intimidated. I shook his
hand. He was a tall man." Akbar raised his hand up in the air. Eddie
imagined Malcolm. "You is a conscious black man. There is things
that Kell could never understand. The Qur'an says that you are not
a Muslim until you want for your brother what you want for yourself. I live by this." The woman was nodding, as if she'd heard Akbar
quote the Qur'an before; her face was sincere. Eddie wondered if
she were a Muslim, too, one of those spooked-out white California
Muslims. "There are temptations in Vegas," Akbar said. "We got to
protect your spirit, boy. You'll have money and women coming after
you, and come on, Eddie, you is the rawest ghetto nigger as I ever
met. Ghetto niggers can't handle money, not at first. You need another ghetto nigger like me to guide you. We are building in Vegas,
Eddie, an empire. Boxing is just the start."

"I'll need a couple weeks. Finish out the competition, wrap things
up in Phoenix. Unless you want me sooner."

"A couple weeks is fine." Akbar was smiling at him; the woman
was smiling. "We ain't going nowhere, boy. We'll be right there in Vegas when you're ready, Eddie."

"All praises be to Allah!" Eddie said, shaking Akbar's hand, and he
left them, took the stairs down to the twenty-third floor. He rushed
down the stairs, smiling, laughing out loud.

He found Tommy standing before his door. "Kell ran out," Tommy said, shaking his head. "I looked in the lobby, but he wasn't there. The night before your first day! He said he saw one of his old buddies from New York, and I left them in the lobby. I went to the managers' meeting by myself."

"He'll come back, then," Eddie said. "Let him alone."

"Come on, Eddie." Tommy was shouting. "He said he'd stay here. You know he ran off drinking. You stay, you need your sleep."

"Let him go and drink, Tommy. He'll come back. He always do."

"And black out somewhere? Fuck."

"I'm coming, then."

"Fine," said Tommy. Kell had snuck off to put liquor in his blood, and Tommy had enough. Eddie chased Tommy down the hallway. In the elevator Eddie wondered why Tommy would not let Kell sneak off and drink. It did not matter now. He'd been scouted. In two weeks he'd be fighting pro. The boy from Kansas City was a punk. He'd beat him on an hour's sleep.

"You know he fucked you," Tommy said as the elevator drifted down to the lobby floor. Tommy ran out of the front lobby into the dark streets of Chicago, in his U.S.A. cap, his outrageous Hawaiian shirt. Eddie ran after him, smiling.

Eddie followed Tommy through the streets; he kept thinking of Johnny Tapia, yesterday at the Hilton bar. Until tonight his life had been Johnny Tapia's life, filled with misery, only now things had turned around for him. He ran after Tommy down side streets, praying that Kell had gone by foot. In a dark patch Eddie took Tommy aside and looked at him. Tommy stared at him, panting.

"I met this guy," Eddie told him. "A manager from Vegas. Akbar Muhammad. He offered me a contract. I want you to come with me, Tommy, to Vegas. You can be my cut man."

Tommy ignored him, hurried forward, breathing through his mouth. They searched one bar after another.

They stood before the front doors of a bar called Stocks & Bonds. The doors were of black leather with gold rivets. The bar seemed too plush and too close for Kell. Tommy turned to Eddie. "Eddie, don't start telling me about some manager from Vegas. You should be sleeping," Tommy told Eddie. "We'll talk to Kell about the man when we find him."

"No, you can't tell Kell about him. Kell won't like him. Kell won't understand. It will hurt his feelings, Tommy."

"What's wrong with you? You got to investigate stuff like that." Tommy opened the front door. "I don't want to hear nothing more about it right now. We got to get you to sleep in an hour."

Eddie followed him, whispering, "We can be rich, Tommy. We can send money back for Kell. The stable mothers will watch after him. Don't be a cop, Tommy," Eddie said and grabbed his shoulder. "I hate cops. You ain't no cop, Tommy. The cops beat me one time. Come with me to Vegas. We can be rich together." Tommy ignored him. The bouncer looked at Eddie. Tommy flashed his ID. The bar was filled with graduate students; business school types sat in the table next to Kell. John Cougar Mellencamp sang "Jack and Diane" on the jukebox.

"The kid is with me," Tommy told the bouncer. "We're just looking for our friend. The kid won't drink nothing." The bouncer gave Eddie a look and let them pass. Kell sat at the end of the bar. Kell was not drunk, but buzzing. Kell saw them come in and shook his head.

"I could not stop myself," said Kell, playing with a napkin.

"You fucked Eddie," Tommy said. "We wasted hours looking for you in every damn bar in Chicago."

"Tommy, you didn't have to take Eddie with you," Kell shouted. "It's a free country. I know the way back to the Hilton."

"Get the check and let's go." Tommy waved his hand. "You messed up Eddie's sleep, and I still got to prep for tomorrow."

Kell looked at Eddie. Tommy got Kell's check and paid it at the bar. "This bar used to be called something else," Kell said. "I don't remember what. But it sure wasn't *Stocks and Bonds*. I went here once, twenty years ago. My wife and I. My daughter went to Northwestern. She kept changing her major. She dropped out ten credits short, unmarried, knocked up, and she calls me irresponsible. We stopped here one weekend, my wife and I, a parents' weekend." Eddie watched him. "Hey, fuck you, Eddie, I could not stop myself. Look at me. Eddie," he said. "There are parts of yourself that you cannot conquer no matter how hard you try. Ugly parts. Now you got me feeling guilty. Look at you. You'll be fine tomorrow. I will make it up. Give me a year to get it together." Kell waved his hand. "Redemption is around the corner."

Tommy came back from the bar, folding his wallet. "You are an old bag of shit," he said.

"Leave him alone, Tommy. He can't help it."

A gray-haired Asian man shoved a vacuum across the patterned lobby carpet. In the hallway Kell vomited on his left arm, and Tommy started shouting. Tommy ordered Eddie to get to sleep, keyed the lock on his hotel room, and ran to the bathroom for a towel. Eddie followed him into the room. The old man lay back and shut his eyes and lay sobbing.

Tommy heard Kell crying and stood up from the floor and shook his head at Kell. "Shut up," he shouted. "Shut up! Ain't nobody gonna feel sorry for you here. Stop your crying."

Kell set a spotted hand on his crying face. "I can't."

"Call his children," said Eddie, watching Kell sob. "In Connecticut."

"He was a lousy father," Tommy said, shouting at Kell to shut up. "He had the good life and he ruined it. Nobody likes him but us. One day one of Kell's old friends came to the gym while he was passed out, and he said that Kell is a self-defeating man. Do you know what that means?"

"But his children grown now. They need to take care of him."

"He's a self-defeating man. No one can help a self-defeating man."

"I'm not," shouted Kell from the bed. "I'm not a self-defeating man!"

"You're a self-defeating man," said Tommy, like a man scolding a dog, "and you need to stop telling Eddie you can take him to Vegas when you can't!"

"Get out, you redneck! Get out! Get out!" Kell shouted.

"And then who will clean up after you?" said Tommy.

"Eddie will. Eddie won't let me down. Eddie is a good boy. Don't listen to him, Eddie. I can take you to Vegas. You're gonna win tomorrow. We'll be in Vegas next year. But Tommy can't come. Tommy is a no-good son of a bitch."

"Who washes your clothes and runs the gym? You fucked up your life, old man. Tell Eddie how you fucked up your life. How your family left you for your drinking. Cause you killed that little girl," said Tommy. "You make me sick! Some poor little Mormon girl, jack-knifed her. Some little student at Mesa Community College in nineteen seventy-nine. You stupid shit! You never told Eddie that, did you?"

Kell began to sob again. Eddie looked at him.

"Why you think he can't drive, Eddie?" Tommy said. "Why do you think he works in that shithole gym back in Phoenix? He was a big-time engineer for McDonnell Douglas. He earned seventy thousand dollars a year. Had this big old house in Paradise Valley. I seen it once. Used to build fucking helicopters. Think, Eddie," Tommy said, wiping the sweat from his brow, his own shirt covered in Kell's vomit. "Look at him lying there. He can't even clean up after himself no more. And you was buying him booze before you went Muslim. And you think he can get you to Vegas?" Eddie looked down upon Kell, his deliverer, drunk, now unconscious, old Kell, his atrophied arms crossed, now snoring on the bed in the dank room, and his face grew hot.

Akbar had saved his life. He lay in his suit and did not sleep. He read the auto ads in the *Chicago Tribune*, imagining the car he'd buy when Akbar made him rich. He imagined buying a house for Mama and Nana. He imagined visiting Turtle in suits as beautiful as Akbar's and designer sunglasses.

He waited in darkness beneath a section of empty bucket seats the next morning. Kell nudged him, and they marched up the stairs, Tommy after them, squinting in the light. The boy from Kansas City stood in the north corner, the smiling, mild-faced boy from Kansas City, who gave Eddie his back and whispered a prayer to Jesus. Eddie noticed the minor boxing celebrities. They were watching him now, some of them. Sets of 106- and 125-pound fighters waited in the two adjacent rings for the simultaneous bouts. Eddie searched for Akbar in the dark crowds, and Johnny Tapia, finding neither. No one came on the first day. Johnny Tapia would be a sign, Eddie thought. Because his life, too, was pitiful, only Tapia's was so much worse. Like a joke it was so bad: the cocaine, the depressions, the hundred-foot bus crash at the age of seven, daddy murdered the week before he was born, mama raped, hung, and stabbed to death in the next room while he slept, at age eight. It was enough to make you cry, but Tapia was not here. Eddie searched for Akbar, but there was no Akbar. The boy from Kansas City was praying to Jesus. The lights dimmed. The boy wore an obnoxious black robe with his name stitched in sequins. A white man whispered in the boy's ear. The boy was polite for a 256-pound superheavyweight. "I'm sorry," Kell whispered, "for all the times I fucked you, Eddie."

The boy from Kansas City was tall. His hair was cropped short, out of style, and he fought without tattoos and gold teeth and he fought for Jesus, and there was a purity to his hunger. He would not cuss in the lockup. The robe came off and his body was dark, rock-hard muscles. Eddie would beat the boy hard. The referee appeared, a bearded Hispanic man in a shirt without stripes, mouthing the instructions, and the boy from Kansas City went quiet.

Back to the corners. Kell tightened Eddie's face guard and left Eddie with the boy. The bell rang. Eddie and the Kansas City boy merged in the center, the boy ducking, circling, Eddie throwing straight jabs that fell off into black space. The boy was shorter by two inches; he tried to get inside with double jabs, rushing the next minute. He was clinging, whispering prayers under his breath; then he was double jabbing again, appearing under Eddie's chin. He got inside, connecting, smacked Eddie's mask, threw shots that echoed in the crowd. There was that stinging on Eddie's chin. He raised his gloves to his jaw, but already the boy had knocked Eddie down. The boy appeared again under Eddie's face, slapping; Eddie's cheeks rippled in concentric circles, waves of undeviating force. Eddie blundered at an uppercut, knowing the boy from Kansas City would slip his punch. Judges jotted on clipboards below, jotted, jotted, jotted. The ring doctor, Dr. Rosenfels, looked uneasy. The referee watched Eddie's eyes from across the ring. Finish the round. Now Eddie ran at the boy: they almost collided in the middle of the ring, the boy jabbing, raking Eddie's gut. Eddie lay on his back, on the canvas in the hard light. He did not see it. He heard the boys in the adjacent rings fighting on. *Tss, tss, tss!* The boy from Kansas City raised his meaty arms, but he was too humble to dance. The referee bent over, staring at Eddie, and called the fight. "Twenty-six seconds," said a beautiful woman from the crowd at his left. Her husband shushed her, saying, "The boy can hear you." Dr. Rosenfels came into the ring, looking wary, Kell and Tommy behind him.

But it had only been twenty-six seconds. Eddie could stand now. He was not even winded. He could stand and beat the boy from Kansas City now. He was taller than the boy; he had reach. Dr. Rosenfels flashed a penlight in Eddie's eyes. "Are you okay, kid?"

Eddie nodded. He thought of Akbar. Akbar was somewhere in the audience. He'd ruined it with Akbar. He opened his mouth to tell Dr. Rosenfels, and blood spilled out across his shirt.

Kell took off Eddie's bloody mouthpiece. A woman in the crowd gasped. Eddie felt the eyes of strangers on him; he waited for them to forget him, to look at the boys fighting in the other rings, but they would not. Then there was a flurry in the ring to his left, a 106-pound boxer taking down his opponent, and the crowds forgot Eddie and they looked and there were "oooh's" and "ahh's" in the darkness. An official came into Eddie's ring and raised the glove of the boy from Kansas City. Kell looked at Eddie now and picked him up from the canvas, and took off his face mask, and then, for the first time in Eddie's memory, hugged him, saying nothing, squeezed him until the lights again dimmed, and there was laughter—he heard it, heard it from boys, Kronk boys in robes waiting to fight. Laughing because he'd fallen so fast. A record, Eddie thought. He wanted to beat the laughing boys; he wanted to start the fight again. He could beat the boy from Kansas City now. Tommy leaned over the ropes; a Gloves official told him they must leave the ring now, and Dr. Rosenfels patted Eddie on the back, and Tommy waved at them, and they went out together as the decisions came in the adjacent ring, to applause. Janitors dressed in white with latex gloves came to scrub the canvas with Pine Sol, to clean the blood, dry up the sweat.

Eddie hurried down the stairs, the doctor behind him, feeling his cheeks, staring into his eyes. He wondered if Akbar would hear about this and take back the contract.

In Dr. Rosenfels's makeshift office the doctor put ointment on Eddie's tongue to stop the bleeding, passed him a capful of Listerine to wash the blood out of his mouth, and Xanax because there was gloom on his face.

"Go on, take it, Eddie, you look fazed," said Tommy.

Eddie swallowed the Xanax down with a Dixie cup of water. "They was laughing," Eddie said.

"No, they wasn't," said Tommy.

"Nobody was laughing at you, son," said Kell.

"They was," Eddie said. "I heard them. The Kronk boys and the other ones. They think they is the shit."

Dr. Rosenfels had that reserved look of melancholy, like the elegant people in front rows. Eddie turned to Dr. Rosenfels. "They was laughing, wasn't they, Doctor? You heard them."

"I don't know," said Dr. Rosenfels, turning to Kell. "I can leave more Xanax with you for the kid."

Kell nodded.

"We're flying back tonight, to Phoenix, Dr. Rosenfels," said Tommy.

"Then watch him, watch him on the plane. Physically, he is fine, but watch his mood. Some take it hard." Dr. Rosenfels tapped out Xanax pills from a pillbox in his jacket into a business-sized envelope, and passed the envelope to Kell. There was a rise in the crowds outside, the sound of applause—already, a boy had fallen in the second round, and he was this moment climbing to his feet. They waited for the crowds to go quiet, then Tommy and Kell escorted Eddie outside, down the hallway of waiting, nervous boys in robes, down the street to the taxi, which took them back to the Chicago Hilton and Towers, and they flew back that night to Phoenix.

Book Four

Straw Men

*T*hree letters, little, colored, scented, in envelopes, the city of Phoenix misspelled, lay on his pillow. He sat at his desk and swallowed another Xanax, staring at them. Tessa had written him from California, over a space of months, but the letters were all postmarked April 22, 1995. She'd waited so long. He wondered why. Had she met a man? Was she coming back to Phoenix? April 22—the very day the sheriff bused Turtle off to Florence.

Eddie, Im out. Turtle fuckin crazy. Im goin back to Oak Town. I run out the dead womans house from Turtle and I run up 27 Street. . . . I seen Turtle shoot Jules. I take my purse and run out. I spitz up in the weeds. Turtle be yelling at me. He be chasing afer me. I goes way way up north to Indean School Rode. I ♥ you Im scarred.

She'd run from Turtle, out of the dead woman's house that night. She'd gone to the Bank of America the next morning, closed her account, bought a used car at a car lot, and drove to California. The first letter came in a Motel 6 envelope, the return address an obscure California town, but the last two envelopes had the same return address: *Room #6, Aegis Motel, Oakland, CA.* He knew Tessa lived at this motel now; he imagined her slow migration to California, from motel to motel, Tessa driving along I-10. That she might live in one certain place, he thought, and offer this news to him now, when just this morning he'd failed in Chicago, when Akbar might not sign him now. He had to get to Vegas soon and sign Akbar's contract before Akbar changed his mind. Twenty-six seconds. He read the other letters; they were dark, like Tessa's moods in the months after she'd fled . . . a daily account of sorrow, boredom, each day walking Dwight St., in Oakland, the sun beating on her face, of seeing old high school classmates at the grocery store, at the gas station, dressed in hooker clothes. *They smile at me and pretend like they dont remember me.*

Then he searched the letters for a phone number, her pager. She said she loved him, but she did not leave a phone number. She was struggling in Oakland and she could not see him now. He had nothing to offer her anyway. He had to make his life in Vegas first, find her in Oakland, coax her back to Vegas with him. He would be in charge of things now. This was the situation. She would have to accept the situation. The boy would be a problem. Why did she not give up? he wondered, when they could make a child together, a child to replace her child, and it, their new life, the new child, would drive him, make him hard and focused like Johnny Tapia at the Hilton bar, the suspension lifted, plotting his comeback.

I folowed the hiway to Cali. I thot about you the hole way down. God I love you. I love you and I alway loved you. It hurted me to run from you without saying it, without telling you good-by. ♥ Tessa. ♥ ♥ ♥

He lay on the bed and slept. He had to get out of the city soon, to-morrow or the day after. He did not have time for good-byes. He would save the good-byes for Vegas pay phones.

In the morning he scribbled a flowery, frantic letter to her on note-book paper. He promised her he loved her for real like a grown man. He was a man. He was a broken man. Turtle had ruined his life by shooting Jules for no good reason, sent her, his true love, running away from him again, sent Detective Patricia after him. Detective Patricia had ambushed him, Eddie wrote her, had cops beat him with clubs. He'd joined the Nation for that, and the Nation was like the army: they taught you to dress and act and clean yourself and talk and carry yourself with respect, but now he had to do things his own way. When she saw him he would have the big money, he promised.

Akbar said his weaknesses were blatant. He had to work on them. Vegas would be like Chicago seven times multiplied. *Then I go to the Bank of America and close my acount. I lay low for a cople days. I feel lik Turtle will kill me Eddie. I bot me a car at the Auto Sale a old Bonvil '81 for $600. It run good.*

He was staring out his window at the park. He went to see Mar-chalina one last time. He bought her flowers from the Roosevelt St. rose peddlers and trekked to her town house in the afternoon. She took the flowers and set them on the bed. Her face was red. She was crying. She'd just gotten off the phone with Wilma. Marchalina was studying for finals. Every conceivable schoolbook was splayed open on her bed. Marchalina cleared the bed, sighed, and sat Eddie down on it. Wilma had said something, and Marchalina was furious. "Wilma is a bitch," Marchalina said. "I'm moving out of here this summer. Wilma is a fucking snob. We can get an apartment if you want."

"What happened?"

"She won't be happy until I'm a bitter black self-hating bitch like her. She wants to ruin my life, you know." She wiped her eyes. She looked at him. "Oh, she doesn't understand why I'm still talking to you. I told her you were competing in Chicago. I told her you might go to the Olympics someday. She doesn't even know you, Eddie. She's never said one word to you."

He lay on Marchalina's bed while she crammed for finals. He'd never gone back to school. He did not belong with her. If he didn't make it big in Vegas, he'd have to get his GED. He squeezed his eyes shut. ♥ *Tessa.* He'd read the letters the night before, memorized them, brought the paper to his nose and sniffed. He should be with Tessa now. He should tell Marchalina that he was leaving for Vegas in a few days, but he did not want to watch her crying again. He should run this moment from the little brown-skinned girl, take the next bus. Then he forgot Tessa, for in a moment Marchalina was atop him, bending down in the darkness, kissing his mouth, staring. "I'm still mad at you." She laughed. "You didn't call me from Chicago. I knew it hadn't gone your way when you didn't call me. I'm mad at you. You didn't tell me what it was like, Chicago. I am supposed to be the one you tell. You don't tell me anything, anything."

Drifting to sleep at night on Marchalina's floor, he imagined the Aegis next to a highway of rushing cars. He was naked atop Tessa, and they were making a child together on the faded Aegis Motel sheets to the sound of the traffic of the street outside, sunshine flashing through the window, a child to be the child he was, watching her from the closet in 1987, the once muted child screaming into his palm. Tessa lay naked beneath him, his face pressed against hers; he'd never felt so close to another being, so connected; and he woke to the most pleasant sensation, the rawest joy, of making love to Tessa after the long highway journey to California, on her motel bed, a sensation all the more perfect because he came without a single unfocused thought, a single distraction . . . the elation of making a child with her, and he woke atop Marchalina, Marchalina staring at him in the darkness. "Where's the condom?"

"I was sleeping."

"You just got me pregnant!" Marchalina whispered. Eddie looked at her clock. It was three in the morning. She pulled her nightshirt down to her knees, cracked the door to see if Wilma was up, and darted down the hallway to the bathroom. Eddie sat up. He heard the bathroom fan, Marchalina running the faucet. The little brown-skinned girl was in a panic, washing his sperm out of her, every trace of him, the future flashing before her. Marchalina came back and shut the bedroom door behind her. Her voice was sharp. "You dick, you were trying to get me pregnant! Like I'm some hood rat. I'm a fucking junior, Eddie. Wilma said you'd try something stupid like this." She'd washed herself in the bathroom, washed him out of her.

"I was sleeping. I didn't mean it." He wanted to run. He would pack his bags and run down to the bus station tonight.

He stared at Marchalina in the faint window light. The high school crush was grown, his live-in girlfriend, the little brown face that once seemed forever trapped between adolescence and adult-hood the face of a worn-out woman, dirty children at her legs; she'd gained thirty pounds; he worked at an AutoZone. He sold brake pads. He herded boys for Kell, mopped his floor. Hauled soda pop in crates around the city.

She had only herself to blame. Her mama told her so. "You want me to be like Sherice?"

"No."

"She takes food stamps. I saw her use them at the Albertson's one time. I wanted to cry."

"No."

"You want me to drop out to have a baby? God, Eddie, is there anything you won't do to push me away?" He put on his jeans, his shirt, his sneakers. He opened Marchalina's window, sticking his leg out. "That's it," Marchalina said. "That's exactly what you should do." Marchalina was sobbing, and slapping his arm, almost shout-ing in the dark room, but even this could not wake him; he was still, half sleeping, lost in the fantasy of Tessa just five minutes before, the motel bed in Oakland. He felt dirty. He'd ruined the little brown-skinned girl's life. Allah would punish him.

"Go on, run away," Marchalina told him. "I'll have to ride my bike to the clinic tomorrow morning and skip first period, take the morning-after pill!" She was staring at him, wiping her eyes with another Kleenex.

He climbed out the window and went down the fire escape and ran south down the street. He imagined Pops running to Amarillo in 1987. Who could blame you for running from a cruel city, a screaming black woman, when you had no prospects? He ran home, went through the front door, inside his room, ran to his desk, and opened Dr. Rosenfels's business envelope of Xanax, scraping his finger along the bottom and finding it empty.

He looked up. Adolpho was tapping at his bedroom window, waving him outside.

Pink sunlight broke over the mountains. "Come on," Adolpho said, and he drove Eddie to an IHOP. They ate pancakes, alone in the empty restaurant as the sun came up. Adolpho had spent forty days in the Los Angeles County California State Prison for stealing a BMW and for being in possession of stolen property. Adolpho got seventeen months, but the prison was so overcrowded that Adolpho was out in time to come back to Phoenix for his baby son's third birthday.

Adolpho drove Eddie to his farmhouse in the morning. They slept in the living room, and Eddie woke on Adolpho's sofa at noon, Adolpho beneath him on the floor sleeping on a blanket. Uncle Balthazar set a plate of Juanita's fresh-made lunch before him, pulling at the shocks of his hemp-colored hair. Eddie and Adolpho, spreading door beads with their bodies, went into the kitchen, where Juanita stood, beaming at Eddie. By afternoon there were mamas and their babies in the backyard, Adolpho's sister Elvira, Adolpho's boy running around naked on the dirt. Eddie sat next to Adolpho on a beach chair. Adolpho pointed at a boy running about in diapers. "He don't recognize me no more," he said, sipping a beer. Adolpho's baby son kept swinging at a piñata with a broom handle until dusk, when the piñata exploded to the laughter of brown naked clapping children, exploded on its string, streamers, candy, crumpled dollar bills, coins bursting out, Adolpho's baby boy screaming in laughter as the piñata came unseamed, the boy snatching candy from the dirt. Adolpho stood. "Come on, Eddie, let's go," he said, and they were winding down the hill to Adolpho's hooptie, Juanita, Uncle Balthazar waving good-bye.

Adolpho drove drunk on beers and high on tabs.

They stopped at a Circle K so Adolpho could get some cigarettes. At the Circle K, a tired Mexican man in a Dalton, cowboy boots, and denim shirt stood, whispering something to the clerk, who pushed a nickel, a penny, and a dime across the counter. "I don't speak Spanish," said the clerk.

"*Marquetta, por favor,*" said the man in the Dalton.

"I don't speak Spanish."

"*Marquetta, marquetta.*"

"He want a receipt," Adolpho shouted from across the store, squeezing a bag of Wonder Bread. Adolpho was staring at the cashier. The clerk tore off a curl of receipt and passed it to the man in the Dalton, who thanked Adolpho from the door and jogged out with a pack of generic menthols. Adolpho bought his own cigarettes and waved Eddie outside.

Adolpho's body was covered in tattoos, gothic prison tattoos. In the parking lot, lighting a cigarette, Adolpho lifted up his T-shirt and flashed his brown belly. *Black Indian. Mafioso.* He'd had his hooptie detailed in L.A. before his incarceration. On the hood there was an airbrushed Aztec goddess, floating in an ether cloud. Adolpho was drunk, high, and Eddie was high because Adolpho had snuck tabs in

Eddie's lemonade. Eddie remembered, as Adolpho pulled away from the convenience store, he'd promised Elvira he'd find track marks on Adolpho's body last year, and he'd found them and never told her. The hooptie began to float, to rise from the ground, to levitate . . . it was floating across the street! Black boys gawked, toothpicks falling from their mouths, cigarettes; they were pointing from Broadway Rd., the magic hooptie bathed in foggy light! Adolpho smiled at Eddie. There were fresh tracks. Eddie saw them now.

Eddie had no hint where they could be going, wanted only to return to Adolpho's farmhouse, to fall asleep in the slanted house, the house of cousins and uncles and Tejano music, to feel safe, to exist in memory, to run the next morning across the empty fields with Turtle. But the hooptie was this moment flying. Adolpho turned, looked at Eddie's eyes again. "I see you, man. I see you. You didn't see Turtle off to Florence. I dreamed about you, Eddie Eagle. Good things. Good things. Eddie don't trust me no more. You hate me like you hate your brother." The hooptie floated—floated!—along 16th St. like the buxom airbrushed Aztec goddess on Adolpho's hood. The hooptie floated above the cotton fields, above parked tractors, past St. Mary's, Mary the Mother of God painted three stories tall on its east side. . . . The boxy car floated! floated! floated! thirty feet above, across the black sky, and Adolpho knew it, and Eddie knew it. It was happening to both of them at once, and there was no need to say it. Adolpho wanted to go to Naranja Park to look at the city from atop the hills. He steered left, and the hooptie banked like an airplane.

Eddie cowered on the grassy hill, sobbing. He did not know why. They'd left the hooptie on a street, doors open, headlights on, radio blasting oldies. They made their way to the park, wandered across the grass, and climbed. Adolpho heard barking dogs. Eddie heard them too, taut dog bodies racing to them, paws scraping the grass. Adolpho ran so fast. Eddie bumped his knee against a park bench, tumbled. Adolpho tripped, too. When Adolpho tripped, his kit fell out across the grass, and there was Adolpho searching the grass for his syringe, his spoon.

Adolpho climbed to his feet. "Forty days I got sent up in Cali," he was saying. "Forty days exact. You know, like Jesus and Moses in the desert. The L.A.C. was my desert. I seen my son growing up without me. I seen my son hating on me like how I hate on my daddy. I think I wanted to get sent up in L.A. We all get what we want. Your brother got sent up to Florence, and you didn't see him off."

They had to overcome an iron fence. Eddie jumped into the park. He turned to find Adolpho landing on the grass behind him. Adolpho ran to the hills and began to climb. Eddie found himself running after him, after this drunken, bearded man he no longer knew. The climb was long. Adolpho stood at the summit, Eddie behind him, looking at the city itself. Adolpho's house, the project towers, the back of his own house, the Third Ward, the city of Phoenix, the world beyond. Adolpho touched his arm. "My baby son don't know me, Eddie. I fucked up my life." Eddie looked at him. Adolpho was crying, crying in the darkness. Adolpho was not the same, he thought. Nothing was the same.

A police cruiser burst down the highway in the distance, siren blaring beneath them, riot lights. Eddie ran his fingers through the grass, breathed. Barking dogs in the hills below, nearing. A flashlight appeared in the darkness, a guard, a cop calling to them. Adolpho and Eddie jogged down the hill to the gate, the gate an impossibility now, too high to climb, sharp black spikes! Adolpho knelt with his hands locked and Eddie stepped and climbed—the same moment worrying for Adolpho—and shoved himself over the prongs, falling to the grass, Adolpho after him.

"The cops is after us," Adolpho said. "Right behind us, Eddie! I got warrants out! I can't stop."

Adolpho was steering . . . the hooptie floated over the hills, black boys watching, jealous, because Eddie was floating with Adolpho, and they, the poor boys, could not float. . . . Eddie began to laugh, to shout as the car rose from the street. He was floating with Adolpho! Adolpho landed the magic hooptie in the middle of Central Ave. like an airplane on a runway. Eddie jutted his head out of the window, vomiting into the rushing air. "The cops!" Adolpho said.

Eddie wiped his mouth, looked for cops. "No, Adolpho, no cops."

"I need you do me a favor. I just need a place to be alone and shoot up. I feel a seizure coming on." Eddie nodded. "There we go. I see you, nigger." The hooptie was hurling across Central Ave. Adolpho stopped the hooptie before a flophouse on Adams St. Eddie looked at his own jeans; there were grass stains; he was sliding down the slippery grass hills of Woodland Park on a bag of ice, Adolpho behind him, laughing, laughing until the bags crashed.

Inside the flophouse Eddie paid the clerk. How the piñata had burst apart in the waning light the hours before, into a thousand bits, Adolpho staring at his baby boy. The clerk buzzed them in. The stairway seemed six stories high. At the top a bare, bone white lightbulb, blinking. Adolpho leaned on Eddie. A couple of drunks lugged a little brown refrigerator down the stairs.

On the second floor Eddie unlocked the door for Adolpho and walked him inside the room. There was a window and a mattress. Adolpho opened the kit, felt his pocket for his Zippo, removed his belt. "Call my mama." Eddie wiped his mouth with his shirt, nodded, leaned against a rotting wall as Adolpho latched the belt around his tattooed biceps. "Take me to the window," Adolpho said. Eddie carried him there, sat Adolpho on a radiator. He stared out. Laid his kit out on the windowsill. A car sped down Adams St. Adolpho tightened the belt tourniquet with his teeth, peered at his tattooed wrist of Mary the Mother of God. Shaking spoon over Zippo flame. Heroin bubbles. Eddie had not seen it before, how it looked, bubbling heroin. Akbar would save him in Vegas. Like he promised. They would make prayer together out behind the gym. He would go to

Mecca, like Malcolm in the movie, and pray for Adolpho's soul. Adolpho poured the warm heroin juice into the syringe, shoved the needle into Mary's bosom. Adolpho tightened the belt with his teeth. "Push it for me, brother. Push it for me, Eddie Eagle. I can't go home tonight. I see you, man. I see you, Eddie Eagle. I know you hate your brother. God, why couldn't you see Turtle off to Florence? He is your brother."

"You are my brother," Eddie said, pushing the plunger. Adolpho's head flopped back in joy. Adolpho wept, removed the syringe, and set the syringe in his kit, the kit upon the checkerboard tile floor. Adolpho began to shake, Eddie kneeling above him. Adolpho clutched Eddie's foot. There was Adolpho shaking on the floor beneath him, knowing, waiting. Call my mama. But I can't. The spasms will break, Eddie thought. Please stop. Please stop. He waited, Adolpho panting, shaking. But the spasms did not stop. Someone passed down the hall outside. Adolpho's legs beat against the floor. He shouted, mouth filled with dark blood. Old drunks banged at the door. Adolpho stared at Eddie, squeezed his hand. *I love you, Eddie.* He was dead, Eddie thought, dying! And the flophouse attendant, the old men in the hallway, had seen him walk Adolpho up the stairs. He felt Adolpho's face. You is dead! I can't go to jail right now. The face was warm, but there was no pulse; he could not be certain because his own heart was beating so hard. Call my mama. No, I can't tell her you dead. Eddie stood, in a panic, rubbing his fingerprints off the doorknob, like a criminal, wiping the barrel of the syringe, the plunger, with the bottom of his T-shirt. He rushed down the staircase, old drunks watching him, and out the lobby door.

*H*e woke in Woodland Park under the tree the next morning, the money in his pockets stolen, dried vomit on his mouth. He wandered up the hill and into his house. Mama and Pops were both at work. He found Nana in the kitchen, scrubbing the counters with a rag. "A man called for you," she said. "It sounded official. A boxing thing. Where you been at, boy?"

"Adolpho's house," he told her. "Adolpho come back yesterday."

Nana looked at Eddie and squeezed her rag in worry.

"Who call me, Nana?"

"A man from Las Vegas. There is a spot opened up for you, he say, or something, but he needs you there by tomorrow. You better call him right back."

Eddie ran to his room and called the telephone number on Akbar's card. The sultry woman from Akbar's Hilton suite answered the phone, asked Eddie for his social security number, his date of birth. He wondered if Akbar had heard about Chicago. He must know. He wondered if he should tell her now, just to be honest, make sure Akbar hadn't heard about the KO and changed his mind, but there was no time. The woman was speaking so fast. "Okay," he said. "I can be there." She told him to bring his driver's license with him. She was this moment filling out his Nevada boxing license. Eddie told her he would be there tomorrow afternoon.

He couldn't go to Vegas without Tommy. He packed his bags. He took the number 87 bus up north that night to Tommy's job. He'd never seen Tommy at work before. He found him in a Sizzler line-cook uniform, a hair net pulled across his stringy hair, in a back kitchen, throwing pads of meat on a grill. "What are you doing here?" Tommy said. "Is Kell okay?"

"I got a Vegas N.A.C.-sanctioned bout, Tommy. Akbar said he could get me others, depending."

"Who?"

"The man in Chicago. Akbar Muhammad."

"Come on, Eddie. When?"

"Saturday. I need you to come with me, be my cut man. Whatever he pay me, I'll give you half."

A server appeared and gave Tommy an order. Tommy looked at it and threw a frozen chicken breast on the grill.

"Saturday, as in tomorrow? Fuck you. Eddie, I don't know." Tommy flipped a pad of beef. "Have you seen Kell? Have you gone by there? They shut the place down. The landlord put a bolt on the front door. Kell ain't got nowhere to go. The old man had to sneak back in through the fire escape. All the boys went over to Ricardo's gym. I bring Kell food. The stable mothers check on him, but you don't." Tommy gave Eddie a look. "I just got an apartment off Indian School Rd., Eddie. I like this job. They don't fuck me with the hours. I been riding this busted-up ten-speed around, but I'm saving up for a car. My cousin is a deputy in Apache Junction. He's going to help me study for the police officer exam this time." Tommy looked at Eddie.

He turned around in a jolt and put his hands on the aluminum counter behind him, staring at his reflection. "Goddamn it," he shouted and ripped off his hair net, his apron, and tossed them both in the hamper.

They found Kell in the foul boiler room. They had to climb the fire escape and go through the top window, run down the mezzanine stairs, because the landlord had bolted the front door. Crunched beer cans sat around Kell's sofa like a moat. He was passed out.

"We leaving now," Eddie told the unconscious man. "We left liquor for you."

"Ain't like you can use the van," said Tommy.

"I know you'd have gotten me up to Vegas if you could," Eddie said, "and I don't hold nothing personal against you for all your lapses and your lies, and the things you promised, except that it would have been better that way." They left Kell a store of marked-down booze from the Liquor Giant and ran out to steal the club conversion van.

In the parking lot Tommy unlocked the passenger door for Eddie.

They swung by Tommy's apartment at midnight. Tommy packed his country music tapes, his boxes, emptied the refrigerator of sandwich meat and wheat bread, stuffed all his belongings in two duffel bags, set them in the back of the conversion van, and he drove Eddie back to South Phoenix. He parked before Eddie's house, and Eddie ran inside to get his bags. Pops's Cadillac sat running in the driveway, trunk open. He was running back to Amarillo.

"Hey, Eddie, huh?" Pops whispered on the front lawn, a box of his clothes in his arms. "Thought you left already, huh? I guess you see me running away again. What? What? I'm going to Amarillo, son, back to stay with your uncle for a while. I suppose you disappointed at me."

"No, Pops." It was natural to run when there was nothing left. He took the man's bags and set them in the backseat of his Cadillac for him. Pops smiled at him, went back into the house, took another laundry bag of his clothing, fresh from the dryer, and set the bag in the trunk. "I suppose your mama will be happy now. Have the house to herself. You take care of her, huh?" Pops said. "She don't, huh, know about this just yet," he whispered, "but your nana will explain it. What you say?"

Now Pops climbed into the front seat of the Cadillac and unlatched the parking brake, backing out of the driveway with his headlights off. "And always be your own man in life, huh, huh? And, and you walk with the angels now, you hear? And remember what I taught you, huh! There wasn't nobody like you before you, and there won't be nobody like you after. Yes sir," said Pops. "My boy. Huh? Huh? What?" And with that, Pops gave Eddie a crisp salute, started the Cadillac, turned on his headlights, and drove away down the dark road.

Eddie hurried into the house to get his bags and found Mama in her bedroom, her pretty face lit in the light of the window. "Goodbye, Mama, I'm going to Vegas now to be a fighter for real." Eddie bent over and kissed Mama's cheek.

"Your nana told me. You just gonna leave me like that? You be safe in that city. You call."

They looked together out her window at the empty driveway. "He'll come back again," Eddie said.

"I know he will," said Mama, shaking her head, "and so will you."

With Tommy he passed through the dark South Phoenix streets, the van rushing past one-story houses, music pounding from curbside boom boxes, boys in tank tops on lit stoops huddled and staring at Eddie inside, as if to call him back to Phoenix. The two-room houses rushing past his window seemed like far-off outposts to him now.

Tommy took the exit ramp. When they'd driven two hours north, too far to turn back, Eddie turned to Tommy in the van. "Listen," he said, each word occurring to him as he spoke it, "I ain't got nothing but this."

"Go to sleep, Eddie."

The van was nearing Yuma, hurling across the spine of the road. It was two hours before dawn, light falling over the dust fields. "This guy in Vegas," Tommy asked as Eddie drifted to sleep. "This Akbar. You didn't ask him about the money? You didn't even sign the contract? You didn't ask about the guy you're fighting, his record? Somebody calls you, tells you to fill in for somebody on the spot, and you just show up?"

Eddie slept until Yuma; he dreamed of Adolpho. He dreamed that Adolpho was sitting in the flophouse where he'd left him, at the window; he saw Adolpho turning from the window and waving at him.

He slept some more until he heard Tommy easing the van to a halt on Hacienda Rd. before a downtown motel above the Arizona Charlie's mini casino, where Akbar had rented them a couple rooms. Old beehived women tugged at slot machines in the blinking darkness.

They had just enough time to unpack, to shower, before running back to the van. Eddie felt his nerves go. He hadn't slept three hours in the last two days. Tommy steered the dying van across the highway. The fight was scheduled for eight rounds. It was four o'clock when they saw it, the auditorium, a gargoyle-colored hangar before them, rusting in sunshine, twenty miles out of the city. Tommy stopped the van before a bunch of beat-up American pickups and then European luxury cars circling the hangar like a moat, whispering, "Come on, Eddie, let's go," jogging with his second's kit across the red dirt, under cacti, Eddie running behind him in the filthy Bumpy's robe.

The auditorium ran five stories high. The ring sat off center, under banks of thirty-foot-tall floodlights. He saw cameras, spectators, middleweights in the fourth round fighting. Blood beat in his temples at the sight of cameras turning on axles, cameras zooming in and out, cameras hung from the skybox, on the ring floor. The upper rows, the ten-dollar-a-seat rows, were wild, of angry shouting, ugly men in caps and T-shirts, drinking beer, concessionaires running between them, tossing bags of popcorn, selling nuts and beer. Eddie's mouth went dry. Eddie followed Tommy through ranks of beautiful people sitting at the ringside tables, who saw him in the robe, knowing, whispering into cupped ears about him. Continental Boxing Federation banners, blue and gold, fluttered on the tall aluminum walls.

He found Tommy before the locker room door, a converted employee kitchen. An hour passed. The fights were running thirty minutes behind schedule. Inside, a defeated middleweight undercard, a wiry black man with sideburns, stripped out of his robe, his trunks, offering his naked brown buttocks to his cussing manager, his second, and strode barefoot to the showers, the manager, the second having just whispered something calm and assuring to his tattooed back. There was a rise in the crowd outside, shouts and applause, and the second and manager of the showering middleweight went to the door to look at the fight, in its third round, another middleweight undercard bout, of fighters a tier below their own man, in which they took only passing interest, confiding to each other that neither of the now competing fighters were good enough to fight him, even now, on his second straight loss. Tommy laid Eddie on a towel on the bench and rubbed his shoulders. Eddie looked up. Akbar appeared in a silk shirt and jacket, smelling of musk, his hand outstretched. "You realize that fight was just cable televised, boy."

"No sir." Eddie sat up and shook Akbar's hand.

Tommy shook it, too. He introduced himself. "I know the kid was amped to fight," he said, "so he didn't talk to you about the money so much, but I guess we best talk about the money. Like how much is the purse, how much the kid get otherwise? I imagine you charge us for the registration, about which I'd like to be informed."

Akbar was frowning. "The boy takes an AIDS test next week." He turned to Tommy, who watched him, squeezing a towel. "And fills out a psychological evaluation test, true-or-false questions. 'I like to play with myself.' 'Sometimes I think I am a fruitcake,' et cetera. Does a sit-down with some people from the Nevada Athletic Commission. As a favor to me, they let him fight tonight without the prelims, but they watch us close, the N.A.C.'s.

"Fellas, those N.A.C.'s don't like us. They don't want to see no more governing bodies. You see, fellas, the C.B.F. is about the common man, which your involvement only demonstrates, and Tommy, Tommy, is that your name? That is the truth cause we don't pimp our fighters. So, boy, they will ask you questions about me. I'm an uppity nigger in their book. 'What kind of cologne does that baldheaded nigger use?' they'll ask you. 'Who did he vote for for governor last election?' Just remember the N.A.C.'s are as corrupt as a two-cent ho. They got motherfuckers selling rankings, fixing fights, you understand, but they want to look at Akbar. They got cats fighting with gonorrhea, fighting coked-up and all that, in them so-called establishment bodies, but they want to pin something on Akbar, dig? Purse is two thou, the show-up is a thousand, which you best split between the two of you cause we told the kid he didn't need no management in the C.B.F."

Eddie slapped Tommy's shoulder. "A thousand dollars, Tommy, two thousand more if I win!"

"I told you I would take care of you, boy," said Akbar. He produced documents from his attaché case, Eddie's Nevada boxing license, the C.B.F. contract, which he placed into Eddie's hand with a pen, glaring at Tommy.

Tommy stared at Eddie. "Go on, sign them, bro."

Eddie took a pen from Akbar's hand, signed the documents, page upon page, a sense of his own significance welling. He signed the documents, the waivers, and the releases; he initialed. Akbar disappeared. Eddie watched the ring from the dressing room, the card girl traipsing about the ring in the ninth round. One of the fighters got stung with a stiff jab; he bled from the mouth. Eddie watched the blood go splat across the apron.

Tommy rubbed Eddie's neck, waved him out of the locker room, into the giant room, and they strode down between the small front-row candlelit tables, under the banks of men chanting from the high, ten-dollar seats, in the direction of turned heads, the crowd meager, as an old chubby white janitor knelt on the bright springy apron, wiping the blood with ammonia and bleach, the auditorium smelling now of malt beer and perfume and ammonia. Eddie watched the exhaust fans turning on the dark ceiling above; his muscles felt cold.

It was easy work. His opponent was out of shape, a Quechen Indian named Clyde Williams, from Yuma, who hopped about in mismatched Pony boots. The bell rang and Eddie raced to him. Pads of fat hung from Clyde's back, from his corpulent stomach. His black hair was tied in a ponytail. He bit down on his worn blue mouthpiece as Eddie beat him. Now the rushing darkness. Eddie beat Clyde from the start, all nausea draining out of him as he struck the Quechen's plump chest, his burnished cheeks.

The round over, Eddie sat on a stool as now Tommy whispered into his left ear and then his right, sponging water across his face, prepping him in the meager light, as Eddie stared at the card girl's high-heel shoes. Clyde was standing in the opposite corner, without a second, his shorts hilted to one side, belly hanging, biting on the chewed-up mouthpiece, gasping for breath, watching the card girl's bouncing breasts as she waved the round card before the upper rows and the candlelit tables. Eddie noticed the judges watching him, suspicious. Then he saw them jotting again, making slashes with the tips of their no. 2 pencils (the bell had rung), and he was jogging through a cloud of perfume left by the descending card girl, sending Clyde back in little flurries, the pencil tips slashing across notepads below, slashing for him, the Quechen grimacing, the bell sounding again (the round—it had only lasted a second), another card girl climbing inside, Eddie watching her round, happy face as Tommy sponged his head.

A good fight, Eddie thought. The crowd was amped. He stood, ran at Clyde. He thought of how he'd spend the prize money. He sensed appreciation in the crowd. He counted the dollars Akbar would pay him in his mind's eye, $3,000 divided by two, $1,500. Tommy fed Eddie water. At the bell Eddie ran to Clyde and cut him off at two corners, squared his shoulders to him, beating Clyde's stomach with his fists, slapping the crown of Clyde's head. The men in cheap suits and the women in bright lipstick stood, the robed fighters, Dr. Testa, the ring doctor, the judges, now knowing, now believing, leaning forward in the dark and revolving periphery; and Eddie went at Clyde with his fists, sent them into his cheeks, finding in each jab, each hook, a kind of redemption for it—the ward, his boyhood, a kind of stretched-out torment, his life—for whatever it was, whatever he felt now rising in his throat, the innumerable sufferings, pummeled into the Quechen's cheeks; and above the poverty and above the now realized and now surmounted degradation, the longing and hunger, the realization that he would be rich, for the card girl, staring half naked from darkness, saw it, setting the useless posterboard at her feet—and how he pitied the girl because she'd fixed a sum of money to her own degradation—smiling in the backdrop because she saw it, his redemption, as the Quechen fell on his back.

Tommy ran into the ring and squeezed Eddie, each of them thinking of the money. The men in the ten-dollar seats roared from the high walls. Tommy set the robe on Eddie's shoulders, laughing, whispering happy words about how proud Kell would be when he found out, and followed Eddie down the scaffold. People tipped glasses, cups of beer, cigars, and cigarettes at Eddie. A glamorous brunette smiled at him from a candlelit dining table. The referee stopped him at the locker room door to shake his hand.

Eddie found his opponent in the locker room, the yawning Quechen, changing into his street clothes, wiping the sweat from his shoulders with paper towels, preening himself in the dressing room mirror, spraying his unshowered body with cologne, combing his beautiful black hair. He was rushing off somewhere. Eddie approached him, calling him now by name. "Clyde," he said. "You fought good."

Clyde glanced at him and spat chewing tobacco in a brown paper bag. He put on a white button-down shirt. "I let you win," he said, going through a worn duffel bag.

"Hey, don't be so hard on yourself."

Clyde climbed into a red valet vest with CLYDE stitched on the left side. He shut his locker. "No, I threw the fight. Mr. Muhammad paid me to do it," Clyde whispered, shouldering his gym bag, strutting out of the dressing room in his valet uniform.

Akbar met them along the Strip at eleven with women, two administrative assistants, and a large-bosomed escort who went by Amanda, who stared at Eddie from the middle seat of Akbar's Expedition as the casino lights burned through the window tint. Eddie wondered why Akbar had brought an escort along unless it was to test him. He stared out the window at the unknown streets, seeing Turtle in the conk-haired pimps in roll chains along certain streets, who stared at the Expedition from dark corners, from parked, souped-up cars.

Akbar's driver dropped them off at the front entrance of La Fleur. The wind blew hot. Akbar led them inside, into booming violins and across a maize rug, where the maître d' recognized Akbar by face

and seated them all at a long covered table, waiters offering dark
jackets to Eddie and Tommy, who sat across from the big-bosomed
escort—Tommy kept staring at her. The maître d' returned and took
Akbar to select a few bottles from the wine cellar. Akbar darted
across the room of clanking utensils and glass, as from every other
corner one silver-haired man or another waved at Akbar furiously.

Akbar returned with two bottles, which orbited the table, the bald
man now tasting, now sipping. Above the violins Akbar raised a glass
with the table and made a toast. Eddie stared at him from across the
table. He watched the sultry blond woman make a sexy face at Akbar, and he realized she was his girlfriend, his mistress. Then five
minutes later there was the same exchange with Akbar and the brunette, and Eddie gasped. There would be no pilgrimage to Mecca, no
trips to the mosque. The bald man would not save him; he main-
tained only the minor tenets of the religion, ignoring the larger ones,
like sobriety and fidelity, but asked about the pork content of the
mushroom-and-carrot sauce on which his baked filet sat, fondling
the thigh of each mistress through the evening, yet mumbling Arabic
prayers under his breath before consuming his meal, which he did
in the Muslim way, beginning at the perimeter, right hand moving
inward, the same meal he consumed with red wine. He wore tonight
a black shimmering collarless smock shirt under his jacket, something reminiscent of a Middle Eastern djellaba Eddie'd seen the
bearded, orthodox brothers wearing in the hood, but silken, shining;
he appeared as if drawn from one of the old-time paintings Eddie
had seen in the Islamic art book in the mosque library, the Moor
leaning against the wall, his black head shaved bald, and he wore a
dark mustache, darker than his skin, his voice slurring with slowly
sipped wine.

A couple appeared at the table the next hour, a brawny, good-
looking man with linebacker shoulders and a cowlick. His redhead
wife sat beside him, dressed in a bright conservative blouse, sitting

down in the center of the table across from Amanda. Akbar raised his glass. "This is Van Brett, previously of the Arena Football League, the Nashville Kats, and Ronnie, his wife."

"You signed?" cried one of Akbar's mistresses. "Akbar signed you with C.B.F.?"

"To box?" said the other.

Van Brett was nodding, his wife with him.

"He's in a lull," said Ronnie Brett. "His agent said the boxing might be good between scripts. And Van's a born jock."

"Beautiful!" said a mistress, sipping.

"Why not?" said Van Brett, flexing his biceps. "Kick some ass in the L.V."

"What about the show, the pilot, what about living in Hollywood?"

Ronnie Brett drew a finger across her neck.

"Oh, oh, no!" said the first mistress.

"But I just saw him on TV, last week," said the other. "He was a cop—no, a detective!"

"That was a walk-on. That was the detective deal. That was not the pilot. They cut the pilot, hon. But he'll make it," said Ronnie Brett. "This is the important thing. He's got the look they're looking for. It's like you made the cutoff, you know, to have the look they're looking for. My girlfriend, she works at this spa they have down there in Hollywood called Epiphanies, so she knows all this stuff. And she was saying the week before Van and me come down how your average successful actor makes one, two failed pilots before he comes into a winner."

Akbar's mistresses nodded in unison. Van Brett took up a menu, Ronnie Brett after him, whispering to Van Brett, patting his flat belly. "No steak tonight for you," she said. "This is not your cheat day, and no wine." She slapped his hard biceps with her polished fingernails, her voice a singsong Tennessee burr. She slapped his arm each time Van Brett gaffed, smudging her lipstick on the wineglass, and smelling of flower perfume; only her tanned face offered any proof of their California life. Ronnie Brett spoke to almost no one but Akbar as Van Brett chewed his broiled chicken, stared out the window at the Stratosphere, a long unfinished silhouette above casino lights. The lights, Eddie thought, how they resembled carnival lights, the swirling colors everywhere, so many that Eddie felt drunk in the lights, now thinking of the money, the money . . . he would take a Peter Pan to Oakland, how Tessa would love the lights, how one day he could take her here, a champion, to see the lights. Akbar lit a cigar, and Eddie stared at Van Brett through Akbar's Davidoff smoke, thinking of the money, until the escort leaned over in the smoke, her breath moist with wine, saying, "My name is Amanda." Eddie blushed, causing the escort to laugh until she was coughing, patting her pale cleavage with her plump fingers, laughing and coughing.

In the La Fleur bathroom Eddie offered the escort to Tommy, Tommy drunk and whispering from the adjacent stall with grave certainty. "I do not get Amanda, Eddie. You get her. No question she is pretty, but Akbar bought her for you. He find out I took the girl . . ."

"I'm going to California to see a girl in a couple days. You take her."

"Here, Eddie, here is the money," said Tommy, passing him a 7-Eleven bag with $2,000 and a pack of lubricated condoms under the wall. "I swung by a check-cashing joint. Now, don't spend none of it. I'll talk to Akbar in the morning. I took a third cause a cut man can't just take a half, cause that's not how it works, and just take it now while I'm stoned on wine. Now, count it, Eddie. Count it right now. That's how it's got to be between us. You beat that Indian real good, and this is your night, brother, so you take sixty-six percent and you take the hot girl, and you fuck that girl cause it's your night."

Akbar found Eddie in the hallway, pulled him aside, twisting a cigar in his mouth. "You understand there's no such thing as a perfect Muslim," he whispered. "Women ain't forbidden to us, brother. I still make my prayers. What is a man without a woman? Come on, boy. I saw you frowning at me. The Europeans' ways are not our ways," Akbar whispered as a silver-haired man passed by, slapping his shoulder. "You was a white man," he whispered, "I'd piss on your foot and call it rain. Like that bumble clot football player over there with his stank wife. Think he can come down to Vegas having never seen the inside of a ring and go back to Hollywood with a professional ranking. Fuck that cracker over there, son. I'm trying to put you down with an empire in the making, this C.B.F.! I knew you'd turn Amanda down." Akbar's face, his dark and beautiful face, became contrite; he lowered his cigar. "I want you to save me, brother, the way I saved you from those pretenders in the Nation of Flimflam in Chicago. I want you to save me from myself, from the little *sheitan* that beats in my heart. You will be my escort to the mosque each Friday. Those women, those women," Akbar whispered, pointing his cigar at the drunken table of women circulating pictures of Van Brett's terriers, at his two mistresses, "they are my wives, you dig? Had this cat from Saudi Arabia marry us at the Lux, you know. So we ain't legally married. So we ain't married in some white man's church! Fuck the white man. Let me tell you, I been in this boxing game since the sixties, okay. I knew Muhammad Ali. I knew all them. I told you I knew Malcolm. I knew Huey, Farrakhan, H. Rap, all those cats. I knew segregation. I got an anger in me that even you could never know, boy. This C.B.F. is not just about making money; it's about uplifting the black man. You remember that. You learn to trust Akbar Muhammad. Akbar Muhammad is a smuggler—er, *struggler* for his people!" Akbar began to laugh, a wild laugh. "Akbar Muhammad don't subscribe to the white man's uptight ways! Take as many wives as you can afford, brother." Eddie nodded at him. What a phony Akbar was, he thought. A hypocrite. At that moment

Akbar's two "wives" stood from the table, strolled past them to the bathroom, one of them saying to Akbar as they passed, "Darling, Van's dogs are so gorgeous, and he loves them like children." Akbar pressed $500 into Eddie's pocket.

The next hour Akbar appeared with two more bottles from the wine cellar. It was only ten. "The Strip is dull till after one," Amanda confided. Akbar sat down. Van Brett put a flame to Akbar's cigar.

"Akbar worries about water consumption," said one of his wives, sipping wine. "It's a crusade with him."

Van Brett lit his own cigar; Ronnie frowned at him. "It's a big deal in California, too," he said.

"Akbar had a plumber install this, this water-saving contraption in the condo," said Akbar's other wife, the blonde, making a rectangle with her hands. "This, this thing! It recycles the bathwater! It costs twenty-four thousand fucking dollars."

"Yuck." Ronnie Brett pinched her nose. "Now, girls, I'm all for the environment, but I will not drink my toilet water."

"It is recycled. You can't taste it."

"Whatever," said Ronnie Brett.

A violinist appeared behind Akbar and played *Boléro*. Akbar said, "I was telling the mayor last year: 'You want to bring all these families to Vegas, and ain't nobody dealing with the water issue.' I am one of the few Las Vegans who worry about water consumption. I read this book by Rachel L. Carson when I was in Prague with the girls last year, and it turned me on to the environment problem." Akbar lost his train of thought and waved at Eddie. "Look at this boy! This boy ate a real steak tonight. This boy has never eaten so much, never eaten so well. That's a fifty-dollar steak. My boy come down here on the fly and lit up the C.B.F. Now, how does it feel to make three thousand dollars in twenty-four hours on a few rounds' work, Eddie?" Eddie watched Akbar. Eddie nodded. Tonight was a gift, the Quechen. Akbar was preening him; he could feel it. The table was looking at him now, and they understood this, too. "Just remember where that money come from." Akbar pointed his cigar, smiling. "The C.B.F. *The Colored Boxing Federation!*"

"Akbar!" said the blonde, fingering her hair.

"No wonder they won't let us up in that MGM Grand. No wonder all them N.A.C.'s buzzing around! Too many coloreds, too many niggers, too many Indians, and too many spics! Got us fighting in factory buildings, broke-down hangars."

"Don't say that," said Ronnie Brett, applying lipstick to her mouth, staring into a compact. "Don't pretend it isn't about money, Akbar, when it is."

Tommy took a sip of wine and turned to Akbar. "I know a guy over at the Tocco. This guy. Say he gets the kid something in the I.B.F., something local that don't interfere?"

"Say I put you out in the street!" Akbar broke into laughter. The actor rubbed a tattooed biceps. "I am worth eleven million dollars. A straight nigger from East St. Louis. You don't come into eleven million dollars by making half-ass decisions! I have accountants and lawyers, preppy college boys working for me. My lawyers have lawyers! We pay our fighters. We ain't like them other so-called governing bodies. This is about the little man. We ain't like the others, the alphabet-soup, three-letter, three-judge panels. We cultivate, we make an investment, keep the promoters at bay, the referees, the old heads. Opportunity! Time to leap in, Tommy, while nobody looking. This is U.S. Steel. This is Microsoft. This is the Stratosphere."

"Over time, I'm saying. I was thinking of the kid."

"Oh," said one of Akbar's wives. "It's sweet. He's thinking of the kid."

Akbar went simpatico. "I'm about to sign the kid to three more fights at three thousand a pop. You think you'd be making that kind of money fighting in the I.B.F., the W.B.O.? I know about the little man. There's no money in this life. You got administrative, you got licenses. You got to feed your boy three times a day, get your boy a cot, and a fighter got to sleep. Meanwhile, you got other people with real backing, serious development, you got MBAs standing behind them, making financial calculations. You got seasoned trainers who can size a fighter up in five seconds, see the deficits, correct. Somebody's making an investment in them." Akbar jabbed his cigar in Eddie's direction. "Last week all he had was my phone number."

Tommy looked at Akbar. "Just that the C.B.F. isn't as, as established as the other governing bodies. I mean, C.B.F. fighters ain't recognized by the others yet."

"Five years ago, the W.B.O. was three letters and a fax machine! Look at it now. Do I look like some dumb spook to you? When Akbar makes money, everybody make money. I have what they call a *fiduciary interest* in the motherfucker! I founded the C.B.F. This kid is C.B.F. exclusive for the next three fights. That goes in writing. That is number one on the agenda when we have our sit-down. Number two at our sit-down: Tommy learns to trust Akbar Muhammad. All Akbar wants is to make you a rich white boy. Cause I like you, Tommy, you country motherfucker, you corn-fed redneck." The table erupted in drunken laughter.

It was one o'clock. The women sat in the lobby, on ruby red cushions, while Akbar spoke to his CFO, Duane, on a cell phone, shaking hands with men of importance, giant gray-haired men striding outside with wives, mistresses, into the blinking city.

Van Brett removed a cigarette from his pocket and waved Eddie out, striding forward to the cusp of the lawn in long easy movements before an array of expensive cars, and lit the cigarette.

"My eyes red?" he asked. "Akbar just signed me with a guy who's fought one hundred and fifty-something amateur bouts in Kentucky and thirty professionals. I ran to the rest room and puked. I gave the toilet jockey a dollar for an extra swig of Listerine so Ronnie wouldn't smell the puke on my breath." Van Brett turned, still preening, rubbing his turnip-colored cowlick, staring at his reflection in the window of the Lexus parked before the grass. Eddie wondered why he'd waved him out. "Can you see the fear in my face, Eddie? This is my fear face. I am an actor, Eddie. I am memorizing this face, Eddie, this feeling right now." Eddie looked at Van Brett. He thought it was easier than it was; his muscles would mean nothing in the ring. "All this fear," Van Brett continued. "This city. I am putting it to memory, so that I can use it in a role. Ronnie says we will never get a bead on this city. Hollywood was like, like a mirage in the first few months, the phoniness, like you find out some small-time actor lives in your building, that you're standing behind him in line at the 7-Eleven, the desperate people, the auditions, the rejection, then you get used to it. You build a wall, you become habituated to it because there is so much rejection, because Hollywood is all about rejection. But this place, I can't get a bead. The lights and the big fake boobs, man, and all the strippers, nickel machines at the gas station, right?"

"I feel sorry for you."

"You feel sorry for me?" Van Brett turned around on the grass. He looked startled. He took the insult like all the large, physical men Eddie had known, flexing his muscles, shifting his body. "Why?"

"Cause you don't know what you getting yourself into."

Then Van Brett turned from Eddie and watched the skeleton of the Stratosphere, new, unlit, under way; Eddie felt the whole city staring at it; it hung in the air, dark against the blinking skyline. "Hey, I like to try new things, Eddie. All this fear I'm feeling now, like maybe I can use it in a good role. I was freaking when I signed those papers for Akbar. I wouldn't have signed nothing if—I mean, two weeks ago, I thought my pilot was going to be picked up. I thought I was going to have real options again. You don't make so much in the Arena Football League. When your wife don't work. If you live the lifestyle. All this fear." Van Brett took a sigh. He leaned against the front rake of the Lexus. "All this fear!" he muttered to himself. "Take it, Van, take it! Accept it!" He grunted. "Eddie, I want you to know that I am a totally progressive white dude. Professional football teaches you that."

Eddie rolled his eyes. "I am going back inside."

"I'm broke, Eddie," Van Brett cried. "Fucking Ronnie spent all my money. There's no fucking money left. I haven't told her how broke we are. I went through all the arena football money. I went through all the pilot money. Ronnie thinks I'm here on a lark, to get some Hollywood play out of it. I'm broke. Do you think I would do this if Akbar wasn't throwing serious money in my face? I mean, you know what it is with women and money. Got a girl, Eddie? Say, there is the one club around here where all they play is hip-hop. The Shark. I was trying to get Ronnie to go, but she's a country-western girl. My little redneck. Akbar said you were from South Phoenix. I imagine I'd get real street cred I rolled out with you a little bit. That's what they want in Hollywood now, real street cred. Say, bring your girl by the apartment, and Ronnie can cook Southern for you."

"No. We can't be friends."

Van Brett laughed. "Why not?"

"We is in the same weight class."

Van Brett considered this for a moment. It had not occurred to him until now. "I played arena football for the Nashville Kats and the best man at my wedding played for the Red Dogs." Van Brett rubbed his tanned cheeks. "Well, fuck. God, what am I doing? I don't know shit! Look at you. I couldn't beat you. I ain't fought once! I'm not in shape. I'm not even in arena football shape, how can I be in boxing shape?"

"Don't talk to me no more," Eddie said, watching Van Brett from beneath the flapping awning. Eddie left him; he went to the door, a couple stepping inside before him.

Van Brett looked as if he would cry, the giant man. Eddie went back to him. Van Brett was gazing at the hulking unfinished skeleton of the Stratosphere. "Don't never let another man know how afraid you is," Eddie whispered to his back. "Don't never let on to nobody, not your trainer, not Akbar, not people at the gym. Don't tell nobody, not even your woman. Keep it inside; it makes you hard. You got a few weeks, a month. Step up your conditioning, run in the mornings. It's all instinct. So, half of what the trainer teaches you you'll just as soon forget. Learn one combo and work your straight jab. Don't think cause you played football and you got some size your shots will sting the other guy. When the shots come, don't look away, and don't hold your breath."

Van Brett nodded, his back turned, smoking.

*T*he purse money poured through his hands like water. Eddie fought twice more in the space of four months, won each time, and bought a used '87 Mazda. He sent money home to Mama. Tommy discovered slot machines. In the afternoons Eddie knocked about Hacienda Rd., the Strip, the busy walks of tanned, bobbing heads and cream blazers, until he knew the hookers, the escorts, the card girls by face, even at night in Vegas lights, men who'd watched him from the chairs, shook his hand, the C.B.F. ring doctor, Dr. Testa, in his suits, so handsome, so rich.

One day he found Amanda in Tommy's motel room packing Tommy's duffel bag. Tommy came out of the bathroom, a toothbrush in his mouth. "Akbar cut us loose, Eddie," Tommy said. "He stopped paying for these rooms. We can't stay here no more. Get your things. Mandy and me is going back to Phoenix."

"No. I'm staying, and you can't just leave me, Tommy. I made you money."

"Akbar cut us loose. That's it. Come on. Time to go back to Phoenix. Kell needs us."

"No. Let me talk to Akbar, then."

"Don't think," said Amanda, stuffing a shirt into Tommy's suitcase, "he doesn't care about you, Eddie. You're all he talks about. Vegas eats your soul. Come with us, Eddie. I'm going, too. We can all go back together."

"Akbar wanted you to take a dive for that football player, Eddie," said Tommy. "I told you not to mess with him. Come on. Kell needs us. We'll regroup. Vegas will still be here when we come back."

Eddie did not believe him. Eddie thought Tommy was only chasing Amanda back to Phoenix. "I made you money." Eddie pointed at Tommy. "I made you money. I made money for you. You're fucking me." Eddie watched them standing together, Amanda and Tommy, once pumping hands before him. Amanda finished packing. The room went silent. Tommy felt inside his pocket and threw his room key on the unmade bed, walking out with a duffel bag. Amanda touched Eddie's shoulder as she walked out.

Eddie called Akbar at his condo. There was a misunderstanding. One of Akbar's wives answered, pretended not to recognize Eddie's voice. Eddie looked at his room. He couldn't afford another two days at Arizona Charlie's without the comp. He'd have to find a cheaper place or sleep in his car. The cleaning woman came into the room. Eddie took his things and walked out. He ran down the steps as the manager was running up to check on the room. He wandered the Vegas streets with his bags. He sat in the lobby of a thirty-story theme hotel across from the MGM Grand, reading a *Newsweek* somebody'd left behind into the afternoon, watching vacationing families traipse in, waiting for someone to ask him to leave, but no one did, and fell asleep. He slept a few hours on a comfy chair. Clyde Williams woke him with a tap on the chest, standing above him in his red valet uniform.

"You work here?" Eddie asked him.

"Across the street," Clyde said, leaning on his broom. "I'm scheming on a chick over here, a bell girl." Clyde looked at Eddie. "Akbar dropped you, huh?"

"I need to talk to him, it was a misunderstanding."

"Akbar's like that. I know a guy who can get you a sit-down. Look at you. You ain't got nowhere to sleep."

"You know a cheap place?"

"I got a place." Clyde smirked to himself. "I'm working a double shift. I don't get off till one. You hang tight."

Clyde ran off. At one in the morning he returned, smelling of cigarettes. Eddie packed his suitcases in his car trunk, and drove Clyde down the strip of blinking casino lights and away until the car was hurtling beneath the night sky, the horizon opened up before them three miles out of the city, the casino lights behind them, the moonlit road curling under desiccated trees, wiry limbs stretching out in silhouette. Eddie watched the side of Clyde's face. He wondered what his angle was, how Clyde could be so kind to him, now, after he'd knocked him out. Clyde stared out the window, watching the cacti blurring past along the roadside.

When they'd come into such a patch of darkness that Eddie could see nothing except stars, Clyde told him to stop, and Eddie wondered if Clyde was going to jack his car. Clyde opened his door and ran across the desert. He took a Swiss army knife from his pocket, scraping the edge of a cactus; he returned with a bit of raw peyote, cutting the cactus and the peyote into small bits, stuffing them inside a dime-store corncob pipe, mixed with pipe tobacco, and lit it.

"How come you left Yuma?" Eddie asked him.

"You try Yuma, Arizona." Clyde inhaled.

"You lived on a reservation?"

"Yeah. So."

"I didn't mean nothing," Eddie said. "I got Navajo in me on my father's side."

Clyde rolled his eyes. The pipe smoke made him giggle. After a while he said, "My big brother was a very important person where I'm from, let us say, and, let us say, that I was a very important person just for being his brother, and, let us say, where I lived not one important decision was made without his input. If a man was in a predicament, he visited my big brother. When the first well run dry, they consult my brother though he had no official position in the town; when the politicians come, they visit my brother before they visit the tribal president; and when the hucksters come selling my people casinos, they visit my brother first. All the while I am standing beside him. Then my brother got sick with the diabetes, and stuck in his bed, and all the people started looking to me. Then he got sicker and sicker, and the people start coming my way. Then his kidneys failed and he died. So the very morning after his funeral, when town people come knocking at my door, I slipped out of my bedroom window, Eddie, and I ran away and hitchhiked to Vegas."

Clyde rolled down the window. The smoke seized him so hard that for ten minutes he lay back without speaking. He was so long silent that Eddie went off the narrow road into absolute darkness, lost in cacti, hoping he'd not gone too far astray, hoping that they were close.

A town appeared before them. The town was not a town, but a pharmacy, a motel, a restaurant set side by side on hard desert. Clyde pointed to the motel, which read in neon NOCHE DE PAZ, and Eddie drove into the empty parking lot. Eight-foot white stucco walls surrounded the motel like the walls of a fort. Though it was three in the morning, Eddie heard raucous laughter inside, the sound of men and women frolicking, splashing in a pool. When Eddie climbed out of the car he smelled beer and oranges, menthol cigarettes, and the odorous perfume of ladies of the evening.

"Sleep on my floor for a while," said Clyde.

"I don't have no money," Eddie told him.

"Chill out, Navajo. This is the Paz. *Paz* is, like, Mexican for 'peace.'"

Eddie nodded at him.

He woke on a floor the next morning to the smell of oranges, the chubby Quechen eating oranges from a crate at the side of the bed. Clyde saw Eddie waking and held out an orange. "You want breakfast? Oranges is free."

"No," said Eddie. "Not now." Clyde waved him into the hallway. Eddie followed Clyde down the hall, Clyde checking the doorknobs of every door with his brown hands, his feet sweeping along the patterned carpet. Tossed magazines, trash, cigarette ashes ran along the hallway, which reeked of beer and cigarettes and oranges; and there was rowdy acid metal rock music from both ends of the hallway. A tattooed white man passed the two of them buck naked from one door, crossing the rug to the room across the hall, nodding at Clyde.

The town was of dust swirls and sunshine, tilting palmettos, stucco walls, hedgehog plants. Not once did Eddie see people from the town appear at the front wrought iron gates of the motel, or in the restaurant, or coming out of the pharmacy; the hotel staff was a longhaired guitar-strumming concierge and a gaunt Guatemalan janitor, a devout Catholic, who crossed himself before lugging every box, emptying every trash can, before cleaning each side of the pool.

The next morning a palmetto fell outside, and Clyde and the concierge went down to the bottom of the hill to look at it.

Eddie found Clyde at the pool that afternoon with other boxers, now floating in the overchlorinated pool, squinting at him from beach chairs. "I need to get a sit-down with Akbar."

A boxer floating on an inflatable cushion looked at Eddie, looked back at Clyde.

Clyde turned to Eddie, squinting under his palm. "Hang tight. Somebody might come talk to you tomorrow." Eddie nodded. "It's easy," said Clyde. "You ain't got to train. I drink a beer the night before each fight, watch the porno channels."

In the morning Eddie found Clyde and the other boxers eating oranges in Clyde's room before the twenty-seven-inch television, the room smelling of oranges and coffee, the men peeling oranges before the television, digging their dirty fingernails into the rinds, their yellow teeth into orange skin, eyes shut. Eddie left them eating the oranges they'd unloaded from the back of the beeping orange truck. The longhaired concierge wandered down the hall strumming his electric guitar.

An old man appeared at Eddie's side a few minutes later, as if he'd scheduled the meeting with Eddie in a calendar. Eddie drove the old man into Vegas; they got coffee outside the Strip, shared a bag of powdered doughnuts for lunch, and the old man said, "Look, this will be easy for you, I'm going to be your trainer, your manager, your father, all that shit." He turned his wrist to check his watch, revealing a tortuous gecko tattoo. "Get to Duane early is what you do. Be proactive. Duane and Akbar is like this. Boy, we gonna make you rich. We'll get you three, four fights, for five hundred each, my take notwithstanding." They came into the city, staring at the rushing buildings as they got onto the highway, the old man directing him with his finger.

"It ain't like there's something wrong with it."

"Who said there was nothing wrong? This is consenting adults, right? This is America. This is consenting adults."

The old toothless man finished his coffee and tossed the paper cup out of the car window. "Look here, I saw action in the Korean War. I never thought I'd come back." The old man leaned over and whispered, "I'm gonna take care of you just like I took care of the Indian. I like to work with Duane. Akbar don't intimidate me, but Duane and me gots rapport. Akbar was setting you up for the actor. Duane and Akbar feel like the actor is good publicity for the C.B.F. An opportunity for you, boy. You got to take the brass ring if you can get away with it." The old man snickered. "You got someone offers you five hundred a pop—and maybe more—who are you and you don't take it?" They climbed out of Eddie's car and drove to the parking lot of the Mirage. Eddie waited for guilt to wash across him, but it didn't. With the money he could run to Tessa, take her out of Oakland, run away. "Look at this place," the old man said, shutting the car door, "blows my fucking head every time. Duane lives high on the hog. See, that's why you can trust Duane. Duane practically runs the C.B.F. That's how I know I can get you five, maybe seven hundred a pop, minus my take."

Inside the hotel they rode the gold-trimmed elevator with a beautiful escort still dressed in an evening gown, her heels hanging from her fingers. She looked at the floor. The old man stared at the woman's cleavage until the elevator stopped at her floor, and she stepped out in stocking feet.

Eddie walked down the hallway. The old man grabbed him by the elbow. "We square? Don't fucking do nothing funny. Duane is a businessman. Duane handles the finances. We said five hundred a fight. I'm going in there talking that number."

"I want ten thousand."

"What?"

"What about your take? Expenses? What about administrative? Gym fees, registration? I want ten thousand dollars."

"That would be twenty-five hundred a fight! What you know about administrative expenses, boy!" The old man wiped his forehead with a handkerchief.

"I know what the manager takes," said Eddie, "the second, I know about the taxes. Laying the hotel bill and gym rental on the fighter. I know what they is paying the actor."

"Don't talk uppity to Duane. You'll offend him. I've got to maintain a working relationship."

"I want ten thousand straight up for whatever I do or I drive back to Phoenix tonight."

"Ridiculous. You'll never get it. And fuck you for asking, you ghetto fuck," the old man whispered, folding the handkerchief, inserting it in his pocket. He turned his back. "What's so special about you?"

"I know the actor gets fifteen thousand a fight."

"He's the actor. Akbar didn't cut him loose."

"And my take don't come from your take, either. Your take is your take. My take is my take."

The old man stared at him.

"Ten."

"No wonder Akbar cut you loose." They went down the hall. It was a beautiful hall, accent lights glowing against the gold trim of the rug. The old man was more nervous than Eddie.

Duane, a dark-haired man in a rugby shirt, baseball cap on his head, opened the door and led them inside. Whiteboards with numbers, black and red, and makeshift grids lined the walls. Eddie saw Duane take two ornate sitting chairs from a wall and position the chairs before his desk. Eddie sat down next to the old man. Duane seemed too young to be Akbar's partner, his face too boyish. He looked like a fraternity chapter president. Duane had lined seven beepers against the wall and three cell phones. Several times a beeper would vibrate, and Duane would climb off the table, examine the face of the beeper, cursing or smiling, crawl across the thick rug to the whiteboard to erase a number with his fingers, and fill in another—*KS: 14* or *NYY: 22* or *BRS: 0* or *FLP: +2*—with such concentration and without once excusing himself, as if the vibrating message were excuse enough. The old man saw Eddie staring at Duane, watching his movements, and slapped his knee, then sat with his head hung before Duane, like a servant. When the pagers went quiet Duane returned to the table, the old man smacked Eddie's knee again and whispered Eddie's C.B.F. record.

"Undefeated." Duane nodded. "I remember."

"His trainer pissed Akbar off," said the old man, rubbing his chin. "The boy wants a new contract." The old man peered at Eddie, his chest, his thighs, his forehead, his ears, his long feet, as if Eddie stood upon a block.

"What's up, Eddie?" Duane said. "We haven't been formally introduced. I signed your purse checks."

"Mr. Duane, I think Tommy said something to Akbar last week cause Akbar stopped paying the bill on my motel room. He won't take my calls."

"Tommy was negotiating ex parte, Eddie. Akbar has a short leash. Of course. The C.B.F. is yet another alphabet-soup governing body, and Tommy wanted something more established. Nobody likes us right now until the commission cools its heels. Me and Akbar put the C.B.F. together in a Denver motel room two years back; we scribbled the business plan on cocktail napkins during a Dolphins game." Duane nodded at the old man. He turned back to Eddie. "But we just signed a two-point-five-million-dollar contract with a local cable sports station, VSN. That's legitimacy. Look at me, Eddie. Do I, ha, look like I'd break your legs? I love boxing. I have a deference to it. I love all sports, football, baseball, basketball, but prizefighting is my heart. I mean, don't you love it?" Eddie looked at him. No one had ever asked him this question before; it had never seemed relevant that he might love it or not; it was what it was; the gym was across the park. The old man had loved him. Said there was money in it if he applied himself. Michael Carbajal won a silver medal in Seoul with only his big brother training him in the backyard. Eddie looked at Duane. "But you're so good at it," Duane said. "What are you, eighteen? Regional champion. Part of me is saying: Send this kid back, send this kid on his way. He might be something. Maybe Tommy was right, maybe we should consider the karma." Eddie sat in the chair, stone-faced. Duane rocked back, and his eyes went a moment wide.

"You want me, I'd take a fall against the actor," Eddie said.

"Wo, now!" The old man slapped Eddie's knee.

Duane looked over his shoulder. The old man had been talking about three or four fights, but Duane only needed him for one. He turned to Eddie and put a finger to his thin lips. "October. Against the actor. If I was flipping channels, I'd watch Van Brett go up against a guy who looked like you."

"October," said the old man. "I could prep him nice."

"Some people," said Duane, "take a fighter like you, waste him on a bunch of no-count boxers, and waste that record of yours, your amateur wins, and your intangibles."

"That means your looks," the old man told Eddie, "your size, your personality."

"Your last name is pure Hollywood."

"He could play the good guy or the bad, huh, Duane?"

"Some guys, Eddie, put you on a losing streak, right away. You see, Eddie, there are fighters who take longer to develop in the pros. But sometimes they are worth the investment."

"Like when a guy starts peaking." The old man leaned over. "Lord Jesus, can't take your eyes off them. Like Tyson before he got rid of Kevin Rooney."

"And look how long it took Tyson to perfect his knockout skills," said Duane. "No one ever talks about that."

"So Duane got a guy," said the old man. "A Hollywood flake."

"A television personality," said Duane. "Akbar kept you pretty clean. He popped your cherry with the Indian and then he left you alone. You met the actor. He's undefeated, too. He beats you. He's champ and you stay two. Next year, we branch out, get him W.B.O. matchup. Nice publicity."

"And send the actor back to Hollywood," said the old man, "with the fruity-toots. Eddie boy sticks around."

"Well, maybe that could be me," Eddie told Duane, "if I got these in-tangibles. Think of what I could do with some backing. You run the C.B.F., Duane. I could make something out of the C.B.F. I could

make you big money. I could fight real dudes, you give me some
backing just like I been doing."

"Akbar said you went down pretty quick in Chicago." Duane
shook his head. "I keep my guys real viable, Eddie. Maybe the actor
catches you on a bad day, but the next two are all yours. And there'll
be a place for you. The C.B.F. is growing. I've got lots of work for you.
Security, collection, telemarketing, offshore betting, Eddie, you
name it. How'd you like to run down to the islands for us next year,
watch the telephone banks, sit on the beach? And that's just the beginning," said Duane. "The future is computers, the Net. Internet
sports betting."

"Windows Ninety-five," said the old man, waving his fingers. "Give
Eddie something administrative, Duane, a résumé builder. I like
him."

Eddie turned to Duane. "I want, want ten, ten thousand dollars,"
he said.

"For the actor?" Duane shut his notebook. He shook his head.

"I want ten thousand dollars, a straight ten, no cut, no expenses,"
he said. It was impossible. Duane was smirking. Eddie did not care.
Nothing he'd ever said had made him feel so important.

Duane looked at the old man. "I was thinking more like three."

"I told the boy to be reasonable, Duane."

"I'll drive back to Phoenix," said Eddie.

"Stop it, Eddie."

"Eight."

Duane was not smiling. He stared at Eddie. "Okay. How about I
give you one thousand right now, and three thousand to fight?" He
took a roll of hundred-dollar bills out of his desk drawer and passed
it to Eddie. "You play along with the actor. There's no walking away.
I'll call Akbar tonight." Duane stood and shook Eddie's hand. "This is
it. You don't talk to the N.A.C., neither, and your professional career
as you knew it will be over."

Eddie swallowed. "No expenses, no administrative, no regis-tration." He pointed at the old man. "You pay him what you pay him. I get my three to fight the actor. I work out of the Tocco, not some broke-down no-name gym with busted-up heavy bags and no shower." Duane glared at him for a moment; then he nodded in agreement. Duane's pagers went off on the rug, and Duane crouched down, searching the text display of each pager.

Eddie drove back to the Paz through dust with $1,000 in his pocket, the old man beside him, his hat on his lap, staring at the cacti. He'd squared away four thousand; he'd squared away the Tocco. He could train with the real boxers there. He should feel happy, he thought, but he wasn't. He was no better than Turtle, a crook; nothing separated them now. He had to find Tessa. At the edge of the little town the old man touched Eddie's arm. "You got what you wanted, boy. You's a rich young man."

"Tell Clyde I went to see a girl in California," Eddie said, and he left the old man on the hard broken dirt and turned the car around in the direction of the highway.

He took Tropicana Rd. to I-15 as light rain fell on the curling highway—clouds going the color of tangerine—the highway sweeping underneath him. He was in Oakland by late afternoon, shuttling down 9th St. to the Aegis, winding through streets of convenience stores and intersections, Million Man March posters on telephone poles.

He parked before the Aegis at dusk. He looked at the flat one-story apartment building. An old white woman in a floral print dress watched him from a picnic chair climb out of his car and hurry up a sweep of Kentucky grass. He went up the hill to the motel lobby until he saw her, Tessa, running to him in a T-shirt and cutoffs, her flip-flops slapping under her bare feet, calling his name. She dropped her laundry basket on the walk.

She hugged him. Cars passed down the four-lane street beside, heading from the small office building pavilions west to better parts of the city. Tessa squeezed his hand. He gazed at her now in the low light. She looked horrible and beautiful at once, ten years older than she was, her cheeks drawn, pale. He'd longed for her all this time, dreamed about her, set out to save her when now her face looked worn. She was ugly and she was old. Tessa kissed him. Then she held him in a sort of desperation and stared at him, as if knowing he'd sold himself cheap in Vegas. How with a look she could know this. He held her; her body was frail. He remembered how as a boy it was enough for him to touch her, to feel safe, wrapped under her arm. She'd lost weight. She was smiling at him, standing on the dirty walk of her slum motel on Dwight St., on the very street she walked each day. Her motel room was around the other side of the building. She took her laundry basket, and he followed her.

She opened her door, set the laundry basket on her rug, and shut the door. "I knew you'd come," she told him. "I wanted you to wait till I was ready. Look at this room," Tessa said, "at my new room, look at all my new stuffed animals." She held up a teddy bear. "This is Wendell right now," she said, waving the bear. "Actually, he just up the street with his grandmother. You can see him tomorrow." But he did not want to see the boy. Her pager went off on her hip. Tessa peeked at it. She sighed and kissed Eddie's cheeks, his mouth, kissed him long enough that he might sense she could love him still, but not so long he might forget that she was suffering. She clung to him, pressed her body against him. She'd written the letters, and the letters had sustained him, called him here. He looked out her window. "I been thinking about you all this time," he told her. "Making my way to you. Your letters come when I was so depressed. Tell me that you love me now, like you wrote. That's what I come for." Tessa was watching him. "I grown now," he told her, as he'd told her a thousand times in his oft-repeated fantasy of this reunion. "I can love you like a grown man," he told her. A thousand times he'd fantasized saying this to her, but not once had he considered what it meant—*love you like a grown man*—for in the fantasy Tessa only kissed him, only nodded, the next moment begging him to love her like a man, to save her.

In the fantasy she gave up on the boy, left with him without complaint the next morning after a night of lovemaking. *Four thousand dollars*. She did not in the fantasy look at him like this, lost at his meaning, head tilted, silent, face tired-looking, turned-out and old. A motorcycle raced down the highway beside them. He shook his head. "Tell me that you love me or I'm leaving right now."

"Stop it." Tessa giggled into the palm of her hand. She laid Eddie on her twin-sized bed, which sat against the long window; she laid her worn body atop him and stroked his hair. He felt the city at his shoulder. This was California. Another long slum street. No different from Phoenix. "Silly boy," Tessa was saying. "Love don't work like that." Now he wondered what she meant. He sensed her hesitating, the three hand-scribbled letters a sort of ruse to lure him, and felt stupid. He'd imagined she would confess her love to him by now, without any buts, any strings like in the letter, and the moment he saw her he'd feel no longer worried, no longer this emptiness. She traced her finger along his chest. She stared at him. She was still so pretty to him. She did not look like what she was.

"I love you," Tessa said, but it came too late. Eddie stared into her soft, creamy face, her brown hair brushing against him, and he was that moment certain he loved her only in memory, when she was more beautiful, and how he'd pitied her; but this thought, that he pitied her, that he'd always pitied her, only caused him to love her more. "You can't just demand," Tessa said, "that somebody act and say all kinds of things like they life straight when they is suffering. I'm trying to get my boy back, Eddie. I'm close."

"Why did you cut me off all them months?" he asked her. "Do you love me, or not?"

"I done what I could. Yes, I love you. I wrote you them letters. My life messed up right now, Eddie."

"We gone through so much, and you just cut me off, make me worry about you."

Tessa's warm breath swept across his face.

He shook his head. "Why did I even come? You don't love me that way. I thought you loved me. That time when we messed around in your motel. Look, there is things you got to understand. I grown now, Tessa. Don't treat me like a boy. Do you love me like a man?"

"My life be messed up." Tessa pulled her curly hair back, stared at him, and kissed his nose. He stared back at her. "I told you I love you."

"My bags is in the trunk," he told her.

"Go get them, then."

He climbed off the bed, stood. She loved him; she loved him. What more did he want from her? Now his chest felt light, as if filled with weed smoke. He went out to get his bags.

He came back, set his bags on her rug, shut the door. But she did not love him. "You be loving someone else?" he asked her. "Tell me now. One of your men? The men you be with? A pimp?"

"Listen to you." Tessa was laughing. She came to him and touched his mouth. "You is so young. You know I don't love nobody but you. You know I is just a body to those men." She stared at him. He did not understand her. He lay on her chest, and she stroked his head. Every moment was precious, frantic, slipping from him. Nothing worked as in his fantasy, the way he'd imagined it driving from Vegas.

"Can we go somewhere to talk? I mean for a little while. Just somewhere to talk."

"Come on," she said. "Let's walk." They went down a sidewalk of broken cement. Million Man March posters hung from light poles. The march was Monday, he remembered. Tessa said she'd said seen men boarding buses last week at work. Eddie walked beside her, watching the dirty walks, walks devoid of black men. Eddie wondered what it would be like if one day all the black men in the world were swept off the streets, and the streets looked like this. He looked at her now. He tried to imagine her in a head scarf, reformed, a Muslima, but he could see her only in her street clothes, her hair un-combed and dry as straw.

They went back to her motel room. He'd wasted the walk. He'd said nothing, convinced her of nothing. It was not like he'd imagined it. In the car he'd known what to say to make her love him, follow him back to Vegas. He stopped at the parking lot and touched Tessa's hand. She was hurried now, on her way somewhere, to a date. "I need to talk to you," he told her. Tessa keyed the lock and opened her door.

"I'm going now." Tessa looked at the pager on her hip. "I'll be back late. You can wait up. You can watch television." He grabbed her wrist. She turned from him, her face meek. "It's just some old white man, a doctor, up in the hills in Berkeley. All wrinkled up." Tessa laughed. "He always feel guilty after he bust. Then he tell me he wants to save me, to get me educated at a community college, buy me a car. Then he tell me it is the white man's fault, what I do. That I am, what's that word? I just go quiet ex, exploited. Ha! and he pay me extra."

He should stop her, he thought, but he could think of nothing to say, nothing that would convince her this moment to stop and fol-low him back to Vegas. He sat on her bed and watched her change into a simple blood-colored skirt, patterned with leaves, her face made up, but no longer powdered white. No wonder this doctor wanted to send her to college. She looked this moment like a college student in her skirt. She did not look like what she was. How happy he was that she need not walk Dwight St. every single day, that she could on weekends venture into the hills of Berkeley. How happy that she'd found some stability, rich white men. Tessa's pager went off, and she realized she was late. She went to the bed and gave Ed-die a kiss good-bye. This was not what he'd envisioned. He'd imag-ined that they would get coffee somewhere. He'd imagined there would be time to talk and make love on the bed, or at least, now after all, make a commitment. He could save her if she let him. He had only a few days before he had to return to Vegas, to train for the fight. He could not coax her back if she spent every minute working. Eddie kissed her lips now. He held her soft, worn, freckled face to his until Tessa was drawing away from him, saying, "Oh, Eddie, I must go."

He lay on the strange bed, wondering how he could get her to follow him back. It did not seem possible until Tessa shut the door behind her and drove her car away, until she was gone, and he could think to himself. But she need only love him, he thought. She need only give him a chance, follow him back for a weekend. Later he could reform her and marry her, convert her. He sat on her bed watching her thirteen-inch television.

He waited for Tessa until he fell asleep. At midnight he heard Tessa standing at the door, fiddling with her keys, and he climbed out of bed and opened the door for her. A short, pimpled teenage black boy in an overlarge football jersey, sixteen, stood before Eddie with a motel room key in his hand. The boy had a roped, gold-plated neck chain, the letter N encrusted with fake diamond bezels drooping at his belly. The boy saw Eddie standing at the door and looked at him without fear and snickered, his mouth filled with gold.

Then the boy saw Eddie's bags on Tessa's rug. "Where Tessa at?" he shouted. He spat on the ground, turned, and left Eddie. Then he stopped and ran back, flashed a handful of foil heroin bags in his palm for Eddie to see. "Can you be setting her out like me, nigger! Can you be giving her these, nigger! Huh!" Eddie looked at him. "Tell Tessa Nitro come by." And he traipsed off in his bright, unlaced sneakers, across the dark gravel and down the grass.

Eddie shut the door and sat on the bed. He looked at the floor. He put on his jeans and took his wallet from the dresser, his keys. He stood and got his bags. Then he climbed out of his jeans and lay in bed. Tessa came home the next hour. He watched her wash her face in the bathroom sink, climb out of her dress, and there it was, her naked body, as in his fantasies, still beautiful, there she was, the woman he loved, a moment naked, a liar, everything Turtle said. He should fuck her now, he thought, and go back to Vegas and be done with her, but she was so pitiful, so pitiful, he could not think about sex. She climbed into a T-shirt. She lay against him, touched him, touched him; he stopped her. Driving back from Berkeley she'd been thinking. She whispered, "I love you. I love you. I love you. I will go anywhere with you, anywhere but Phoenix."

Toddler children shouted somewhere and woke him in the morning. Tessa went out that morning, bought eggs and flour at the 7-Eleven, disappeared in the common kitchen behind the laundry house, returned with fresh pancakes, which Eddie took down with instant coffee. Eddie shut the door and sat next to her on the bed. "I got a big fight coming. It's big money," he told her, but he did not tell her how much. "It's money for you and me to go somewhere, to be together."

"You ate your pancakes so fast," Tessa said. "Ate so many. Well, come on boy, let's go."

They went out into the sunny parking lot, and Tessa drove him around Oakland, circling, and he watched the streets, streets emptied of black men. He wanted Tessa to know he had money now. He wanted her to know he had $1,000 now and another $3,000 coming. He wanted her to know it wasn't like before, when he could offer her nothing but his Golden Gloves jacket. Tessa stopped the car across from her grandmother's house on Sample St. and she watched her son's window from the steering wheel.

"I like to look on Wendell sometime even when I can't visit him. He should be out right now. She keep him in too much. I bought him a bike. He should be riding it right now, on a day like this. Hold on," Tessa said, and in a moment she'd run out of the car and across the street to the window on the side of the house, throwing twigs at the window screen, waiting, waiting. Tessa ran back. "Grandma must have tooken Wendell to his daddy's."

"People is watching," Eddie told her, whispering, "from their porches."

"Relax. Ain't nobody care. I come visit Wendell at his window all the time."

The car lunged down Sample St. Eddie imagined Tessa the months before running to Wendell's window, knocking on the glass with her painted fingers, the boy stabbing his round head out to look, as children ran, shouting down Sample St. outside. Eddie had told her of the money. It was not enough. Tessa was singing radio songs, her head bouncing over the steering wheel as she drove her old Bonneville north to the beach.

They went to a public beach. There were potbellied, middle-aged men reading newspapers, project girls lying on beach towels, their baby boys barefoot, in diapers, wobbling to the cold water. They stayed an hour, until it seemed too crowded. Then Tessa drove him north away to a beach she knew, a quiet beach, and as she drove he slept, his head resting against the window, as she hummed soupy love songs, and when he woke, they were at the beach, the sand cold, colder than he could have imagined, but after a long march across the sand they came across a stretch of desolate beach, and Eddie lay upon his belly and he was very soon asleep, Tessa's fingers rubbing his shoulders.

"Will you take me anywhere? Wendell, will you love him?"

Eddie lay silent on the blanket.

"Someday, I'm going to steal that boy out of his window, Eddie."

"I know."

"It's illegal if you with me. You'll be a felon. But I ain't going nowhere without him. I'm gonna steal Wendell and run away somewhere. I don't care what my grandmother do." He slept on his stomach. Tessa did not sleep. She'd waited to tell him this. She did not eat the chicken she'd packed; she did not drink the Minute Maid. He heard her take a foil package from her pocket, open it, put it to her nostrils, and sniff the heroin; he thought of the boy in the neck chain; he remembered the hurt on his face. At least Tessa don't shoot up like Adolpho did, he thought, and there was Adolpho staring at him silent, from the flophouse floor. Eddie woke to find Tessa watching him in silhouette from a blanket. "You think I should leave him behind. Wendell." He watched her from the sand. He rubbed the sand with the tips of his fingers, felt it. "But I won't. You know that. But I can't leave him." She packed up her blanket. She wiped the sand from Eddie's stomach. She rolled the blankets. College kids danced around a bonfire to the east. Tessa went forward, and he ran after her. They danced before the fire to wailing alternative music. The college kids were cool. "You both go to Santa Rosa?" asked a young blond-haired man, and Eddie nodded until Tessa was giggling, the white boys watching her. The white boys offered them beer and tabs; Eddie shook his head. Tessa took the beer, swallowed down the tabs; the beer, the tabs made her voice bend, dart, and snap like the bonfire flames. Eddie looked at her and she was old, withered, and ugly again. She had lied to him. She'd fucked the boy in the neck chain for drugs. She would never leave with him. How stupid she was to think of Wendell now, when he could take her, and with the $3,000 they could live in an apartment in Colorado or Texas, another California town. His thoughts oppressed him. He should give the up-front money back to Duane and go home to Phoenix. His face went hot, and he was crying, unnoticed to Tessa in the music, her high, the darkness. The college boys shouted, and the girls giggled in clouds of marijuana smoke, and they had run already, run naked into the dark water, leaving their bathing suits upon the sand. "They done left they wallets on they blankets," Tessa whispered to him, giggling. "We should vick they shit, but they was cool to us, huh?" Tessa's eyes went loose and she was lost, drunk and laughing. She did not see him crying. He wiped his eyes. She stood, ran to the fire to dance. He watched her silhouette dancing before the bonfire. And she was high and giggling, as if the liquor or the weed had now overcome the melancholy pull of her desperate thoughts. He stared at the flames. Then he ran after Tessa, happy at least that she'd not vicked the white boys' wallets, as if this made her redeemable.

"You always was so good to me," Tessa said. "So good. Oh, how I love you, Eddie. Oh, I'm so happy now," she shouted, eyes shut. "I feel so safe. Even when you was a boy, I felt you protecting me." They sat inside her car, sand in their shoes. Eddie watched the bonfire over the dashboard through the dirty window.

"Whatever happens, I got to have Wendell with me," she told him. She watched his eyes, watched him taking solace in her words. The distant bonfire lit the side of her face. "He has to come. You can go back to Vegas. And if you do not come back, I won't hold nothing against you," Tessa whispered, until the tabs seized her again, and she was giggling.

"Three thousand," Eddie told her. Tessa's eyes shot up. "Four."

"Four thousand! For real? We could go to Baltimore," Tessa shouted. She was smiling. "Los Angeles, the ATL." Tessa went quiet, and they listened to the waves from her car. But they could not take Wendell. They would live where no one knew them. Now Tessa sighed, keyed the ignition, and Eddie watched her stare forward as she drove.

Tessa's left front tire blew out a mile down, and Tessa let out a low scream. Eddie guided her with soft-whispered instructions to stop at the side of the road, got out, and changed the tire while Tessa watched him from the grass, keys clutched in her hands. He wiped the grease from his hands on the back of his shorts. Tessa started the car. On the radio the DJs talked about the Million Man March. "It's tomorrow," Tessa said. "I will make you breakfast. They is putting it on TV, can you believe that? I make you breakfast, and we can watch it. I don't work on Mondays now." The car arched forward on a lean. Eddie washed his hands in Tessa's bathroom and slept hard beside her.

In the morning he woke before her and watched her from a chair. He stared at her. He sat on her chair and stared at her for an hour, for as long as he could, knowing now he would not ever see her again. Turtle had been right. (And Turtle had loved him, he thought; he'd been so cold not to see Turtle off to prison.) He climbed to his feet and went to her, touching her sleeping face with his hand one last time, putting to memory her sallow face. He went out the door and shut it softly behind him.

Hurrying down the hill to his car, he turned back to find Tessa staring at him from her motel window, just woken, her sweet face watching him, waving good-bye.

uane got him his old room at Arizona Charlie's. Eddie sat in it, staring at the unfinished Stratosphere through the window. He ran the city walks in the morning, trained at the Tocco on alternating days.

He trained in boredom. There was nothing else to do. He'd never trained so hard. He skipped rope and beat the heavy bag until he'd burned off all the fat from his belly in five days. He imitated the Tocco boys.

On fight day he checked out of Arizona Charlie's, changed into his robe and trunks in the bathroom of a Burger King, drove his car down Las Vegas Blvd. until he saw a satellite dish in the backyard of a distant house, and he realized that it would be televised, that he was wearing the Bumpy's club robe, Kell's robe. Cameras. Anyone might see him, Tommy, the Chicano boys, the stable mothers, anyone. He stopped his car at the roadside and turned the fuzzy robe inside out, and stood in the robe beside the car and watched the traffic until he could wait no longer and sped to the ugly, gargoyle-colored hangar, around the parking lot, parking in the back beside card girls and concession men, hurried in through the back, through the delivery door, down a low ramp, sitting alone in the undercard locker room, searching for the old man. He waited on a concrete bench, reading the *Spider-Man* comic book someone had left behind.

The old man appeared with his second's kit. He yanked the tape across Eddie's hand until his knuckles turned white. The old man said, "I did a tour in Korea. We didn't think we'd come back. Gave us an edge, made us free. All us moved out the Paz last week. I miss them oranges. Now give us five good rounds," and he spat in a nearby sink. An N.A.C. official came in and inspected Eddie's wraps and signed each hand.

Eddie went out of the locker room to the ring; he went up the scaffold indifferent to the music and the crowd, the cameras. A woman watched him from a table, her raven hair tied up, smoking a cigarette tipped with her lipstick. New chairs ran high up the hangar walls. Men in stripes meandered through the chairs, selling popcorn, nuts, and beer, and darting through the crowd. Dr. Testa exchanged phone numbers with a man in a striped suit. The *Round 1* card girl in a white bikini watched the ring from the edge of the dressing room curtain. The lights in the skybox fluttered a moment, and everyone stared into the ring. "I'm proud of you for getting that four," said the old man, rubbing his beard. "You deserve it. I knew you'd ask for more." Eddie stared at the blinding white apron, the polished scuffs on the surface. A camera flashed in his eyes. Ronnie Brett coughed in the second row. Eighties rock moaned across the room. "One of my other boys fought the actor last month, you know. He was fourteen and twenty-seven, but it was still a strain upon the poor boy to lose to that fruitcake." Eddie searched for Akbar in the dark corners, in the skybox.

Van Brett went into the ring from the other side of the hangar, a Clint Black song thudding from the speakers. The raven-haired woman at the table stabbed the cigarette into her mouth. Van Brett marched to the ring, a three-man entourage behind him, his turnip-colored hair cut short in a military buzz, his face drawn and moist with Vaseline, in a silk robe, affecting courage. Strangers filled the ring, a cameraman, the referee, a drunken card girl, Akbar and Duane, with officials from the N.A.C. and others, and Eddie pitied Van Brett because he had looked at the crowd, and the crowd had stared back at him, and now Van Brett was spooked. Now Akbar, Duane, the others abandoned the ring, and the referee, a squat Chicano, shouted the instructions at Eddie and Van Brett. Eddie did not hear the instructions; he watched Van Brett: how handsome he was, how handsome even in his fear, how he looked the part, Eddie thought, surely he looked rugged and mean, and surely he was handsome. Van Brett watched Eddie, his face passive, and Eddie thought, What a good actor he is, for Van Brett appeared the next moment fearless—then Eddie remembered that he had nothing to fear. Eddie touched gloves with him. They turned their backs to each other, going back to their corners, and Eddie felt naked in the hard light, and only the money made this sufferable. He stood at the corner, a moment taking deep breaths as if it were real, as if the ending had not been determined in advance, and the card girl in the white bikini pranced drunk up the scaffold and waved the card in four directions and pranced back down. Eddie ran at Van Brett and twice beat his shoulder, to which the actor took a sort of personal offense, once swinging back, and glaring, his arms at his sides until Eddie struck his chest and a single jeer came out of the crowd, and Eddie went backward until Van Brett realized he must chase Eddie; he did this, swinging. The crowd was clapping, the autofocus cameras whirring beneath them, judges slashing pencils against their score cards. Van Brett did not look tired until the old woman in the rhinestone dress beat the ten-second cane against the apron, and Eddie realized he'd not hit Van Brett twenty times, and the crowd seemed impatient. Now the bell rang and the actor shot his muscled arms into the air, and the card girl took a breath and went up the scaffold.

The old man fed him water. Eddie spat in a bucket. The card girl left the box, and Eddie drank more water. Eddie stood and charged Van Brett, who stood with his arms hung in fatigue, then punching, like a bar fighter, slack-jawed, telegraphing, punching with his shoulders, punches dulled by massive muscle, ambling to Eddie like a zombie, and Eddie sensed in the crowd a disbelief, almost laughter at the clumsy hunky-looking man. He locked up with the large, dim man, whispering, "Stop punching with your shoulders, Van." The referee yanked them apart, his Pony boots squeaking across the apron, and gave them each a caution. Now Van Brett drove at Eddie, crouched, keeping his form until Eddie hit him twice in the stomach, and then Van Brett fell over, red-faced, grimacing in shock. In the stands men stood on their feet, shouting. The referee ran over and gave him a ten count, Van Brett staring at Eddie, standing on the count of five. Eddie knew Akbar was shouting in the skybox. Van Brett stood, opened his mouth, and ran at Eddie, panting.

Van Brett lowered his guard. He did not bother to hit Eddie. He was too tired. He stood with his hands hanging at his sides. A profane noise shot up in the crowd. There was boredom. Van Brett was exhausted already. He'd not conditioned himself. Eddie went to him, striking him once or twice in the cheek, letting down his gloves for Van Brett, who after a second let loose a reckless flurry into Eddie's face, sending up cheers from the swirling crowd, the judges slashing their no. 2 pencils under them. The old, craggy woman in the rhinestone dress beat the ten-second cane against the apron, sagging arm fat shaking as she did, and Eddie dug in his feet, wrapping his arms around Van Brett's wide, perfumed body as the referee came to them. "Just hit me, Van," Eddie whispered.

The referee grabbed them each by their shoulders, prying them apart with a groan. They locked up again. "I can't, I can't!" Van Brett whispered after many hard breaths. "I'm too tired to win. You can keep the money. I'll let you have it. I'll tell Akbar." The bell rang. The referee broke them apart with another caution; the smiling card girl wobbled up the scaffold.

Eddie went to his corner. He felt Akbar peering at him from the skybox. The old man rubbed Eddie's cheeks with Vaseline. "Let him hit you. And quit talking to him in the lockup, you stupid ghetto fuck. Looks funny. You fall in this next one. You let him fucking hit you!" he whispered, snatching the water bottle out of Eddie's mouth.

"He can't. He too tired. He can't."

"You stupid, stupid boy! He can't, or he won't? He could, you let him. You fall on the next clean punch." The rock music faded. The card girl stumbled on the third stair. Eddie jogged to Van Brett, who struck him twice, and he took solace in the shots, and he struck Van Brett and sent back his head, his cleft chin, his good-looking face, his glove slipping across the actor's wet, turnip-colored hair. Van Brett caught his breath, chasing Eddie in a blunt, red-faced desperation, arms waving about him. The actor knew nothing of the sport. There were rules and conventions to which he showed no veneration. He'd not even conditioned himself, and the crowd knew it, the riotous black shouting wall of noise, of wailed profanities. From the dark floor below, the old woman in the rhinestone dress frowned at Eddie, the ten-second cane shaking in her bony hand. Then Van Brett was upon him, so close Eddie could smell his hair spray, Van Brett flurrying in his face. Eddie let himself be struck upon the cheek and the chin, let himself fall back, plunge to the canvas scarred with boot leather.

There was noise, camera flashes from ringside. Eddie lay on his back and almost smiled. The referee came now, the ten count. Eddie looked at the ceiling lamps. Van Brett watched him from the other corner, gloves hanging at his sides.

The referee finished the count and waved his arms. Another camera flash went off. Then a boo rose from the ten-dollar seats. Men were shouting, standing. Eddie stood and looked at Van. The referee looked at the judges at ringside, who themselves looked at the ten-dollar seats, the shouting men. A beer bottle came flying through the darkness into the ring, slapping against the canvas. The crowd set up a low shriek. Van Brett and his second watched from their corner. Beer and popcorn rained into the ring, crumpled napkins, pink lemonade, paper cups, Coke bottles from the high black walls. The card girl who'd been waiting at the corner ran out under her poster-board. Ashtrays came flying into the ring, more beer bottles thrown at Eddie and Van Brett, who slipped through the ropes, out of the ring, Ronnie Brett behind him covering her head with her Gucci purse. Eddie went through the ropes, and down the scaffold. Tossed beer and Coke and pink lemonade stuck to his skin. Men on each side slapped him with their fists in the darkness. A glass ashtray struck Eddie in the back of his head. The hangar lights seemed to flicker. Blood ran into his eye, causing the room to go red and pink as demon-faced men from the ten-dollar seats, their faces contorted, cussed at him from every direction, and on the floor men spat at his head, tossed their beer bottles at his torso. He went to the locker room, shut the door behind him. He caught sight of himself in a distant bathroom mirror. The old man followed him and slapped Eddie with his hat. "You won't get no money, now!" the old man said. They waited for Akbar. Akbar entered with silver-haired men in suits. Akbar went up to Eddie and squeezed his neck. "We told you to make it look real! You was supposed to wait for a clean shot."

Van Brett stepped out from behind a wall of lockers with Ronnie Brett, his silk robe covered with popcorn and soda and beer and litter. "Akbar, give Eddie the money," he said. "Give him whatever you promised him."

"He was tired," Eddie told Akbar, pointing at Van Brett with his wrapped hand. "He couldn't do it. He was tired. The old man told me to fall."

"Jesus God, the young man is bleeding," said Ronnie Brett, wiping the popcorn out of her hair. "Get him a bandage, Akbar."

Akbar stared at Eddie.

"Duane said three thousand," Eddie told him. "I done what you told me."

Akbar shook his head. "Fuck three thousand dollars, fuck three thousand dollars, fuck three thousand dollars."

"Give him the money, Akbar!" shouted Van Brett. "He did what you told him."

"Please, Akbar," said Ronnie Brett. "He's bleeding, and it's over, and me and Van are going back to California."

Akbar stood in the locker room, staring at Eddie. Akbar opened his wallet. He gave Eddie $900 in hundred-dollar bills, then shoved him against a locker.

"Your head is bleeding," Van Brett said, walking to Eddie. Ronnie passed him his wallet, and he opened it with taped hands. "Here." The actor took all the bills from his wallet and he passed them into Eddie's sticky hands, passed $200, and Ronnie Brett came forward, in shock, and presented her Gucci purse to the actor, who opened it with his taped hands and removed from her wallet $161, which he offered to Eddie, and a Kleenex from Ronnie's purse for his bleeding head, the room silent save for the crowd outside. Eddie went to the locker. Akbar and the old man and Ronnie Brett and Van Brett watched him rush out of the locker room, through the back.

He raced back to Vegas with the radio off, into the city of blinking lights, down the Strip, dirty, sticky with pink lemonade. He drove twice down the Strip until he caught sight of Clyde working his night shift in the valet parking lot of the MGM Grand. He drove up to valet parking. Clyde was coming from the garage in his vest; he saw Eddie and came running.

"I'm leaving the city, I'm leaving for Arizona."

"I'm leaving, too," Clyde said, staring at Eddie in his robe. "Soon, next week maybe. I'll ride back with you then."

"Look at me, I'm leaving tonight, right now."

"Hold on," Clyde said. He ran into the garage and emerged with his duffel bag, stopping only long enough to toss his red valet jacket on the sidewalk, and climbed into Eddie's car.

They drove out of the Strip. Soon they were nearing Yuma. Clyde asked him to stop for a few minutes. Eddie stopped the car. Clyde got out and sat on the hood. Eddie sat next to him, feeling the warmth of the engine beneath him. He watched Clyde light his peyote corncob pipe and smoke it.

"The girl in California," Eddie told him. "I lost her."

"Everybody loses the girl in California," Clyde said. He sucked in the peyote smoke. "I'm scared to go back, Eddie, but I have to go back. This feeling, this feeling," he said, exhaling. "This feeling is how I always want to feel. This how I want to feel tomorrow," Clyde said, "when I walk into town," and he giggled, "when they see me, and they ask me where I been all this time, and I tell them, Eddie." Clyde exhaled. Eddie wondered if he could stay with Clyde. He would stay in Clyde's town for a few hours, a few days, live there until he was ready to go back. "I am ready. I ain't afraid no more."

They followed U.S. 89, Eddie realizing that he would too soon come upon the town—in seconds—and he would never see Clyde again.

The water tower hung in the sky. They came into the town at ten at night. Litter swept across the town, dead trees, broke-down cars. The oldest of men upon horses rode up beside them, one man on each side, and stared at them through the car window. Clyde watched them and went silent, looking at the town without regret.

"Maybe I could stay here a little bit," Eddie told him, "seeing as you run this place, maybe just to visit."

"No," said Clyde, "you cannot visit me, Eddie. I cannot visit you. Not for a long time. We have things to do, Eddie." Eddie drove Clyde across the long dust roads between leafless trees until Clyde went silent, until the horses and the men were long behind them.

"I lost all my friends," Eddie said. "I got so much pain for me in Phoenix. I don't know why I'm going back."

"You know why." Clyde looked at Eddie and touched his shoulder. "Later, Eddie," he said, grabbing his duffel bag, climbing out into the dusty street.

He came into Phoenix from the north at three that morning, his car covered in Nevada dirt. He got off I-17. He found Marchalina's development, parked his car in the parking lot, and climbed her fire escape, the robe sticking to his dirty skin. She woke and found him hovering at her window. She opened it and kissed his cheek, pulled him inside. She squeezed him, looked at him covered in dirt and filth and popcorn. She snuck him down her hall, into her bathroom, where in the mirror he stared at himself, the reddish film sticking to his brown skin, his neck, his chest, his stomach, like a tar, bits of the popcorn, rubbish. Marchalina ran the shower and put him in it. She wet rags and rubbed the filth off his shoulders. She washed his back, his shoulders, kissing, kissing. She soaped his neck, his chin. She kissed his mouth and drew a rag across his stomach. She cleaned the cut above his eye with rubbing alcohol, put a Band-Aid on it. She took the crumpled, pink-soda–covered money from his hands, and washed each bill in the sink, folding them in a warm towel to dry.

She peeled the dirty gauze tape hand wrap off each hand, yanked off his boxing shorts, put him naked in the hot shower, scrubbing him beneath the water, toweled him dry.

They lay on her bedcovers until morning broke. Then, when she'd fallen asleep beside him, he went out of her window, saying, "I'll come back tonight."

He throttled his car south in the direction of skyscrapers, down Central, to the edge of the city, the red-rock mountains, and he was home. Junked cars along the streets of windswept trash. Van Buren. The police cruisers turning into the narrow morning streets. Black boys rising aimless, leaning against the redbrick project walls. Now the New State Variety; now Woodland Park, filled with brown children streaming across the hills; now his pink corner home. Now the dead woman's house.

Mama met him at the front door and hugged him. She took him inside and sat him down at the kitchen table, where she'd been clipping coupons. "You need to see your brother." She was frowning.

"I don't know."

"You need to see your brother."

"Why? I just come back."

"We don't go see him but twice a month, boy, and we is going tomorrow after church." Eddie looked at her. He could not go, not yet, when he'd just failed in Vegas, but Mama was firm. Turtle was suffering at Florence. It was in her face, Eddie thought. Mama set a kettle of water on the stove. It went off. He drank coffee with her, staring out the windows. Driving from the north, the streets had looked different, his streets. He could not explain it. He wanted to see the streets again. Mama touched his face. "They beat you up. Look how they beat you, baby, my beautiful boy. What did they do to you?" She measured the bridge of his nose with the nub of her thumb like she'd done when he was a boy, laughing. She stared at him from across the kitchen table into the afternoon, until he heard the shouts of boys in the park, and he must go out to see it, his hood, for himself. He felt something pulling him outside, down the street. Some thought, some memory. He did not know what.

He went down Woodland, like a stranger, walking, watched from windows; he watched park mothers push their children in strollers up the winding hill, boys on bikes down the streets. There was Van Buren just across the park, just as he remembered it. He stood now before the dead woman's house. A fifteen-year-old boy, a boy with a fresh fade, in a T-shirt two sizes too big, in baggy jeans and brand-new Reeboks, stood at the gate, glaring at him, as if he did not know the house, this street, his street. A prostitute called to the boy from the open doorway. The wind shook the giant yellowed bushes above the gate. Again the prostitute shouted at the boy from the doorway, her corpulent figure leaning on the doorjamb, shouting, shouting. The little lord of Woodland Ave., Eddie thought. King of the dead woman's house. The sight of the boy was maddening now. In his hood. On his street. He hurried back to his house and stood on his porch. Through the screen door he saw Mama and Nana in the kitchen making sandwiches for tomorrow's trip. It was this. It was this. Yes, he must go with them tomorrow, he thought. He could not wait to see his brother now. There was so much to tell him.

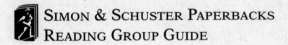
Night Journey

1. The novel is driven by many personal and social themes. Did you react to the book largely as a personal story or a larger, societal one? If you had to choose one theme that is most strongly played out in the novel, which would it be? Why?

2. The differences between Tessa and Marchalina are mostly obvious, but discuss the similarities they share. What does Marchalina represent for Eddie? Also, much of the novel concerns Eddie's sentimental obsession with Tessa. What does she ultimately represent for him? What draws him to her? Where is the true love story?

3. Black novels often make reference to other novels written in the black tradition. (The literary critic Henry Louis Gates Jr. calls this phenomenon "signifying.") Where do you find *Night Journey* responding to important black novels—in its treatment of the black condition, spirituality, culture, sexuality, and politics? Other common elements of the black novel include the presence of a trickster figure, the quest for literacy,

and allusions to the experience of slavery. Where do you find these in *Night Journey*?

4. What keeps Eddie from the same type of trouble that plagues Turtle? What formative events do most to shape Eddie when he is younger? What role does his talent for boxing play? What people or incidents influence the decisions, and how does this differ from Turtle's experience?

5. The novel is filled with irony at many levels. Discuss the irony in Turtle's treatment in the criminal justice system, in Eddie's relationship with Jules, Tessa, and Akbar, and with the Vegas boxing world.

6. How do Eddie and Turtle react to the disappearance of their father? How do their reactions most significantly differ from each other? How does this desertion kick-start the events that make up the rest of the story?

7. What is the importance of Eddie's involvement with the Nation of Islam? What specific changes come about in his life because of that involvement? Is his attraction to the group initially a spiritual one, a social one, or both? Does it remain that way? What does the impending Million Man March add as a backdrop to the rest of the novel?

8. Sports-themed novels often use athletics as a metaphor for the struggle for individuality or autonomy in American society. How might this be true of *Night Journey*?

9. In the end, when Eddie returns home, what has he learned? What do you think his purpose is in coming back to Arizona? Where do you think his life will lead after the novel leaves off?

10. Discuss the power of memory, fantasy, and self-delusion in the novel.

11. Is *Night Journey* a protest novel?

A CONVERSATION WITH
MURAD KALAM

Q: Eddie and Turtle are such strong central characters. Do you think of the novel as primarily Eddie's story?

A: Yes, I think the novel is Eddie's story. For me, *Night Journey* is a novel about youth. Thus, I chose to write about a young man who is impossibly naïve, an innocent thrust into the ugliest atmosphere. (So much of youth, so much of American culture, is about naïve fantasy and self-delusion.) He is also the character who most reminds me of myself. I always found the idea of writing about myself to be a little narcissistic. Only a few writers, like Proust, can write beautifully about themselves and approach something transcendent. I thought Eddie's life offered more depth, weight, and importance than my own. When I conceived the novel, I was struggling to understand the crisis of the young black man in America. I translated my experience of youth into Eddie's experience.

Yet, this question is really about Turtle. Turtle is based on several people I knew. Turtle is one of those characters a writer encounters who takes on a life of his own. He is perhaps more compelling than Eddie. He is without any illusions about himself and not reined in by any morality. In this way, he is a rebel. Yet, I think it is in his contempt for phoniness that he is most charming. Ultimately, however, he is ignorant, violent, and dangerous. He exists without Eddie's painful enlightenment and self-discovery.

Q: What was the significance for you of setting the book against the backdrop of the impending Million Man March? How do you think current events can best be utilized to enrich fiction?

A: The significance of the Million Man March is that it encapsulates the book. It was during the Million Man March that we, as a country, really looked at the condition of the young black man in America. For Eddie, like so many young people, including myself then, the Million Man March captured the imagination. It represented the possibility of self-actualization, dignity, responsibility, and full-fledged participation in America.

So, using this event as a backdrop allowed me to be true to a particular time, which is how a current event can help give structure and meaning to a novel. This was also a time when Islam, as it still is, was so popular in the black community.

Yet, social politics should always come second to the rules of narrative. The function of the Million Man March and the Nation of Islam in the novel are literary: the power of a popular ideology on a young naïve, dispossessed man. I was conscious of novels like John Dos Passos's *U.S.A.* trilogy, which deal with powerful ideologies, here communism. So, I thought it best to understand Islam, the Nation of Islam, and black nationalism, in this way, as ideologies and organizations, which is not to be reductive. This let me focus on a common theme, a young person seeking escape or transformation through a possibly liberating ideology, but also the inevitable disappointments of any ideology or organization to someone who has not confronted himself.

Q: The novel seems driven, partly, by the idea of father figures. What male figures have been strong influences in your life, and how did they help you?

A: My father is easily the strongest male figure in my life.

My father's stories of his life were the first stories I heard. By chance, his story is a Dickensian story: he was born in a small country town called Buff Bay, in Jamaica, and injured his eye on a breadfruit tree. Baptist missionaries took him to Amarillo, Texas, for medical treatment at fifteen. He lost his eye, but, by thrift, stayed on, living in the black community—in the late fifties, , it was inconceivable that he live with a white family—and attending segregated high schools. He later supported himself through college and became a doctor and received a Ph.D. As a black man in the segregated south, he saw America at a very interesting time. (I think that I inherited much of his anger about American racism.) Yet, as an immigrant, he never let go of his optimism. In that way he was a bit naïve.

When I was growing up, my father talked a great deal about his life and the life of people in his childhood village, and I think it was in this way I learned the rules of narrative. It was the story of the third world, of post-colonialism. So, there was absurdity. You felt the influence of the Bible. People mostly got what they deserved. There were logic and humor.

Q: The spiritual themes of the novel are often subtle, but always present. What role did you see faith and belief playing in the story? Are your characters' lives driven by their ideals, or vice versa?

A: Oddly, I don't know how much of the novel is really about spirituality or religion. Eddie comes to the Nation and Islam simply as a political reaction against racism and an expression of his frustration with his life. At some other point in the future, he might, if he stuck with it, engage Islam as a faith, but the novel is not concerned about religion at all. Rather, I am trying to be true to an experience.

I don't know if it is at all possible to write well about genuine faith. I think it would be impossible to write a decent, interesting book about a faithful person, excepting a novel à la *The Idiot*. For some reason writing about the loss of faith is possible. To write about religion is really to write about hypocrisy.

Ultimately, faith, like boxing, was the vehicle through which I could play on the most American of themes with Eddie: naïveté and self-creation.